P A N T H E O N   B O O K S

April 1998

Dear Bookseller,

I'm enthralled by this debut novel—a compulsively readable, literary love story set within the white expatriate community in Kenya—and I'm not alone.

Rules of the Wild was one of the most talked-about books at Frankfurt last year, and foreign rights have already been sold in England, Germany, Sweden, Italy, Denmark, France, Holland, and Brazil. In-house excitement is steadily growing: my colleagues are finding in this novel the dark political wit of *Mating*, the decadence of *White Mischief*, the sweep of *Out of Africa*—and a narrative voice unlike any they've encountered before. Esmeralda, the Italian expatriate at the center of *Rules of the Wild*, is a woman of dazzling ironies and introspections: piercingly intelligent and self-deprecating yet romantic and decidedly under the spell of Africa's beauty and horror and mystery.

Francesca Marciano—a woman of enormous personal charm—is herself an Italian expatriate living in Kenya. A documentary filmmaker, Marciano has concentrated on contemporary African life in her films. And with her intimate knowledge of the place and the people, she has imbued *Rules of the Wild* with an extraordinary sensual and emotional richness. It is a stunning first novel, and I hope you'll be as excited by it as I am.

With best regards,

Sonny Mehta

RULES OF THE WILD

RULES OF THE WILD

FRANCESCA MARCIANO

Pantheon Books • New York

Library of Congress Cataloging-in-Publication Data

Marciano, Francesca.
Rules of the wild / Francesca Marciano.
p.   cm.
ISBN 0-375-40358-2
I. Title.
PR9120.9.M36R8   1998
823—dc21   98-10963
CIP

Random House Web Address: http://www.randomhouse.com

Book design by Trina Stahl

Printed in the United States of America

First Edition

2   4   6   8   9   7   5   3   1

I thought, if you're really going to live in Africa, you have to be able to look at it and say, this is the way of love, down this road: look at it hard; this is where it's going to lead you. I think you will know what I mean if I tell you love is worth nothing until it's tested by its own defeat. I felt I was being asked to love without being afraid of the consequences. I realized that love, even if it ends in defeat, gives you a kind of honor; but without love, you have no honor at all.

RIAN MALAN

PART ONE

ADAM

CHAPTER ONE

To wake up at first light, a flea in the prairie of rock and sand
each morning, is to realize that one's own importance
is something one highly overrates.
One was mad, all right, after a year of it.
One sees that now, looking back.

GERALD HANLEY

In a way everything here is always secondhand.

You will inherit a car from someone who has decided to leave the country, which you will then sell to one of your friends. You will move into a new house where you have already been when someone else lived there and had great parties at which you got incredibly drunk, and someone you know will move in when you decide to move out. You will make love to someone who has slept with all your friends.

There will never be anything brand-new in your life.

It's a big flea market; sometimes we come to sell and sometimes to buy. When you first came here you felt fresh and new, everybody around you was vibrant, full of attention, you couldn't imagine ever getting used to this place. It felt so foreign and inscrutable. You so much wanted to be part of it, to conquer it, survive it, put your flag up, and you longed for that feeling of estrangement to vanish. You wished you could press a button and feel like you had been here all your life, knew all the roads, the shops, the mechanics, the tricks, the names of each animal and indigenous tree. You hated the idea of being foreign, wanted to blend in like a chameleon, join the group and be accepted for good. Didn't want to be investigated. Your past had no meaning; you only cared about the future.

Obviously, you were mad to think you could get away with it without paying a price.

It's seven o'clock in the morning, and I smoke my first cigarette with sickening pleasure at the arrivals hall of Jomo Kenyatta Airport in Nairobi.

She is on the early-morning British Airways flight.

Her name is Claire, I have never seen her. I was told that she is blond, long-legged and sexy. She will be looking for me. She has probably been told to watch out for a dark-haired chainsmoker with the look of a psychopath, or at least this is the only honest description that would fit me today.

I hate Claire, she is my enemy, even though we have never met. Yet I am here to greet her and welcome her as part of our family, the baboon group whose behaviour I have finally managed to make my own. I guess this is my punishment.

She has never lived here before, but she is coming to stay for good. She will eventually learn all the rules and turn into another specimen, like all of us. That is what everyone has to learn in order to survive here. She is coming to live with the man I am in love with, a man I haven't been able to hold on to. Another possession which slipped out of my hands to be snatched up by the next buyer.

The tourists start pouring through the gate, pushing squeaking carts loaded with Samsonite suitcases. They all wear funny clothes, as if each one of them had put on some kind of costume to match the ideal self they have chosen to be on this African holiday. The Adventurer, the White Hunter, the Romantic Colonialist, the Surfer. They are all taking a break from themselves.

She comes towards me looking slightly lost. I notice her long thin legs, her blond hair pulled tightly into a braid. Her skin is pale, still made up with London fog. She is wearing a flowery dress and a thick blue woolen sweater that makes her look slightly childlike. I wave my hand and she lights up. It's true: she *is* beautiful. She has destroyed my life.

It's like musical chairs, this secondhand game. When the music stops, one of us gets stuck with their bum up in the air. This time it must have been my turn.

I steer her cart out of the airport towards my old Land-cruiser.

"Did you have a good flight?" I try a motherly tone.

"Oh God, yes. I slept like a log. I feel great." She smells the air. Thank you so much for coming to pick me up at this hour. I told Hunter that I could have easily gotten a taxi—"

"Don't even say that. There's nothing worse than arriving in a place for the first time and having to start haggling for a cab. I believe in picking up people at airports. It's just one of those rules."

"Well, thanks." She smiles a friendly smile. "Wow, you *drive* this car?"

"Sure." I hop in and open the passenger seat while I hand a ten-shilling note to the porter. "Watch out, it's full of junk. Just throw everything on the back seat."

Claire looks slightly intimidated by the mess in the car. Tusker beer empties on the floor, muddy boots, a panga on the dashboard, mosquito nets, dirty socks, rusty spanners.

"I just came back from safari," I say matter-of-factly as I pull out on the main road.

"Oh."

She looks out the window at the grey sky hanging low over the acacias. Her first impression of Africa.

"What a nice smell. So fragrant."

She sits quietly for a few seconds, letting it all sink in, her weariness mixing with her expectations. Her new life is about to begin. I feel a pang in my stomach. I didn't think it would be this hard. As usual, I overestimated my strength.

"Have you heard from Hunter? He's still in Uganda, right?" I ask, knowing perfectly well where he is; I have memorized the hotel phone number.

"Yeah. He thinks he'll be back next week, unless there are problems at the border with the Sudanese troops. In which case he will have to go in."

She sounds so casual, the way she has picked up that hack slang, as if the outbreak of a war was the equivalent of a night club opening. Just something else to report, another two thousand words in print.

"Let's hope not," I add more of the motherly tone. "I'm sure you don't want to be left here alone for too long."

"I'll be all right. It's all so new, I'm sure I won't be bored." She turns to me and I feel her eyes scanning me. "I knew when he asked me to come here that he wouldn't be around a lot of the time," she adds nonchalantly.

She's tough, I can tell already, hard inside, under the fair skin and that blondness. She'll get what she wants.

"You live with *Adam*, right?" To put me back in my place.

"Yes. He's still at the camp up north with the clients. I've just come back from there. You'll meet him when he comes down on Saturday."

"I've heard so much about him from Hunter. He sounds wonderful."

"He *is* wonderful."

We take the Langata road towards Karen. She looks out the window taking everything in: the tall grass shining under the morning sunlight that has pierced the clouds, the old diesel truck loaded with African workers which spits a cloud of black smoke in our face, the huge potholes. She will learn how to drive a big car, find her way around town, she will learn the names of the trees and the animals.

"I'll drop you at home, show you how to turn on the hot water and things like that, and then leave you to rest. If you need anything just call me, I live right around the corner from you."

"Thank you, Esmé, you are being so kind."

She will fall asleep in the bed I know so well which is now hers.

I am glad to hate her. Now I will go home and probably cry.

This is a country of space, and yet we all live in a tiny microcosm to protect ourselves from it. We venture out there, and like to feel that we could easily get lost and never be found again. But we always come back to the reassuring warmth of our white man's neighbourhood in modern Africa. It's right outside Nairobi, at the foot of the Ngong hills where Karen Blixen's farm was. It's called Langata, which in Masai means "the place where the cattle drink."

There's no escape; here you know what everybody is doing. You either see their car driving around, or hidden under the trees in their lover's back yard, parked outside the bank, the grocery shop, filling up at the gas station. A lot of honking and waving goes on on the road. You bump into each other at the supermarket while you are shopping, the post office while paying your bills, at the hospital while waiting to be treated for malaria by the same sexy Italian doctor, at the airport where you are going to pick up a friend, at the car repair shop.

Even when you are out on safari, thousands of miles away from everybody, if you see a canvas green Landcruiser coming the other way, you look, assuming you'll know the driver, and most times you do. It's a comforting obsession. So much space around you and yet only that one small herd of baboons roaming around it.

This is our giant playground, the only place left on the planet where you can still play like children pretending to be adults.

Even though we pretend we have left them behind, we have very strict rules here. We sniff new entries suspiciously, evaluating the consequences that their arrival may bring into the group. Fear of possible unbalance, excitement about potential mating, according to the gender. Always a silent stir. In turn each one of us becomes the outcast and new alliances are struck. Everyone lies. There's always a secret deal that has been struck prior to the one you are secretly striking now. Women will team up together against a new female specimen if she's a threat to the family, but won't hesitate to declare war against each other if boundaries are crossed. It's all about territory and conquest, an endless competition to cover ground and gain control.

You always considered yourself better than the others, in a sense less corrupted by the African behaviour. You thought of yourself as a perfectly civilized, well-read, compassionate human being, always conscious of social rules. The discovery that you too have become such an animal infuriates you. At first you are humiliated by your own ruthlessness, then you become almost fascinated by it. The raw honesty of that basic crudeness makes you feel stronger in a way. You realize that there is no room, no time for moral indignation.

That this is simply about survival.

Nicole and I are having lunch in a joint off River Road, where you can get Gujarati vegetarian meals. You have to eat off your aluminum plate with your fingers. There is a lot of bright-coloured plastic panelling, fans, flies, and a decor straight out of some demented David Lynch set. Wazungus, white people, never dream of coming here and that is exactly why we do, because we like the idea of two white girls having a lunch date on the wrong side of town.

"You look sick," Nicole says, gulping down chapati and dal. Her skin is a shade too pale for someone living in Africa and covered in a thin film of sweat. She's angular, beautiful in an offbeat way.

"I *am* sick."

"You have to get over it. I can't stand to see you like this."

She has just had a manicure at the Norfolk Hotel beauty salon and her nails are painted a deep blood red. She's wearing the same colour lipstick which is rapidly fading onto the paper napkin and the chapati, a skimpy skirt and a gauze shirt. Looks like she has just walked out of an interview for an acting job at the Polo Lounge in Hollywood and driven all the way to the equator in a convertible sport car.

"You didn't have to go pick her up at the airport. I mean, someone else could have."

"I guess I wanted to test myself. And in a way it was symbolic."

"Did Hunter ask you to do it?"

"Yes," I nod quickly. But it's a lie.

"I can't believe it. He's such a—"

"No. Actually it was my idea."

"You *are* sick."

"True. But it's all part of our private little war."

Nicole sighs and takes another mouthful of vegetable curry, her wavy hair hanging over the food.

"What does she do? I mean what is she planning to do here?"

"I haven't a clue. Articles for *House and Garden?* Maybe she will start a workshop with Kikuyu women and have them weave baskets for Pier One. She looks like she could be the crafty type . . ."

"Oh *please.*" Nicole laughs and lights a cigarette, waving her lacquered nails in the air. "She must be better than *that.*"

I take a deep breath, fighting the wave of anxiety which is about to choke me. I am actually drugged by the raw pain. It is almost a pleasure to feel it inside me, like a mean wind on a sail that any minute could wreck me. If I survive it it will eventually push me to the other shore. *If* there is another shore.

I feel as if I have lost everything. It isn't just Hunter. I have also lost Adam, myself, and most of all I have shattered the silly dream I had about my life here: I have lost Africa.

"When I saw her this morning," I have to say this, to get it out of my system, "the way she was looking at things, so full of excitement . . . you know, everything must have seemed so new and different . . . it reminded me of myself when I first came down here. Of the strength I had then. I felt like Napoleon on a new campaign, I wanted to move my armies here, you know what I mean?"

She nods; she's heard this a million times, but has decided to be patient because I guess she loves me. She knew beforehand that this lunch would require an extra dose of tolerance.

"She'll fight her battle, and learn the pleasure of annexing new territories. And I don't mean just sexually. She will start to feel incredibly free. Whereas I am already a prisoner here. Like

9

you and all the others. We fought, we thought we had won something, but in the end we are all stuck here like prisoners of war. And we still can't figure out who the enemy was."

"Oh please, don't be so apocalyptic. You are just in a seriously bad mood. I think you need a break. Maybe you should go back to Europe for a while."

"Nicole, why is it that after so many years we don't have any African friends? Can you give me an answer? I mean, if you think about it—"

"What does that have to do with—"

"It does. We're like ghosts here; we can't contribute to anything, we don't really serve any purpose. We don't *believe* in this country. We are here only because of its beauty. It's horrifying. Don't you think?"

Nicole picks up my dark glasses from the table and tries them on, looking nowhere in particular.

"Look, there's no use talking about this again. I hate it when everybody gets pessimistic and irrational and starts ranting about living here."

She stares at me from behind the dark lenses, then takes them off and wipes them with a paper napkin.

"Haven't you noticed the pattern? We're like this bunch of manic-depressives. One moment we think we live in Paradise, next thing this place has turned into a giant trap we're desperate to get out of."

"Yes," I say, "it's like a roller-coaster."

"I think what we all do is project our anxieties onto the whole fucking continent. This has always been Hunter's major feature and you've just spent too much time listening to him. He loves to ruin it for everyone else because he hates the idea of being alone in his unhappiness. He will ruin it for Claire as well, just wait, you'll see."

This thought makes me feel slightly better. I am not in a position to rejoice at anybody's future happiness at the moment, I feel far too ungenerous. I am acting just like Hunter: working to create as much misery around me so that I don't feel completely left out.

Nicole smiles.

"Come to the loo. Then I'll take you to Biashara street. You need a bit of shopping therapy."

Nicole is cutting a line of coke on her compact mirror inside the pink Gujarati washroom. I envy the way she always seems to be completely unaffected by her surroundings and carries on living in the third world as if she's simply browsing through an ethnic sale at Harvey Nichols.

She snorts quickly, holding back her curls.

"Wow! It's such bad stuff, but what the hell . . ."

She watches me while I inhale my portion of rat poison, then puts on a naughty smile.

"We'll turn Claire onto this really bad coke and transform her into an addict, that's how we're going to get rid of her. We'll persecute her till she gets a bleeding nose."

I finally laugh. The rush makes me feel warmer. I'd like to hug Nicole now, but she is suddenly looking serious.

"You know, Esmé, I never told you, but in a way I feel like I should tell you now . . ."

"What?"

"I did sleep with Hunter as well. Long before you came out here."

"Oh."

Her cheeks are lightly flushed. I drop my eyes from her face.

"I had a feeling you had," I say. But the revelation hasn't shocked or hurt me.

"Why?"

"Just because . . . oh I don't know. Because of a certain intimacy you two always had."

"Do you mind me telling you only now?"

"No. It doesn't make any difference. Really."

We pause and smile at each other. I feel my heart hammering wildly, and the sudden urge for a cigarette. But I know it must be the cocaine, not her revelation. Strangely, if anything it makes me feel closer to her. She lights two cigarettes and hands me mine. We stand, our backs against the pink tiles, inhaling smoke and scouring powder.

"I am not unaware of what you said before, you know. We are all trapped in some kind of crazy white-people's game here," she says in a soft voice. "I just don't want to get completely engulfed in that kind of dissatisfaction because I don't have any alternatives."

"What do you mean?"

"I wouldn't be able to go back to Europe and function at this point. That's what made me so unhappy about sleeping with Hunter, now that I think of it. I felt he was constantly drawing energy out of me. His bitterness was poisoning me; that's what made me get away from him."

"Hmmm . . . I guess I am the one who has been poisoned now."

We stand in silence, smoking our cigarettes.

"I'll tell you exactly what it is that hurts, Nicole. The absolute certainty that I don't, and probably you don't either, have the determination, no, wait—the *faith*—to redeem someone like Hunter. We both would rather be poisoned than try to detox him. I never believed I had the power to make him happy. Isn't that stupid?"

"Why, what makes you think this girl will?"

"She has that strength. She will simply drive him out of whatever hole he's trapped in and bring him to the surface. She will love him, it's as simple as that."

"You love him too."

"But she's fearless. Young. And she will have his children."

"Yes. She's a breeder . . ."

"Right. We are not."

"No. We'd rather snort coke in the loo."

We pause, meditate for a few seconds. Then we do another line and go shopping.

I have to go one step back and try to put things in order. To fabricate some excuses for myself.

You have tried to leave before.

You have woken up in your bed in the middle of the winter, rain furiously pounding on the *mabati* roof, and felt like everything including your brain was turning to mould. You hate the idea of being so far away, forgotten by your friends at home, oblivious to the political changes in the world. You are starved for magazines, sophisticated conversation, films and good clothes. The person lying next to you is a man who was born here, for whom all that is simply nonexistent. Before falling asleep he has told you how much he loves the sound of the rain pounding on the tin roof at night, how it reminds him of his childhood. You hear him breathing peacefully, wrapped up in the blanket while you are going mad. In the morning you walk out in the garden, holding your hot mug of coffee close to your chin, your last good pair of boots deep in the thick mud. You feel as if your entire soul is going under. Everything around you has the bitter taste of decay: the mangoes rotting in the basket, the corrupted policeman at the roadblock who wants a bribe to let you pass, the headlines in the paper about new tribal massacres in the desert and piles of bodies liquefying in the heat. Suddenly the hardness of Africa reveals itself to you. Senseless and without redemption.

When you look in the mirror your face looks drained, armored, no trace of lightness left. You look older. That's when you think there may still be time to save yourself.

You want to leave. And you believe you will never come back.

Nobody is happy to let you escape, since everyone shares the symptoms of your disease. Someone will take you malcontentedly to the airport, in full Kenyan style, still wearing shorts and sandals, opening one Tusker beer after another, hitting the cap on the door handle and throwing the dripping empties on the back seat. They will sway and swear overtaking *matatu* buses on the way, they will be rude with the porters who are too slow to take your luggage.

You don't care.

You are already on the other side of the ocean, shielded by what's left of your good European clothes, the list of phone calls you have to make tomorrow.

You are out of here.

You check in with a smile, handing your ticket to the pretty stewardess in flawless uniform, the efficiency of Europe already welcoming you behind the airline counter.

You think you will come back, sure, but just as a tourist, to see your friends and your ex-lovers. To see all the places you loved. The Chyulu hills, Lake Turkana, the beach of Lamu, the Ewaso Nyiro River.

You don't know yet that you won't be able to get away.

So many people have tried to define the feeling the French call *mal d'afrique* which in fact is a disease. The English never had a definition for it, I guess because they never liked to admit that they were being threatened in any way by this continent. Obviously because they preferred the idea of ruling it rather than being ruled by it.

Only now I realize how that feeling is a form of corruption. It's like a crack in the wood which slowly creeps its way in. It gradually gets deeper and deeper until it has finally split you from the rest. You wake up one day to discover that you are floating on your own, you have become an independent island detached from its motherland, from its moral home base. Everything has already happened while you were asleep and now it's too late to attempt anything: you are out here, there's no way back. This is a one-way trip.

Against your will you are forced to experience the euphoric horror of floating in emptiness, your moorings cut for good. It is an emotion which has slowly corroded all your ties, but it is also a constant vertigo you will never get used to.

This is why one day you have to come back. Because now you no longer belong anywhere. Not to any address, house, or telephone number in any city. Because once you have been out here, hanging loose in the Big Nothing, you will never be able to fill your lungs with enough air.

Africa has taken you in and has broken you away from what you were before.

This is why you will keep wanting to get away but will always have to return.

Then, of course, there is the sky.

There is no sky as big as this one anywhere else in the world. It hangs over you, like some kind of gigantic umbrella, and takes your breath away. You are flattened between the immensity of the air above you and the solid ground. It's all around you, 360 degrees: sky and earth, one the aerial reflection of the other. The horizon here is no longer a flat line, but an endless circle which makes your head spin. I've tried to figure out the trick that lies behind this mystery, because I don't see any reason why there should be more sky in one place than in another. Yet I haven't been able to discover what is the optical illusion that makes the African sky so different than any other sky you have seen in your life. It could be the particular angle of the planet at the equator, or maybe the way clouds float, not above your head, but straight in front of your nose, sitting on the lower border of the umbrella, just on top of the horizon. Those drifting clouds which constantly redesign the map: in one glance you can see a rainstorm building up north, the sun shining in the east, and grey sky in the west which is bound to turn blue any minute. It's like sitting in front of a giant TV screen looking at a cosmic weather report.

You are travelling north, towards the NFD, the legendary North Frontier District, and suddenly it's as if you were looking at the landscape through the wrong side of binoculars. The ultimate wide-angle lens, which compresses the infinite within your field of vision. Your eyes have never cast a glance so far. Flat land that runs all the way to the distant purple profile of the Matthews Range and then, just when you thought you had reached an end to the space, right when you imagined that the landscape would close itself around you again, that you would feel less exposed, another curtain lifts up to reveal more vastness, and your eyes still can't catch the end of it.

More land stretching obediently under your tires, offering itself to be crossed. Your tracks become the endless flag of your conquest. You fill your lungs with the dry smell of hot rocks and dust, and you feel like you are breathing the universe.

You see yourself as you are driving into this grandiose absolute geometry: you are just a tiny dot, a minuscule particle advancing very slowly. You have now drowned in space, you are forced to redefine all proportions. You think of a word that hasn't occurred to you in years. It sprouts from somewhere inside you.

You feel *humble*. Because Africa is the beginning.

There is no shelter here: no shade, no walls, no roofs to hide under. Man has never cared to leave his mark on the land. Just tiny huts made of straw, like birds' nests that the wind will easily blow away.

You can't hide.

Here you are, under that burning sun, exposed. You realize that all you can rely on now is your body. Nothing you have learned in school, from television, from your clever friends, from the books you have read, will help you here.

Only now do you become aware that your legs are not strong enough to run, your nostrils can't smell, your eyesight is too weak. You realize you have lost all your original powers. When the wind blows the acrid smell of the buffalo in your nose, a smell you had never smelled before, you recognize it instantly. You know that its smell has always been here. Yours on the other hand is the result of many different things, from sunblock to toothpaste.

Le mal d'afrique is vertigo, is corrosion, and at the same time is nostalgia. It's a longing to go back to your childhood, to the same innocence and the same horror, when everything was still possible and every day could have been the day you die.

As I said, I am making excuses for myself.

I am trying to put everything on a grander scale, in order to feel that I haven't lost all I have lost for nothing. I have been driven out of the Garden of Eden but the apple wasn't something I wanted to eat out of simple greediness. Now I know that no human being will ever resist that temptation.

Chapter Two

Fear always remains.
A man may destroy everything within himself,
love and hate and belief, even doubt,
but as long as he clings to life,
he cannot destroy fear.

JOSEPH CONRAD

I come from the Old World.

I grew up under the shade of thick-walled family houses, behind crumbling façades, among old furniture inherited from my grandparents. I went to school walking through dark alleys that opened between buildings built by Michelangelo. On hot summer nights my friends and I used to jump in the cool water springing from fountains and swim among tritons and mermaids whose tails were intertwined in frightful knots of marble. I lived my whole life in a world that testified to the extraordinary talent of the human mind. I didn't grow up just in civilization: I grew up surrounded by beauty, which I took for granted. Mine must have been a geographical destiny.

My father was the perfect product of twentieth-century Europe: a poet. A Neapolitan poet, Illuminism coded in his DNA. Ferdinando had only one faith in his life, and that was faith in the power of words.

"We'll sell everything but the books," he used to say whenever we ran out of money, standing proudly, his back to the library, like a warrior before the walls of the city.

And sell we did: stereos and carpets and paintings and TV sets. There was a constant flow of items in and out of the pawnshops, which we always regarded as humorous rather than humiliating. But the books never went. No one would have been interested in buying them anyhow.

I must make some space for Ferdinando, because I wouldn't have ended out here, and then I probably wouldn't have been expelled from the Garden of Eden, had he not been my father.

Ferdinando was a beautiful man. Handsome in the way only passionate people are, when the energy is all concentrated in the face and radiates from their eyes. His were like the eyes of a falcon. Ferdinando looked to me like an aging medieval knight. Strong features, pronounced nose, graceful lines spreading like a thin fan around the corners of his eyes, dark thick hair, always too long, hair which later had streaks of white curling around his neck. And his hands, of course. Nervous and strong, woven with blue veins, his hands were the terminus of his brain. Words flew straight from his head into them, then slid from the pen onto the paper. Ferdinando never believed in typing, he had a very particular relation to his handwriting. He needed to see his words scribbled in his notebook, tentative words lingering for days on one corner of the page, patiently awaiting their destiny. Maybe they would go in or maybe they would be crossed out. His notebooks looked like a mad chart, one phrase here, another there, everything on standby in different positions. Poems are a bit like puzzles, he'd say. One wrong choice and nothing else sounds right. Eventually he would find the perfect sound he had been looking for and instantly that scribbled page would come alive, wipe itself of all indecision, and remake itself clean, in the form of a few beautiful lines.

Ferdinando wasn't interested in nature. He was too decadent, too much of an atheist, a soul possessed solely by Attic furies. And, needless to say, he was an alcoholic.

Harmony and balance had no appeal for him. He was attracted by chaos, by the inscrutable disorder that rules life in modern cities. He knew degradation, he didn't fear squalor. He could look the black bull in the eye.

He met my mother in New York in the fifties. They drank, went out to the clubs, hung out with interesting people, argued about politics, experimented with all that was available. With her red hair and white skin, my mother always looked frail, as if she was always on the verge of breaking down. I still can see her endlessly torturing her hair, biting her nails: she looked always as if she wasn't quite there with you, but rather thinking about someone else. Maybe in love with someone else who was making her unhappy. She always seemed to be devastated by a pain that had nothing to do with you, with the life you and she were sharing.

I remember my mother as a young woman—we were living in New York at that time, in an old apartment on the Upper West Side—stretching her bare legs on the sofa, looking out the window, oblivious to the noise of her children's games. She just lay there, listening to jazz, wrapped up in her secret obsessions, waiting. I never knew what she was waiting for. Maybe for the phone to ring, for her lover to call. But it never rang.

I don't know what it was; I guess nobody ever knew. Maybe it was her way of playing with Ferdinando: in order to survive him she had to escape him. Every one of us watched her constantly, followed her movements around the room as if she could just vanish from one minute to the next. We were always on guard.

I was only eight and my brother was four when she died. She crashed into a guardrail and flew off a bridge driving back from a friend's house in Connecticut late at night. She had drunk too much, they said.

That night it was snowing. I don't remember much else. Only how the phone had woken me and my brother up in the middle of our sleep, and kept ringing nonstop while the house slowly filled with people. I could feel their hysteria in the next room, and from the texture of their voices I knew something must have happened. Something big and dark, something frightening. Something totally new, which had never happened to us before. We sat patiently in the kitchen in our pyjamas, waiting to be told. Someone finally came in, hugged us and fed us chocolate chip cookies.

I remember pressing my nose against the window, trying to concentrate on the way the snow whirled and drifted under the orange streetlights. It's going to be such fun in the park tomorrow, I kept thinking.

Ever since then I always liked to think that she had flown into the river just like that. Pirouetting in slow motion like a dancer, like one of those snowflakes waltzing in the night.

I don't think it ever occurred to Ferdinando that my mother could die. After all it was he who was the dangerous one, the alcoholic, the poet *maudit*, he the one bound to be killed in a car crash. Instead my mother's death had stolen the scene away from him, and left him speechless. He felt he hadn't been cast for the role of a widower with two children.

So he took me and my little brother back to his house in Naples, where we led the extravagant life of two children tended by another older, pestiferous child.

He often overslept and forgot to take us to school, there was never any food in the house to feed us with, he never remembered to buy us new clothes. He simply kept handing me and my little brother wads of sticky crumpled cash, so that we could look after ourselves with it. But he read us bedtime stories from the *Iliad*, taught us how to cut open and eat the inside of sea urchins straight from the sea. He used the ruins of Pompeii as our private playground, making believe we were the only survivors of the volcano's eruption and had been left with a whole ghost city at our disposal. We loved him, maniacally. He was our king. I went through my Electra complex without the smallest hesitation. After all, I had nothing else to hold on to. Ferdinando married again twice, he couldn't bear to be without a woman in his life. Both his wives, in different ways, kept their doors shut to both me and my brother, as if we scared them. Or maybe it was we who preferred to keep away from them. They all reminded me of my mother: somewhat haunted, beautiful and aloof.

All of them held back something Ferdinando couldn't grasp

and which all his life, with the fury of a hunting dog, he tried to dig out.

I know the trick to get rid of pain: whole chunks of my life dissolve like a drop of ink in water. But I do remember one of the last times I saw Ferdinando. Not much else after that, when it was all over and all that was left was excruciating pain.

I'm driving to the house out in the country where he lives with his third wife, Louise. It's February, and there is that particular clear winter light just before sunset, when everything looks sharp like cut glass, as if sealed by the cold. The house sits on top of a round hill; only three cypresses break its circular outline. So unlike Ferdinando to live in such a tamed landscape as Tuscany, I can't help thinking. But Louise couldn't bear to live in the city. And he's too ill now, too weak, to put his foot down and force her to live in one of his casbahs.

As I'm slowly entering the driveway I am saying to myself, *Maybe this is the last time I will see him.* It sounds absurd: you are not supposed to know this beforehand, you only know it was the last time afterwards.

Yet as I gently brake on the gravel, I am overcome by a feeling of total estrangement. This is going to be some kind of scientific experiment: I must imprint in my mind every single step into this tragedy which is taking shape before my eyes. I am not yet able to perceive it as a whole, I can only take in one small fragment at a time.

The house looks just the same: the overloaded bookshelves, the yellowing lampshades, the faded cotton print on the sofa, the smoky scent of the fireplace. He's sitting by the window, silhouetted against the fading light. He hasn't turned the lights on. He has grown a three-days' beard, his hair hasn't been washed. He has rolled up the sleeves of his old sweater, eaten by moths. He is disheveled. As usual, he looks beautiful.

I sit in front of him and I stare. We keep quiet like this, just looking at each other, while the room falls rapidly into the blue winter light which follows the sunset. I brush his profile, the high cheekbones, his lips, with my eyes. His fingers fiddle with a button. He's been prohibited from smoking, and it's odd to see him without a cigarette in his hand, without the familiar cloud of smoke floating around him.

I think: The way he's dying doesn't look anything like what I expected. He stares at me, perfectly lucid, while every day another bit of him crumbles away. Only his anger hasn't crumbled yet: I know he is furious at the idea of having to die.

Each day the brain tumour deletes another sound from his speech. His thoughts are all there, witty, complicated and twisted as ever: it is the language that is slowly sinking. Every morning he wakes up to discover that another letter has vanished from his mouth. He's now left with only vowels. Horrific growls, animal-like. I try to decode him, he gets impatient. He can't stand the humiliation of not being understood.

Louise is upstairs. I can hear the muffled sound of her footsteps on the wooden boards and the faint sound of classical music. Everyone around him has to pretend that nothing is happening. None of us is allowed to acknowledge the fact that he is dying. This is the deal we were all forced to strike with him.

A few weeks ago, when he still was able to speak well enough, he put his arm around my shoulder and drew me close to his neck. He stared into my eyes.

"You know this is no longer *me*, don't you?" he whispered.

That was the only time he ever said anything about it.

The absurdity was that Ferdinando died mute.

It was as if some karmic punishment had descended upon him. Like a Greek hero suddenly deprived of his shield by the will of an angry god and left naked before the spear of the enemy on the battleground.

Ferdinando's body was weak, translucently white, abused by too many cigarettes, alcohol and sleeping pills. It was a lifeless receptacle, a forgotten carcass which required no care. It had never mattered to him. It was his head that had made him invulnerable.

Ironically, that neglected body was what betrayed him in the

end. Slowly, incessantly, every little bolt and screw came undone, bits and pieces at a time, until the whole thing went to
pieces and was no longer recognizable. Until it lost its dignity.

His illness forced him to recede into the most primitive form
his body ever had: Ferdinando died like an infant without language, forced to wail in order to attract other people's attention.
He died in such a way that we would all learn that the shelves
loaded with books we were never allowed to sell—the Shake-
speare sonnets, Dante's quatrains, Piero della Francesca's paintings and Brunelleschi's laws of perspective—were of no use at
all. We realized that there must be some other way to face one's
death. But not even Ferdinando, who always seemed to know
everything, knew how to do that.

When I stared into his eyes that evening, in that quiet moment of transition before the night falls, I saw something I had
never seen before.

I saw his fear.

He wanted to know. What was going to happen? What was
this *thing* going to be like, once the darkness fell upon him?

I didn't want him to know how terrified I was to see him like
this, so I closed my eyes and held his hand for a long time, until
we were both in the dark.

I still don't know about my mother.

All I am left with are some black-and-white photos that I
used to keep looking at when I was younger, in the hope they
would tell me something more about her.

There is one I particularly liked, in which she sits on a win-
dowsill in a light crumpled linen dress, barefoot, where she has
the look of a circus girl. A trapeze artist, a failed dancer. The determination and sadness about her. That strength in her calves,
and the vulnerability in her eyes.

I used to search my own body for her. I looked for those
same arched eyebrows, lean feet, high cheekbones, slanted
eyes. But she had gone. Even her genes seemed to have vanished like fish sliding out of the net, so that I could never claim

her back.

Many years after her death I found a note she had written to Ferdinando around the time they had first met. It was scribbled on the back of a faded postcard.

It is not in the nature of love to be so daunting. I don't want to have to fear you, especially when your wit can be so unkind. I've never been good at being afraid, and you know what scared animals are like. Stop talking, just hold me. Even better: marry me.

That scrap of paper was the only thing I found in all these years which made my mother come alive, in the flesh, which made her real to me. She had to marry Ferdinando in order to lose her fear of needing him.

Marry me, she had ordered him. Release me from fear.

He obeyed. My father always showed great respect for acts of courage.

The way Ferdinando was so clever with words gave him power to make his way into anything, and he knew that well. In that respect he was an arrogant conquerer.

After he died it suddenly occurred to me how I had lived all my life shielded by his personality: I had been hiding behind his genius, his provocativeness, without inheriting any of his talent. If anything, I had grown weaker and weaker in his shadow, and now without him I felt stripped bare, unable to cope.

I needed to find myself a place that wouldn't remind me of him, a place full of emptiness, without a written history, where language had very little meaning. Because without Ferdinando, beauty, intellectual exercise, artistic talent, literature no longer made sense to me.

Later on, as I was leaving all of it behind, I felt like it had never even existed: all I could remember was that expression of fear in his eyes, and that silent question, to which of course, I had no answer.

In fact all his loss left me with was the realization that in

Ferdinando's world—the world where words have power, where culture means control—one can only postpone fear. All one actually is able to do, is to freeze it.

I needed to go somewhere where my body would be the only tool required to survive, a place where I would be able to test my fear, rather than putting off the moment I had to face it.

Only by going there did I feel I might be prepared for whatever happened.

CHAPTER THREE

Nature, Mr Alnutt, is something we were
put on this earth to rise above.

KATHARINE HEPBURN IN THE AFRICAN QUEEN

It is now Adam's turn to come into the story.

If it's true that, as I always believed, names hold a destiny in themselves, Adam couldn't have been called anything else.

To me Adam was like the first man of the world, the man Leonardo drew inside the circle with his arms spread. The basic principle. In baboon language: an alpha male.

I came to Africa with the wrong guy, which turned out to be the best possible thing.

In the midst of a bleak April, only a month after my father's funeral, I was shipped to this continent like a postal parcel, sedated by sleeping pills, in the company of a young man—we'll call him P.—with whom I had had some desperate sex right after Ferdinando's death.

I had been crawling into his bed every night with my eyes shut, wrapping my legs around his body the way a parasitic plant strangles a tree, and with the same determination I had clung on to him hoping I'd find some sunlight at the end of the tunnel. But no.

P. loved it, he hadn't a clue how sick my mind was, how completely crazed I had become after my father's death. He believed in distractions and insisted on taking me out all the time.

P. was a yuppie with literary aspirations, tall, dark-haired, smelling of Eau Sauvage, impeccably dressed. Probably good-looking, but without a face. He had been going out with harmless girls all his life and had learned about the bad ones only in books. So he quite enjoyed my lunacy, my terrory, and most of all my cruelty. He believed he was going to learn something new from me.

He took me to Kenya on holiday and scrupulously paid for everything: money had always been his only means of having things under control.

For all I cared I could have been anywhere.

I lay in different beds in different five-star hotels, placated only by the soothing sound mix of air conditioning and CNN, ordering room service while P. was out exploring nature in zebra-striped vans, with a happy crowd of tourists who wanted to get their money's worth and wouldn't stop until they could take a good shot of a lion's kill. They all came back just before dark, exhausted, comparing what they had managed to get in the shot, loud and proud, hungry for more.

I hated all of them and kept ordering chicken sandwiches.

Africa lay out there somewhere, a secret entity which revealed nothing of its nature. I could feel its vastness creeping in from the window. Something big was certainly going on out there, but I couldn't be bothered to find out what it was.

On day six, P. accused me of sabotage.

"Esmé I really don't think it's a good idea to lie here all alone, it'll just make you more depressed. You must make an effort. Trust me—"

"Listen, I am perfectly all right, I'm just not in the mood to see other people, I want to rest."

"Sometimes I have the feeling that you are doing this on purpose. You don't *want* to feel better."

I was lying on the bed among ashtrays, magazines, crumbs

and empty plates. I looked up at him.

"It's all right not to feel good all the time, you know. Happiness is not *mandatory* on this planet."

P. had been a tourist all his life. He liked to browse around, take pictures, and eventually head back home. He had had high expectations about his voyage into my personality, but I guess I had disappointed him. In his mental brochure, taking the neurotic daughter of a famous dead poet to Africa must have seemed an appealing cultural choice. He had put a copy of *The Green Hills of Africa* in the Fendi briefcase, in case he ran out of inspiration.

Unfortunately I turned out to be a rather flat country, not much action there. Plus our sex life had come to a halt. I couldn't stand it anymore and had asked him to move to the other twin bed. He didn't look happy but he took it with savoir faire. After all he was a well-bred Italian and wasn't going to claim his money back.

I didn't care about being a fraud. I just wanted to be left alone.

On day seven we moved to the middle of the Masai Mara, to a luxury tented camp surrounded by more ferocious American tourists. With no CNN to hypnotise me, I couldn't sit inside the tent all day, so I agreed to go on a game drive before sunset.

I remember smelling the rain. I could see dark clouds heading our way, thick lead against blue sky. That incredible sky, which I was seeing at last, took my breath away. I had no words to describe it then, and don't now.

In the stillness before the storm, the plains opened before my eyes. The gentle shape of the acacias, the herds of zebra and wildebeest and buffalo dotting the yellowing grass in the distance: it all came alive and whatever had been dead inside me slowly started to breathe.

Then we saw the elephants. About thirty of them. I asked the driver to stop the car and turn off the engine. I stood up through the open roof, feeling the gusts of wind blowing through my hair, and watched them slowly come my way.

"God they are huge!" said P., clicking away. "Esmé! Look at

the size of those willies!"

"Just *be quiet,* will you?"

He did.

The elephants came closer, all in a line, very slowly, the old female clearing the way for the others. They were all around us now. I closed my eyes and smelled them, listening to the gentle sound of the grass being torn by their trunks. No footfalls: just the grass and the wind, and the smell of the rain coming closer every second. The sun disappeared behind the clouds, flashing a last green acid light on the plain. A colder gust of wind, then the sky turned black.

It came down torrentially, with lightning and thunder, and the sound was deafening.

Water was running down the rumps of the elephants, dripping down the backs of the muddy buffaloes. It didn't change their slow motion; I could still hear the muffled moans of the wildebeests, grazing peacefully under the downpour.

"We should go, don't you think?" P. whispered nervously in my ear.

He's the kind of man who hates to get wet.

I didn't answer. I was still standing out of the open roof, water running down my cheeks, flowing down my neck, choking my nostrils, my hair stuck to my temples. Breathing, feeling the space, the rain, the smell of the animals, of the soil releasing its richness.

Crying. At last.

P. sighed and retreated inside, shaking his head, not happy with what I was doing.

On day eight I was feeling, if not better, at least different.

I sat at our luxury-camp breakfast table with determination, and proceeded to X-ray P. in the bright morning light.

As he was helping himself to scrambled eggs and bacon I had a clear vision of what it was that I loathed about him.

There is a vast tribe of men like P., who manage to live all their lives within their self-imposed boundaries, and are perfectly resigned never to cross them.

They are uncomfortable at the mere idea of having to come out in the open: in fact they don't even seem to be capable of getting out of their own clothes with ease. They seem perpetually sealed in their Brooks Brothers shirts, even when they are naked and breathing heavily on top of you. Nothing will change them, not death, nor disaster, not war, nor a broken heart. But the saddest part is that beauty will not change them either. They can't take it in, let alone open up to it. They are perpetual spectators. They just take pictures.

It was intolerable: the thought of being exiled from beauty, of having to look at it with the same resignation as when you look at something you know will never have, something you are not worthy of. That really killed me.

The possibility of yourself becoming that beauty, even if only once, simply by wading into it, letting it flow in through the pores of your skin; rolling in it, mud, dust, rain or sand, *smearing* it all over you—suddenly I was feeling wild—how could anyone exclude that possibility from their life?

Now I don't know, but it seemed very clear then at that breakfast table, watching the Calvin Kleined troops of tourists loading their money's worth of breakfast onto their plates, eyes fixed on the bacon, comparing it with the quality of bacon back home. They seemed completely unaltered. Whereas I had been released from the sealed package I had come shipped in only fourteen or fifteen hours earlier and was already delirious. There was no way I could climb back into my cardboard box and ignore what I had seen.

"Our plane leaves from the strip at three," said P., hoping that after my wailing with the elephants he had seen my absolute worst and that I would spare him more dysfunctional behaviour. "We could go for a quick game drive, come back at one, get some lunch and then pack."

His meticulous tiny plans. I felt like smacking him in the face. And why was this total stranger using "we" all the time?

It was like surfing. I had been underwater so long, waiting to drown, and now—totally unexpectedly—I found myself on top of the wave, out in the sun again, terrified of losing my balance, because the thing was going so damn fast. But it was my only chance and I had to keep riding it, regardless of how frightening it was and how poorly equipped I felt. I knew I didn't want to go back under.

"You know, I am not coming back with you," I heard myself say to him, brightly, my mouth full of toast. I quite liked the sound of it. "I am going to stay here on my own."

"Here *where?*" He looked frightened.

"Here. In Africa. In the bush. I don't know." I waved my hand around, pointing vaguely at the trees. "Right here, maybe."

He stared at me.

"You can't do that."

"Why?"

"Because we have a ticket which you can't. . . . it can't be changed and—"

"Everything can be changed."

He looked at me in disbelief. He wasn't ready for this kind of thing so early in the morning.

"And what about money? I mean it's going to cost you a *fortune* to stay in a place like this on your own, I just don't see how you . . ."

I smiled at him and eagerly began buttering another slice of toast.

He gave up. He was finally starting to hate me.

"Esmé, why do you always insist on acting so *strange?*"

I shrugged. It felt good to be back on the wave. I would find ways to manoeuvre and keep my balance.

"I'll be fine. Just lend me three hundred bucks, will you?"

More silence, more resentful stares.

"Listen, I feel responsible for you. Actually, I *am* responsible for you and I am not going to—"

"Oh, fuck *that.*"

This is how it happened. Everything had been moving very slowly inside me for months. Then my life turned around over a plate of scrambled eggs.

I took P. to the airstrip, with the air of a scrupulous secretary seeing off her boss. He had left me five hundred dollars in cash and had paid for an extra night at the camp. He asked me "But exactly *how long* do you think you'll stay on?" about a million times.

The fact that I didn't have a plan, that I was no longer going to act like a tourist, obediently following the orders of his travel agent, that I was going to plunge into that unknown landscape on my own and disappear from the map, seemed to terrify him. I was escaping from the tyranny of schedules and vouchers, like some mad Russian anarchist.

"Call me as soon as you get back. I will be very concerned until I have news from you. Actually, call me collect as soon as you are near a phone."

I gently patted him on the back, blew air kisses on both sides of his cheeks, waved goodbye with a smile and watched the six-seater lift him out of my life.

I felt light and euphoric as the Land Rover drove me back to camp with the latest batch of Texans. I no longer minded them, even when they anxiously asked me whether I had seen any rhinos around.

When I got back, Adam was sitting on one of the bar stools under the thatched roof of the mess tent. I didn't notice him right away, because I was too busy checking my latest secret experiment. Was I, the guinea pig, going to freak out, lose my grip on my surfboard and crash into the waves, or was this the beginning of freedom? Monitoring myself closely for any sign of anxiety, I sat down at the bar and ordered a shot of tequila. I needed to feel warm. I figured the best way to go about it was to take one step at a time and check my body temperature every half hour.

The night was closing in, filling the air with its different sounds like an orchestra pit before rehearsals, each animal carefully tuning in from a distance. The shrills of crickets, the hoarse frogs, the intermittent grunt of a hippo followed by its splash in the muddy water, the baboons playing in the trees. And in the distance the muffled moos of the wildebeests, thousands of them grazing on the plain, always heading towards greener grass like an army moving camp.

I felt Adam's eyes on me. We were the only two people left sitting at the bar; everyone else had moved to the tables and was busy wolfing down food. He smiled.

"Not hungry?"

"What? Me? . . . Oh . . . well, no . . . not really. Slowly getting drunk on Camino Real."

He chuckled.

"Can I collaborate and buy you another?" His voice was like velvet in the semidark.

"Yes. Thank you. My name is Esmé."

"Adam. What kind of name is Esmé?"

He moved closer. He smelled good. I couldn't make out his face very well in the dim light of the mess tent, but his presence felt nice.

"Actually it's Esmeralda. A rather pompous Italian name. But Esmé is also the name of a character, an appalling little English girl in a J. D. Salinger short story . . . my parents *loved* Salinger."

"'For Esmé with Love and Squalor,' is that right?"

"You know that story?"

"Absolutely. The American soldier and the little English girl in the tearoom. Then he goes mad, or something."

It surprised me that he had read it. I must have assumed everyone in Africa would be illiterate.

Adam spoke gently to the barman in Swahili, which sounded like some kind of children's secret language, full of *ahs* and *ohs* and *uhs*, a bit like Italian in the way it sang, but not as flamboyant. The barman laughed, as if responding to a good joke, and poured two Camino Reals.

"Are you on holiday or what?" he asked.

I smiled.

"A good question. Actually I don't know what I am on."

The radio in the back of the bar started its raucous unintelligible sounds, and Adam leapt out of his seat and disappeared behind the counter. I heard him speak more Swahili, dropping in a few English words, like "spark plugs," "alternator" and "starter motor," lots of "over," and back he was on his stool, smiling.

"That sounded very efficient," I said in a friendly tone.

"I need a spare part from Nairobi for my car, and hopefully they will fly it in tomorrow."

The barman lit a hurricane lamp and put it on the counter. I looked closely at Adam's face. Now I could make out his sandy hair, the strong neck, and his beautiful lips. He looked straight into my eyes. His could have been green. He looked so unexpectedly handsome that I blushed: I was not prepared to be stared at by such an attractive man. I noticed his hands around the glass. Strong and flat. I quickly downed a second tequila.

I have a camp just a few miles up the river. My clients left today and I'm stuck until I can fix my car. This camp has a very good mechanic, someone who used to work for me. They stole him from us, but thank God he's still around.

I suddenly felt too nervous to say anything.

"So, Esmé," I loved hearing my own name in that voice, "what are you doing in a place like this all by yourself?"

I gave him a brief, confused account. I told him that I had no plans, that I didn't know anything or anybody, that I was on some kind of mission but hadn't figured out yet what it was. He didn't look puzzled. We drank more tequilas.

He told me a little about his family, how he was a second-generation Kenyan, how his Scottish grandfather had had a coffee estate upcountry, then his father had been a hunter in the Northern Frontier District, and how he was running luxury tented safaris for upmarket American tourists. He bombarded me with questions, as if I was some kind of exotic specimen he had never come across before, which pleased me. By tequila number four I had completely forgotten about my surfing ambitions; I had switched to automatic pilot and was smoothly gliding into the night in the company of this beautiful stranger.

34

The next morning I woke up at dawn alone in my tent, my heart racing, trying desperately to disentangle myself from seriously morbid sexual dreams. It still looked pretty murky down in those depths where my unconscious was free to roam like a wild animal. I walked out of the tent and sat in front of the river watching the hippos still asleep on the bank, one on top of the other. Such a happy family. I wished *I* could have had a night like that. I drank cups of coffee until I had palpitations, carefully bathed and chose something nice to wear, then set out to look for Adam.

I found him in the staff quarters of the camp, among a busy crowd of Africans wearing overalls, Zairean music screeching from a transistor, looking intently under the hood of a big four-wheel drive.

"Good morning." He smiled. His hair was still wet, and in the morning light his eyes definitely were a dark shade of green.

"You look very nice in that dress, *Esmeh*." The way he pronounced my name, his velvety deep voice lingering on it, made my heart stop for a split second. It surprised me that I had already become something he could call by name.

"Do you mind if I watch you fix the car?"

Adam laughed.

"Not at all. You're most welcome to *watch* me," he said, as if I had made a sexual proposition. And he was absolutely right.

I sat cross-legged on the ground and proceeded to dissect every muscle in his body, registering the shape of arms, calves, ankles, following every nerve, contraction, drop of sweat, as if I had never seen the body of a man before. I was hypnotized by his rhythm, the careful movement of his hands, screwing and unscrewing inside the hood, gently pulling out wires, then wiping the grease on his old khaki shorts; the gently quick way he spoke with the guys who kept handing him tools like a team of doctors to a surgeon. Now and then he would look over at me and smile, as if making sure I was still there.

I am remembering this scene so clearly because it was a key to my attraction to Adam. His body had such a vibrant vitality, everything seemed to be so coordinated, and yet in its simplest

35

form. Adam's shoulders were the archetype of shoulders, so were his legs, the veins in his forearms, the solid roundness of his kneecaps.

There are bodies—the majority in fact—which are mute, their purpose merely to transport and protect their contents. Arms and legs have no life of their own, no hints of personality or secret disposition will be revealed by a close study. The main purpose of those bodies without a character is to conceal rather than to express.

P. had a completely mute body, which took shape and sent a message only when wrapped in designer shirts or pastel cashmere sweaters. P.'s body made itself intelligible to the world only through basic fashion-coded signals, which had to be added, like software. Otherwise his body had never developed a language of its own.

This body here, the body of this man fixing the car—I had to sit down in order to take it all in, it made my legs weak.

It didn't talk to me: it sang. Every tiny bone in his wrist, the shape of his fingertips—the whole thing was like a symphony.

Suddenly I couldn't bear watching that body another minute unless I could blend into its music. I felt that my anxiety would finally be sedated for good only when that body embraced me and took me in. I wasn't thinking of having sex. I wanted this man I didn't know to make love to me. I knew that if he did there would be fresh air and light at the other end of the tunnel. I knew it by looking at his body, and I knew it by the way he had pronounced my name. Obviously I was losing it: everything was getting out of control. But the determination I felt in my folly had started to please me.

"Esmé, what are your plans? I mean, where do you think you will go after this?" He had lit a cigarette and come to smoke it next to me while the guys in overalls were welding an obscure piece of burnt metal.

I felt a wave of heat rise up in me.

". . . Oh, well . . . I'm not sure. I should . . . have to . . . leave this place today."

"If you'd like you can come and stay at my camp." He kept

his eyes on the welding job, making sure his guys were not fucking up. A pretty concentrated guy, I thought.

"I don't know what to say. It sounds great, but . . ."

"The place is empty, there are five big tents. And a fully stocked bar."

The five-tent bit meant that we had the choice of sleeping in separate tents. The full-bar bit probably meant that there was plenty of booze to make the choice we really wanted, which was to sleep in the same tent.

"Well, thank you," I answered noncommittally.

There was a pause. I didn't dare look at him and pretended to have taken a sudden interest in his spare parts.

"Good," I heard him say, "we are almost done with the car. We can leave whenever you're ready. It's only about forty-five minutes away."

I relaxed and felt the heat wave cool down. There was some hope after all at the end of this manic tunnel. At least I thought that was what my body was trying to tell me.

I don't remember much of my first day with Adam. I kept looking at him, rather than at the landscape which he was constantly pointing out. We drove in his car all the way up the escarpment, through the zebra and wildebeest migration.

"It looks like Genesis, day four, when God decides to add the animals to the landscape," I said. "I can't believe you are called Adam, on top of it all."

He grinned with a naughty twinkle in his eyes.

He never tired of stopping the car to point out a Thompson's gazelle or a zebra, or even a tiny bird on a branch, with wonderfully colored wings and a very complicated name. He wasn't class-prejudiced, unlike those avid tourists who only cared to see the big guys like rhinos, elephants and cats, as if the rest of the animal population, being in such abundance, was working-class, peons not worthy of attention. Adam loved everything with equal passion, pointed at the light through the acacias or the shape of the hills with such pride that it was as if he had personally designed them that morning. I pretended to show interest in all that he showed me, nodding but looking at his beautiful mouth, wondering when he was going to kiss me—after sunset?

His camp looked like the real thing: everything was well done but in a rustic way, so that it felt like a camp and not a hotel in the bush. There was a big mess tent with a wooden table and safari chairs, kilim carpets and cushions scattered around. The tents were made of thick green canvas; mine had a huge double bed in it, a charming writing table and an old wicker chair on the verandah.

What I remember of the rest of the afternoon gets a bit confused. I think he took me for a walk, along the river, we took a nap (separately), had a shower (separately), and while the animal orchestra was tuning in right after sunset we headed for the bar. We sat around the fire with double gin and tonics, made our way through dinner with a few beers, had an after-dinner cognac around the fire, and finally, just when I thought I had no more endurance, when I was beginning to lose hope, bliss came in the form of his arms gently pulling me towards him.

I waded into him slowly, as he embraced me, and took me into the tent. He undressed me slowly, wordlessly, and held me and looked at my naked body. When we touched and kissed and loved each other it was as if we had done this all our lives. There were no angles, no bones, no tension: every particle of our bodies was round and soft, hands and lips like feathers. We flowed and floated into each other, and I knew this was right. I felt I had finally started to reach shore.

And then he said my name again, looking into my eyes.

"Yes?" I asked, my voice broken.

"I love the sound of it," he whispered.

I wanted more of that. I so desperately wanted more of that love that I closed my eyes and thought, Please be good, don't fuck this one up. *Please* save your life.

I didn't.

But then, how does anyone learn?

Chapter Four

Why do I travel so much
when I am so terribly frightened of travelling?

SVEN LINDQUIST

Nicole and I are driving around aimlessly in my car, our shopping on the back seat. I have managed to spend an astronomical sum of money on things I don't need. I now own a new set of espresso cups imported from France, an Italian wine carafe, a very expensive piece of fabric from Rajasthan in case I feel like making new cushions, a string of old West African beads to add to the collection, another silver Ethiopian cross, Brie, Camembert, German rye bread and a case of South African wine. I've shopped the world and still I could go on. We have raided Yaya Center, the open town market, the Ethiopian shop and the new delicatessen on the Ngong road in only two and a half hours.

Someone said that in Africa one becomes avid. You always want more, it's never enough. Your house will always look tentative, unfinished, too rustic; your closet too empty, your car too old, your CD collection pathetic. You become obsessed with what you lack in life. It's always another repair, another essential piece of furniture, another kitchen tool, another step up the ladder before you reach inner peace. Material possessions haunt you. It could be a Wonderbra or a chunk of real Stilton cheese; the nature of the object is irrelevant. The object becomes the mantra on which to meditate whenever you feel your identity is starting to fade away.

We buy three-months-old British *Vogues* stolen from the post office. The street vendors on Uhuru Highway push the glossy magazines through the car window at rush hour. Another display of material necessities opens before our eyes while we quickly flick through the sticky pages.

The feature on "Sensual Bathrooms" covers six whole pages. The list of items you need in order to fully enjoy your bath is specific and extremely expensive. Scented amber candles £10, Moroccan white cotton towels labeled "Hammam" £24, rose-petal bath salts £18, a stainless steel rack designed by Philip Starck £150.

Anything will do, in order not to turn into one of those desperate expat housewifes in jogging pants and sneakers, who long ago have lost hope and keep just one yellowing jar of Pond's night cream on the bathroom shelf. Or those diplomats' wives running around in pretty dresses and a string of pearls, attending yoga classes and parenting courses at the Lighthouse Center, lunching on yoghurt and alfalfa sprouts, desperately holding on to some kind of routine in order to make their life here remotely comparable to the lives of their friends back home.

Nicole and I firmly believe in frivolity as the ultimate form of rescue. Ours is survival consumerism, at times strictly voyeuristic, an unwritten rule we observe devoutly in order to keep our sanity.

We pull into the Karen gas station, next to the bank and the post office.

Karen got its name from Isak Dinesen, better known here as Karen Blixen. It was here that Baroness Blixen had her now internationally famous coffee farm. In her time, it took half a day by horseback to reach Nairobi from here. Today it's only a thirty-minute drive to the center of town, and it has turned into a rather affluent, mainly white suburb, which still retains a slight bushy atmosphere.

The Karen shopping centre is the epicentre of our lives. We come here every day to pick up the mail, bank, shop, meet a friend at the Horseman's restaurant, buy flowers for dinner parties, check with the mechanic, order wood or paint at the hardware. This is where we find out what everyone else is up to. A constant flow of cars pulls in and out in front of the stores: station wagons loaded with dirty barefoot children just picked up from the Banda school, neurotic young mothers in shorts who have just bought provisions for a week; Kenya cowboys in sandals loading the back of the car with beer cases and ice blocks for the next safari; decrepit couples who have lived too long in the sun, rigid as embalmed terrapins, tipping the shop boy one shilling only, in memory of the good old days.

It's the epitome of small-town suburban life, but with a twist: the echoes of Karen Blixen and the colonial architecture of the stone buildings give a romantic aura to the hopeless triviality of our activities. Right here, at the foot of the Ngong hills, is where it all began: Baroness Blixen has become Nairobi's Statue of Liberty.

"*Habari, mama.*" The guy smiles at me as I give him the keys and he starts filling up the tank. "*Wapi* Adam?"

"*Alienda safari. Atarudi weeki ingine.*" I am who I am to them because I belong to Adam. This is definitely a man's society.

"Where have you girls been all day?" Suddenly Nena appears at the car window, biting a green apple. "I've left messages everywhere."

She's wearing an old secondhand dress tied tightly at her waist with an old Turkana beaded belt. Her long dark hair is tied up in a knot with a pencil stuck into it. She holds Natasha, her four-year-old, in her arms.

"Hi darling."

"We've been cruising around." I stroke Natasha's hair. "Hi baby."

"Listen, I'm having a dinner party tonight," she says.

"Great."

"I love your necklace," she says to Nicole.

"Thank you. What time?"

"Nine-ish. I thought I'd ask Hunter's girlfriend as well—didn't she come in today?"

There is an almost imperceptible pause.

"Yeah. Esmé picked her up at the airport," says Nicole nonchalantly.

I feel Nena's inquisitive eyes on me as I fiddle busily with the cigarette pack. I've never known whether she knows. I guess she does, because everyone here always knows.

"Don't you think she'd like to meet some people? Hunter told us to take care of her until he comes back from Kampala."

"Absolutely." I smile efficiently. "I'll call her up and give her a lift in my car."

Nena throws the gnawed apple over her shoulder.

"What's she like? Claire, right?"

"Yes. Claire. She seems sweet," I say, "blond. You know, kind of pretty."

"Oh, okay." Nena is disappointed by the lack of interesting details. "I've got to run to pick up Toby at school. I'll see you later, then."

I drive Nicole home without saying another word.

I am thinking that maybe I will have to go away again soon, go back to Europe and really try to get used to it this time.

"Are you all right?" Nicole is watching me closely.

"No. But I will be."

"For God's sake, I wish you'd stop trying so hard to be in control."

"What do you mean?"

"I mean that if it's ripping you apart the way it seems to be, stop pretending that you can bear it. Call him up now, tell him you are going to die, tell him you can't live without him. Fight for it, it's your fucking life!"

"I will *not* die without him. That's the whole point. He knows that too well."

"*Aw Gawd,*" Nicole lights a cigarette, "this is *such* a bad soap opera."

I drop her home. Her verandah looks so peaceful, her canvases piled against the wall, the brushes resting neatly in the jar, the smell of turpentine floating in the air. I am so jealous that she comes home to something she cares about.

"Do you want to borrow my green dress for tonight?" she asks cheerfully as she steps into the house.

"No, thanks. Another time."

"Do you care for another line?"

"Not really."

"Are you sure you want to go and pick her up? Why don't you just leave her behind? We don't need to—"

"I hope everyone hates her. I hope *you* hate her."

"Of course I will. Don't you worry about *that.*"

I drive home in the golden five-thirty light. The magic hour. It's your moment of peace, when the clouds clear the sky just before sunset.

The Masai *askaris* walk along the side of the road, going to work wrapped in their red blankets. The Kikuyu maids are on their way to catch the *matatu* which will take them home, away from the idyllic silence of this white neighbourhood, into the smoky and crowded confusion of Ongata Rongai, reggae blasting from the *hoteli*'s windows, kerosene lamps shining in the dark, deep into the husky and festive noise of the African town.

I stop by the side of the road before honking at my gate and meticulously begin to remove the price tags from the espresso cups, the carafe and the South African wine. The money I have spent on these items equals the monthly salary of both Wilson the cook and Alice the maid. I don't know which makes me feel more guilty: when I forget to perform this operation and I catch a glimpse of Wilson's and Alice's expression while they empty the shopping bags in the kitchen—it's not resentment nor spite, more like a sort of reverential terror towards an object so inexplicably expensive—or when I remember to do it and find myself crawling in the back of the car, frantically ripping off tags like a

44

thief about to be caught.

On the equator there is no light after sunset, night falls over you like the shadow of a giant.

Inside the house Alice is lighting the fireplace, and the candles on the mantelpiece. All of a sudden I feel cold.

I sit by the telephone. You never know whether it's going to work. I lift the receiver. It does. It may not tomorrow.

He's only ten digits away.

I can't. I can't dial, ask for his name, wait until they put him through, breathe, say Hunter it's me, I love you, please let's stop this killing game, let's just be together can't you see we're meant for each other please send her away this is crazy I will make you happy I just want to love you.

I never could and now it's too late. We have squandered the time we were given, too busy fencing each other off. Now our time is up. We made it too nasty.

Wilson creeps into the room and asks me in a whisper if I am eating at home.

"No, I'm going to mama Nena, thank you Wilson."

I'll run a bath and forget about it.

Claire has also had a bath and her long hair is still wet.

"Ready to go?" I dangle the car keys from my fingertips.

"Yes. Do you think I'll need a sweater?"

"Probably."

I watch her while she goes to the closet. She is wearing a wide-pleated skirt that makes her look like a schoolgirl. She is sexy in that mysterious English way, as only blond girls with a good family background and an aptitude for outdoor activities can be, fresh as a rose yet hard as a nail. I feel so different, dark and wounded like Saint Sebastian pierced by arrows. I'm surprised no blood is seeping through my dress.

The phone rings and she leaps to pick it up on the second ring.

He's calling from that hotel room in Kampala where only an hour ago I had set my imaginary scene, my failed love declaration. He's lying on the bed, fluorescent lights full on, sipping a Coke, just as I had pictured him earlier, except he's talking to her.

Claire whispers, her body curled around the receiver like a snail.

"Well . . . just fine . . . going out . . . Nena . . . Jonathan Hart called for you . . ."

She doesn't mention my name, as if I'm not even in the room.

". . . will go to town . . . when do you think . . . coming back . . . fine . . . me too . . . yes, me too."

I am sitting in the red armchair, my back to their conversation.

Nothing could be worse than this.

I actually pronounce these words, very slowly, whispering so that she can't hear me talking to myself.

I am an impostor in this house, I shouldn't even be here.

She comes back towards me with a smile.

"That was Hunter; he may come back the day after tomorrow."

"Oh."

We walk outside in the dark, the *askari* flashing the torch to the car. We drive in silence; I am too drained to make any effort at conversation. The car lights flash on the wild hares jumping in the grass, stars are shining in the cold sky.

She smells of coconut body lotion. What a silly scent to wear.

I know I will never heal from Ferdinando's loss. In fact I miss him more and more: when he was around I was able to look at things through the lens of his intelligence. I was always allowed to borrow it, like a child is allowed to play with his father's glasses, and every time I did, things people said or did somehow stopped frightening or confusing me. He had a way of putting things back in their place. It was like having our own private observation point. He was the one in charge of the focus; I just had the privilege of making use of it. Ferdinando saw through people, nobody could fool him. He often ridiculed them to the point that they were forever destroyed even in your memory. Often I felt that he acted like a child whose favourite game was ripping my dolls to pieces. But in the end, once he had performed his wild open-heart surgery, I was forced to admit that there was nothing inside but plastic.

I guess that this was his only means of protecting me and my brother: he never seemed to have the inclination to take care of us in any other way. His observation point was the safest place we had.

Now, without him, I'm back in the blur, I am no longer capable of redefining the contours. I guess I'm back to mistaking plastic for gold.

I had never felt so passive as after that first time Adam and I made love.

For one thing, I couldn't sleep, I wanted to stay awake, lying next to him, in order to study his proximity, his smell. I wanted to absorb it, to get to know it quickly. I watched his body breathing slowly next to mine, his ribcage rising rhythmically, I inhaled the warmth of his nakedness without fear. Nothing about him felt foreign or intimidating. I wished I could stop the clock and never have to get up again, say anything, make any decisions. I just wanted to lie still in the dark next to him and hear him breathe.

I watched the sky lighten slowly through the tent netting, listened to the first birds waking in the trees. Against the white light Adam was silhouetted in profile, still wrapped in his quiet dreams. I watched the colours come alive in slow motion, greens and blues superimposed on the black-and-white of night, the pink light of dawn glazing the sheets. Once the tent had turned into a faded watercolour Adam opened his eyes without a stir. I looked at him expectantly and saw the same expression in his eyes as the night before. His sleep hadn't washed it out. The expression, I believe, was of total happiness.

Later we sat very quietly next to the smouldering coals of the last night's fire and drank hot tea.

He then said simply, "Are you going to stay?"

It wasn't clear what he meant: that day, that week or beyond.

"I'm not planning to go anywhere. I hope you don't mind," I said, trying to sound just as Sphinxlike.

"Great. So we can relax."

It sounded like a good plan. I just didn't know whether I was ready to relax.

The mad surfer in me was still ready to kill in order to survive. Since the death of my father I had been intoxicated with pain, feeding off fear and rage. Now, for the first time, I was desperate to get rid of them. I felt like one of those characters in an adventure movie, aboard a ship in the southern seas wracked by a typhoon at night—waves smashing the ship to pieces, masts cracking and falling, screams, bodies being thrown overboard, lightning and wind tearing the sails—*then cut to* the next morning, dead calm, blue sky, our heroine is beached on a sandy shore fringed with coconut palms, and is rescued by natives with flowers in their hair.

I have always felt grateful to Adam for the way he welcomed me in his life. I never had to ask, to push, to knock. He was this big open door right from the start.

I had never thought of myself as a good person. Too twisted, too unhappy to be good. But now I wanted to be tamed. I needed to revive my integrity. I knew I could be a better person than the one I had been lately.

Adam and I ended up spending nearly two weeks in the bush. He broke camp and sent his truck with his guys back to Nairobi, and the two of us took off alone, wandering towards the north.

What struck me immediately, as with no other man I had met before, was that Adam knew how to do everything: he was the most competent man I had ever seen. He never got lost, never looked at the map, he simply *recognized* the shape of mountains, rivers, junctions in the middle of nowhere. He remembered trees, boulders, springs. The landscape was imprinted on him, and it was obvious why: it had never really changed since he had been a child. I liked the way he *owned* it. It was his, he had been roaming it all his life. For me, on the other hand, the bush was such a foreign environment—I knew absolutely nothing about it—that I couldn't even make up my mind whether I should be in a panic or not. I lay awake in the tent after Adam had fallen asleep and listened to the presence of animals around us. I heard branches creak, distant grunts, close growls, strange hisses. At times I could swear I felt the back of an animal brush the canvas along my side of the tent. I never knew which was what, but I could definitely *smell* them. I managed to lie perfectly still in a sort of frozen exhilaration, feeling the warmth of Adam's sleeping body next to me, bewildered more by my own reaction than by the possibility of sleeping between a man's body and a lion's. The next morning Adam would spot their tracks on the sand around the tent. Hyenas, baboons, hippos, leopard, he would announce matter-of-factly, and in the daylight the marks of their hooves or paws seemed totally harmless. It didn't seem possible that all that activity had taken place while we were inside the tent. At night he would point his torch in the river to reveal the shining yellow eyes of the crocodiles, or the smooth back of a hippo. He loved the feeling of being surrounded by game; he was actually disappointed when a camp felt too quiet. I was confused; I didn't know how to behave and I didn't want to disappoint him, so I never complained. I had no idea if what we were doing was mad or absolutely normal, but I trusted him totally and made it a point to like anything he seemed to enjoy. My secret experiment on that first safari was to keep testing my fear every half hour, pushing it a bit further each time and trying to keep its level comparatively low. It was like forcing a muscle: I had never tested how far it could go and I was proud to see it stretch that far.

I remember one particular evening. We had just set up camp

on top of a hill, and set off for a walk. Adam always walked ahead, in complete silence, scanning the hillside with binoculars for elephants or buffaloes. We knew they were there, having seen their fresh tracks, and by then I had developed enough of a sixth sense to feel they must be close, somewhere behind the trees. Adam sat in the tall grass on the ridge of the valley looking down at the forest below us. I was seized by fear. I had visions of furious buffaloes charging at us from every direction. My heart was pounding, every particle of my body was begging me to run for shelter. Feeling exposed and useless, I sat obediently next to Adam while he kept his eyes fixed on the thick of the forest and listened. We sat like that for a very long time and after a while my breathing subsided, my heartbeat adjusted to his. It was as if his calm had slowly poured into me like a blood transfusion. Our silence gave way to sounds I had not been aware of: the wind through the foliage, the chirping of distant birds and crickets. All the screaming particles of my body calmed down and subsided like sand in the river. Now that everything inside me was quiet, I could feel the forest come alive and give out its fragrant breath of moss and fresh soil.

Suddenly a bushbuck appeared in the clearing. Adam smiled and passed me the binoculars. It was such a perfect, beautiful animal. It didn't move at first—it had seen us—but as it realized we were perfectly still and were not going to move, it started grazing timidly. That's when I became aware of how everything had fallen into its right place: my fear had vanished, Adam, the bushbuck and I were breathing together with the forest, we had caught onto its pulse and heartbeat, and nothing bad was going to happen to us. Nothing was going to come storming out of the bush to kill us. Our own silence had made us one with the forest, and as long as we listened to it, we would be safe.

Adam's silence taught me all I know about the bush; now it seems almost obvious. But at the time it struck me as a complete revelation, as something I would never forget.

Everything he did always seemed simple: each night by the campfire he cooked and fed me incredibly good food. I watched speechless as he mixed water and flour and kneaded the dough

which he put inside a blackened pan and covered with coals until it turned into fragrant bread. He winched the car out of the
mud, patched the radiator, fixed the punctures, spoke Samburu.
I probably would have been dead a hundred times without him.

It soon became clear that Adam wasn't the only reason I
wanted to stay. As we drove into space, as Africa opened up and
took me in, I felt that all my vertical fears—the traps, the holes I
had been trying to avoid falling into—were now slowly stretching themselves flat on the ground. Everything was smoothing in
space; even my breathing was slowing down.

I wanted to learn to become competent enough to survive
here, and Adam was obviously the perfect man to teach me. The
key to open the door. It wasn't just the beauty of Africa, it was its
moral geography that I wanted to be part of. It suddenly became
clear to me that this was where I had chosen to be myself again.
Under the glare of that unclouded sunshine, where there was
no shelter, no screen, no shade.

"Esmé, you have the constitution of a mule," he said to me
one day, after we had had to push the car out of a sandbank in
the midday sun. He shook his head and laughed. "Look at you."

He turned the rearview mirror towards me, and I saw myself
for the first time in days; my hair tangled like a Medusa's, covered with red dust, scratches all over my arms and legs, car
grease on my nose.

I felt so happy, as if I had been given a new life.

What was incredibly refreshing—and I remember noticing it
right from the start during that first safari—was that Adam and I
didn't speak the same language, in any sense. By speaking in
English to him I inevitably needed to force something out. Not
only was I obliged to be simpler, less Machiavellian, but by
speaking my second language I was leaving behind a whole
chunk of my history which had to do with Ferdinando. I felt
lighter, as if I had been allowed to unload a weight off my back.

We didn't know anything about each other, we couldn't possibly picture what each other's life had been like up until then. I
tried to imagine his childhood at his grandfather's farm, running
barefoot after the warthogs, learning how to use a gun at the age

of eleven, being spat at in the eyes by a cobra.

He was the result of events and circumstances completely foreign to me.

I was as much of a riddle to him: Naples, Ferdinando and the Communist Party, going to school by cab because my father had never learnt how to drive, baroque architecture, Truffaut's movies, swimming in the coolness of the Mediterranean in the spring. Instinctively we avoided our past histories, feeling that there would be too many gaps, which in a sense neither of us felt needed to be filled. We made love, slept, ate, and drove. We learned how to be close in a physical sense.

I rang Louise, Ferdinando's third wife, collect from the post office in Nanyuki, on the way back to Nairobi. From the window, I could see Adam eating a somosa while checking the water in the radiator. I kept my eyes on him throughout the conversation, almost as if I needed to make that scene as real as possible while making the first contact with the other side.

The picture showed a handsome man I knew almost nothing about, on the edge of a Far West–like African town, across the road from the Settler's Provisions Store. Nanyuki, Kenya, East Africa.

Louise sounded tired and distraught. She said that there had been an incredible amount of paperwork concerning Ferdinando's will, and that I should come back to sign some of the papers. She kept saying "your father" as if now that he was dead and of no avail, I was to blame for the chaotic situation he had left behind.

"We don't even know who has the rights for the American translations, you know your father never kept track of anything, it's such a mess—"

"Did you speak to Lorenzi? He should know."

"Lorenzi is a greedy bastard, like all of them. Goddam vultures . . ."

"Louise, it'll be fine. Don't panic, okay?"

"I just want to get out of here, sell the house and go as soon as possible. I *hate* this country." She was on the verge of breaking down.

I didn't like the way she was going back into her shell, suddenly so resentful towards the place where she'd lived for fifteen years.

"I've had it. Your father's friends are all *grandissimi stronzi.*"

She sounded so bitter, as if without the aura of my father we had all turned back into some kind of barbarians she didn't want anything to do with. She sounded like just another callous American, one who had pretended a liking for excess, for a carefree and bohemian lifestyle, only in order to hold on to a man. At that moment I realized she had probably despised our life all along.

"Are you selling the house? I thought you—"

"That was always the plan I discussed with your father." She was defensive now. "He knew I wouldn't live here alone for anything in the world."

Her betrayal took me by surprise. On the other hand, I guess she didn't have much choice. Was I going to miss Louise? Did I love her enough to give her a reason to stay? The answer was no.

Where I came from there was never enough love for anyone to stay anywhere. Nobody ever asked anyone else to change their plans in the name of something.

I guess I should say in the name of love.

"What does Teo think of all this?"

"Oh God, you know what your brother is like. He doesn't really care one way or another."

I kept my eyes on the dusty road, framed by the post office window.

"Where are you, anyway?" She sounded tired of our conversation.

"In Africa."

"I know *that.* Where exactly?"

"Oh. Kenya. On the equator. I just crossed it in fact."

"Am I paying for this call?"

"Yes, indeed you are."

"When are you coming back? You must sign these papers

53

and your brother of course is completely—"

"—Louise . . ."

"Yes?"

"Please let's not talk about the papers *now.*"

"Right. So is there something else?"

". . . . ."

"Are you okay?}

". . . . ."

"Esmé, this is costing me a fortune."

I hung up on her.

Ten days later I went back.

The logistics of changing my life turned out to be surprisingly simple: I had nothing to go back to. I didn't have a serious job, I shared a flat with a friend I didn't like, and apart from my brother there was nobody I would miss.

I signed the papers. I got my share of the American rights, and Lorenzi, who had acted in perfectly good faith all along, said I would get my royalties every six months. He had been my father's good friend and lawyer and wasn't trying to cheat anyone.

"Don't expect much," he said with a sad smile. "Poetry never sells."

But it turned out that Ferdinando had left very precise instructions concerning me and my brother in the will. Not only did we both have a share in the sale of the house in Tuscany, but we inherited some very good paintings.

On a rainy day I went out to lunch with my brother Teo in a trattoria we had been going to forever, where Ferdinando had always had some kind of special arrangement which basically meant he never paid his bills. The owner came out of the kitchen, kissed us, said he was going to miss Ferdinando a lot and that there was no way he would ever let us pay in the future. The place felt warm, it smelled of minestrone, wood panelling and damp coats, and because it reminded us of many other lunches we had had there we became very sentimental and drank lots of expensive red wine.

Teo is a younger version of the aging knight, with the added frailty and dreamy eyes of my mother. That morning he looked particularly Byronic, his dark curly hair wet from the rain, wearing a buttoned-up oversize shirt picked up at a flea market.

"When do you think you'll be able to join the company again? Can you do the next season?" I asked him.

"God knows. Nobody knows. I still can't bend my leg properly." He looked around the room impatiently. "Maybe I never will."

"Please don't say that."

He had hurt his knee badly and had had to stop dancing a few months back. I knew he suffered, dancing meant so much to him—he had always had such a silvery energy on stage, like a whirling acrobat, an Ariel in flight.

"And what are you going to do with the money?" I asked him.

It was such an unlikely question. We had never before had any amount of money worth talking about.

"I could buy the flat I live in," said Teo with a shrug. "That would be the wise thing to do. Otherwise I could happily squander it travelling with you."

"That wouldn't take us very far. We'd be pretty good at squandering it."

Teo giggled.

"I'd say we'd be excellent."

"It's the only money we'll ever get," I said. "I think we should use it to do something if not wise, at least crucial."

"I agree. Maybe we should buy a bigger flat and share it. We could get seriously organized and attempt to have a grown-up life."

"Right."

I paused. I drank more wine.

A flat in Rome. A brand-new dishwasher. A good stereo. A telephone in the bathroom. Did I want that?

"Teo, I think I want to move to Africa."

He put down his wineglass and stared at me, startled. Then he tried to smile.

"Oh. Well, that's a crucial enough plan."

I kept brushing bread crumbs off the table, without being able to look back at him. Yes, we too were breaking apart now. The observation point had been shut down for good and we both had to find another site from which to look at things down below. The time had come for each of us to do it on our own.

"I don't know. This guy, Adam . . . he . . . wants me to go back and live with him."

He had asked me. In the name of love. As simple as that.

It had happened after we had come back from our safari in the bush, back into some kind of reality—cars, phones, supermarkets, other people. I had started to panic. In only two and a half weeks my five hundred dollars had shrunk to seventy-five; Adam had to go back into his office, book new clients, fix more vehicles, chat on the radio, get a new camp going. Some kind of decision needed to be taken. I felt lost.

"I'm going to have to go soon, Adam. Next week, I think," I had said to him one morning when we had just woken up in his little stone house covered in creepers in Langata.

He hadn't answered. We were still lying in bed. He had kept his eyes fixed on the mosquito net, then had quietly taken my hand in his. That had make me feel like crying. I was surprised to see my tears drop onto the pillow. It was as if my body had decided to produce evidence for my feelings. But Adam didn't see me cry, he kept looking up, as if I wasn't there.

"Don't go," he said quietly.

"But—"

"Listen," he interrupted me, "I just knew it must be you the minute I saw you. It was like 'Oh, there you are at last.'"

He finally turned to look at me. His green eyes looked so serious, almost reproachful.

"One isn't given that chance more than once or twice in life, you know."

"I know."

"Then let's not blow it."

I wiped my eyes.

"All right. I could go and come back, then."

"That's much better."

"He said he *loves* me."

Teo looked at me, surprised.

"Fantastic."

"I don't know. It's a bit scary. I've never done anything like that before."

"Go. Get on the plane tomorrow. This place is dead."

"I feel like I'm going on a secret mission I know nothing about. As if someone has left me instructions on a piece of paper and I just have to follow. It's weird."

"No, you don't understand, that's what's so exciting about it: dye your hair raven black, put on shades and pick up the fake documents with your new identity. Most likely it will be a German name, Baader Meinhoff–like. They'll meet you at the gate and show you what to do next. It'll be an adventure."

"I wish."

There was a pause.

"Wow. Nairobi." He rolled the word in his mouth, as if testing its sound.

"It's a Masai name," I said, feeling suddenly melancholic. "It means 'cold.' The cold place."

"Oh. That's nice."

We fell silent.

"Will you come and see me?" I asked him.

"Yes. But you're coming back at some stage, aren't you?"

"Of course."

Suddenly I was scared.

"Oh Teo, I don't know if I can do this."

"Of course you can, my love. Call me often." He squeezed my hand hard across the table. "Call me collect. I'm quite rich now, you know."

I had the idea that moving out of my life would be a titanic undertaking. Instead my entire history filled up barely nine boxes. I faxed the bank asking them to deposit a small amount of money for me every month in a Nairobi account. I sold one of the paintings. That took care of finances. I was ready to go back to Africa in less than six weeks.

It was the beginning of July. When the Egypt Air flight took off from Fiumicino I felt a wave of panic: I started to feel palpitations; my hands turned cold and sweaty. I tried to control my breathing and attempted to concentrate on the fact that if worst came to worst I could always head back on another flight immediately after landing in Egypt.

But by the time I was sitting in the transit area in Cairo, waiting for the Nairobi connection, the panic dissolved like smoke in the wind. I looked at the other passengers half asleep on the orange plastic chairs under the bright fluorescent light so typical of every third-world airport. American missionary priests, Nigerian dudes in baseball caps, heavily veiled Yemenite girls, Indian families with incredibly noisy children, German backpackers immersed in the Lonely Planet guide.

The transit area: I had reached that neutral zone inhabited only by dispossessed beings—in purgatory en route to final destination—and our common condition made me feel much calmer.

There seemed to be room for a lot of different people. I figured that, in the end, if there was room for the Yemenite girls, the missionaries, the Nigerian dudes and the screaming Asian children, I didn't see any reason why there shouldn't be room for someone like me.

Chapter Five

I sometimes think we've got into a rather bad way,
living off here among things and people not our own,
without responsibilities or attachments,
with nothing to hold us together or keep us up;
marrying foreigners, forming artificial tastes,
playing tricks with our natural mission.

HENRY JAMES

Let's be honest about it.

This is a story about white people in Africa. I am not even going to pretend that it is anything else.

As I said, we don't have any African friends here. Except for those rare occasions—you can count them on your fingers— when we have met this or that young Kenyan, usually from a good family who has studied in England, and each time we remembered them slightly more exciting than they actually were, and made the same mental note that "we must remember to invite him/her next time we have a dinner."

It has nothing to do with preconceptions or prejudice, it's just the way it is, and after a while there's no use even talking about it.

When I moved back here to live with Adam I knew Africans were going to play a big part in my life. I hadn't yet developed a behaviour of my own, but I didn't particularly like any of the white-versus-African behaviour I saw around me. As a result, I overreacted: I was always on guard, too cautious, too kind, too careful never to upset anybody. I distributed astronomical tips to whoever did the smallest thing for me, and never dared protest when I was being taken advantage of. I seemed to be shooting for the award for Best White Girl of the Year.

Then I studied Adam, watched him deal with the Africans who worked for him. He wasn't trying to win their hearts. Didn't have to prove anything. That's when I realized that I was the one who was having a problem.

I still wanted to make an effort, if only to have something to write home about. I persecuted our landlady in Langata, Wambui Wambera, a distinguished Kikuyu widow, until she capitulated and agreed to come for tea on a Sunday. She showed up with her sister and two of their children, both of them decked out in shiny polyester, nylon wigs full on, bright pink nail polish. They sat stiffly on the edge of the sofa, hands resting on their knees, while the children stared at me dully, the horrified look of hostages in their eyes. We politely discussed the weather, school fees, and a Schwarzenegger film they had rented the night before at the video shop. I gave up.

"Just goes to show you the degree of our alienation," Hunter had snapped when, much later on, I described this little tea party with Wambui for him, hoping he would find it amusing. But he didn't.

"We are not living in the real world here. You know what? In the long run it's suicidal to live like this."

In the end, apart from Hunter, who has chosen the best role in the play—our bad conscience—we are content to get along with our staff, and we like to believe we have become indispensable to their lives. We take them to the hospital when they are sick, contribute to the expenses of funerals, births and weddings, we smoke a cigarette with them in the kitchen, laugh at occasional jokes, and that seems enough to satisfy us.

Our relation to the Africans is stricly ruled by money. Obviously we like to think that there is more to it, but at the end of the day, just like Baroness Blixen and her beloved cook Kamante—with the same idiotic benevolence—we are appeased by their gratitude and faithfulness. That's why we keep on tearing off price tags from our extravagant shopping.

We have simply stopped seeing any contradiction in what we do.

So here we are, my enemy and I, walking into another strictly *mzungu* Nairobi party. This is the night of her official debut in the white baboon family. I better watch this closely.

Nena's husband, Peter, comes to open the door. He is good-looking in that plain way most men are around here, ex-boys who have spent all their life breathing fresh air, have had their hair gently streaked by the sun, and have improved their body through a variety of physical strains.

Peter is some kind of ethologist/computer whiz, who follows very closely the growth of the elephant population in Tsavo, producing monthly data which then go onto the Internet and placate the growing anxieties of conservationists around the world.

Will the elephants be all right? That seems the only question about Africa's future the West really cares to know the answer to.

Well, Peter is the man to ask. He is the Elephant Man of Kenya, he's got the figures down and has written books which have won him international recognition. Women readers especially love him because of the jacket photograph where he looks particularly rugged. After all, here is a man only in his mid-thirties, with a beautiful wife and three children, sandy-haired and blue-eyed with a healthy tan, who has a cause.

As a result of this incredibly good image, any movie producer, journalist, writer, any sort of Western half-celebrity who comes to Kenya, rings up Peter and Nena, either in connection with the elephant books or because their house has been featured in *World of Interiors,* giving the definite impression that you need only see that house in order to return home and say you had been treated to True African Ambience.

Nena has this talent of putting incongruous things together to produce a stunning effect. Their house is cluttered with driftwood, shells, Ethiopian headrests, monkey skulls, kilim carpets, Indian fabrics, dried flowers and whatnot. Nena can put a water lily in a glass next to a giraffe bone and make it look like Georgia O'Keeffe has just walked out the door.

Anyway, here she is in her beautiful house with her beautiful husband, the beautiful children in postbath attire, running around in pyjamas, smelling of soap. The table is beautifully set in candlelight and, if all that's not enough, Nena is dressed to kill, her slightly faded Charlotte Rampling look, her dark hair propped up in a bun, little black dress and bright red high heels. She comes forward and leans to kiss me.

"Hi darling."

She then turns to Claire and shakes her hand.

"Welcome. How brave of you to settle in all by yourself."

I turn and look at Claire: she is slightly intimidated by Nena's flair, she is probably thinking that her outfit may be too naive. Which is of course the case and the reason why I brought her here tonight: so that she doesn't underestimate what she is in for. She's obviously not aware yet that the Elspeth Huxley spirit faded out long ago.

The list of participants to this ritual is, once more, a true classic.

We have the Just-Flown-In American Film Writer, researching for a Hollywood movie on a secondary character from the Happy Valley scene. His name is Kevin Steinberg and he apparently has written the script of a Jack Nicholson film which none of us has seen. There is a stunning blond Danish aid worker whose name is virtually impossible to catch, on his way back home after seven months in Ethiopia. We have Allison and Richard Fagen, who run a project up north, close to the border with Somalia, who have been in the country for many years restocking local tribes with goats and camels. There is a middle-aged, rough-looking journalist from the Sunday *Times* I've met before, Ronald Bailey, on assignment on yet another story of corruption, the Old Man having made the headlines again last week re a fantastically expensive private jet he just bought in Texas.

I do the rounds and shake hands, leading Claire from one to the other, and finally land on the armrest of the sofa next to

Miles.

"Claire, this is my very best friend Miles Sinclair, from the *Guardian*."

"Hi Claire. I've heard so much about you from Hunter. Welcome."

"Thank you."

Miles checks out Claire from head to toe and I can tell the response is positive.

"Can I get you girls a drink?"

He comes back with two gin and tonics and lights a Sportsman, ready for the show.

"Hunter told me you and he spent a long time together in Rwanda," Claire says gingerly. "I know your face from some photographs he has showed me. I think it was when you broke into an embassy in Kigali."

"Oh right, the Canadian embassy."

"Yes. You were drinking Dom Perignon straight from the bottle with some Rwandese commander."

"The thing is that everyone had fled. We were very hungry, but we found only champagne in the basement. God, he didn't show you *those* pictures, did he?"

"I thought they looked great."

Miles loves to hear this. It's like being a movie star and meeting a pretty girl who has seen all your films. You've already scored points without having to work at it.

They slide into war talk. Claire is eager to find out the insider's viewpoint. This is the newest subject in her life; she needs to catch up.

Miles is major at telling stories, he's an absolute pro. He'll be amusing all the way through, enhancing the grotesque, the most trivial aspect of what it's like to be in a war. He'll never make the mistake of sounding heroic or brave, he won't allow any distance between the listener and himself; no, he'll keep you right on his side by making you feel that in fact there's nothing so exceptional about what he has been through—it's just men killing one another—and then, just when you're starting to relax, *wham,* he'll hit you in the face with some atrocious detail.

63

Children's bloated bodies piled in a toilet, an amputated arm hitting your windshield as you drive at night, the stench of death in an empty swimming pool. He'll kill you in a second, make you feel the horror with a single stroke of genius: a true master of the coup de théâtre.

Miles is wasted as a hack, he should be a novelist, I keep telling him. He sometimes likes to hear it and sometimes doesn't. He's in his early thirties and has gone into three and a half wars, yet always manages to reemerge with his Peter Pan looks intact.

He's still enjoying the momentum here. I guess it would be hard to give up the status of a Star of the Press in East Africa in exchange for the obscure role of another wannabe writer in Europe. Who could blame him: just this minute Claire is listening in rapture, nodding at everything he says. They are deeply absorbed in Hutu/Tutsi horror stories.

"We had exposed what was going on in the paper by then," he's telling her. "So we run into Colonel Bagosora in the lobby of the hotel, he's the brain behind the "final solution," right?"

"Oh my God! And what did you do?" exclaims Claire.

"Well, you could see the dead bodies from the window, there were at least ten dead children lying in the back yard, right there."

I've heard this too many times, I will have to move along with my drink.

I'm not trying to sound blasé. Just the opposite.

I remember when Hunter came back from Rwanda, how he used to drive me to tears. I don't think I can bear to watch this scene—with Claire playing one of my earlier roles. The repetition is hypnotic, like watching *The Cherry Orchard* over and over again: the actors just shift roles as they outgrow their part.

But I am not jaded. It was very real. They did go to war.

Each time they went in I thought they would come back in plastic bags. Or not come back at all. I couldn't sleep at night, it was so overwhelming.

But they always came back and got drunk or high or laid, and they looked just the same, except for a wilder look in their

64

eyes.

They came to the dinner parties and we all sat, listened, nodded, and eventually got used to it.

Nicole walks in wearing the green dress she had offered to lend me, looking fresh as a nymph. She has brought along another Just-Flown-In specimen, the Young American Female Photographer. Her name is Linda something.

They all come and go in this town, they all do the same things, they always ask the same questions. It's either a book, or a film, or a photo assignment. It's either about animals or war or nomadic tribes. We all obediently display our virtues and our knowledge, we always make a point of sounding impeccably competent. We provide them with whatever they need: phone numbers, locations, Masai chiefs, prides of lions. We take them on safari, we drive them around for thousands of miles, we drink them to death. They usually leave exhausted.

When we go to Europe and look them up, they will sound excited over the phone and ask us to lunch, but invariably after that one time—once the few people you know in common have been thoroughly inspected—their initial enthusiasm will inevitably wear out.

You are their "African friend." An item that will rapidly go off in the European climate. After all, realistically, how many dinner parties does it take before everyone has heard your story of the python chewing up your Jack Russell?

Linda, the young American photographer, is a midwestern beauty, the healthy blonde-verging-on-bovine type. Not knowing exactly what to expect from the soirée at the Elephant Man's house, she figured she would be safe in combat gear, so she's all khaki shorts and caterpillar boots, which is always a winning look if you have good legs. She does.

She and Claire, being the new entries, have instinctively ended up at opposite ends of the room in order to work their way into the new territory independently. Claire is working on the men; she's now chatting to Peter and Miles about some new Iranian film which everyone is mad about in London at the moment. She doesn't know yet what a hopeless subject movies are in this country. She is getting plenty of attention nevertheless, being such a novelty. Linda, more bravely, has decided to test Nena, Nicole and me.

"I would like to move here for some time," she announces.

"What a wonderful idea," Nena says with a considerable lack of enthusiasm. She's lying sideways on the sofa next to Nicole, who's rolling a joint. I detect a slight reluctance in her voice, the reluctance one always feels here before investing time in people one is probably not going to see ever again.

"I have this project on women. I've talked about it to my publisher in New York and—"

"Women? What kind of women?" Nicole asks abstractedly, her eyes focused on the rolling paper.

"Circumcised women. I think the correct term is 'infibulated,'" isn't it?

"Oh. I'm not sure about that." Nicole lights the joint and coughs. "Nena, isn't there a difference between circumcision and infibulation?"

"Yes," Nena stretches her hand to help herself to the joint. "I think circumcision is when they cut your clitoris off and infibulation is when they sew up—"

"Whatever," Linda cuts it in. "In America we call it FGM, female genital mutilation."

She adds this as if we were hot publishing executives she had to persuade to give her an advance on the spot.

Nicole stretches herself on the sofa, her legs leaning on top of Nena's.

"Well, you won't have any problems. There's plenty of that going on here. Masai, Samburus, Rendilles, maybe still some Kikuyus—they all still do it, you know."

I pass the joint to Linda.

"Want some?"

"No thank you, I don't smoke."

"There was this Frenchwoman, two or three years ago—what was her name again, Nicole??" Nena asks.

"Sabine?"

"Yes, Sabine. She came out here and she did exactly the same thing you want to do. Circumcision and all that. A wonderful woman. Didn't she win a Pulitzer or something?"

"That's right. Sabine. She won a Pulitzer," I say.

"Oh."

Linda looks dejected. Most probably her project back in New York had sounded like a truly original idea.

"You know, I'm not sure about this, but I think that only American citizens can win a Pulitzer," she says with a hint of suspicion.

Nicole shrugs, exhaling thick smoke.

"I don't know. Maybe *her mother* was American—"

"Or maybe it wasn't a Pulitzer," says Nena, entirely bored with this already. "But she definitely won *something*."

"Something prestigious. I remember we even had champagne afterwards," I add.

"It was a really wonderful book. I should still have it somewhere."

Nena actually stands up and starts checking the bookshelf.

"Yes. You should take a look at it, I'm sure it would be interesting for you to see it," says Nicole.

"Oh, I think I lent it to someone who never returned it." Nena lands back on the sofa with us.

"Never mind," says Linda. She looks at the three of us. We are completely stoned.

Nicole sighs, her eyes half-closed.

"Sabine. What an extraordinary person she was."

"I wish she would come back." Nena yawns. "She was *such* fun."

There is another long pause. Linda lets the ice tinkle in her empty glass, smiling at us as she tries to figure out fast whether to hate us straightaway or to hang on and see if eventually we will get any nicer.

We are called to the table. Nena proceeds with her artful

placement. She sits Linda between Ronald Bailey and Miles, who are discussing whores and clubs in Kinshasa. I get the Hollywood screenwriter, Kevin, who sets about interviewing me with the determination of a *Vanity Fair* contributing editor.

"So, do you live here?"

That's *always* the opening line. Then there is how long have you lived here (seniority), what do you do for a living (authority), do you live alone (sexual innuendo). I answer obediently, I got my routine down long ago.

Claire has Peter and the stunning Danish aid worker at her side.

"Strips of impala?" asks Peter incredulously.

"Yes. You cut the skin in strips and then you patch the puncture with it. It sticks like glue," says the Dane in his thick accent. He's an expert on the subject: he rode his motorcycle all the way here from Ethiopia.

"It sounds great. The smell is the only thing that worries me." Peter smiles condescendingly.

"That's the point. It sticks when it rots. I promise you, it really works." The Scandinavian Beauty pours wine into Claire's glass as smoothly as an experienced waiter, swirling the bottle. She has been warmed by the wine and the excitement. The presence of men has revived her.

"Where do you find the impala's skin?" she asks. "Do you *buy* it?"

Peter and the Dane laugh. They think it's adorable of her to ask the question.

"First you have to shoot the impala, skin it, then cut the skin in strips." The Danish boy sounds menacing. I picture him skinning cows with a Swiss knife whenever he has a flat tire back home.

"That's quite an ordeal," Peter admits. "Frankly, I'd stick to gum."

Claire laughs, throwing her head back a little. She likes to flirt—and who wouldn't, between those two.

As she takes another swig of wine, I see she will blend perfectly here. I can tell she has instantly perceived what this place is secretly all about: sexual tension. Not only does she enjoy that, but it's clear she knows how to handle it.

Nicole and I exchange a rapid glance across the table. She's squeezed between Bailey (now on the Metropole Hotel in Accra in the old days to Miles) and Richard Fagen (on the advantages of camels versus cows in the pastoralist culture to Nena).

Nicole leans across the table and grins at Claire.

"Tell me, Claire, what are you planning to do here?"

Claire straightens up, as if reprimanded by a schoolteacher, and swiftly puts the innocent look back on.

"Well, I thought it would be a good idea to look around first. Hunter said it will take some time before I'll start to figure out the way everything works here."

I can't bear to hear his name pronounced by her with such familiarity.

"That's very sensible," says Nicole, "even though I'm afraid none of us has figured that one out yet."

"I bet." Claire laughs heartily. Such good technique, this girl.

"Anyway, my dream would be to work in conservation," she adds with a shy smile, eyeing Peter. "I *adore* animals."

Meanwhile, the American Screenwriter is hammering me nonstop. He wants to go back to his room at the Serena Hotel with an answer. Something he can fax back to Hollywood tomorrow which will make his research sound worthwhile.

"Why do you think Kenya has always had this tradition of—how should I say? Is it decadence? Eccentricity? I guess it's *romance*. I mean all these extraordinary characters ended up here, why not in Tanzania?"

"I have no—"

"Exactly! Why do you think Tanzania is far less interesting? *Anthropologically*, of course."

"Oh well, I don't really know. Maybe because—"

He's not even listening, he's just throwing questions in the air.

"You see, *the romance*, this is exactly the point. It's like a cocktail prepared with secret ingredients. There has to be the adventure, the strive for survival and conquest—there's plenty of that in most African countries after all—but what makes this place special is the combination of that with sophisticated people. Hence the decadence, the incredible sensuality! Don't you think?"

"I'm not really sure what you are trying to—"

"The romance is not created by the country in itself, but by the interpretation that certain people—shall we say intellectuals?—like Blixen or Hemingway were able to come up with. They communicated the romance and created the mystique. Don't you agree?"

"Well, personally I—"

"Otherwise," he's impatient now, and looks at me as if I have really exasperated him. *"Why* would someone like *yourself* choose to come and live *here?"*

Miles ends up driving Linda and Claire home. I am too stoned to make it back in the dark, and decide to spend the night in the guest room. Nicole is the last one to leave. We end up in the kitchen with Nena for a last joint and a sip of scotch.

Nena shakes her head.

"It won't last. I can tell you now. She's not equipped for Hunter."

"What do you mean?" I ask, hopeful.

"Too girlish, too naive. He's going to be bored."

"That's what he likes about her. He loves to bully women. It turns him on."

"She's not dumb," Nicole says. She's sitting on the kitchen table, still looking fresh and sexy, post–six joints, three gin and tonics, a bottle of wine and half a gram of bad coke.

"I talked to her. I hate to tell you, but she can be pretty funny."

I look at her in disbelief.

"Funny?"

I can deal with sexy, I can even deal with clever. But funny kills me.

Nicole hops down from the kitchen table.

"Well, girls I'm on my way. Esmé, why don't you come around in the morning on your way home? We can have coffee together."

At the door she whispers, "Darling, I beg you, get your humour back."

"I just hope she dies."

She kisses me good night and I stumble into my room. I slide into oblivion, then I hear her car start and go off in the night, her driving flawless and confident as usual.

I wake up at seven with a splitting headache to the sound of Nena's children playing in the next room. It's drizzling and it feels cold. It's July, the African winter.

I lie in bed, listening to the sounds of the house. Someone is taking a shower upstairs, Juma is setting the table for breakfast.

I try to think about last night's dinner party, and to analyze the reason why I hated every minute of it. It isn't because of Claire; it is because of me. There is something I deeply dislike about myself now, of which I had never been aware before. I have become bitter.

If there is one thing I am not grateful to Ferdinando for, it is having inherited his talent for opening people up and pinning them down with the heartlessness of an entomologist. My father, though, had his contradictions: he said he expected the most from people, but he contented himself with much less in order not to be alone. Thus, even if he had been tearing someone apart, he was still desperate to have dinner with them that night. His weakness was that he always needed an audience.

But whereas he was able to compensate his cynicism with his poetry, me, the fool, I merely learned to mimic his heartlessness without anything else with which to counterbalance it. Now all my toys lie broken on the floor and I'm left with nothing to play with. I wish I could go back to the way I felt before, but unfortunately I've been left with no instructions.

The children open the door of the room and storm in.

"Esmé, look, we have a rabbit!"

"Oh let me see . . . come here, show me."

Toby and Natasha climb up onto my bed followed by the dog, holding a furry rabbit in their tiny hands.

"Does it have a name?"

"Ginger," says Natasha, gravely, "Do you want to hold it?"

"Of course, thank you. Oh . . . it feels so sweet . . ."

"If you want you can hold it by the ears," Toby adds, and proceeds to show me.

They look at me seriously, holding the rabbit, half naked and dirty like angels who have been too long in the sun.

"Come, let's all get under the blankets, it's so cold. We can make room for everyone . . . Ginger will like it a lot."

I manage to convince them to pretend we are inside a tent in the bush, and we all squeeze together under the blankets, dog and rabbit included. I kiss them and hold them tight, feeling the warmth of their tiny bodies, smelling the sweetness of their sleep. They giggle and kick, chubby arms and legs all over me, until I feel warm enough and I have tears in my eyes.

I keep crying throughout breakfast, it's unstoppable, tears just keep rolling down onto my buttered toast. I'm not sobbing or making any sort of noise, I'm crying quietly, in what I hope is a rather dignified way. Nena looks at me, says nothing and keeps passing me butter, coffee, sugar, more toast. Toby and Natasha look at me frozen while the rabbit happily hops on the table. Even Juma looks at me and sighs. Thank God at least Peter has gone to the office.

Nena passes me a paper napkin.

"Why is she crying?" asks Natasha in a frightened whisper.

"Shhh, now you and Toby take Ginger out in the garden . . . put on your shoes . . . hurry."

The children keep looking at me. Toby grabs the rabbit.

"Do you want to hold it?"

"No thank you, darling, it's okay . . ." I blow my nose. "You go out and play with him."

Nena and I remain silent. She is not going to ask me anything; that is her way of letting me know she knows perfectly well what's going on.

"One cannot always be more clever than pain, you know," I say to her after a while. "At some point you just have to give in . . ."

She nods and smiles in a strange way, looking out the window.

She seems to know exactly what I am talking about, and after all why shouldn't she—beautiful Nena with the Beautiful Children, in the Charming House with the Wonderful Husband—Nena who we all assume is not allowed to feel unhappy ever again.

It didn't use to be like this. This place seemed the closest thing to Paradise. I should make an effort, try to remember that time, I keep telling myself while I drive home in the drizzle on the Magadi road.

Suddenly it seems so pointless to remember anything. Isn't happiness such an uninteresting feeling, so dull to describe, once you are in pain?

CHAPTER SIX

*For some the unfamiliar
holds the promise of love, of perfection.*

VIKRAM CHANDRA

When I first moved to Africa to live with Adam I was astonished to discover what a great deal of fascination lies in the realm of physical objects, and what an achievement it is to obtain control over them.

In the first world I had never paid any attention to the physical mechanisms which held my life together. It never occurred to me to figure out how the flush of a toilet worked, which secret route a gas pipe actually took, what a spark plug's purpose was. Their intrinsic nature had never concerned me, I couldn't see any connection between a screw and a wire, a spring and a lever, a fuse and a spark: to me the inner life of mechanical objects was as abstract as a cubist painting. Mechanical objects simply worked, and when they ceased to work they were either mended by expensive specialists or thrown away and replaced.

In Kenya I learned that this was totally unrealistic. Africa is the motherland of mechanical life: in order to survive here you have to be in control of all the components which will allow you to get from A to B. If one little mechanism breaks down you have to be able to repair it. This is a place where the word

74

"spare" has the same ring as "caviar."

Forget improvements; life here is strictly about maintenance.

Your daily task is merely to keep things the way they are, and make sure decay doesn't set in.

Keep the termites away from the roof poles, keep the rust off your car body, keep your skin away from the sun, make sure nothing rots, cracks or comes undone.

How to *fix* things: that's basically what life is all about here, a constant flow of energy aimed at preventing oneself from getting stuck again. This realization put me in a state of panic. I realized I wasn't at all in control of the dynamics, and once more, my intellectual abilities were going to be worth zero. In other words I was stuck from the word go and totally dependent on Adam.

To begin with, I didn't even know how to drive his car. The old Toyota Landcruiser looked to me like a gigantic hostile hound that would growl at me in the absence of its master. The mere possibility of getting a puncture and having to change a tire on my own gave me cold sweats. It was too big, too bulky, too masculine for me to master.

That was when I started to wonder what kind of women lived in this country, and how they managed. If I could just spot them and study how they behaved I might be able to learn the knack as well.

Whenever I followed Adam into the Karen hardware store, I saw him greet and kiss white girls from the neighbourhood. They leaned close to one another on the counter exchanging opinions on spanners, bolts and pipes. I felt shy and awkward. I was a newcomer and an absolute beginner and therefore I always kept two steps behind. I knew I *smelled* like a novice. The girls in the hardware store checked me out thoroughly and I scrutinized them with an equal amount of interest: after all, they were my future role models. Some of these girls were tough Kenya Cowgirls, all baggy shorts, strong calves and no makeup. The prospect of ending up with the same dry dykey look wasn't appealing, but the amazing thing was that in spite of that, I still longed to emulate them, such was my yearning for competence.

It turned out that there was another breed of women, two of whom I spotted in the hardware store. These were incredibly attractive, wore Ethiopian silver bangles, old-fashioned silk dresses and sandals, had a throaty laugh and a dry sense of humour. These women spoke to Adam about drainage and electric fences, while firmly rejecting wrong-size nails and carefully selecting wood planks in fluent Swahili. They were hardware shopping with the attitude they might have had having lunch with a rock star in a trendy restaurant. I found them terribly sexy and wished to learn their language. They were of course Nicole and Nena.

Right from the start there wasn't a trace of antagonism between us. We looked at each other and instantly realized we were kin. A tribe of women who have come to live in Africa merely by coincidence. We had no inbred vocation for this kind of life.

"Do you paint?" I asked Nicole, pointing at the canvas stretchers one of the guys was loading on her roof rack in the car park.

"Yes . . ." She smiled and took a good look at me. "Please come around. Adam can tell you where my house is."

I liked the way she invited me to come on my own, leaving Adam only the task of showing me how to reach her. Nena smiled. I noticed she was wearing a very dark lipstick which matched her nail polish. Rouge Noir by Chanel. Oh no, these two had not been left behind one bit.

"Will you stay for some time?" Nena asked. "We're *desperate* to make new friends here, you know."

They didn't look desperate at all to me; still, it was good to hear that they might enjoy my company.

I had been back in Kenya for about a month, and had spent most of my time following Adam around, attempting to configurate my new life. I was starting to lose hope, but that encounter had been a crucial turning point. Those two women were the first specimens of my own breed that I had come across so far. I figured that if they had survived the climate and the hardships, I

76

had some hope of doing the same. I watched them climb up into the battered four-wheel drive and reverse skillfully out of the parking lot.

Yes, I was going to stay and learn how to be like them.

The one thing one can't help noticing about whites living in Kenya is how everyone is constantly busy working at their "African pedigree," careful never to let others perceive that they are making the slightest effort to improve their skills. That's the trick: it must look like it's imprinted in your DNA. Everything you do here has to look as if you were simply born with it, whether it's speaking fluent Masai, killing birds with a catapult or roping a rhino with a lasso.

When I first arrived everyone I met seemed to be from Central Casting: right car, right clothes, wonderfully adventurous. It all looked perfectly natural to me: the romanticism seemed congenital, the style innate. It seemed as if the players were totally unaware of their glamour and only the eyes of the outsider could detect it.

"I guess one could say we're all held hostage here," Nicole said the first time I went to see her. She shrugged. "Hostages to beauty."

We were having tea on her verandah. It was cluttered with brushes and paint cans, seashells and driftwood, ferns hanging in pots from the rafters. It smelled of firewood and smoke, it looked poetic and bohemian, her canvases piled against the wall, an old kilim faded by the sun. We were drinking ginger tea out of a small Chinese teapot in little cracked cups.

"What do you mean?"

"I mean that we are all stuck here because this place *makes us look good*. Nobody could live like this and have such a good time for the same amount of money anywhere else in the world."

She pointed out her *shamba* boy, kneeling over the flower beds.

"We have servants, we don't pay taxes, we go to lots of dinner parties, we play explorers over the weekend, we look healthy and tanned all year round and we can always blame it on the Africans when things are not running smoothly. It's such a bargain!"

"Well . . . yes, but I suppose there's more to it than *that* . . ."

"Of course there is. But as Hunter always says, here one does a lot of editing. You know, cutting out all the ugly shots and keeping only the good stuff in. And I think he's totally right."

"Who is Hunter?"

"Hunter Reed . . . he writes for the *Independent*. He was born here but has only recently come back from England as their East African correspondent. You should meet him, you'd really like him. He has an incredible brain. Which is a bit of a rarity here, if you know what I mean."

That conversation worried me. I wasn't ready yet to analyse why whites in Africa lived in such denial. It surprised me that Nicole had given it so much thought: since it had been the very absence of intellectual criticism which had attracted me here in the first place, I naively expected everyone else to feel the same way.

That night I clung to Adam's body. He felt strong and hard like a tree. No, I wasn't yearning for incredible brains. I was yearning for something much simpler than that: a way to dig a hole in the ground where I could put my young roots, so that they would grow just enough to bind me to the rich African soil.

Adam's was a luxury camp. The logistics of providing food, adequate shelter, loo and hot shower in the middle of the bush require a lot of planning ahead and expenses. If you expect to have ice in your gin and tonic after sunset you have to pay for all the work that lies behind it. Adam had an office in town, where everything was organized by a small but very efficient group of people. They handled bookings, supplies and any other problem that might unexpectedly arise in the bush. The radio always crackled in the background, while the guys back at the camp would list their weekly requirements: a new distributor cap for the Toyota, coffee mugs, Omo powder, hurricane lamps, wax, matches, rope, towels, silverware and whatnot.

Adam picked up the clients at the airport, dropped them at the Norfolk Hotel to let them sleep off their jet lag and then drove them to camp the next day. He moved the camp around, according to the season and the clients' requirements, but his favourite area was in the north, on the Ewaso Nyiro River, in the land of the Samburu tribe.

The clients were mostly Americans, and were always loaded. They all looked the same when they got off the plane, wearing incongruous hats, gold wristwatches, designer shades. The women had either the ferocious look of the peroxide blonde who hates to age, the glacial stare of the younger mistress or the deadly glare of the resentful wife. The men were graying, gaining weight, losing power. All they had left to impress others with was their money, so they went on very expensive holidays.

This type of client usually came from the Midwest or the South, spoke with a nasal drawl, and insisted on talking to the Samburu with that thick accent, never for a second conceiving the possibility there could be humans on the planet who didn't speak English. They were demanding and irritable if things didn't run as smoothly as in a five-star hotel. There was nothing attractive or sympathetic about them.

There were younger couples too. Californian record or film producers, New York stockbrokers, Miami real estate kings who had made their fortune in the eighties, had snorted masses of Bolivian coke and had now joined the New Age. They had quit smoking, drinking and drugs and had become religious about their body maintenance. Their girlfriends usually bordered on the anorexic, filled their Prada bags with expensive makeup, were determined not to expose their white bodies to the risk of skin cancer, and kept the latest holistic best-seller by their bedside table.

This latter category of clients fell inevitably into the "Short Happy Life of Francis Macomber" syndrome. The girlfriends were always pleasantly surprised when they met Adam at the airport. He was so much more attractive than they had expected: such an added bonus to the exotic adventure. I could see it coming as soon as they stepped into camp. After they had spent barely forty-eight hours in each other's company, the girl would already be ignoring her boyfriend, and addressing Adam with all sorts of questions.

"What kind of snakes live around here? Are they deadly? Are these Masai? Samburu? Do you speak their language?"

When Adam introduced me as his girlfriend I could see a hint of disappointment in their eyes as they shook my hand.

We would dine together in the mess tent, after a round of drinks next to the fire. By the third or fourth day they would usually give up mineral water and have some booze, which loosened them up a bit—not always with positive results.

Usually at this stage the women had become openly flirtatious with Adam. He had turned into the sexiest male icon they had seen outside of Hollywood. By now he had told them what to do in the remote possibility that an elephant attempted to charge. He had reassured them that it was technically impossible for a lion to attack them inside the car. He had patiently explained to them which were the dangerous snakes and how it was possible to prevent the poison from reaching their bloodstream.

So far their boyfriends/husbands had been responsible for many crucial aspects of their life: their social status, their bank account, the interior decoration of the new home. But now this young, handsome man they hardly knew, was in charge of their survival.

Now, that's very sexy. Africa is about danger, about darkness, about fearing the possibility of one's death. And as we all know, nothing is as erotic as fear.

Actually nobody should know this better than me: I had capitulated to Adam's manliness long before these women had, but I still liked to delude myself that I had done it with more style.

"The roaring of that lion today . . . Oh my God . . . I will never ever forget it!" the Anorexic Beauty would recall with a sigh, shaking the ice in her drink and looking at Adam in search of some kind of cosmic confirmation. "I thought . . . wow . . .

this is *really* powerful . . . you hear that sound and you realise we are really worth *nothing* on this planet . . . Do you know what I mean?"

Usually the men had started to sulk by then. This wasn't exactly what they had had in mind when they decided to take Beauty on an African safari. The whole idea of the trip was to make *them* look romantic and macho and glamorous. Instead they realised they were paying a lot of money for this guy to make them look inept.

"How can *you* live here?" the ex–New York cokehead, now living a healthier and wealthier life in L.A., asked me.

It was early in the morning and the two of us were sitting at the table under the mess tent. He had decided to skip the six o'-clock game drive and work on his laptop instead. I think he needed to reestablish his authority by letting the Hong Kong stock market play its role versus nature. He sounded aggressive and was obviously in a ghastly mood. Earlier I had watched him eat his breakfast with an uncanny rapacity. I don't think he was getting laid as much as he had been planning to.

"I mean, Adam was born here, so okay, to him this is home . . . But what do *you* do in a place like this? I mean I would *die*, you know, I would fucking *die* if I had to live so far away from the city."

"I guess I've had enough of city life," I said dryly.

The river, just below us, curved in a narrow bend. I kept my eyes on a big croc on the opposite bank which looked like a mud sculpture. I pointed it out to him. He squinted, and vaguely nodded. He wasn't going to give me the satisfaction of showing any interest in wildlife this morning. He turned to his liquid crystal screen and tapped away for a few seconds.

"You know, this isn't *real*. It's just a big fantasy."

I didn't answer. He bored me so much already I wanted to scream.

"This is just another Disneyland, it has nothing to do with the real world out there. They've let nature take over because they can charge you money to come and see how it used to be thousands of years ago, the hunting and the killing and all that.

The minute they stop making money from nature, they'll destroy it as they have done everywhere else in the world."

I took up the binoculars and pretended to study the river in search of more game.

"They don't need wildlife in Nigeria. You know why? They've got oil there." He sniggered. *"Lots."*

He pointed impatiently at his computer screen as if to remind me of the major financial exchanges taking place in Lagos at that very moment while we were wasting our time watching crocs in the mud.

"You live inside a museum, you realize that . . ."

"Well, you are being pretty Ptolemaic here," I said.

"What's that??

"You know how before Galileo we believed in the Ptolemaic system, the earth being the unmovable center of the universe?"

He looked at me suspiciously. He didn't understand, but he didn't like being called that anyway.

"In other words, why is it always that the West decides what's real and what isn't?" I said.

He shook his head, as if I was being hopelessly ludicrous.

"I mean, this is the end of the millennium, you guys!"

"And so what?" I didn't like the way he called me "you guys."

"Well, it doesn't take a Nobel Prize to tell you that the future isn't heading forward in *this* part of the planet. If I were you I wouldn't like to be left so far behind."

"And what *would* you do if you were me?" I asked, lighting my first cigarette of the day. I knew he found it disgusting that I should smoke so early, and I purposely blew the smoke on his computer screen.

"Well, I would take advantage of all the wonderful technology the West is producing. . . . There's a whole world out there, and believe me, it's fucking fabulous!"

"I guess so," I said dubiously.

"And besides," he said menacingly, his eyes locking into mine, "you are a smart and sexy woman. I would get the hell out of here fast and stop worrying about which bird is which!"

I didn't know which bird was which. I didn't know the name

of anything, and I feared wild animals as much as the Anorexic Beauties because, just like them, I knew nothing about their behaviour or their habits.

But still I didn't like the clients to be around me; their presence irritated me because it reminded me of everything I had run away from. Their inquisitive looks, their nosy questions made me uneasy, corrupted my vision of the landscape. It was as if they were secret agents who had been sent on a mission to handcuff me and take me home again.

There were exceptions, of course. You thought you knew exactly what they were going to be like the minute you saw them step out of the car with their fancy luggage, and instead they proved you wrong.

Tara was in her late forties, platinum blond hair, garish clothes, long silvery fake nails, heavy makeup, Texan hat. She looked like a rich hooker from Vegas. Adam and I couldn't figure out why on earth she had come on safari all on her own. She seemed to hate the bush, jumped at every noise, screamed at every insect, complained about her fingernails splitting, and kept trotting around camp in high heels. I had all these theories about her.

Was she running away from someone? Was she a spy? A transsexual? What was her secret?

"I work in the movie industry, honey," she said to me when I gathered the courage to ask her. "Exotic animals. Animal trainer, my specialty is cats. Every lion or tiger you see in a movie is mine."

"*Tigers?*"

"Siberian, Bengali. Back home I sleep with four of them in my bed. Figured it was time to come to Africa and see a bit of untrained wildlife."

It all fell into place: she had that flamboyant circus quality which some women who love cats have.

Tara knew absolutely everything about big cats. She even knew how to treat their skin problems, worms, vitamin deficiencies. Whenever she spotted a lion or a cheetah in a game drive she would ask Adam to get really close with the car and started whispering to them in an incomprehensible language. The animals would always turn their heads and listen to her, half hypnotized. It was as if they recognized her. Adam was impressed. Now he looked at her with a completely different attitude.

"What are those sounds you make? Is it a language they understand?" he'd ask her.

"It's a secret," she would say, smiling enigmatically. "I'm not going to give it away."

You could tell she would know how to touch them, you could feel her total absence of fear. Next to a wild animal, her grotesque appearance would inexplicably undergo a transformation. Regardless of the garishness of her outfit she suddenly looked regal.

Adam asked what had made her become an animal trainer.

"Put it this way, honey. These days you can get shot in the head any day where I live. I'd rather be killed by a beautiful wild animal than have my brain blasted by some retard on crack. It's a much sexier way to go."

Apart from the few exceptions, when Adam took off with the clients on a game drive I usually preferred to stay behind and take walks along the river or climb up the mountain ridge, escorted by two of the Samburu *askari*s who worked at the camp.

Lenjo always walked in front, holding his long spear and his *rungu*, the short club carved in olive wood which every Samburu keeps in his hand at all times. Diani, barely in his teens, walked behind me. I kept my eyes on Lenjo's back: his long braided hair smeared in cow grease and red ochre dangled gently on his back; the red *shuka*, which he tied over one shoulder like a Roman toga, flapped in the wind; his incredibly long, lean legs seemed to touch the earth with the lightness of a feather. He was a Moran, a warrior of his tribe. Diani had not been circumcised yet and therefore had not acquired the status of a Moran. His hair was still short, his ears had not been pierced, he didn't wear the colourful beads which adorned Lenjo's dark skin.

We walked in silence, listening to the sounds of the bush, feeling the cool morning air brush our arms and legs. Every now and then Lenjo would stop and look out. I could feel his eyes scanning the bush ahead. There was always a moment of suspense, when I would hold my breath not knowing what would happen next. I would turn back to check Diani's expression, and I always found him chewing a twig and looking quite relaxed, leaning on his spear.

"*Ndovu.*" Elephant, Lenjo would announce quietly after a long silence, slowly pointing to the valley below. I could only hear a faint sound of branches falling, and see trees swaying in the thick of the bush.

Yes, there they were. Big elephants with huge tusks. One, two, three—up to twenty, sometimes. We would watch in silence for a while. Lenjo and Diani would speak in Samburu, commenting on the size of the animals. Lenjo, who spoke a bit of English, would then point at an indistinct brown patch in the bush and say with satisfaction, "Very very big one."

He also liked to show me the plants and the herbs the Samburu use.

"This very dangerous; it can kill elephant. You put this on arrowheads, it will finish you in two minutes," he would say of a very innocent-looking green branch. Then he would show me a velvety silver leaf.

"This we call Moran blanket because the Morans when they sleep out under the sky, they rest on these leaves. Very very soft, like a blanket. . . . This one if you smell it it will cure your cold . . . this one will make you very very strong, if you boil the bark and drink it like soup, it will make you very hungry and you will eat one big goat, maybe two. . . ."

I liked the way the young warriors always boasted about what they could do. Yes, of course they could kill a lion with their spear, steal a hundred cattle from a neighbouring tribe, walk thirty miles, eat a whole goat in one night. There was nothing too big or too strong for a Moran.

A Samburu warrior needed to be brave, he was taught this from the earliest age.

"And if you just bend your toes when they circumcise you," said Lenjo with a smile, "oh, you're finished. They will call you a coward, and it will be shame on your family. Sure."

He and Diani laughed at my surprise. Circumcision was the favourite subject of young Samburus.

"You have to be brave and sit still when they cut you with a knife. Everyone is looking at you to see if maybe you bend your toe . . . So you have to sit still, like this."

Lenjo would close his eyes as if he was lightly asleep. Diani would nod encouragingly. They smiled proudly, having made their point.

"*Mape.* Let's go now."

We walked in silence for long stretches, then we stopped and sat cross-legged on top of a boulder looking down at the endless plain. We'd sit like that in silence, listening to the sound of the wind whistling below. I liked to be able to remain that quiet in the company of others, without feeling the need to fill up the silence with chatter.

Lenjo would gently break the silence.

"*Malo.*" Greater kudu, and he would point at a tiny dot in the distance. He and Diani laughed at me whenever they caught me squinting.

I loved the feeling of those walks.

There is a very special bond between humans who are walking close to each other in the wilderness. They have to move carefully, they need to be ready for any eventuality. No one could be further apart than me from those two young warriors, yet as we were sliding silently through the tall grass we looked out for the same signs, we scanned, we smelled, we listened. In the remote possibility that anything was going to happen, it would happen to the three of us, whether it be a buffalo bursting out of the grass, a lion or a cobra. Yes, jaded clients might go on believing the bush was a fantasy world, but nature felt real enough to me.

And so vivid was that feeling that all the rage and pain I had felt when I first arrived now seemed to belong to another life. It was as if the silence of wilderness had seeped into me and had quietened the useless noise of my fear.

Lenjo always smiled when I asked him what we would do if we met a lion in the grass.

"Lions are afraid of men. But you don't show your fear, because animals can know. You always be brave and lion will run away from you. Sure."

We never met a lion, so I never had to test his theory.

Once though, when we had nearly reached camp, he suddenly stopped. So did my heart: I knew this time we had walked upon something. Lenjo turned to me and pointed silently into the trees. I could barely make out a shape and I saw some branches move.

"Elephants," he whispered, and began to step back. For what seemed an eternity, the three of us walked backwards, keeping our eyes fixed on the moving branches. Then we heard the trumpeting. It literally shook the earth, it was so close. Then the branches being broken. A shot of adrenaline fired into my body. Fear in its purest form. Lenjo and Diani froze for a split second, then signalled me to run.

I immediately grabbed Lenjo's elbow, I didn't trust my legs to be as fast as his. We ran and ran, zigzagging through the bush, birds fluttering their wings all around us. I didn't know whether we were still being chased, I only concentrated on the running and suddenly—I don't know where that came from—I knew we were going to be fine.

The incredible thing was that the more we ran, the more we laughed. We kept holding on to each other, laughing hysterically, like children playing a game. We burst into camp panting and shaking with laughter.

"*Huyu, anaweza kukimbia sana,*" said Lenjo to Adam and the other guys, pointing at me and shaking his head with a smile.

"Of course I can run, what did you think?" I replied jokingly, wiping the sweat from my forehead.

And suddenly I felt victorious. It was fun, after all, to be faster than an angry elephant.

Iris materialized one evening in the dusky light right after sunset, in full regalia—that is to say in her battered olive green Land Rover, handbag-size pistol in the glove compartment, old felt hat atop her long blond braid, covered with red dust, Samburu beads and sweat, accompanied by two striking Morans in the back seat.

We had put up camp not far from Wamba. The clients, a group of middle-aged Chicago surgeons with their wives, looked at this wild blond creature in disbelief, and one of them actually took out his camera for a snap. Iris was kissing Adam with passion.

"Oh man! I've driven all the way from South Horr, I'm finished! Let me have a drink before anything else . . . How do you do, Iris Sorensen . . . pleased to meet you . . . sorry to intrude on your sundowner . . . Oh Esmé, finally. . . . There you are, at last!"

Suddenly I was squeezed in her powerful embrace. She smelled of dust and petrol. She took a good look at me and then turned to the clients.

"I've heard so much about this woman!"

Iris was on her way back to Nairobi from further north where she had been travelling for two months, taking pictures for a new book on the tribes of the North. She'd heard over the bush radio that Adam had put up camp on the Ewaso and she'd decided to stop over and rest for a day. How she had found the camp I don't know, it seemed to me we were in the middle of nowhere. But obviously not nowhere enough for a bush woman like Iris.

Adam poured her a drink while she greeted the staff. She seemed to have known them all a long time. Lenjo in particular was thrilled to see her. They went into a very elaborate handshake and joked in Samburu.

"Oh, that one. He's such a star," she said to Adam, returning to her chair and shaking her head. "I'm going to steal him from you one day."

She took out a bag of tobacco and started to roll a cigarette on her lap. We were all sitting around her, our eyes fixed on her like on a screen. She shook her head and smiled at us.

"Let me tell you, it feels great to have reached here. Everyone's pretty nervous around Barsaloi these days, because of the *shiftas*."

"What's that?" asked the wife of one of the surgeons.

"Bandits," she said nonchalantly. Then, licking the rolling paper, "Pretty nasty ones too."

The clients got more excited and began an interview. Was her book going to be published in the States? Yes, indeed.

Who was this woman? Had I ever heard of her? Yes, of course I had, and not only that: I had actually had her first book in my hands not long before. It was displayed in the window of the New Stanley Hotel bookstore. It was called something like *The Last Rites,* and I remembered her picture on the dust jacket. Suntanned, her long hair loose, covered with tribal jewelry, smiling from her muddy Land Rover.

I remember thinking, She can't be for real.

But here she was, the realest of the real, same props included.

Was she born in Kenya? The clients were eager to know more.

Yes, and she had lived most of her life with the nomadic tribes of the North. Her father was a Swedish farmer who had come to Africa in the mid-fifties and settled near Maralal.

After dinner with the clients, the three of us sat by the fire. She was simply wrapped in a Somali *kikoy* and a man's shirt, her long silky hair loose on her back. In many ways she looked like a bleached version of a Moran: the same elegant step, the same gaunt figure.

Adam looked happy to have her there; they seemed to share an intimacy which dated back a long time. Iris was constantly referring to people they knew in common, speaking in shorthand of places they were both familiar with in the bush. They obviously had a common history of safaris and adventures, travels and nights spent under just a mosquito net and the stars.

"You know I got stuck in the Ndotos for a week, my gearshift broke off in my hands, can you believe it? So I had to wait for this guy to come all the way from that mission to fix it—remember that mission where we bought petrol the time we went through the Kaisut desert? What's it called?"

"Yeah, I remember . . . the mission of that Italian priest, the mechanic . . ."

"Well, he's dead now. But there is a Canadian priest in his place, a great guy. He helped me fix it in the end . . ."

"Excellent."

"Remember that bridge, past the big volcanic rock, as you head towards Ol Doinyo Nyro?"

"It's washed out, I know. I went past it about four weeks ago."

"The road is such a nightmare now. I kept getting stuck in the mud."

Their landmarks were rocks and mountains and trees, and water holes and scattered *manyatta*s in the bush. I sat back listening to them talk about the land, redesign it, just for the pleasure of making it a controllable entity again rather than an abstraction. All that land which stretched around us, which had no name or shape and made no sense at all to me.

Their conversation made me think of the the Aborigines in Australia, who believe that the earth was shaped because it had been sung. In the Dreamtime, the Ancestors woke up from total darkness and as the Light began to shine they started walking. They walked about and sang. They sang the shape of each rock and water hole and hill. They sang the trees, the stones, the rivers, the canyons. That's how they made the world: by singing it bit by bit. The "song lines" were their routes, the tracks of their singing from here to there. People didn't inherit land, they inherited songlines. Tribes owned songs.

Virtually all of the Australian landscape can be sung. Where one tribe would finish another one would pick up.

That night Adam and Iris sang their Northern Territory songlines, as if they both owned it by birthright, and on and on they went, until they had sung each hill, bridge, tree, each obscure corner of the African bush.

It was beautiful, listening to them sing it.

"Has she been your lover?" I whispered, enveloped in the darkness of the tent. Adam and I had just made love, and he was lying on his side, smoking a joint. A useless question; I already knew the answer.

"Oh," Adam said absentmindedly, "yes, when we were much younger."

There was a silence. He felt my uneasiness.

"You know, she's like a sister to me now."

I don't know if I liked the idea of Iris's being his sister. If anything, it made me feel even more threatened.

"What am *I* to you?" I asked.

I felt his hand on my temple, stroking my hair, as if he wanted to brush away my doubts. I guess I must have always looked so insecure, but then I never really knew what anything meant. Was I supposed to stay? Was that going to be my life from now on? The life of a museum keeper, as that reformed cokehead had sneeringly said?

"Shhhh," he said and kissed me lightly. "Why is it you are always looking for definitions? You're only satisfied when you're given a label you can stick onto things."

He was right. I needed words, believed in them.

"I love you," he said. "It's as simple as that."

He turned back to put out the joint and the kerosene lamp.

"Now shut up," he said.

I smiled in the dark as he pulled me closer and wrapped his arms around me from behind. I felt his warm hand on my belly and his breath on my neck.

No woman could wish for more. Right?

But I did.

You see, all my life I had been singing different songlines from the ones Iris and Adam had been singing.

In my European Dreamtime there had been no rocks or mountains or trees to be sung, in fact nothing visible at all. I had been wandering aimlessly from one state of mind to the next, designing such an abstract world that now I was completely lost. I desperately wanted my exile to be over: but the minute I thought I had found peace, a home at last, something new would happen and I would panic again. There didn't seem any feeling of comfort, any rest. Why?

I had lost people all my life: my mother, my father, and now even my brother had begun to fade away. I had grown so used to the concept of losing people that I had become an expert at cutting ties quickly in order to minimize the pain. I had learned never to count on anyone who said they loved me: it felt like a bad investment. I simply ignored it, as if their love was something which was here today but could very well be gone tomorrow.

Yet I had been blessed.

That man Leonardo drew in the circle, the perfect specimen. He had no hidden agenda, and now he was mine and he was going to look after me. The gods had sent him; how could I not see it?

But I didn't.

I kept torturing myself, thinking it wouldn't last. My diabolical mind was already spinning at a thousand miles a minute, desperate and defensive, trying to figure out ways to survive without him in this foreign land. It was totally unconscious: like biting one's nails, the minute you realise what you are doing, you are already bleeding.

What can I say? Some brains come with fear built in.

In retrospect I see how Iris's apparition that day triggered most of what happened later. She obviously wasn't aware of this then, and afterwards she never had the time to find out. I wouldn't have told her anyway.

That night by the fire, as they were singing the land where they had grown up, I saw exactly what Adam was going to confirm to me later.

They were brother and sister, born from the same land. They *belonged* there, Africa was in their blood.

I was a stranger and would always be.

The next morning, as I stepped out of my tent at seven I saw Iris, who had been pottering around since sunrise, her hair glistening from the bush shower and smelling of shampoo, a steamy mug of coffee on the hood of her car. She was getting ready to go with her two guardian angels.

"Here," she said gently, "I want you to wear this."

She put a Samburu beaded bracelet around my wrist.

"I'm sure I'll see you back in Nairobi . . . but for the time being, keep it. A small memento. I am really glad to have met you at last."

"Thank you." Her kindness had taken me by surprise. "That's really sweet of you."

I knew the bracelet was a distinct sign of friendship in Iris's language. Her gesture had been genuine, I could tell. I felt bad for having been suspicious of her earlier; it made me feel ungenerous and petty. I knew she wasn't trying to manipulate me or control me. She hadn't come all the way here just to prove a point or to reaffirm her ownership of Adam. That was just my paranoia. I wanted to like her now, but I couldn't just press a button and do it, so I smiled at her as brightly as I was capable of. I watched her as she carefully poured water into her rusty radiator, the early-morning sun shining through the cascade of her golden hair.

"Why don't you stay here another day?" I said. Now it was my turn to make her feel welcome.

"Thanks, but I want to get back now. I have to get on the phone, to the bank, into the bathtub. You know, all those great things you can do in the civilized world," she smiled at me. "Having spent nearly two months in the bush I'm quite looking forward to an urban safari, if you know what I mean."

I thought she meant sex. Well, why not, I couldn't help thinking, she looked like she wouldn't have any problem scoring *that*.

"Plus I am dying to develop the pictures. My entire future is inside here." She gently patted her big camera bag.

I knew from her previous book that her work would be impressive. Her problem was that she looked too good to be true.

93

Her looks were her commodity and her cross, I guess. Meanwhile all the camp staff had come to the car to say goodbye to her. She spoke to them in Swahili and Samburu, tipped each one generously, cracking jokes which had them in stitches. Then she jumped in the Land Rover and drove off in a cloud of dust.

CHAPTER SEVEN

To live in Africa you must know
what it's like to die in Africa.

ERNEST HEMINGWAY

Living off Ferdinando's rights suddenly seemed wrong.

Besides the money wasn't nearly enough, as not many Americans seemed to be interested in my father's poetry.

So, after six months out in the bush I realized it was time to go back to Nairobi and look for a job. I needed something to do which would give me a purpose for staying.

Life at the camp had been thrilling. By now I too knew how to drive a bulky car across a lugger, change a tire with a high lift jack, bake bread on a campfire, recognize the track of most animals. I had learned not to flinch if I met a snake on my path or if a bat flew in my face in the dark. I had mastered enough Swahili to have the guys laugh at my jokes around the fire. Africa had gotten under my skin. But now I had to find something to do which was entirely mine.

While Adam came and went with clients, I settled myself in his house in Langata, a stone cottage on a green slope facing the Ngong hills. It was a cosy little house; I liked the way the dark wood floor planks creaked under my feet, I loved the warmth of the fireplace in the sitting room after sunset, the whiteness of our big four-poster bed. Wilson and Alice welcomed me shyly and looked after me like with a gentleness I had never known.

I knew I had become way too dependent on Adam. So now, even though I missed him when he wasn't around, I felt a strange excitement waking up in our bed alone and having the whole day to myself.

I had time now to put my thoughts into a broader perspective. I was beginning to have a vision of what living in Africa really meant. What had I seen so far?

I had seen whites living in Africa, bathing in its beauty and its wilderness. I had seen Africans—but only as perceived by whites—either proud and noble warriors of vanishing tribes, or faithful servants who looked after their masters with care. And now I started asking myself if what I had seen so far was all there was.

I knew there must be another side to life here, but I didn't know how to unveil it on my own. Any fool could tell it was there, yet it was so difficult to pin down. Nobody I had met so far seemed to want to talk about this hidden thing.

I felt Nicole knew what it was—*we are hostages to beauty,* she had said—but she had chosen to be sarcastic about it rather than serious.

Looking back, I see how all this had been clear to me from the very beginning; I had simply pretended not to see it. An inner voice kept whispering "Don't spoil it yet, just enjoy it the way it is. . . ."

But on my own in Nairobi, without Adam and with time on my hands, the picture was finally coming into focus.

That's when I started to really see the Africans.

The Africans I was looking at now were no longer the noble warriors of the North, adorned in beads and ostrich feathers, holding long spears in their hands. What I saw now, as I passed them on the road, were the average Kenyans in tattered Western clothes: the old beggars on the corner of Kaunda street, the glue-sniffing urchins across from the New Stanley Hotel who would force their bony hands through the car window asking for a shilling, the black middle class who took their lunch break at

La Patisserie, the gas station attendants in spotless overalls, the smiling maids in starched uniforms who served tea in white people's houses, the slow herd of exhausted workmen who walked back home at dusk from the workshops or the factory, covered with grease and dust.

Looking at them I couldn't help thinking of Ferdinando and of his principles. I knew he wouldn't have approved of me. How could I possibly live in the third world, enjoying my privileges as a white person, without taking the time to look around and see what was going on? What had the Africans been doing while I was on safari? What did I know about how they struggled? But most of all: Where the hell were they? Why had we never crossed each other's paths?

I remember once driving Wilson to the hospital where his wife had just had a baby. He looked so different without the uniform he wore in the house. In his everyday clothes, a baseball cap and blue jeans, I hardly recognised him. I must have assumed Wilson was as old-fashioned as the uniform he had to wear. It surprised me that he should carry a Walkman and that he listened to rap.

"How old are you, Wilson?" I asked him. And suddenly felt ashamed not to have asked the question earlier.

"Twenty-eight, Memsahab."

Yes, maybe that was the key. The combination of rap music and Memsahab. Maybe that was what I was failing to understand.

I soon realised that to have an opinion about blacks was a career in itself. Nairobi was throbbing with third world specialists: UN people—UNICEF, UNDP, UNESCO—AMREF, missionaries, NGOs of all kinds, pale men in white short-sleeved shirts who worked for the World Bank. Everyone had a theory, everyone was looking for funds or running a project. The wars in neighbouring Somalia and Sudan had pushed thousands of refugees over the Kenyan borders. Rwanda was about to explode. AIDS was thriving. The Kenyan economy had collapsed.

Experts were flocking in every day.

I didn't know where to start, yet I wanted to know the answer to a very simple question. Something so elementary, you couldn't just ask around: How does a white person live in a black country? And most of all: Where do we stand in relation to one another? I wanted someone to explain the contradictions, to show me the obstacles, to come up with the answer. But nobody did. Everyone around me seemed to plainly ignore the issue.

I think they avoided it for a very simple reason.

Nairobi didn't have a Soweto, you see. There wasn't a history of racial tension in Kenya. There were no more whites in parliament who could be held responsible for overt injustices towards the Africans. So what was the point of crucifying ourselves, when officially we weren't doing anything wrong and not even the blacks were complaining?

Nevertheless whites, within the boundaries of their well-guarded homes, had kept their colonial attitudes intact towards the Africans. Newcomers proved very good at picking them up immediately, as if they had been used to having African servants all their life, whereas back in Europe they probably couldn't even afford a cleaning lady two hours a week. It's amazing how little time it takes for whites to learn how to bully Africans. Once they realise nobody is going to accuse them of wrongdoing, the minute they understand nobody here has ever even heard the expression "politically correct," even the most liberal white turns into a slave master in a matter of days. Whites will forget the meaning of the word "overtime," will refuse advances of a few hundred shillings, will raise their voices and lose their tempers for futile reasons, and sack their staff at whim.

That's what intrigued me. I wasn't an expert, I had no means of coming up with a sociopolitical analysis, yet I wanted to understand why we all behaved like that.

Expats spoke about Africans all the time: referring to the mechanic who was fixing their car, or to the middleman they were bribing in order to get a work permit, they would shake their heads:

"You can't really trust them. They say they'll do it by tomorrow but they won't, unless you're prepared to sit there and make sure they do it."

They would say of the police officer who had come to investigate the theft of their camera, and of the cook who had been with them for years, who had become their prime suspect:

"They always lie, you should never believe a word they say."

All Africans were either liars or thieves if they had no money, or were corrupt and unscrupulous if slightly ahead on the social scale.

Maybe the mistrust was necessary to mitigate the guilt. The more you felt cheated by them the less you felt guilty for taking advantage. I don't know, but it seemed wrong to live with such lack of confidence in each other.

In the last few years Nairobi had become increasingly dangerous. At night people had to watch out while driving home in their new cars. As they flashed the headlights at the gate to signal the *askari* to open, armed gangs would be waiting for them, pointing the guns to their temples. Sometimes, if they didn't get what they wanted, they left the driver dead on the tarmac as they drove off in the brand-new Pajero. Gangs of armed robbers would sneak into the white man's house in Muthaiga at night, club him and his wife until they were unconscious, and steal their money, stereo, television. On the Mombasa-Nairobi road if a tourist minibus had a flat, even in broad daylight, very likely a small gang of hungry youngsters would appear from behind the shrubs at the side of the road and clean the tourists out, brandishing their rusty knifes. You constantly had to watch out for thieves, there was nothing too old or too used for a hungry African. Not even your worn-out spare tire was safe in the trunk. People kept guns in the house and bragged that they would shoot anything that moved if a noise woke them up in the middle of the night.

Security was a subject which never went out of fashion at white people's dinner tables.

"I'm not surprised. Africans have nothing—no jobs, no running water, no electricity; they live in mud huts and have five, six children and nothing to eat. They could feed their family for two weeks just with the contents of our fridge," I said with impetus one evening while everyone fell silent around the table. "I mean, why should we expect to live in peace in a place with such disparities? They have nothing and we always have more than we need. We would do exactly the same thing if we were in their place. We just happen to be on the right side of the barricade, you see."

"And which side might that be, mind you?" someone at the end of the table asked with a vein of sarcasm.

"Well, the side that doesn't need to steal."

I had been invited to dinner at Nena and Peter's. It was my first outing to the Elephant Man's house; Adam was away and I wanted to make a good impression. But somehow the conversation had taken a dangerous turn and I was speaking too impulsively. A man who looked like a butcher, an Argentinian polo champion, I was told, had just described how he had managed to shoot two robbers in the legs and deliver them to the police station in his pickup truck, tied up with rope, like pigs to the slaughterhouse. The pleasure which he exuded as he described how he had wounded them, and the way he sneered recalling the fear in their eyes once he had them tied up with their wrists locked behind their backs and thrown in the back of the pickup, made my blood boil.

"They thought I was going to dump them in the ditch and shoot them dead, the bastards." He chuckled. "And they were lucky I didn't."

I still knew nothing about the rules of an ex–white colony. I had been brought up in a country where nobody would dream of touching on the subject of guns at a dinner table. Nobody I knew had ever even owned one, let alone used it.

I went on ranting, since everyone was now looking at me.

"I don't know, I couldn't sleep next to a gun. It's just one of those things: you use a gun, next thing you know the really bad guys will come because they want your gun. And they will use it on you."

"If you had children in the house and feared for their lives, then you *would* sleep next to a gun, believe me, dear," said Peter, the Elephant Man, who was certainly neither a racist nor a fascist, and to whom I had looked for moral support for my peaceful argument.

No, I didn't have children who slept under the net in Winnie the Pooh flannel pyjamas. Therefore I had no right to inflict my liberal theories on people who had to protect innocent lives on the Dark Continent.

Trying to understand Africa is like being sucked into a black hole. And the more one wants to search into that darkness, the less one is likely to come out of it at the other end. But, as there is no other end, people learn to stay away from it.

When I went back to the house that night and flashed the headlights at my gate, I caught myself looking anxiously in the rearview mirror. For the first time it struck me that maybe it wasn't such a good idea to drive so late at night on my own. Next time I better take an *askari* with me, I thought.

As I lay in bed alone in the empty house, listening to the frightening scream of a hyrax in the trees, I caught myself wondering whether Adam kept a gun in the house. We had never discussed it, even though I knew he had one at the camp. The danger of wild animals in the bush was understandable. But what about hopeless men in the city? I wondered what Adam's reaction would have been to my ranting at the dinner table. Would he have found me naive, as Peter had? I was surprised to find I had no idea.

But more than anything, I wondered, would I have engaged in such an argument at all had he been with me? I realized that I tended to be much quieter when he was around. I always feared that my views might sound ingenuous.

There were still these mysterious gaps between us created by our different upbringings. Sometimes the mystery triggered the attraction, sometimes it only made me feel different and a bit of an outcast.

The wind rattled the window, the wooden floor creaked, and I was covered with sweat. It was fear. And fear in Africa always comes with a black face.

Would it help if I told my murderers about my views on our disparity of wealth? Would they appreciate the way I had contradicted the Argentinian polo champion? Would they stop the panga in midair, pat me on the shoulder with a smile of recognition and call me a comrade? No, of course not. I would be butchered just the same. I was on the wrong side of the barricade because of the colour of my skin. I had what they couldn't have because I was white, and that was the end of the story.

One should just forget about fear; otherwise there is no point in living in Africa.

The morning after the dinner party I rang Nicole.

"Am I imagining it, or do whites in this country tend to become trigger-happy?" I blurted into the phone without even saying hello.

". . . Esmé, what time is it?" she answered in a husky voice. "Don't you have a hangover, for God's sake?"

"Yes, but it keeps me awake, for some strange reason. Did I make a fool of myself last night?"

"Oh . . . that awful Argentinian. He's so gun-crazy, I don't know why Nena keeps inviting him. Of course you weren't making a fool of yourself. He's a total nightmare."

So why was I always the only one to speak my views? Why was it that others never came to my aid, but pretended to be bored by such talk? I was confused.

Life went on as usual, and we all kept paying high monthly fees to private police who were constantly on patrol at night, hiring *askari*s who walked up and down the compound with bow and arrows, and breeding Rottweilers and Dobermans trained to kill.

In the meantime American troops and their high-tech combat gear had turned Somalia into a rerun of *Apocalypse Now*.

"Doin' the Mog" T-shirts, Cobra helicopter stickers on the back of Land Rovers, started to appear. The international press showed pictures of Somali warriors in flip-flops and *kikoy*s waving AK47s from their technicals, while sunburned Marines with crew cuts and Ray bans looked out ahead through the heat shimmers with worried expressions on their faces. The war in Somalia was a romantic war, fought by a bunch of proud and fierce desert clansmen who were not going to let the West interfere. Somalis were not afraid to die; they would point their rusty machine guns up to the sky, determined to shoot down a Cobra rather than look for shelter. Young hacks flew in and out of Somalia aboard the UN planes from Nairobi, and war tales were now topping bush tales around town. Suddenly the Carnivore was bustling with young reporters, photographers and cameramen on break between assignments, holding court at the bar with thrilling stories about escaping bombshells in downtown Mogadishu. They wore green fatigues, mirrored shades, and had taken to chewing *miraa*, the speedy bitter leaves Somalis get high on every day. They stuffed their pockets with small bundles of twigs wrapped in newspaper, chewed the fresh shoots nonstop till they had a ball inside their cheek and their jaws ached, and drank cold beer after beer. They had a haunted look from too many sleepless nights and too much adrenaline pumping through their blood.

The war in Somalia had brought a distinct buzz to Nairobi.

Nicole was a big fan of the hacks. She chewed *miraa* with them and talked politics. The first time I met Miles it had been at her place, together with Bernard, a young French photojournalist, and a wild character called Ruben, a WTN American cameraman. They were good-looking, jittery and vibrant. All of them barely in their mid-twenties. Some had been briefly to Bosnia, some to Eritrea, but most of them had had very little experience of a war situation so far. Certainly none was prepared for what was yet to come.

Having spent such a long time only in Adam's company, I realised I was starved for male friends. I got used to sitting with them next to the fireplace at Nicole's, chewing the bitter leaves until we got a buzz, and jabbering our way through the night. Whenever I made an attempt to go home they would pull me back down on the cushions.

"You can't leave," Miles would say, "it's not even light yet."

I loved the feeling of being their captive. Nicole and I fed off their wild energy: we were seduced by the unsettling behaviour of men who feared for their lives. They looked like they had been on acid for days.

Hunter Reed's name came up several times during those *miraa* nights. He was one of their best hack mates. I don't know why, but right away, any time his name was mentioned I paid extra attention to the conversation. It struck a chord, a sort of premonition, as if I already knew that our paths were bound to cross and leave a mark.

"His mother married one of the BC leaders," said Ruben in an explanatory way. "You know, Steve Biko's party."

"Oh," I said. "I thought Hunter was a *mzungu*."

"He is. That's exactly the point." Ruben smiled, amused by my comment. "He's whiter than white, English in fact; but he grew up in South Africa among African activists. His mother was a reporter for the BBC radio in East Africa, then when they moved her to Johannesburg in the late sixties she left Hunter's father for this Biko man. They're still together now."

"I met her only once," Miles added. "She's a very cool woman. Very, *very* radical."

"Sounds like it," I said.

"That explains his love-hate relationship with Africa," Miles went on. "When we met back in England a few years ago he swore he was never coming back out here again. He said he had had it, that he wanted a normal life. But it's an addiction, he can't stay away from it, you see. And he knows Africa too bloody well for his paper not to beg him to come back, and to push loads of money on him."

So Hunter Reed seemed to be the rock star of journalism in East Africa. Like all rock stars he sounded elusive and unapproachable. I figured one wouldn't just run into him on the street, and the idea of meeting him one day made me unaccountably nervous.

My moment of truth with Hunter Reed finally came via Iris,

of all people.

She had been busy working on her book, and once back in Nairobi I had hardly ever seen her, except for a couple of outings at the Carnivore with "the boys" where we had all gotten completely thrashed.

I can't really say why, but I had a feeling that it was up to me to seek her out and to show her I wanted to be her friend. I felt I should make an effort to see more of her in a sober state, so one morning I pulled into her driveway on my way back from shopping at the Karen *dukas* holding a bunch of tuberoses and a bag of freshly ground coffee. From the outside her cottage looked like a doll's house: wood-shingled roof, pretty flowers all around, pots hanging on the verandah. I pushed open the door: inside it was incredibly untidy: clothes scattered everywhere, magazines, photographic paper, car tools, paint spray cans, piles of prints and sheets of transparencies. It looked like the hideout of a messy teenager.

I heard a man's voice coming from the kitchen. I walked in to find Iris in a pair of striped man's pyjamas, drinking her morning tea all by herself at a small table.

"*G for generosity,*" a voice politely enunciated from a tape recorder in a thick Indian accent. "*The only way money will come back to you is by giving it away as lavishly as you can . . .*"

"Oh Esmé, I can't believe it's you, this is too much!" she said. "Just the person I needed to see!"

"Oh, good. What are you listening to?"

"*. . . all your thoughts and your impulses are made of atoms, and every single action will carry its particular energy into space,*" the voice continued.

"It's this great tape made by an Indian guru, my cousin sent it to me from Europe. You have to listen to it every day and repeat what he says. Basically what it does is teach you how to direct your positive energy so that it all comes back to you."

"Sounds excellent. And what happens once it comes back?"

"Well . . ." She hesitated. "I know it sounds crazy, but . . ."

She pressed the rewind button and started the tape again.

"*. . . basically you listen to what he says, you repeat it out loud, and money comes your way."

"*A for affluence. Affluence has to be a spiritual condition before anything else. Wealth will follow . . .*"

"So what," I said, "you mean all you have to do to get rich is sit here and repeat this stuff every morning? Can I make some fresh coffee?"

"Absolutely, and you don't even have to think about its meaning. The mere repetition of the words sends the right energy wherever and . . . oh thanks, how sweet of you." She took the coffee bag from my hand. "Let me put the kettle on. The principle is that the more you learn how to let go, the more it comes back to you. Money, work, love, anything. It's incredible."

"*. . . let your positive thoughts flow freely and let the universe handle the details . . .*"

"Wow, I like *that* bit," I said.

"It does work, I promise you."

"Is the universe is taking care of all your details?"

"Pretty much," she laughed. "Like now for instance: I was just sent a fax offering me a job, but I'm too busy with the book, so I was wondering just this minute who could do it in my place and you stepped right in. In fact you are perfect to do it."

"What is it?"

"It's French *Vogue*. They want to do a story on war correspondents and they need somebody here to make all the contacts, set up the interviews, the location et cetera. I think they pay well, and anyway I'll tell them you're the ideal person for it. You know, all they need is to shoot all the good-looking hacks wearing designer clothes, so you just have to round up a few of them like Miles, Ruben, Hunter and whathisname, that cute French photographer . . ."

"Bernard."

"Exactly. I'm sure you can handle it perfectly well."

"Oh, I don't know about that. But hey, thanks a lot, Iris. You're a star."

I was thrilled. And I suppose I had to thank the Indian guru for it, too.

This was going to be my first job since I had first arrived in

Kenya nearly a year earlier. Once at home I immediately ran to the phone and called the number in Paris. This very excited fashion editor with a thick French accent sounded delighted to hear I was ready to offer my services. Yes, they were going to come with this very famous Italian photographer and a writer. It was very important of course that the subjects have some *charme*. I guaranteed they would.

"The ones I have in mind are all terribly handsome, don't worry about that," I said, with the determination of an agent pushing her clients with a casting director.

I guess when you are too close to things as they happen, you lose perspective, things slide out of focus. At the time it seemed perfectly normal that a fashion magazine would want to run a story on young good-looking war reporters. So, excited by my newly acquired role in the world of international fashion, I picked up the phone and informed Miles, Ruben and Bernard that *Vogue* was going to run a story on them and they would get to keep the clothes they would be wearing on the shoot. They seemed flattered and were thrilled at the prospect of a free wardrobe. Next I called the German correspondent for ZDF, a handsome man in his early forties who looked rugged and fit, and left a couple of messages on the answering machine of a very good-looking South African photographer.

Then I lit a cigarette and got ready to call Hunter Reed.

"May I speak with Hunter Reed, please?"

"Speaking."

"Hi, how are you, I'm a friend of Iris Sorensen, we have never met . . . my name is Esmé—"

"Yes. I know who you are."

". . . . ."

"Yes Esmé, I'm listening. Carry on."

". . . Oh, well, I . . . I'm working for . . . well, actually I'm giving a hand to . . . let me explain . . . French *Vogue* wants to run a story on war correspon—"

"French *what?*"

"French *Vogue*. The fashion magazine."

"I see."

" . . . They would like to interview some of the journalists who are currently covering wars in East Africa, and take their portraits. I've already spoken with Miles Sinclair, Bernard Marchand and Ruben Torres, I believe they're all good friends of yours. They have all agreed to do it. I'm waiting to hear from the ZDF correspondent, and—"

"French *Vogue,* you said, right?"

"Yes. They are coming out with an Italian photographer and a writer. They'll run a page for each one of you, and you'll get to keep the clothes."

"Which clothes?"

"The clothes you'll wear on the shoot. They are going to use Armani, Comme Des Garçons and—"

"You mean we have to *model?*"

"Well, not exactly—but yes, in a way, yeah. They'll print a full-page portrait of each one of you wearing the clothes they choose. That's how it always works in fashion magaz—"

"Esmé, how long have you lived here?"

" . . . . ."

"Do you read the papers? Are you aware of what's going on?"

"Of course I am. Why do you ask me that?"

"Because people are *getting shot* on the street every day in Mogadishu, *that's* why, Esmé. How Armani comes into the picture, I don't—"

"Listen, I'm just *working* for them; it's not my idea. I have nothing to do with it, you understand?"

"I assumed you were calling on their behalf."

"Oh, listen, you don't *have* to do it if you don't feel like it, I just thought I'd ask you. If you hate the idea, then that's fine, I understand perfectly well."

"Yes. That's exactly the point. I hate the idea. I *loathe* it."

"Great, okay, no problem. I'm very sorry if I've bothered you with this."

"Not at all. No problem."

"Well, then goodbye, Hunter, thanks anyway."

"Goodbye, Esmé. I hope everything works out for you."

"You don't need to be so patronizing, you know."

"Am I being patronizing?"

"Yes, you are."

"Sorry about that."

"Oh, never mind. Just forget about the whole thing, okay?"

"As you wish."

"Goodbye, Hunter."

"Goodbye, Esmé."

I slammed down the receiver. Fuck you, Hunter Reed, I thought. My God, what a prick you are.

About a month later, in the middle of Mogadishu, a group of hacks ran to the site of a building which had just been shelled by Cobras, where they had heard many Somali civilians had been killed. As they arrived, cameras ready to shoot, an angry mob assaulted them. They were stoned to death. The story of their bleeding bodies being dragged through the streets of Mogadishu made headlines around the world.

A gloomy shadow enveloped all of us.

"Why them, of all people?" asked Nicole, her face white as a sheet, tears streaming down her face. "They had nothing to do with it."

But had that stopped the stones in midair? Had the angry mob realised that these young men were not the enemy, that all they wanted was to report what had just happened? No, they had killed them just the same because, once again, they were on the wrong side of the barricade due to the colour of their skin.

Ruben and Miles came back to Nairobi on the UN plane. They were feverish and haunted, and couldn't stop talking about it. They cried and got drunk, they sobbed until they made no sense and fell asleep wet with tears and reeking of vodka on Nicole's cushions by the fire. All of them knew each other, had all been like brothers bonded by the experience of danger and lurking death. It was something which we couldn't grasp, and this only made us feel more helpless. Hunter Reed's best friend had been killed. He was coming back the next day on a special UN plane carrying the bodies. There would be a memorial service for the victims in a church in Hurlingham, and a wake. All of Nairobi would be mourning.

I didn't go to the service; I didn't want to intrude on their grief. For me there was no face, no body, no memory over which to shed my tears. And somehow I didn't think I could face seeing Hunter Reed for the first time, as he cried for his best friend who had died on the streets of Mogadishu.

So now you can see that things were beginning to take shape before my eyes; but the result was disheartening. The more I saw what living in Africa implied, the less I understood where one was supposed to stand. Maybe my mistake was standing in the middle: I should commit to one side and stick to it. But would it be the side of Iris and Adam, who loved Africa because of its wilderness and its primordial innocence, or that of the Argentinan polo player who feared Africa's hunger and its hatred? Would it be the side of trendy European magazines, which chose Africa as the perfect backdrop for fashion shoots, or the side of those grieving young men, gathered to mourn the death of their friends stoned by an angry mob? That side, it seemed, revealed how hopeless and mindlessly cruel Africa could be.

It's strange how people come into your life, which back routes or shortcuts they choose to take before they join the main road you're travelling on. Somehow you know they have been on a parallel journey for some time, and any minute you may cross each other at a junction—you can feel them coming your way. Sometimes it takes them forever to show up and you become almost impatient. By the time Hunter Reed and I met, we already knew too much about each other to be surprised.

But there was one thing I didn't know, and for some strange reason I had made a point of not asking. I had no idea what he was going to *look* like. I didn't want to know that he was attractive, and the thought he might be, annoyed me.

Adam was in Tanzania on safari with clients. In the last few months I had seen very little of him. His voice had become a distant crackle on the radio I'd hear at given times from the office in town. He'd come home between safaris for only a few days, always physically exhausted, worried about the next trip, sad to have to leave me again.

I felt almost like a soldier's wife: there wasn't much I could do about it; I could only train myself to accept it. The few friends I had made had become very precious.

One rainy night Nicole had invited me for dinner, Nena and Peter were there, and Miles showed up with Iris, which annoyed Nicole.

"I think they've been fucking," she said while in the kitchen adjusting the salt in the potato and leek soup. "It drives me *nuts*."

"Oh . . ." I was baffled. "I hadn't realised you and Miles were . . ."

"Well, just slightly, you know. More like cuddling, really. But the minute Iris comes to town you always end up back in the kitchen wearing an apron, while she's gulping down your tequila in the living room performing her 'Once we were warriors' routine for the boys. By the time you bring out coffee they are all dying to fuck her. She always makes me feel like such a *house-wife*."

Iris did look particularly sexy that night, in a short suede skirt which showed quite a bit of her golden brown legs, a belt made of cowrie shells tied around her waist, her long slick hair loose on her back. She was in top form, and every man in the room couldn't help but respond to her flirting.

Just as we were about to sit at the table the door was flung open and Ruben walked in with a stranger.

"Sorry, Nicole, but we had a flat," were his first words.

He wore heavy boots, a brown suede jacket, and was dripping wet. He looked thin and bony and his skin was very white against his long black hair. His hands were smeared with car grease, his fingernails bitten to the quick. I knew immediately this must be Hunter.

"So *you* are Esmé," he said as we were being introduced. His dark eyes were just as I had imagined during that conversation we had had on the phone. Glittering blades, which pierced me right through. He smiled at me as if he thought it was amusing that I actually dared to exist and had a human shape. He patted his pocket and took out a pack of Roosters, the cheap brand of nonfilter cigarettes he was smoking, that only Africans buy. He lit up, exhaled the smoke in my face and smiled.

"I hear your father was a poet."

"Yes."

"You know, I think I may have read some of his poems."

"I doubt it . . . he's not very well known outside of Italy. He's only just recently been published in America."

"That's it! A friend of mine, an American journalist, left one of your father's books for me to read while we were in Somalia. Can't remember what it was called. I read it about two months ago."

"Did you really?" I tried to sound blasé, but I was impressed.

"I loved it."

"That's very bizarre."

"That I read the book or that I loved it?"

"That of all places you should read my father's poems in Mogadishu."

"Things happen. Nothing happens by coincidence, as the Buddhists say."

He stared at me with a smile, as if expecting a reaction which I didn't give. I had no idea what that remark was supposed to mean, and I couldn't make out why he was suddenly being so friendly or why he had decided to act as if our telephone conversation had never taken place.

Yes, I should have said it right away—Hunter Reed *was* very attractive. More attractive than I had been prepared for. His features were sharp. He looked like a creature who didn't like to venture out in the sun, but woke up late, drank coffee and smoked cigarettes indoors until dawn. His beauty had a mercurial quality, his skinny body seemed to vibrate like a violin string. One could actually feel the electricity which enveloped him like an aura. The only softness in Hunter's persona was his full lips.

We sat around the dinner table which Nicole had set with flowers and candles.

"So, Hunter," said Peter, "I hear you've just been in London for a week; it must have been a good break after Somalia."

"Not really. It's actually very confusing, especially if I'm there for such a short time."

"No fun parties? No babes?" Peter insisted.

Hunter fixed his eyes on me from across the table.

"No. To be honest I find London full of girls with very exciting lingerie and very boring lives."

Everyone laughed. For no reason, I flushed as if his sexual innuendo had been directed at me.

Meanwhile Iris was on a mission, its target Miles. She was explaining how up in the North, while she was shooting the photos for her book, the Morans had given her a Samburu name. That was to be considered an honour. They only gave names to people who belonged to their tribe. Miles was impressed.

"And what does your name mean?" he asked.

"'The Rich One.'"

Hunter sniggered.

"No doubt about *that*."

"It means *spiritually* rich," Iris said coldly.

"Oh, sure," Hunter rolled his eyes. "And what would be the Samburu equivalent for 'spiritually'? I am really dying to know how you got that bit of elucidation, Iris."

"I happen to speak their language quite well, you know."

"So I hear, and since none of us does, nobody can prove the contrary." He turned to Miles. "She's the Unquestionable Authority on Tribal Boys, don't ever mess with her on that subject or she'll be at your throat."

Everyone except Iris laughed. I saw how she lacked a sense of humour when it came to herself.

"And Hunter is the Unquestionable Authority on Tribal Wars. Everyone here has his own African doctorate, I suppose. I happen to care about the destiny of these people; is there anything wrong with that? Or do you think nomadic tribes in East Africa have a lesser right to survive than Tutsi or Dinkas?"

"Nobody I know of is threatening their existence—"

"Of course they are! Their culture is about to disappear. This is probably the last generation who will undergo their initiation ceremonies. The schooling system is destroying their tribal identity, they will lose their traditional knowledge and become—"

"Oh, *please* don't give me this bullshit, Iris," Hunter interrupted with a sneer. "I can't bear another minute of these clichés."

"Really? Well then tell us, what's so cliché about trying to preserve their identity?"

"I'll tell you: the time has come to quit drinking blood and slicing their dicks, my darling! It's time your beautiful Samburu peacocks leave their beads and spears behind, join the rest of the world and learn how to operate a computer if they don't want to be seriously taken advantage of!"

Iris raised her voice.

"Who are *you* to know what's better for them?"

Hunter could sense he had made her uncomfortable, and seemed to enjoy that.

"Right, and who are *you* to know, may I ask?"

"I *grew up* with them, Hunter."

"Oh yeah? Well, a lot of us did. Maybe it's time you grew *out* of them and started reading the *Economist* instead, if you care to have a larger picture of the future in the third world. Which I am sure is the last thing you'd want to do. Much more fun running around wearing beads with good-looking warriors and cashing in on their wild looks. One thing's for sure: the minute they cut their hair and get a job, you are out of yours. So I'm not surprised you want them to stay where they are."

Iris reddened with rage.

"And the minute they stop killing thousands in tribal wars *you* are out of a job. Give me one reason why it's more ethical to write about guerrillas in the bush armed with AK47s."

Hunter smiled and lit a Rooster. He exhaled very slowly, studying the smoke which he blew upwards.

"I never even *dreamed* of making ethical comparisons here. I just wish you would stop inflicting your tales of stardom in the bush on us." He turned to Miles. "We've had to listen to it for years."

Nicole grinned at me across the table. She was enjoying the rampage. At last someone was putting Iris in her place.

"Come on, you two," said Peter, "stop bickering."

"Fine with me," said Iris glacially and turned to Hunter. "What would you rather talk about? Wars? Viruses? Coups? Ecological disasters? Corruption? You're such a big star on all these subjects."

"Could we take a break?" said Nicole. "Will you stop ruining my dinner party, *now*?"

"Right. One last question, forgive me." Hunter raised his glass towards Iris with a naughty smile. "One thing I've always meant to ask you is: do you actually get to *fuck* them, or—"

"Will you stop it?" said Iris, grinning at last, as if he had finally given her the cue. "God, Hunter, what's wrong with you tonight?"

Now that the conversation had turned sexual, back up her alley, she was amused. Her little payoff.

Turning to Miles, she said with a radiant smile:

"I never have sex with my subjects. I just like to look."

Hunter sat next to me on the sofa as we sipped coffee after dinner.

"You don't talk much, Esmé."

"Well . . . it depends." He made me feel uncomfortable, on guard, as if he could start tearing me apart any minute, so I sat still in my corner ready to spring. One thing I knew for sure: I wasn't going to be his next victim. But surprisingly, his eyes lit up and his voice became very soft.

"Your father's poems are wonderful. There was one about birds . . . the green feathers of birds?"

"The green . . . ? Oh yes, I think I know the one you mean."

"Do you have a photograph of him by any chance?"

"What? . . . Yes, of course. Would you like to see it?"

"Very much. I always want to know what people look like

when I like their thoughts. Do you look like him at all?"

I blushed like a teenager. The thought that he had read Ferdinando moved me immensely. For the first time in months someone here on Planet Mars had connected with my past. My father's poems in Mogadishu. I just couldn't get over it. And Hunter Reed of all people.

"Yes, I think, a bit. I'll show you the photo."

I didn't say come around, I didn't explain where I lived. I figured I'd let the universe handle these minor details. I just assumed that if he really wanted to see me, he would find me. Because now I knew that Hunter Reed wanted to see me, and the photograph was just a pretext. I just *knew*, the way people sometimes know about each other even before they meet in the flesh. You can smell the other coming your way, as if the physical attraction shows up before the body.

In retrospect I think we both knew this that time on the phone when everything went wrong.

But I didn't admit to myself that night how much I wanted to see him again. Adam came back the next day from Arusha, tanned, covered with dust and smelling of bush. I was relieved to see him and he was relieved to be home. The clients had been a nightmare and he couldn't wait for the safari to be over.

We sat across each other in the hot bathtub, the room filled with steam, vapor dribbling down our backs.

"It's horrible to be captive to people you loathe just because they've paid you to show what you love."

"You talk about the bush as if it is your lover," I said.

"It's all one has when you grow up here. So in a way it's all you can give to others."

Yes. Trees, birds, tracks, rocks, rivers, elephants, buffaloes; smells, sounds in the night—these were Adam's belongings. He had presented them to me like gifts when we first met, like wedding presents. I had taken them with gratitude because I believed his love for Africa was going to teach me how to save my life.

But something had happened while Adam and I had been apart: in the course of my private explorations I had begun to discover another face of Africa, one where I could see no wild animals, landscape, or sunsets, no trace of beauty or love. This face was harsher, uglier.

Nevertheless, though I didn't know why, I was attracted to it.

Now, with Adam back at my side, I felt guilty for having secretly enjoyed Hunter's cynical views of the future. Yet I couldn't help thinking how his tirade against Iris had reminded me of the destructive game I had been so familiar with all my life: wasn't it Ferdinando's favourite pastime to destroy everyone's hope?

We stepped out of the bath. Adam went to the kitchen and came back to our room with a drink. He asked me what I had been up to and I told him about Nicole's dinner party.

"Hunter? I haven't seen him in ages. How is he?"

"He seemed all right," I said, "except . . . I don't know . . . he was simply horrid to Iris. Is he always so aggressive?"

Adam grinned.

"Oh no, he just likes to get on her nerves; it's his way of teasing her."

"I don't know about teasing. It was more like he was making fun of her in front of everybody, like she was some kind of *moron*."

"Those two are always bickering. It's one of those ex-lovers' syndromes; they can't help it."

"They were *lovers?*" I was surprised at how much that news took me by surprise.

"Oh yes. For years. Long time ago."

I suddenly felt irritated.

"My God . . . everyone seems to have slept with everyone else here."

Adam pulled me close and kissed me lightly on the lips.

"Yes, there's no way around that. It's a big place with very few people. One has to get used to it."

"I hate it. It's too incestuous."

He laughed. I tried to move away from him but he wouldn't let me go. He whispered, teasing me:

"All we're doing here is striving to keep up our population

rate and reproduce our species in this very unfriendly environment. How can you blame us?"

We fell on the bed. I closed my eyes and smiled as I felt the
slow pressure of his knee between my thighs. It felt good to have
him back again.

That's what Africa does to women: it puts us right back in
the place we were trying to escape. In that position where
women need to have men around or are bound to feel helpless.

No, I didn't want to be a single woman in Africa and I was—
surprisingly—totally ready to admit it.

CHAPTER EIGHT

What would I do to divert myself
if I had not language to play with?

JOHN BANVILLE

"It could be the solenoid switch or the pistons," says Mr Kilonzo, head down under the hood. "Unless it's the distributor cap."

"We just changed *that*," I say, sipping my tea.

I say "we" because by now Kilonzo and I feel like a team of surgeons who have tried unsuccessfully to revive a terminally ill patient through a long series of wildly imaginative operations. We've replaced every possible organ inside the ancient body of my car, but unfortunately our personal experiment keeps relapsing into a deep coma. At this stage we feel utterly discouraged.

It's only eight thirty in the morning, the day after Nena's dinner party: the car has just died again on me as I was driving home from her house after breakfast. All I wanted to do was to slip under my duvet at home and fight my hangover in the dark, but instead I had to flag down a truck in last night's party dress and slingback shoes and ask the driver to tow me all the way into Kilonzo's repair shop.

"If it's the pistons then we're in deep trouble, aren't we?" I ask, trying to decipher his absorbed expression.

"Let's not jump to conclusions and cry wolf," says Kilonzo, who has a definite philosophy against making his clients unnecessarily depressed. "It may be just the points after all."

"I wish, but frankly I doubt it."

I'm sitting on a stool in the darkness of his shop under the neon light. As usual Kilonzo has offered me a cup of his strong masala tea and a cigarette. I enjoy sitting here in the shop, breathing car grease and oil and watching Kilonzo mend the crumbling organs of my car. It reminds me of when I was a small child and I used to sit in the kitchen in our house in Naples watching Silvia, our old housekeeper, iron clothes. She was a large woman who smelled of Vim powder. I remember inhaling the aroma of cleanliness that emanated from her body and the freshly ironed clothes. There was always a radio on in the background, just like in this shop. Silvia would make me a cup of hot chocolate and I would sit on top of the washing machine and watch her pile the crisp shirts, one on top of the other.

There is something soothing in watching people transform matter with their hands, as happens every day in every kitchen or repair shop in the world. It's the job of the magician and of the healer to make inert matter go from lifeless to crisp, from broken to whole. But this morning I feel crumpled and broken, like an old rag Silvia would have ironed, or a rusty exhaust pipe Kilonzo would weld.

Kilonzo is a stocky Kamba man in his early fifties, who wears thick glasses and immaculate blue overalls. He's an unusually well educated and humorous ex-cop, with strong ethical principles.

"You know, Mr Kilonzo," I say, "you have become one of my best friends. I don't think I spend as much time with anyone else in this town. The sight of you checking my engine has come to be familiar."

Kilonzo laughs.

"Maybe you sabotage the car in order to come and spend time with me."

"I enjoy your company immensely, but I couldn't afford that. At this point it would cost me much less to take you out for dinner."

Kilonzo chuckles and reemerges from the engine holding something small and greasy between his fingers, which he checks carefully by the neon light. He then screams something in Kikuyu to his spanner boy, who comes back with a tiny screwdriver.

"Can I make a phone call?" I ask. I want Nicole to come and pick me up.

"Sorry, but the phone is down today."

"Okay, I'll run to the box then."

"The whole area is down. Since yesterday."

He tries to start the car, shouting orders to the spanner boy, who is holding the battery cable, but nothing happens. Suddenly the main power goes off and we fall into darkness.

"Now what?" I ask, with a hint of irritation.

"Now we wait for the power to come back," says Kilonzo somewhere in the dark.

Someone lights a kerosene lamp.

"How long will that take?" My depression is giving way to anger, the anger I know so well, when everything decides to die on you and you are stuck again, back in the deep African mud.

"Oh come on, Esmé, how can I know? It could be one hour, four hours, the whole day." I make him out in the dim light of the lamp: he has just lit a cigarette and is smiling as usual. "They are rationing."

"I can't bear another minute of this! How can people work like this? Don't they lose their business?" I think I am screaming. Kilonzo pours himself some tea and keeps smiling at my impatience, which he has learned to recognize. He senses it each time I ask him to fix my car with the same amount of anxiety I would have as if I was asking him to fix my life, and to fix it for good.

"How is it possible to send a fax, to operate a computer? Do you realize that this whole place shuts down *kabisa*? It's totally ridiculous! Tell me, how can one get any work done?"

"It is not possible, of course," he says with his polite African inflection, "but it doesn't help to get upset about it."

"Yeah, sure; I just don't have that kind of personality, I guess," I say, furiously dragging on my cigarette.

"Then I'll tell you a story about *your* kind of personality," says Kilonzo with a grin. I can see his white teeth shine in the dark. "When I had a *shamba* near Nakuru, we had a neighbour, a *mzungu* from Germany. He was always complaining that this didn't work and that didn't work; and sometimes I used to go and fix his pickup or the water pump, but you know in those days it was more difficult to get hold of spares, and the road was really bad, so sometimes things broke and stayed broken a long time. The *mzungu* was always in a very bad mood and blaming others for it; he always complained that his workers didn't take proper care of things and that anything brand-new he gave them to use was in pieces in a matter of days. So one day he was building something or making a small repair, and he went to the hardware in Nakuru town and bought a red bucket. A red plastic bucket, okay? He was very happy with it and gave it to his workers, right? That evening he went back to check the day's work and he found that the workers had destroyed the new red bucket."

"How did they do that? It's not easy to destroy a plastic bucket . . ."

"That's exactly the point, you see? He came to see me, holding the bucket in his hand. 'You tell me, how is this possible?' he kept asking me, and he was nearly choking, that's how furious he was." Kilonzo laughs and slaps his leg with his hand. "'I am leaving this country, I cannot live in a place like this!' Oh my God, you should have seen him! And he did that. He packed up all his things that very same day, he moved out and never ever came back."

Kilonzo is laughing so hard he has to take off his glasses and wipe his eyes with the back of his hand, his fat body shaking.

"Oh, no," I say, laughing with him. "The bucket was the last straw!"

"Yes! He left everything because of the plastic bucket! So my wife and I, whenever we've had a difficult day, and things didn't go the way they were supposed to, we say we had 'a red bucket day.' You get the point?"

"Absolutely. That's what I am having today. A *totally* red bucket day."

Kilonzo cackles approvingly.

"Good! Now you don't need to leave the country, you see? You just get yourself a new red bucket! It's a lot easier than packing everything and starting a new life, isn't it?"

"Right. But I don't need a red bucket, so what it is it I need to get?" I ask Kilonzo with the hopefulness of a disciple to his guru.

"Oh well . . . I'll have Ndegwa give you a lift to the Lenana Forest shops, you go to the hairdresser for a couple of hours, do something new to your hair and read some ladies' magazine, so you relax a bit. You get yourself something nice to eat as well. By the time you are finished the car will be ready and you'll be a happy woman again."

I follow his advice and I let Ndegwa drive me to Heather's, the Karen beauty salon. I order a sandwich from the delicatessen next door, and I let Sheila, a plain blonde with a Cockney accent, cut my hair. I gulp down my taramasalata and cheese sandwich while devouring old issues of *Hello,* where I find out what everyone was wearing at the Academy Awards, learn that Jerry Hall and Mick are still not getting along, and that Pavarotti is on a diet. Sheila tells me that she has just come back from UK and the haircut she's giving me is the latest. I close my eyes, falling back into the familiar world of girls' chitchat, exhilarated by the smell of hair dye, nail polish and glossy magazines, the world where every woman feels at home no matter how far from home she is, and I finally relax just as Kilonzo predicted.

Ndegwa is still waiting for me outside Heather's when I come out, ready to drive me back to the shop. This is the only country in the world where your mechanic is willing to drive you to the hairdresser in order to relieve your tension. The absurdity of it all makes me smile again. At Kilonzo's the power is back on and my car is ready to go. It wasn't the pistons after all, so the bill is not as bad as I feared. What started out as a red bucket day is turning into an African success.

"I told you: never jump to conclusions," Kilonzo says, patting the hood. "You love drama too much, Esmé!"

Yes I do, Mr Kilonzo, I think as I drive out of his shop, it must be the Italian genes or something.

It keeps drizzling and it's damp and grey. I stop to buy firewood on the side of the road and, as the guys load the logs in the back of the car, I smell damp wood, smoke and wet soil, the pungent aroma which always remind me of my life here.

This wintery weather actually suits my mood, it makes me feel self-indulgent and cold. Now I can finally light a fire, lie on my bed and stare at the ceiling, laying out all the bits and pieces, all the memorable scenes, the fragments of conversations and the turning points, everything I can recall—like a child taking all the toys out of the box just to make sure he still owns them— all that has been happening without any apparent order or reason but which nevertheless has ended up shaping my life here. I am now the result of all these mechanical actions, which at the time didn't seem to be taking me anywhere in particular, but which in actual fact have dragged me into a treacherous territory from which I no longer know how to escape.

I didn't see Hunter again for a long time. He never came to look at Ferdinando's photograph. At first I was slightly disappointed—I hadn't expected to be ignored like that—but after a few days I actually forgot all about Hunter Reed. Or at least I thought I had.

Weeks passed, and around Easter the dry weather suddenly gave way to the rains. Soon after that Adam closed down the camp for the season and came home. The first rain announced itself with distant thunder one morning, and it was such a relief, after months of scorching heat and dust, to see it dancing and bouncing on the dry leaves of the garden. Everything started to breathe and come alive, thanks to the moisture. After that first day the rain never stopped and kept furiously pounding on the *mabati* roof, drenching us mercilessly every time we ran from the verandah into the car. All of Langata had turned into a giant mud puddle.

In the evening the rain would stop and in the stillness of the night bullfrogs started croaking incessantly. There were frogs everywhere: black and orange ones which lived inside the pipes and peeped from the washbasin's drain hole while I brushed my teeth in the morning.

Adam couldn't stop moving even under these floods: he was either repairing or welding something in the workshop in the back of the plot, running to get a spare somewhere in the industrial area, building a fence or having new tents made. I realised this man was hooked on physical activity: he couldn't bear to sit still. But we did manage to spend time together in the evenings, watch a video, chat in front of the fireplace or go out to dinner in town, like normal people do. Our life as a couple was slowly taking shape and I was beginning to get used to it.

Every now and then, if the wires hadn't fallen off the trees because of the weather, or the Masai hadn't stolen them to make jewelry, I rang Teo. As he described the coming of spring on the Amalfi coast or in the countryside in Tuscany, I could picture yellow *ginestre* and dark blue lavender. I found myself yearning for the fresh smell of new grass and wild roses, for the soft April light when plants and people wake up from the winter delicately stirring their limbs. Meanwhile at my end, rain kept pouring while all kinds of horrid insects were performing unsettling mating dances around the lampshades. Sometimes thousands of flying ants would cover the entire wall in just a few minutes like a thick black buzzing carpet, and Wilson and I had to literally sweep them off the wall with a broom. Nature had woken up from the dry sleepy season and was furiously mating with cruel determination, in order to survive another six months of lifeless heat.

"Everything is so extreme here. It goes from life to death with nothing in between," I complained to Adam.

"What do you mean?"

"You don't have middle seasons, like spring or fall . . ."

"I love how you say 'you' as if it was me personally who was responsible for the whole African climate. We do have seasons, Esmé; you are simply not looking carefully enough. And we have beautiful seasons too, just like in Europe: the sky changes, the wind turns, the colours are different and you can smell the grass and the flowers. I'll show you once we go to the coast."

At the beginning of the summer, the rains slowed down. All the expats were leaving to go to Europe for the holidays.

"Let's go to Italy together," I said to Adam one morning. "I want you to meet my brother."

"I want to, I really do," he said, a hint of guilt in his voice, "but I can't afford to now. I have to go to the States and book next season. We'll do it next year, I promise."

So there was a next year. A future. That pleased me.

Adam was planning his yearly promotional trip to the States in order to hunt down rich clients for next year's safari season, by holding a series of "bush lectures" with groups of possible clients at their local Rotary Club or whatever it was called. He was going to be away for six weeks: he would be going out to dinner with travel agents and magazine editors and coming back with the bookings. His slide shows showed not only the wilderness and how close they would come to the game, but above all the facilities his camps provided. In general first-timers on African safaris are terribly nervous about ablutions in the bush, and fear that they might have to squat behind the shrubs, which ends up being their main objection to this type of voyage into the darkness. Adam made sure to show them exactly what to expect in his very expensive "luxury tented camp." They all sighed with relief and sometimes applauded enthusiastically when the bush bathroom en suite slide appeared in all its splendour, with porcelain tank, wooden seat and all.

The whole thing sounded like a nightmare to me.

"I have to do it," he said with a shrug, "otherwise the company just goes dead. Everyone else does it, and believe me, it does work."

In a way he was like an actor going on tour to give a sneak preview of the show, showing just the teaser of the film to sell the plot and the good looks of the main character. Everyone wanted to buy the *Out of Africa* dream, but nobody wanted the dust, the warm beer, or to have to take a crap in the bush. Adam with his itinerant slide show was there to prove that it was possible indeed to buy one without the other. Knowing how reserved Adam was, I realised how much he must hate doing this, and at the same time I was surprised at how much he was ready to put up with. On the other hand, he made very good money.

"I can't do this much longer," he said. "I just need the money to buy myself some land, and then I'm out of the business. I want to enjoy the bush without having to *explain* it to people with videocameras. I want to sit around the fire and be silent."

I guess the reason why I could afford to be a snob and keep away from the hideous rich couples in full Banana Republic safari gear was that I didn't have to make my own money. I had chosen a luxurious dependency on Adam's income and my father's posthumous recognition.

Before he left for the States Adam and I decided that the two of us were to go on a safari and planned a trip to the coast, where his family had a house near Mombasa. His parents were spending most of their time there now, even though they still kept a small farm upcountry near Rumuruti which was run by Adam's older brother Brian.

I had never met Adam's parents, and I was nervous. It felt kind of official to go and stay with them, but after all he and I had been living together for almost a year now. I had heard their voices on the phone whenever they called to talk to him.

"My parents are cool, just relax," said Adam as we were driving south on the Mombasa road. "We are just going to swim and get a tan, it doesn't mean we're getting *married,* you know."

I jumped in the seat. The sound of the word kept buzzing around my brain as we dived down from the higher lands into the plain and crossed Tsavo National Park, lush and covered in blue wildflowers.

"See?" said Adam triumphantly. "This is the African spring. Can't you smell it?"

Married. I'd never even conceived of it before. But now, looking at Adam driving next to me and sniffing his beloved African spring, I thought it could actually be possible. He had taken such good care of me, he had healed me. I never wanted to go back to my earlier state, to the fears and the loneliness which awaited me back in Europe, not to my mother language or my way of thinking. Adam put his hand on my knee, and I brushed it lightly with mine, feeling a wave of tenderness. Once again we were traveling in the midst of nothing, flying in empty space, feeling the vastness all around us, and inwardly I said yes, I could live with this man, marry him and have his children; with so much emptiness around us it was a comforting thought to one day become a small group of people who felt close and safe together.

That was what Africa seemed to be doing to me: putting things back into place, probably where they should have always been but never were. In a place where to love seemed finally necessary and to trust a relief, a place where it seemed pointless to fight to be in control, because it was clear you couldn't control any of it. A place where having children and marrying a man didn't sound like a middle-class choice.

A place where Ferdinando would probably have gone mad.

Adam's parents' property was south of Mombasa, near the Tanzanian border. It sat on top of the coral cliffs overlooking the Indian Ocean, in a staggering cove which for some mysterious reason had been left behind by the fast and furious development of the last fifteen years. Their property bordered on a *kaya*, the Swahili word for sacred forest, which allowed wild game and indigenous plants to thrive all around. It was a magical place, one of the last to be spared by mass tourism. His mother, Julia, was a landscape gardener and had a nursery of rare plants and palms in the back of the property. She was tall and lean and pretty in that plain English way which I had become so familiar with since being in Kenya, a kind of beauty that brought to mind the particular daintiness of movie stars of the late fifties. Women of

Julia's generation, who had lived on their fathers' coffee farms most of their lives, didn't seem to have gone past Doris Day or Joan Fontaine. They had all slid happily out of fashion forty years ago, still wore pastel cotton prints and sunglasses which made them look like a faded Kodak ad. Her husband, Glenn, was a big man, with the same strong physical presence as Adam. His face was pleasantly wrinkled after too many years in the sun. They kissed me warmly, as if they had already known me a long time.

"Come, there is tea on the verandah," said Julia.

"How about a serious drink, Mum?" said Adam. "I've been driving all day in the heat."

"That's a much better idea!" said Glenn. "Esmé, come sit down, you must be exhausted. It's such a hellish trip from Nairobi. I always hated that road."

He put his arm around my shoulder and led me through the house, to the verandah overlooking the sea.

The house was old and charming: a whitewashed Swahili style A-frame with a thatched roof. Inside the furniture was sparse and simple: Lamu four-poster beds, old hardwood tables and chairs, white curtains flowing in the breeze. The bookshelves were loaded with old editions of Graham Greene and Daphne du Maurier, ancient issues of *National Geographic,* and damp-smelling leather-bound volumes. Some impressive trophies hanging in the living room testified to Glenn's younger days.

"The biggest impala ever shot in East Africa," he said proudly, pointing at a gigantic head. It was bizarre, seeing all those dead bush animals at the sea.

"Aliiii!" called Julia in a high-pitched voice. *"Tafadhali, lete drinks na barafu!"*

A young man, barefoot, dressed in white, appeared with the drinks tray. He yelled with excitement when he saw Adam. They patted each other's shoulders and shook hands with affection. Soon the rest of the staff turned up to greet him: all had been with the family a long time and had known Adam since he was a child. I took an immediate liking to all of them. Rajabu the cook was a stunning *mzee* with a white beard and almost green eyes. He was a bit of a witch doctor, Adam said, and his knowledge of local plants for medicinal use was amazing.

I had felt exhilarated from the moment I stepped out of the car, I think it had to do with finally coming down from five thousand feet. My whole body stretched, the pores of my skin opened to the warm moisture in the air, everything smelled sweet and rich, like frangipani and rotting mangoes. How could I have stayed away from the sea for so long? It seemed that nothing cruel or desperate or mindless could ever happen at the ocean.

This was the South, and like every other south in the world it was softer and gentler than its north, had an ancient and more sophisticated culture. When Adam took me to Mombasa I felt completely at home: it reminded me of my own Italian south, it had such a Neapolitan soul. It was hot and noisy and crumbling, but it was vibrant, cosmopolitan, and every single old man sitting cross-legged among his heaps of vegetables in the shade of the fruit market had the face of a Sufi philosopher or a sultan. You felt right away that this place had a history, and a written one at that. The coastal tribes were so different from the tribes of the central provinces, like the Kikuyus, the Kambas or the Luos. Their blood had been mixing with Arab, Portuguese and Indian blood for centuries; their ancestors had sailed between Zanzibar and Oman, Lamu and Mombasa, Karachi and Pemba, trading ivory, hardwood, slaves and spices on their dhows. These men still dressed in white and wore embroidered Muslim caps as they sat under the shade of a tree in the evening, sipping tiny cups of cardamon tea. The old *wazee* still greeted you in the most wonderful old-fashioned ways, whispering the loveliest *salamas* as you passed their way.

"*Shikamuu* . . ."
"*Maharaba* . . ."
"*Salam alekum* . . ."
"*Salama sana* . . ."

Every morning Adam and I took long walks on the beach, and watched the fishermen lay their nets within the reef and clap the water all around to trap the fish inside. Their silhouettes dotted the horizon, and one could hear the sound of the distant clapping coming from every direction. The dogs always came down with us and ran after crabs and birds while we sat in the shallow pools at low tide, and talked for hours. I realized how little time Adam and I ever had to *talk*. I knew so little about his life before we met. During that week, his childhood on the farm and at the coast slowly took shape before my eyes. He showed me all the secret places where he used to play as a child; and every rock and tree and waterpool was still there, just as he had left it. He showed me the ruins of the old mosque hidden in the thick of the *kaya*, where he used to hide and play in the afternoons when the sun would filter through the foliage and light the ruins like an illustration from an adventure book. He took me to the "swallow pool" below the cliffs, where the birds always nested in the cold season and filled the air with chirping sounds. One could swim there even at low tide, and snorkle over the most amazing collection of brightly colored starfish which lay on the white sand like a scene from *Fantasia*. We would snorkle next to each other, and I loved the feeling of our bodies underwater, the shimmering light reflecting on our skin, my long hair floating like seaweed and brushing his arm. I loved the taste of salt on his mouth when we kissed.

Before sunset we always walked to the point, where the reef reached the shore and the surf pounded against the cliffs. There was always wind, and the sea spray covered us in mist as we stood on the edge of the cliff looking out at the view of the bay. It was heaven.

"Why don't we come and live here?" I asked. It seemed so logical and so easy to do.

"This is exactly where I want to buy land," Adam said. "That's why I need another year or two. Then we can build our own house, right here."

Never before had anyone said anything so simple and definitive to me. Never had anyone dared make such plans with me. *Buying land, building houses.* I had only heard such lines in one of those movies where Henry Fonda plays a pioneer. I held

Adam's hand in the wind, incapable of replying, feeling slightly guilty, as if I had taken someone else's role by mistake and they were just about to come and throw me off the set.

But another part of me, deep down, knew that even if it had been a case of mistaken identity, I had grown to the point where I was *becoming* that other person, and it was time to stop worrying: nobody was ever going to find out. My old self had been buried long ago and far away. Nobody would ever trace the body. I was going to be fine. I smiled and thought, Yes, I am going to be happy ever after.

I like to think I got pregnant that same night. My body felt such a wave of gratitude and trust, I let myself go so completely, like someone who is willing to drown, that I remember thinking as we were making love, yes, yes, yes, here I am, here I come, I will not hold back ever again.

I remember closing my eyes and falling asleep to the distant sound of the ocean breaking on the reef and thinking that I felt just like those waves: after such strong currents I had come to break against the coral barrier and was ready to turn into still water.

That night, nestled in Adam's arms, I dreamt of our bodies diving close together into the green. My limbs felt fluid, my skin smooth like a dolphin's. As the water turned a darker blue, I looked up towards light at the top. But I no longer needed to reach the surface: I could hear my slow breathing underwater.

CHAPTER NINE

Well, that was the river,
this is the sea.

Ferdinando had once written a poem called "Sirena." It was about a woman—*nè carne nè pesce*—a creature of darkness with a cold stare. A mermaid who smelled of algae, pulsed and wriggled like a fish. The siren was a hybrid of warm flesh and cold blood, animal and human, sex and death, yet condemned to be neither—not fish nor flesh, nor old nor young—forever caged in its sexless fish tail, never allowed to breed.

For some strange reason I had always believed my mother had been the original inspiration of the poem, probably because of that cold stare she had, the long red hair against the whiteness of her skin. There was something obscene and desperate in the concept of a woman siren, and I always felt fascination mixed with horror at the idea of her sexuality trapped in the fish scales.

"Your mother?"

I remember how Ferdinando had raised his head from the book he was reading and had tipped his glasses further down his nose as he looked at me. It was a late summer afternoon. I must have been sixteen or so, a skinny teenager sitting on the parapet of the terrace across from him. I hated the way he was able to read like that for hours, completely unaware of others around him.

But my question had amused him, because he put his book down.

"Why not? She would have liked that. She quite liked the idea of being dangerous."

"But why is a siren always dangerous?"

"Because she will possess you not by bearing your child but by taking you down in the deep and never releasing you again. She's sterile, you see, and sex with a siren bears no fruit, is an act against nature."

"But Mother had two children."

"True. But she was a siren at heart. It's a mental category."

He paused, then he looked at me.

"You are one too."

"Why do you say that?"

"Because I can see it in you."

I frowned.

"I don't think I like that very much."

"Well, you are wrong. It's meant to be a compliment. At least from *my* point of view."

"I think it's morbid, it sounds so sick." I suddenly felt irritated.

"It's not sick at all. You are just being puritanical."

"No, it's awful." I raised my voice, now I really wanted him to take it back. "It's like being an outcast, some kind of monster."

Ferdinando sighed. I knew how much I bored him when I was like that. He never liked it when I wanted to be like everyone else. So he tipped his glasses back up and opened his book again.

Looking back on it, there wasn't anything particularly puritanical in my not wanting my father to associate me with the idea of ruin, rotting algae, dark murky water, let alone my mother. I didn't like to feel doomed. But I couldn't help thinking of that poem as my very personal curse: neither fish nor flesh, cold-blooded, sterile. Taboo.

What now I think Ferdinando meant then was that he didn't see the breeder in me. He saw the same restlessness, the same torment which persecuted him and the women he had loved. On the other hand, he never believed peace was something worth pursuing to begin with; he didn't think it was realistic to seek happiness and fulfillment. He found it a rather dull and useless task and had no sympathy for those who strived at it.

But my body didn't turn out to be a siren's after all. I had secretly wriggled out of the fish tail and had been walking on dry sand for a while, out of the murky water and breathing fresh air.

Usually I feel like keeping myself at a safe distance from tight family clans. I never know how to fit in; I simply lack the experience. I never baked biscuits in the kitchen with my mother, or went shopping with her, or on picnics, never had candles to blow out on birthday cakes. On Christmas day Ferdinando would take us to a restaurant, preferably Chinese, since he hated all religious traditions with a passion.

But Julia and Glenn had been so open and welcoming towards me that I surrendered to their warmth. They insisted that I should come visit them even on my own, whenever Adam was away with clients and I was bored with Nairobi. It was their way of showing me that I was now part of the family.

"They loved you," Adam said proudly as we were driving back to Nairobi. "My dad especially, he's crazy about you."

"Really? Do you think so?"

He nodded.

"He took me aside as I was packing the car and said, 'Whatever you do, don't let her out of your life, son.'" He shook his head with a smile. "Typical of my father, he loves making that kind of patriarchal statement."

We laughed. But I knew that his parents' approval had meant a great deal more than I might have expected.

After our trip to the coast I felt suddenly unprepared to be without him again. I dreaded the time we would be apart in a way I never had before. When, only a week later, he had to leave for the States, I drove back home from the airport and found myself crying like an abandoned child. It was ridiculous, but I couldn't bear to be left alone any longer.

One morning I looked at my waist, felt my breasts, and had a distinct feeling that something completely new had been happening inside me for God knows how long. It was time to check. I sat on the edge of the bathtub holding the pregnancy test tube in my hand, and looked at the bright blue colour in astonishment, my heart pounding, sweat breaking out under my armpits. I was going to have Adam's baby.

"I can't believe it," said my brother Teo from the other side of the world. "Please stop crying; this is so beyond my reach. Please darling, don't be in such a panic."

"I *am* in a panic, I can't help it." I sobbed from my side, feeling the Indian Ocean pounding mercilessly inside the cables which connected my phone to Teo's. "I have absolutely no idea what to do."

"You mean you don't know if you want to keep it?"

"Of course I want to keep it! I just don't know what's going to happen to me. I never thought I could be a *mother*."

"Neither did I," I could feel him smile at the other end "but hey, maybe it's time you stopped being the child. You'll stop thinking about yourself all the time. Sounds great."

"Please, this is *not* funny. You have no idea how this feels."

"No, I wouldn't. But I mean it. I wish I had something else to think about other than me, me me. Really Esmé, I envy you."

"It's as if your body has taken over your brain overnight and from now on will be in charge of everything. It's like a coup d'etat. You can't stop it from doing what it's doing. It's scary, I promise you . . ."

I put a hand on my belly. No, there was nothing I could talk my body into doing any longer. It was going to produce another human being regardless of whatever advice I was willing to offer. I didn't particularly feel better equipped for turning into a parent than, say, Teo did. But being a woman implied that my body could go ahead and carry out what I had merely fantasized while holding Adam's hand on the cliffs.

"Stop being such a control freak, Esmeralda," Teo said. But I could tell he was moved.

"But nothing will ever be the same! You realize that?"

"Yes. That's exactly the point. That's why people have children: to move on. It's wonderful. You're no longer the honorary boy."

The more he said that, the more I sobbed. I wasn't unhappy, only terrified at the idea of change with no return ticket.

"My whole body has gone haywire: there's this incredible amount of activity going on inside me nonstop, my hormones are in a frenzy. I feel hot, cold, nauseous, tired, hungry, weepy, it's *insane*," I said, dragging hard on my cigarette.

"Go see a doctor. He'll explain it all to you. And you are still smoking, I can hear it."

"Yes, like mad."

"You better quit and sign up for one of those breathing classes fast," he giggled.

If having a baby meant no more turning back, on the other hand, since I had first arrived here, I had always wanted to blend in, belong, grow roots. Now I was going to have a child in Africa and make Africa his or her home. So what was the point of crying? Unexpectedly, I felt lonely in my trip into motherhood. Not only was I leaving Teo—I knew he would never be an adult, he didn't *need* to—but I was leaving behind Ferdinando, his poetry, his way of looking at things, in other words *my own tribe*. Now that I had buried my earlier self for good, it felt scary and completely insane to have done so.

But my panic proved only temporary. It vanished—miraculously—as soon as I heard Adam's voice later that same day.

He was in Santa Fe. It felt like millions of miles away.

"Should I come back?" He sounded awestruck, like a little boy.

"I'm perfectly all right, don't be silly."

"I . . . I . . ." He struggled for words. "I can't wait to see you. I want to hold you."

"You will." I found myself beaming, proud as a hen.

I had finally *done* something. And it was going to be *ours*, forever and ever. Even Adam was overwhelmed by it.

I had proved Ferdinando wrong: I was not going to be another doomed marine monster who lures men into her dark waters. I was going to be a mother, a breeder, under the bright African sun. And it felt like deliverance.

I sat in Dr Singh's waiting room holding a leaflet in my hand: "Prenatal yoga classes, every Thursday at the Light House Center." It showed a picture of a pregnant woman in the lotus position. I sighed.

I scanned the room and carefully examined each of the women sitting around me, immersed in old issues of *Cosmopolitan*. They all seemed confident and relaxed, most of them well advanced in their pregnancies, their full round bellies concealed under flowery frocks, their legs slightly swollen, all of them Aryan white. I felt that irritation come back again: why was it always like that in Nairobi? Why did *mzungu* women all share the same hairdresser, gynecologist, dentist, aerobics instructor, masseuse? Why did we huddle together in these waiting rooms like a flock of retarded sheep, joined in a common effort to avoid any African hands touching our Sacred White Bodies? We did this all the time and never even noticed.

I had gotten Singh's number from Nena.

"He's very good," she had said to me. "He's a Sikh. I went to him when I was pregnant with Natasha. You'll like him."

I waited hesitantly for extra reassurance. Which came in the form of:

"He studied in Oxford. Moved back here only a few years ago."

Oxford. How soothing that sounds when it comes down to letting some stranger mess around with your body in a faraway country.

So there I was, herded into the flock of young white mothers-to-be, waiting to blow up like all of them into a giant pudding, slip into the same hideous dresses and get to know them all by name at the Thursday evening yoga classes. I felt a pang of anxiety as I envisaged them as my future buddies.

"You are in perfectly good health," my newly acquired doctor said. Dr Singh *was* cool. He displayed a confident charm which would have made him fashionable among the New Age Hollywood crowd. In his mid-forties, a golf champion as shown by the several cups on the shelf, he wore a neatly pleated red turban and a blue blazer, turtle-rimmed designer glasses, italian moccasins. He scribbled something on a piece of paper.

"Here. This is the address of the lab for the scan. It's in Lavington, near the BP petrol station. They are the best in Nairobi, I recommend them."

"Great."

"After eight weeks we should be able to detect the heartbeat. So go anytime after the next ten days. We won't be able to see much before then."

I liked the "we." Singh and I had instantly become a team, a twosome aiming for the same result.

"Should I do anything in particular?"

"Like what?"

"I don't know . . . like not driving, not smoking?"

Singh smiled. He must have been so used by now to paranoid *mzungu* mothers assailing him with their fears.

"Basically you can do everything you feel like doing. With measure and caution, of course." He grinned. "You will be just fine."

How amazing that this perfect stranger—from a faraway land, different religion, foreign language—suddenly had turned out to be my guide in the most intimate, revolutionary journey of my life.

I walked out wishing dead every mother-to-be in the waiting room. I wanted Singh to concentrate exclusively on my case. If *we* were a team, and this mission was major in *my* life, how could *he* devote equal time and attention to all those insignificant, freckled, overweight, uninteresting UN wives?

It's extraordinary what pregnancy does to you. First you become incredibly selfish and mean. I think it happens because all of a sudden you feel extremely vulnerable, easy prey of medical malpractise, malaria, snakes, mad *matatu* drivers, giant potholes. You soon realize how fragile a receptacle your body is, how thin and immaterial the layer which separates your floating dormant creature from the dangers awaiting outside. You find yourself ready to scream for protection at every corner but determined to rip apart anything which could threaten what is going on inside you.

In the following weeks, waiting for Adam to come back, I led a very peculiar life. I had fallen under the tyranny of my new physical state: I moved in slow motion and felt as if I had cotton wool stuffed inside my brain. I would curl on the couch under a blanket with no thoughts, staring at the jacaranda trees outside the window until it grew dark. Wilson would slip into the room to draw the curtains and turn on the lights, and that would finally shake me from my trance.

I found the company of others exhausting—plus I would fall into a narcosis by nine thirty at night—so I wasn't much fun to go out with. The first thing I did every morning was dart to the mirror and study the profile of my belly. Yes, it was a small—insignificant to the untrained eye—but perfectly round belly. During the day I busied myself with a list of useless errands. I dyed all the mosquito nets, covered the armchairs in a new material, obsessively repainted my finger and toe nails.

I started calling Teo more often than usual.

"Help!" I said to him, "I'm about to redo the curtains! Do you think pregnancy alters one's personality for good?"

"No, I think you are just sliding into temporary hibernation," he sighed. "It'll pass. I read it somewhere."

We discussed names. We planned my trip to Italy to show off the baby. We ran up astronomical phone bills.

Meanwhile Africa had started making the headlines again.

Blood was pouring out of Rwanda and it looked like it would never stop. The Hutus were determined to wipe out the Tutsi, and what had started out seeming to be another African tribal war had swiftly escalated into a horrific genocide. Everyone in the West got used to photographs of slaughtered children, dismembered bodies on the first page of their daily paper. To them it must have looked like a remote nightmare, something which could only happen in a wild, godless, savage place like darkest and deepest Africa. It felt equally alien and faraway to us, the white tribe who lived around the corner.

I stayed away from the papers, I couldn't look at the photographs, they made me nauseous. My survival instinct had turned me into a sort of thick-headed selfish housewife, who pushed her shopping cart away from the upsetting covers on the magazine stand and headed for the ice cream instead. I just couldn't handle death. Especially death in Africa.

The "boys" had all gone in. They were flying in and out of Kigali, and each time came back in a darker trance. I had seen Miles and Ruben a couple of times. They no longer bore any trace of the vibrant Mogadishu buzz. This war was very different than what they had experienced in Somalia.

When the UN troops had pulled out of Mogadishu a couple of months earlier, the hacks knew that was the end of the story, at least for the press. The world wasn't going to give a damn about Somalia once the whites were out of there. The last time they flew in and met in the legendary Sahafi Hotel in downtown Mogadishu it had felt like the end of a glorious year in school. From now on they would be scattered in different parts of the world on new assignments. It was the end of something. Their Age of Innocence, in retrospect.

So when Rwanda broke out, so soon after the end of the Somali story, the press corps almost rejoiced. Great, they thought, back into action with their pals once more. Their rite of passage wasn't over yet.

At the same time they were anxious to see what this would look like. They had sensed this one wouldn't be anything like "Doin' the Mog." This time there would be only death and despair awaiting them.

"They will never recover," said Nicole. "What they have to

see, photograph, will never leave them for the rest of their life."

We were having lunch on the terrace of the Norfolk Hotel. The restaurant was busy with the usual herd of khaki-geared families on their way to the Masai Mara.

"I wonder how much of this they will be able to take," she said.

She had spent the night before with Bernard, Miles, Ruben and Hunter. Bernard had shown her some of the photographs he had taken. "Too shocking to be published" had been the response of his agency. They had all left again that morning at five, back into Kigali, hunting for more despair.

Nicole looked pale, drawn, as if she had witnessed a murder. She shook her head.

"I don't know . . . It all feels so wrong."

"What feels wrong?" I asked.

"To be sitting here, having Caesar salad."

"There isn't much else we could do. Is there?"

"No . . . of course not. But at least they are *dealing* with it. It's a nightmare, but it's what's happening in Africa. Whereas," she looked around, pointing at the tourists in "I love Kenya" T-shirts, "*this* is such a fucking joke."

I felt defensive.

"It wouldn't make you feel any better going with them to Rwanda."

"No. It's not a matter of better. *Better* is not the point." She looked tired.

"I know, it's so disheartening." I sighed, and then I looked at my watch. "Darling, I really have to be going."

I put a few shilling notes on the table.

"I have my appointment in ten minutes. The scan."

"Oh right. The scan." She raised her head and looked at me as if from the bottom of a swimming pool.

I was lying on the table, my eyes fixed on the ceiling. The lab technician and his assistant were staring at the monitor. Their silence felt too long. I tried to raise my head and look at the monitor, but I couldn't see much. The technician coughed nervously. He was very tall, I remember thinking he must have been a Luo.

"There is nothing here, madam."

"What do you mean *nothing?*"

"No heartbeat."

I didn't move. I waited a few seconds, but he kept silent.

"What do you mean, no heartbeat?"

"I think the baby is dead, madam."

I stormed into Singh's office, without waiting for his secretary to announce me. I had driven from the lab feeling faint, my vision blurred. I had put my shirt back on inside out.

I flung open his door like a killer.

He looked startled.

I sat down across the desk from him and I distinctly remember his steadily tapping his pen on his notepad as I blurted out what had just happened. The sound maddened me to the point that I felt like smacking him.

"Isn't there anything you can do? I asked aggressively."

"Nothing," he said politely. "These things happen, especially in the first three months."

Then he lifted the scan against the light of his desk lamp and studied it carefully. I held my breath. Maybe, after all, there had been a mistake.

"I'm very sorry," Singh said. And put the scan back into its folder.

"*I* haven't done anything wrong. *You* said it would be okay to drive," I said accusingly.

Yes, he had said that. But even though I hadn't done anything wrong, still it happened frequently.

The phone rang. He spoke quietly, rapidly. The results were perfect, he said, would you come in two weeks' time for another checkup? He then turned back to me. Unsympathetically, I thought.

I felt like a black sheep who had drifted out of his flock, and whom he no longer had reason to care for.

The technician he had recommended so highly had been incredibly rough, I complained, forcing back the tears. He had shown no tact. *The baby is dead,* he had said. Now, that language would be unheard of in Europe and—

"Yes," said Singh. "You are absolutely right. That's unacceptable and I will make sure to reprimand him about that. But now it will be necessary for you to check into the hospital. This afternoon. We must remove the—I don't remember the word he used, but it was a technical term. It was no longer a living being. It had become a *thing.*"

I drove home like a stone. Like a stone I picked up my toothbrush and my pyjamas, told Wilson that I would sleep out. Like a stone I lay in my bed in the maternity ward of the hospital, took the drug, went to sleep. When I woke up an hour later, it had been done. It had been painless. It was over.

At home the phone was down, so I couldn't call Adam to tell him. But it was better that way, because I didn't feel like speaking to him. I didn't want to have to say, Hold it, reverse, nothing has changed, we're back to square one. All that future, which had stretched from now to the end of our lives, all that future which was going to make us one thing—a couple, a mother and a father—till the day we died, had shrunk back.

I was back to not knowing what would happen next, to not belonging anywhere or to anybody. I could easily get used to that again, no problem: that was the way I had felt all my life.

I didn't feel like calling my brother either and saying, You know what? I was right: I was never meant to do this. I was never supposed to bury my earlier self and wriggle out of the fish tail. What a foolish thing to believe: I'm back down there swimming in murky waters, cold-blooded, covered in seaweed like all the women from my tribe.

PART TWO

HUNTER

CHAPTER ONE

He put the Belt around my life—
I heard the Buckle snap—
and turned away, imperial,
my Lifetime folding up—

EMILY DICKINSON

I'm still lying here, eyes on the ceiling. Everything feels quiet and white. Clinic-like.

I am slowly taking all the bits of the story out of the box and putting them one next to the other, hoping to make some sense out of it. Hoping to find at least one answer to the many unanswered questions we have been asking each other relentlessly. Me, Adam, Hunter. We have been torturing each other, relentlessly unloading our grief onto one another, and yet unable to find a single answer which could at least seal the bleeding wound. Where was the mistake?

But then, do we really make mistakes, do we actually take the wrong turn, say the wrong thing? Is it possible to isolate the moment where we made the mistake, so that we could—theoretically—go back and undo it? Or is it more like losing a grip, a sense of direction? Is it maybe like falling asleep and letting it all happen while we keep our eyes closed? Yes, it is a bit like that, isn't it? We pretend not to have seen or heard. Like children who lie frozen in their beds at night, eyes shut tight, while their parents shout angry words in the next room. Whatever it is that hurts, we want to keep it apart from us as long as possible, until the poison makes us so ill that we can't fake it any longer.

When did this poison start dripping slowly into my blood? Was it after the child? Was it after Iris? Was it because of Hunter or was it ultimately because of me? Now, on this winter morning, in the starkness of this white room and the emptiness I feel inside me, I finally see it clearly.

It was because of me, and nobody else.

Wilson knocks gently at the door.

"Unataka kula nini kwa lunch, mama?"

"No, thank you Wilson, no lunch. A cup of coffee, maybe."

He looks at me, lingering in the doorstep. He knows something is not right. I try to smile.

"Hakuna tabu, bwana. I just feel a bit tired."

"Then rest, *mama."*

He moves gently to the window and pulls the white cotton curtains, to soften the piercing white light. His footsteps are light, like the steps of a dancer, as he leaves the room.

Yes, it was because of me, but not me alone.

This is not a gentle place.

Don't let this soft light fool you, nor the light steps of Wilson; there is no warm nest here where you can curl up and feel safe. This place will first take you in and then spit you out in the desert. You'll be on your own, without shelter or shade, but you'll know that it was always meant to be like this, since the beginning of time. This raw, this stark. Don't let its beauty fool you.

I didn't think about the child. I wanted to forget as fast as possible.

Adam called the night after I came back from the hospital— he was in Colorado, he said, he sounded excited—he had been invited to stay an extra week to give a lecture at the university there. Had had a lot of bookings and—

I told him. Quickly, matter-of-factly.

I could feel the disappointment in his silence. He said he was sorry, said he loved me very much. Should he come home?

"Don't worry, I'll be perfectly all right."

"Are you sure?"

"Absolutely. It's over now. There's nothing we can do about it. I'm fine, really. *I mean it.*"

I think he was relieved to hear that I could manage. It would be a problem to interrupt his trip right then. He explained to me how crucial this lecture was going to be for a number of reasons that I can't recall now.

"Of course," I said, "you don't need to explain. And as I said, even if you came back now, you wouldn't be able to change anything."

He tried to cheer me up by telling me he had seen the Grand Canyon and how it had made him homesick. He said again he loved me very much and he missed me. All I remember thinking about that long-distance phone call was how long-distance it actually felt.

The next day Iris appeared at my door. She had pulled her hair back into a tight braid, wore a crisp white shirt with khaki drill pants and looked as immaculate as a water lily.

"Are you all right, for God's sake? Nicole just told me what happened. You should have rung me, I would have taken you to the hospital. It's mad to have gone all on your own."

She handed me a plate covered with foil.

"Here, this is for you."

"I'm fine, really. I preferred to be alone. It wasn't such a big deal. What's this?"

"A cake. I just baked it. Watch out, it's still hot. God, I can't believe you didn't call any of us. This is what friends are for."

"I know, but . . . *you* baked this? Amazing. I didn't think you baked cakes."

"Why?" She winked. "I'm a pretty average Swedish farmer's daughter, you know."

149

We sat on the carpet around the coffee table in the living room and had her delicious spice cake with tea. It cheered me up to see her, and her attention touched me. She was quiet and low-key, which was pleasantly in tune with my mood.

She said she was on her way to England in a couple of weeks, to see her publisher about her book.

"They want it out before Christmas." She absentmindedly flicked a cigarette ash into the empty teacup. "Which is great, you know, sales-wise."

Somehow she didn't sound as self-confident as usual.

"When will you be back?"

"Oh, I don't know. I was thinking maybe, I'd do research for a new project there. I think I've done all I can on this side of the ocean."

"You mean you may just *move back* to Europe?" I asked incredulously. It sounded like such an unlikely plan for Iris to make.

"Well, why not? If it looks good. If the book sells. You know, at the end of the day there is just so much one can do in Africa. How many more subjects for a book can I come up with? Plus, I have never lived in Europe, so I wouldn't be moving *back*. I would be moving for the first time."

"That's right. Funny how that always escapes my mind."

"You see, people like me or Adam, we went to school here, we've never had a life other than this. He's making a living out of it, and he can carry on like that as long as he likes, great, but I don't want to turn into some pathetic matriarch running around with warriors until the day I die. I think I can do better than that. Don't you think?"

She looked at me expectantly. Her honesty had taken me by surprise.

"Yes, of course you can . . ." But then I wasn't so sure. "Like what, though?"

"I don't know. That's why I want to go. I need to see museums, art galleries, films. I want to be able to walk into a bookstore and buy photography books, look at other people's work. Compare. How can I do any original work if I don't compare it with other people's?"

"Compare, yes. That's essential." I had a feeling, judging by the assuredness in her voice, that she had been lectured about all this by someone else.

"You should go to Italy and spend some time there," I suggested. "You must see Piero della Francesca, Giotto, Masaccio. You should go to Venice, Florence, Palermo, Naples. Oh yes, the south, you'll love it there."

The thought of Iris, famished for knowledge as she was, going to Italy for the first time, thrilled me. Suddenly the quantity of beauty, of elevation, grace, harmony, in the art of my homeland, seemed unbearable. I felt dizzy thinking of it.

"There's so much to see! You'll die. You'll never be the same again, I promise you: you'll look at this place in a completely different perspective afterwards. . . ."

It would be the equivalent of what had happened to me, I realized: the way I had fallen apart when I saw the sky and the vastness of northern Kenya. It had been as if all the curtains had dropped simultaneously and left me there, center stage, thunderstruck.

"It'll change you forever," I insisted. "Promise me you'll go. You must look up my brother. You'll love him."

"Yes, I will. I'll try." But she was already thinking of something else. She looked around the room, her eyes staring off out of focus.

"I was wondering whether I could borrow some books from you. I feel like reading something."

"Books? Yes, of course. What kind of books?"

"I don't know. I was thinking of poetry, maybe? T. S. Eliot, Whitman, whatever . . . and a Russian. I would like to read a Russian."

"A Russian."

"Yes."

". . . Which one?"

She shrugged.

"I don't know. Any one of them. Whoever you think is good."

I went to the bookshelf and took out an old paperback copy

of *Crime and Punishment*.

"Well, if you want to get into the Russians you may as well start with this one." I pushed the book into her hand. "How did you get this idea about the Russians?"

Iris was busy scanning the back of the paperback.

"Oh . . . I had a conversation with Miles a couple of nights ago. He said I would really enjoy them."

She slid the book inside her back pocket and slapped it, boyishly.

"You know, all those guys think I'm such a retard because I haven't read anything." She smiled mischievously. "Which, by the way, is the absolute truth."

"Which guys?"

"You know, the Nairobi press core. Yack yack yack, they're always yacking about *Heart of Darkness*. I can't bear them." She sighed and shook her head. "Anyway . . . at least Miles is the only one who bothers to advise me about what to read. I really appreciate it. It makes me feel like I'm not completely hopeless once I step out of the bush."

I realised she had a crush on Miles. He must have been the trigger to her European mission. She looked so different now, on the eve of her trip to London, than when I had met her for the first time at the camp. Suddenly I saw how unworldly she would appear among the London glitterati. How untrendy her clothes would seem, how out-of-date her conversation. How she could have been easily misjudged for just another Swedish farmer's daughter who baked delicious cakes. One felt like giving her a lot of advice.

She stood up, ready to go.

"Thanks a lot, Esmé. And by the way, my birthday is the day after tomorrow and Nena offered to have a dinner party for me at her house. My place is too small."

"Great." We started to the door, but I suddenly turned back. "Wait! I want give you a little birthday present now."

Afterwards I wondered why I had had that intuition—to give it to her then, rather than wait for the day of her birthday. I ran to the bookshelf and took out an English translation of Ferdinando's book. I scribbled on the first page.

"You said you wanted to read poetry. Here, this is my father's."

She lit up and flicked through the pages.

"Thank you! Oh this is so amazing!" She read my inscription. "Hey! Thank you *so much*."

"If you want you can borrow some of my winter clothes before you go off," I said. "I've got so much stuff in the trunk."

"That would be incredible." She gave me a squeeze and kissed me on both cheeks. "You are so wonderful, thank you."

I watched her hop into her car and reverse, screeching the tires. She drove as aggressively as a man. I smiled and waved.

Another hybrid, I thought. Half boy, half princess; half warrior, half child.

There we were, in our pretty party dresses once again.

Even by Nairobi standards it was getting late, and Nena was starting to get annoyed.

"Typical Iris," she said, looking at her watch, "to show up late for her own party."

We heard a car in the drive. I saw Hunter walk in and instantly felt a shot of adrenaline: my heart beating like a hammer in my chest, my knees weak. My reaction amazed me. He took off his glasses, and brushed back his black hair with his hand. I could smell the cold air from his face: he must have come in an open car.

He went to kiss Nena.

"I'm so sorry to be late." He held out a bottle of wine. "Shall I put this in the fridge?"

"Yes please. You're not late; Iris hasn't made her grand entrance yet." I could tell she was angry. Iris always had this amazing talent for irritating other women, I thought.

I couldn't have cared less that dinner was late. I gulped down my vodka and felt a pleasant tingle. Hunter came towards me with a drink in his hand.

"Haven't seen *you* in a long time," I managed to say flirtatiously.

"I haven't been around."

He looked pale and tense. He forced a smile.

"Unfortunately I have been to some very unpleasant destinations." He raised his glass and looked straight into my eyes.

"To your obviously fabulous health."

I laughed.

"And to yours."

The phone had rung in the noisy room, and Nena went to answer it. It wasn't her tone of voice, or what she said, which attracted our attention. It was the quality of her silence: it made us silent all at once. We listened.

". . . What? . . ."

Her eyes went blank.

". . . When? . . ."

The room was hushed now. We all looked at her. She put down the receiver in a stupor.

"Iris is dead."

Nobody said anything. Nobody moved. We waited, frozen, for her to come towards us and sit on the sofa by the fire. She looked at the floor, her hands clutched between her knees.

"She had a car accident. She is . . ." Her mouth quivered.

She looked at us, imploringly, like a little girl.

"She is *dead*."

It falls like a rock. When that word rolls down it takes only an instant to smash everything forever.

We stood, a frozen crowd of party guests—toasts still in midair, leg of lamb roasting in the oven—like crystallysed Eurydices on the threshold of Hades. The word had been spoken. And now there would be grief, tears, desperation.

We turned into a group of panicked ants, frantic, frenzied. We started ringing different numbers, drove into town, ran first to the hospital, then to the morgue. Peter, Hunter and Miles spoke, argued, bribed, handled the Kenyan bureaucracy which had taken possession of Iris's body and had turned it into a *thing*, something which now required forms, certificates and

154

signatures. Nicole, Nena and I sat numbly in every waiting room—the hospital, the morgue, the funeral home. We let them deal with it—overhearing their tense conversations with police officers, hospital staff—and smoked in silence under the fluorescent lights, red-eyed, our mascara streaking down our cheeks, like a spooky trio from a Venetian carnival.

The next day Iris's parents came from the farm to complete the formalities. They were both blond, strong, simple, their English hardened by a Swedish inflection, their skin thickened by upcountry sun. They spoke little and, as if their grief had sunk into them too heavily, couldn't manage to lift their heads.

I couldn't get hold of Adam. I had no number for him. All I remembered was Colorado. I rang up the college in Boulder. When I asked the operator whether she would know of an upcoming lecture about East African safaris, she laughed at me.

"We've got hundreds of lectures, thousands of people stepping in here every day, honey. Which department you want?

I hung up.

"We are gathered once again because of the death of a friend."

Hunter looked at all of us assembled in the small church, his voice quiet and clear against the fresh stone of the walls.

"And it is not an unusual occurrence. We who live in Africa have had to learn to grow accustomed to death. People we love die, we keep losing them all the time. Yet each time death strikes it leaves us speechless, it seems impossible that it should have happened again. And yet it must be this very death, this darkness and this lingering fear, that makes people here feel so close to one another. It is the ever-present possibility of losing each other that makes our bonds so intense and so tight.

"Iris was killed the day of her birthday. She was only twenty-seven, but she had more experience than many older men in this country. She could shoot a gun, and she would have known how to handle a charging buffalo or a bandit. But instead she was killed by a drunken Kikuyu at a traffic light in Westlands, in broad daylight. Her shopping bags were still on the back seat. So this reminds us that when death comes, it always comes unannounced, it is always cruel and ravenous. It is always mindless and absurd." His voice quivered slightly.

He paused and looked at the ceiling.

"Iris had been given a name by her Samburu friends. They called her "The Rich One." I used to tease her about it. In fact sometimes I know I teased her a little too hard. But now I see how right they were."

He stopped again. One could hear muffled sobs, whispers. Then, in the back of the church, the Morans started heaving and hissing, and the heaving became an undulating dirge. We turned to look at them. They had come from very far to say farewell to their friend. Some of their faces we knew from her photographs. They stood erect on a line, wrapped in their bright red *shukas*, their long hair smeared with ochre, holding their spears, unflinching like a lost legion of the Roman Empire. The sound their lungs emitted was like the wind through the trees, like the water of a stream, like the breathing of a running animal. The vibration of their syncopated breaths rose like an organ blowing inside a cathedral.

We stood shoulder to shoulder in the tiny church holding each other's hands while the Morans kept singing.

And it suddenly felt right, to be so close—all of us—mourning another death in Africa.

Late that night I heard a car pull into my drive. I was still awake, I don't know why, but I knew it must be him as soon as I saw the headlights against the trees.

"I couldn't sleep," he said. "I was hoping you'd still be awake."

"Come in. Yes, I couldn't sleep either. Nobody can tonight, I'm sure."

"I figured you and I would be the only two left on our own. Miles went to stay with Nicole."

"How is he?"

"A wreck."

"He really fell apart, didn't he? Sit down, I'll make you some tea."

He followed me into the kitchen, not looking around. He didn't seem curious to take in where I lived; he just walked in as if it was the hundredth time he had come to see me. He sat on the wooden table and watched as I filled the kettle.

"I'll tell you what. Tea is great, but I'm starving. I haven't eaten in two days."

"Oh. Okay."

I opened the fridge and took out bread and cheese, leftover chicken curry, salad.

"Now that you mention it, I haven't had anything to eat either," I said, feeling a sudden pang of hunger. "Forget tea, let's have wine with this."

In the cupboard I saw the leftovers of Iris's cake. I took it out. It felt so odd in my hands, wrapped in plastic. Still fresh.

"She baked this for me," I said hesitantly. "It's . . ."

I stopped and looked at him, not knowing what to do.

Hunter stared at me gravely and then took it from me.

"Let's have it."

We pulled out two chairs and sat down to eat. The sight of food had made us so rapacious that we didn't bother to warm up the chicken. We ate and drank in total silence, looking at each other as we ate, until there was nothing left. The previous forty-eight hours had drained both of us so much that I don't think we had any energy left to feel uptight or nervous about being alone together, for the first time, that late at night.

The wine had warmed us and had fueled a feeling of peaceful exhaustion. We moved to the living room and I revived the fire.

"That was *so good*," he said as he stretched out on the sofa, lighting a Rooster. "I couldn't face another night of insomnia in my cold, empty place."

I curled up at the other end of the sofa, at a safe distance from his body.

"I'm glad you came. I didn't want to be alone tonight either."

We didn't say anything for awhile. I lit my cigarette and I listened to the sound of our breaths exhaling the smoke.

Suddenly I realised how long—somewhere inside me—I had been wanting to see him like this. The two of us alone, on my sofa.

"It moved me, what you said in the church. About how people *die* here." Hunter didn't stir.

"Back in Europe you go home at night and all you worry about is how many messages you'll find on your answering machine. Here you come home and you wonder if your friends are still alive."

"You know," Hunter flicked an ash on the floor and propped himself with his elbow. "If she had been told she was going to die like this, oh man, she would have *hated* it."

"Why?"

"To die like a housewife coming home from the supermarket? Very unsexy." He lay back on the sofa and looked at the ceiling. "She was *so vain*."

I heard him sigh.

"Did that annoy you?" I asked.

"Sometimes. I guess because I felt that, like many other people here, her life was this perfectly planned magazine ad. If you buy it, this is what's included in the price: adventure, sex, beauty, old colonial charm. And instead—this is probably what I was trying to say in the church—a fucking *kikuyu* runs her over in the middle of town. And do you know what that tells us?"

"No."

"It tells us, *this* is Africa, sweetheart. The rest is crap, interior decoration, advertising. Because Africa is a fucking drunk *kikuyu* in a Nissan, you see? In the end that's what did her in. That's what I mean when I say this country is ravenous. It didn't even give her the chance to make the exit she deserved. It doesn't fucking care to make you look glamorous the day you die—"

"I think she thought the world of you."

"I *loved* her," he said angrily, almost snarling. "There was more life in her than inside a kindergarten. I was madly in love with her when I first came back."

I flushed. Just hearing the sound of the words *madly in love* coming from him made me uneasy.

"And what happened?"

"I couldn't follow her, she couldn't follow me. We were living in the same country but we were seeing different things, all the time. Because of my job I had to put up with a lot of ugly stuff, and Iris—well you know how she is—she . . ."

We both noticed his use of the present tense, but ignored it.

". . . she was too busy creating the perfect ad campaign for her life—the Beauty and the Vanishing Warriors mystique—and I resented it. She didn't want to be brought down. She was never interested in the truth, if it meant seeing the ugly side of things. She hated that. She said I only liked her when I succeeded in making her unhappy."

He paused, looked at the ceiling and then at me.

"Maybe she was right, who knows." He sighed. "Maybe I got a kick out of spoiling her fun, but I believe there is a *truth,* and most of the times it is very ugly, very unjust and very cruel. Especially in this part of the world. And I believe in not ignoring it; otherwise I wouldn't choose to do what I do."

"I know," I said. "It must be very difficult for you to join our little Karen dinner parties after being in Rwanda."

He shrugged.

"That's not the point. It's very difficult to come back to *anything* after that."

We were silent for a long time. Then he started again.

"The first time I saw the body of a dead man, I was shocked. It was in Somalia. It was bloated like a cow, the stench was unbearable. I said, There you go, your first corpse. When we arrived in Kigali at the very beginning, we could feel right away it was going to be a really ugly story, very different than Somalia, but we had no idea that we were going to witness a genocide. The first two days I would count the number of dead bodies on the streets. Then I stopped counting. All of us did. We didn't even talk about it anymore."

He looked at me so seriously, almost like a child caught doing something wrong.

"That first week in Kigali, the killing was so heavy, we couldn't believe it was happening. The morgue was filled up to the ceiling, blood was streaming out of its shut doors. You would drive through a group of sobbing women at a checkpoint and know that they would no longer be there on the way back. Sometimes you did see them again, but lying dead on the ground. At night we climbed on the roof of the hotel and listened, horrified, to the screams of people being butchered all around us."

"How do they . . . I mean, what do they use to . . ."

"Kill them? They carve people up with machetes or club them to death with these huge wooden *rungus* covered with nails. Apparently, when they break into a house and start putting the whole family down, people bargain and pay them money to use bullets instead. These Hutus are high on it. They run around in gangs of twenty or so, covered with blood, high on the violence and the physical strain. You know these guys' job is to kill *all day*, with their bare hands, people who are fighting for their life. It's an incredibly hard physical task. You can see they are possessed, but at the same time it's impossible not feel the thrill, the immense energy that is produced by their blood lust."

He stared at me, with a blank look. I reached for his lighter and he passed it to me mechanically, barely touching my hand. I think he wasn't even seeing me any longer.

"The frightening thing is when you realise that a threshold has been crossed," he continued, resting his chin on his knee and staring into the fire, his dark hair covering his eyes now. "The boundary which rules our lives and tells us every day how far the limits are set. These people have smashed that boundary and are running amok on the other side of it. That other side has no limits, there's no turning back once you have reached it."

He pulled his hair behind his ear and looked at me, as if almost surprised to find me there, listening.

"And it has nothing to do with being African. It has to do with being a human being. Only I guess in Africa the veneer between rational behaviour and madness is much thinner and quicker to wear out.

I was starting to feel nauseous, overwhelmed, but there was no way I could stop him now. He wasn't talking to me; he was talking to himself, as if performing a ritual, where by naming the horrors one by one he could make them disappear.

"Dead bodies are dead bodies. What kills me is wounded children. Sometimes you walk among what you assume are dead people, and suddenly you feel these small hands clutching at your ankles, or hear their cries in the distance. You can't take wounded children in the car because the militia will stop you, the men will take them out and kill them before your eyes. So we stopped doing it."

"Oh God, Hunter . . ." I covered my eyes with my hands.

"It's the truth. I am not saying this to impress you. I only say it because it's the truth." He sighed heavily. "When I saw *her* body at the morgue . . ."

"Yes." I nodded, and I felt a lump in my throat.

"Christ, I had *made love* to that body, but it was just another bloody corpse. My mind refused to register it as *hers*. I don't know what it is that happens to your brain, it finds its own devices to survive, to keep functioning. It has nothing to do with cynicism; it's survival instinct."

He kept looking into my eyes as I sat frozen, feeling my pupils dilate, as if I had taken some hallucinogenic drug.

"Life has to go on. Nothing stops life, nothing. Not even the nuclear bomb. Two weeks ago in Rwanda, Ruben and I arrived at a church near a village. People had been hiding inside, hoping to be spared. Well, we got there very early in the morning, he had his camera rolling. Outside there were hundreds, I mean *hundreds* of bodies. The smell was so bad you couldn't breathe. *That* smell you never get rid of, it'll stay with you for the rest of your life. Inside there were decomposing bodies piled up one on top of the other up to your *waist*, all right? There must've been thousands in there. Women, children, everything. Your ankles were six inches deep in body fluid, in liquescent . . . matter. The dogs had already been in there and had done their job. I've never been crazy about dogs, but after that . . ." He flicked his cigarette into the fireplace. "Anyway. The place of course had been evacuated, but the Catholic priests had tended this small rose garden in back of the church, all right? Miraculously the flowers had been spared, they were perfectly intact, like nothing had happened. I stood in front of the roses, and watched them for a long time. It was the only thing I could concentrate on to keep my sanity. You know, it was a sunny morning, and the bees were busy as on every other morning, flying from rose to rose. This little parallel world was going on as ever, completely untouched by it all. Ruben was shooting everything on his Betacam. The thing about a Beta mike is that it picks up the oddest frequencies, it's totally arbitrary in picking up sounds. The only soundtrack to that scene—one of the largest, most horrifying scenes of carnage I've ever seen, or humanity has seen as far as I'm concerned—was the buzzing of bees and the chirping of birds.

I felt the warmth of tears as they started streaming down my face.

"We kept driving across the countryside passing through the villages, sobbing like two idiots, and everywhere we went we met this eerie silence. Just the birds. Literally, we only needed to stick our noses out the window to find more bodies. The incredible thing was how animals had taken over the houses. In every house you'd find the cows in the bedrooms, pigs in the bathroom. Feeding off whatever was left. The owners lying in pools of dried blood on the floor. The animals quietly roaming about. Everything wrapped in this endless silence."

He saw that I was crying, and that, I think, woke him up.

"I don't know why I'm telling you all this. Sorry, Esmé," he said. "I didn't want to—"

"Don't be sorry. *I'm* the one who is sorry."

"For what?"

"For you. For everything . . ." I started sobbing.

He leaned towards me and wiped my tears softly with his fingertips.

"Don't cry, please."

"Why not? Why shouldn't I?" I asked almost angrily. "When

is a good time to cry, then?"

It was coming down like water tumbling into a ravine. I was crying for him, for Iris, for the bodies in the church, for me, for my child, for my father, my mother. For everything that had been broken, taken away, lost, for all that had been forgotten.

"Yes," he said. "You're right." Cry, but come here.

He pulled me on top of him. I felt his arms wrap tightly around my shoulders, his fingertips rest on my cheekbones. We stayed like that for a long time, until I stopped crying. We sat listening to each other's breath and heartbeat, learning each other's smell, afraid to move, to say anything. We listened as one listens for every stir, every creak, every murmur in the dark, our heartbeats thumping faster, as if distant footsteps were getting closer in the night. I was afraid of what I wanted. I was longing for those footsteps to stop at my door and come in, and afraid they would fade away instead.

Finally he said:

"Let me sleep here with you."

"What?"

"You heard me. I don't want to go."

"No . . ." My heart was pounding furiously. "I mean, yes. You can stay."

I let the words fill the room, I let them carry every hidden possibility. Then I broke away from his embrace and looked into his eyes.

"You can sleep here, on the sofa."

"Yes, that's okay. The sofa is *fine*," he said, the condescending tone creeping back into his voice.

I realised he had probably meant that all along. He smiled as if to ease me out of my embarrassment.

"I just don't want to leave you now and drive home. I want to sleep close to where you sleep."

"Yes." I nodded. "But why?"

"Because there's no reason to be apart, you and I, on a night like this."

I laid my head on his chest again. I felt his heartbeat gradually slow, his muscles relax, until he fell asleep. When I heard

163

the first birds in the trees I stood up, pulled a blanket over him and slipped into my bed.

I couldn't sleep. I tossed and turned, hopelessly attempting to detect any stir coming from the living room. His physical presence right beyond the door perturbed me beyond my wildest expectations.

It was driving me mad not to be making love to him.

The realisation that this was what my body was aching for terrified me. I kept turning over, hoping the feeling would abandon me and I could fall asleep. Instead I saw the sky grow pale behind the trees and cast a white shadow in the room. Then I heard the roosters in the distance.

"Fucking hell!" I whispered, pulling the sheets over my head in a desperate attempt to seek deliverance in darkness. But there's no escape from light: it comes, at the same time every day, shining upon all the things you are not yet ready to discover.

I must have been asleep for no more than half an hour when the phone rang. I heard the long-distance beep.

"Hi darling, sorry to wake you," said Adam, "but I wanted to catch you before going to sleep."

The sound of his voice startled me. I sat bolt upright, sweating, my heart bursting in of my throat.

"It's very late here and I've just come back from this insane party at—"

"Adam," I cried, "Oh *Adam* . . ."

"What is it?"

"Something terrible happened. Iris . . ."

"What?"

"She was in a car accident."

"Oh, no. Is she badly hurt?"

"No. No . . . she is . . ."

This time it would have to be me saying it.

"She's dead."

There was a very long silence. I listened to the beeps, the rustle of the line.

"When did it happen?" His voice sounded flat, robotic.

"Three days ago. The funeral was yesterday. I didn't know

how to get hold of—"

"I'm coming home. Now."

"Yes, *please*."

I heard a click and the hissing of the international connection came to an end.

In the living room all that was left was a dent in the pillows.

I stepped into the kitchen. Saw the empty mug of tea on the table. Wilson turned to me from the sink and smiled.

"Good morning, Wilson. *Habari?*" I tried to act as normal as possible.

"*Mzuri, mama.*" He caught me looking out the window in the drive.

"*Bwana Hunter ametoka saa hii.*"

His car was gone.

"*Amewacha barua kwa wewe.*" Wilson handed me a piece of paper.

His handwriting was very small and neat.

"I'm off. I'll be thinking of you." Just like that. Imperial.

Yes, everything was back to normal. Adam was coming back home and Hunter had vanished once again, somewhere out of my reach.

I sat in the kitchen, my eyes on Wilson's swift movements as he poured hot water from the teapot and took the toast out of the oven.

Another breakfast for the living, I thought.

But I didn't throw away the note. I wanted to keep it to go over later on.

I'll be thinking of you, was what I would read over and over in the vain hope that the phrase would disclose more of its meaning.

You cannot help searching for a hidden surprise if all you are left with is a small piece of paper.

I rang Nicole.

"Are you awake?" It was still before eight.

"*Awake?* Are you joking? I never slept," she said. "I've smoked two packs of cigarettes and had six mugs of espresso."

"And Miles?"

"Unconscious. Sleeping the sleep of the just. Come over and let's smoke some more together."

She was sitting on the verandah, wrapped in a faded kimono, her nails still covered with old polish.

"Oh," she said when she saw me, "thank God you're here."

She looked wired, her dark hair disheveled. Her bare arms were white and sinewy, streaked by blue veins.

"What's wrong?"

"Nothing really. I've just spent this endless night with Miles, and now I'm worn out. I had to console him for not having paid enough attention to Iris, for never telling her how wonderful he thought she was before she died. Then," she sighed. "We had sex. Passionate sex."

"Oh."

"Vicarious sex, of course."

Everyone must have had sex last night, I thought. It's what usually happens when somebody dies. To counteract the loss, to reaffirm the principle of life. It's only natural, a basic instinct.

"But you know, it shook me up a bit. Even though I knew perfectly well why it was happening. She's probably laughing at all this," said Nicole with a grin.

"Who, Iris?"

"You bet. All the women in this town get laid by proxy by her ex-lovers the night of her departure."

I looked at her stunned. Had she seen Hunter's car in my drive? Anything was possible in Langata.

"Hunter came around last night," I admitted like a suspect who thinks it better not to hide anything from the cops.

"Ah-hah! Hunter," she said, Holmes-to-Watson-like. ". . . And?"

Nothing. He slept on the sofa, he didn't want to sleep alone at his place. He needed some warmth, I guess.

"One can't really refuse *that*, right?" said Nicole sadly. She looked away, somewhere out of focus. "Especially on a night like last night."

"We didn't . . . nothing happened," I added in haste.

"Much better that way," she said and then sighed, thinking of her own misjudgements. "Much wiser never to cross that line. Sometimes snapping back into your original position is much more arduous than you'd think."

"Yes, I totally agree. Much too dangerous," I said, a bit too vehemently.

That woke her up: she looked at me, surprised. I stared back, holding her gaze without flinching. That's when she knew I was gone for him.

CHAPTER TWO

Good walking leaves no track behind.

GEOFFREY ORYEMA

"What are you doing still in bed?"

Miles barges into my room, disrupting my daydreaming.

"Oh God, Miles, you gave me such a fright. What do you mean, *still?* I've been up since seven. I was just relaxing. I had to fight off a bit of a hangover, but I'm fine now."

I have been lying in bed since coming back from Kilonzo's shop, staring at the ceiling, as I had planned. My mind has been going around in circles, and has brought back surprising details I thought I had lost forever.

Miles sits beside the bed and looks at me closely. I'm slightly annoyed at this intrusion.

"What have you done to your hair?"

"Got a haircut. Do you like it?"

"Kind of." He looks undecided.

"Oh well, too late now." I don't like anybody sitting at the side of my bed staring at me like I'm sick or something. So I get up and head impatiently towards the living room.

"I didn't say I *don't* like it."

"Hey, my hair is the last worry on my mind." I shake my

head. "Got a cigarette?"

"Yes." He promptly lights me one. "How about a cup of coffee?"

I can feel by the tension in his body that he hasn't turned up, like he usually does, just to have a chat and hang out. He needs something, and once he gets it he'll be out of here. I pour two cups of coffee from the flask which Wilson has left in the kitchen. Miles follows me, keeping up a bland chatter.

"Great dinner party last night, wasn't it? Was the American film writer fun?"

"Not exactly," I answer sullenly as Wilson takes out the cold milk from the fridge. "Thank you, Wilson. Come Miles, let's sit out on the verandah."

"Oh. He seemed like a cool guy to me," says Miles, disappointed by my bad mood.

"Maybe. Not *my* idea of cool, anyway."

"Okay." He sips the coffee and tries to look relaxed, stretching his legs on the low table. "That American photographer, Linda. I liked her a lot."

"Really?"

"Quite a babe, I thought."

"Mmmm."

I hope he's not going to go through the whole guest list.

"I saw her work. Not bad, I must say."

It's infuriating to me that he should even mention her work. I am thinking of Iris, and I am furious on her behalf. Why do we replace people, why do we forget so easily?

"When I took the girls home last night . . . her and . . . Claire," he clears his throat, sheepishly, as he pronounces her name. "Linda showed us some of her most recent work."

"Really? She travels dragging her portfolio along?"

"Oh, come off it, Esmé," he says reproachfully. "She was just carrying some back issues of magazines where her work had been published. So she could show people here."

"How convenient." I enjoy getting on his nerves. "Was it exciting stuff?"

"Well, average," he concedes. "We had a few drinks and a

couple more joints at her hotel."

"Sounds like you had quite a late night."

"Yes. They kept asking me stuff like I was some kind of survival kit. These girls are total urbanites, it's their first time to Africa, basically it's freaking them out."

"I bet they loved every minute of it."

Undaunted by my lack of response, he grins.

"Linda was trying to act like she was more of an expert, right? Like she knew more about the bush and stuff. Then she goes into the loo, sees a spider and all hell breaks loose." He sniggers. "She had *such* a fit."

"And what about Claire?" I ask nonchalantly.

"I took her home. We talked a bit in the car. She's very intelligent, extremely well read."

"Is she?" I say, trying to look bored.

Wilson appears with a little plate of homemade biscuits. He smiles as he puts it on the table between me and Miles.

"Thank you, Wilson," I say. "What a great idea."

Miles starts wolfing down the biscuits.

"Anyway, I'm going to take them both to see the sunset on top of the Ngong hills later today. I was wondering if I could borrow a cooler for the wine . . ."

"You know, Miles, I wish that when you came to my house you would bother to say hello, thank you, how are you, to my staff. They are not *objects*, you know."

"What?" He looks at me in disbelief.

"Just now. You've seen Wilson twice and didn't even acknowledge his presence, like he was a sheet of glass or something."

"Hey, listen, I'm sorry. There's no need to get so upset—"

"No! You're wrong," I snap, "*there is*. Someone should get upset. For once."

I think I'm about to raise my voice. I can feel my face warming.

"I can't *bear* the way everyone is always so careless. Like nothing matters, like nothing makes the slightest difference! Like no one fucking cares!"

I'm screaming now. I see my hand pick up the coffee mug and I watch it as, in perfect slow motion, it flies over the lawn and blows to pieces. Miles is horrified.

"For Christ's sake, what's wrong with you?" I detect panic in his eyes.

"Nothing is wrong with *me!* Does it ever cross your mind there could be something wrong in the way *you* behave?"

"I . . . I haven't the faintest idea—"

"Forget it. Go in the kitchen, ask Wilson to give you the cooler, get what you need fast and get the fuck out of here."

"Esmé, please, what is it? Listen, I'm sorry about Wilson, I didn't mean to . . . But *please,* tell me, what did I do that—"

"No, you didn't do anything. Nobody ever does anything wrong here. I'm imagining it. All the time."

I kick a safari chair, which crashes on the floor. Miles stands up, in all his Britishness, horrified by my Anna Magnani–like behaviour.

"'Bye Miles. Enjoy the sunset."

I step back into the house and close my bedroom door behind me. I count to fifteen, then I hear the engine start and the car pulling out of the drive.

Adam came back from America distraught, tensed and hardened by pain and physical exaustion. As I drove to the airport to pick him up, less than forty-eight hours after his phone call, I couldn't help thinking how different his homecoming was going to be than the one I had imagined only ten days earlier, when I was still running around in supermarkets, checking out what baby food looked like. In the meantime I had been through a fast spin in a tumble dryer, and had reincarnated into at least three different people since those happy days sitting in Dr Singh's waiting room. I couldn't tell which one of them I was at the moment, but I was certainly not the person Adam had left behind five weeks earlier.

When I saw him at the airport he too looked different. He was thinner, his eyes were bloodshot, his skin whiter than I had ever seen it. He felt remote, not quite there.

"I rang her parents from Boulder," he said on the way home in the car. "I want to spend a couple of days with them at the farm. They said she is . . . in this beautiful spot under a tree. I just want to sit there for a while."

"Yes."

"Could you be ready to go tomorrow morning?"

"Yes. Are you sure you want me to go with you?"

"Yes, why not?"

"Maybe you want to spend time alone there. And I think it would be easier if it was only you with her parents. They've known you since you were a kid, you're like family to them."

"Oh, but . . ."

"I think you should go alone. I've already said my farewell. Really, I mean it."

He knew I was right.

That night, as we lay in bed, I could feel the weight of his pain, somewhere deep inside him where I couldn't reach. I held his hand in the dark.

"Fuck," he said. "I'm really going to miss her."

It's so difficult to admit, it feels demeaning. But I couldn't help thinking that now there was no space left in him to mourn the loss of our child. He'd said nothing to me about it since he had come home. I knew that for him, being so far away, it had been an abstraction. A phone conversation.

But for me—it had been inside me, it had changed the shape of my body. Nothing could have been more real. And there I was, competing with Iris's death for his attention. I was making a stupid mistake; nobody can win such a battle.

Now I see it more clearly: everything was happening at the same time, there couldn't have been a worse moment to be demanding. But in the last ten days I had lost a child and a friend. The harder side of Africa had slapped me in the face and I was deeply wounded.

Very early the next morning, barefoot and clad only in one of his shirts, I stormed into the garage where Adam was checking the car with one of his mechanics before taking off for Maralal.

"Will you come inside for a minute? I need to talk to you," I said rudely. He looked at me, surprised, and followed me into the bedroom.

As we sat on the bed I burst into tears.

"Oh God, Adam, I have had it. I don't know, but I think I want to go back. I am so tired of this."

"Back where?"

"Home. To Italy, away from here."

I had begun to sob.

"Hey!" He pulled me closer, alarmed. "Hey Esmé, what's wrong? Please tell me."

"You . . . you do these things all the time—"

"What do you mean, *I do these things* . . . like what?"

"Driving, fixing things, rushing here and there . . . I can't stand it anymore."

He looked at me in shock. He had no idea what I was talking about.

"You know," I went on, "where I come from, in my family, people use words to describe their feelings. And—guess what? —it does make a difference. After all that's happened, all you do is check if the radiator has a leak. It's barbaric, it drives me fucking nuts."

"I'm sorry." He let the air slowly out of his lungs, then raked his fingers through my hair a few times and looked intensely into my eyes. "It's just that I feel so bad too, I don't know how to—"

"You never *say* anything," I interrupted him.

"True. You're so much better than me, that way."

He fell silent.

"I wanted that child, too, Esmé."

Suddenly I felt ridiculous for throwing such a tantrum. I wiped my eyes.

"I know that."

"Good. You bear that in mind, will you?"

I nodded.

"I love you," he said.

I looked at him with a blank stare.

"I . . . love . . . you . . . Esmé," he repeated slowly, as if he feared I no longer understood English.

"I know."

"I don't know how to show you in any other way. *Please* don't get upset like this."

When Adam came back from Maralal a couple of days later, I was feeling calmer and he looked himself again.

"I want you to come with me on safari," he said. "You look like you desperately need to get out of here."

He wanted to find a new site for his camp before the season started again. He'd come back with lots of bookings, and business looked very good.

"A lot of clients from last season have booked again. I want to take them to new spots, where no one's ever been."

"No one, ever?"

"You'd be surprised how many parts of this country have never been visited by man. You'll see: we'll to be travelling on some pretty godforsaken tracks."

We got ready for a rough safari. Electric winch, serious tool kit, car spares, maps, guns and ammunition. I bought the most extravagant provisions: oyster sauce, Thai green curry and lemongrass in brine, just in case one felt like stir-fries, chocolate syrup and all the imported crackers I could get my hands on.

Adam was inhabited by a strange fury. I could see that five weeks in the "civilized world" had made him restless, like an animal in a cage. But beyond that, I sensed that he needed to get rid of something—pain, frustration, I can't say what it was. He needed to wrestle, and not having an enemy to vent his anger on, he set off for safari with the resolution to defeat any obstacle that came his way.

Nature took up his challenge and showed us its teeth.

Only one day's drive away from Nairobi we entered a flat country which seemed to stretch for ever and ever. It was rocky, dry and dusty. There was nobody in sight, not even a child looking after his goats. It was like going into a furnace. Every track we took disappeared into nothing, but Adam never once turned back the car. He just went on, unrelenting. We had to literally rebuild with a shovel bits of road which had been washed out by the rains. We winched the car out of dried riverbeds, cut the bush with a panga when it got too thick for the car to go through, pushed stones and branches under the tires to pull the car out of the sand. Every day we worked like slaves to gain a few miles into virgin territory. And the deeper we waded into the bush, the harsher it got. It was a thick thornbush, impenetrable and stifling. The river, which I had been so looking forward to reach, was muddy, crawling with crocodiles and infested with mosquitoes.

"No one has ever been here before," he said with pride, as we sat under the stars, when the night finally gave us a break. "Isn't this beautiful?"

No, it didn't look *beautiful* to me. It looked harsh, eerie, hostile. There was no peace or bliss among those spikes. My skin was slashed and cut; flies buzzed around the sores; I felt exhausted and filthy. The meat we'd brought rotted in the heat, and we ended up feeding fillets to the crocodiles.

One night after dark, as we were collecting firewood, we nearly stepped on a huge snake moving slowly through the grass, close to our tent. The snake was startled by the torchlight and sat dumbly in the grass. It was enormous.

"Don't move," said Adam and he left me there, frozen, to frame the snake with the torch beam. He ran back with the shotgun.

"What a fucking monster." And he shot it.

It was a puff adder. The biggest he had ever seen, he said, shaking his head. I had never seen anything remotely like it in my life. It must have at least been five feet long, as thick as a boa constrictor, and weighed more than ten kilos. Full of deadly poison. We slashed its head off with a panga and threw it into the fire, where it sizzled, spreading an acrid smell. Adam set off into the bush holding the headless snake, which kept wriggling in spasms.

175

"Where are you going?" I asked faintly.

"I want to put this as far away as possible from camp."

"Why, do you think the hyenas will come and eat it?

"It's possible; they eat everything. I just don't want to sleep close to this *thing*."

It was the first time that I'd heard Adam express not fear, but revulsion for something.

At night the baboons kept me awake with their spooky human cries.

"They're just baboons," said Adam in the dark of the tent. "You've heard them a million times."

"No. These sound like screaming children; they're horrible."

I knew the bush was snarling at us this time. I could *feel* it. But Adam would never admit something like that. He was determined to seek salvation in the perfection of nature, and wasn't going to let nature turn its back on him like that.

I studied him as he washed himself in the muddy river. He looked so strong and handsome standing naked in the soft evening light. He smiled and stretched his hand.

"Come," he said. "It's so beautiful."

But the water looked too murky, the riverbanks too slimy, to bring me any relief. What Hunter had said about himself and Iris suddenly came back to me: I couldn't help thinking Adam and I also had started to see things differently now. The realization that this might be the beginning of a distance between us deeply disturbed me.

We moved from the river at last and started climbing up into greener country, into the hills. The air got cooler, the palms gave way to ferns and tall grass. We met herds of impalas, kongoni, elands. We saw them run on the ridges and scatter among the grass. The freshness in the air was a relief, but more than anything it was exhilarating to see open country and sky again, after the oppression of the thick bush.

It took us a whole day to climb to the top of the range. It was an incredibly hard drive. The track to the top was so steep we felt like we were fighting against gravity. We climbed up agonizingly slowly, in low gear, the wheels of the Toyota fighting to hold their grip on the rocks. We jolted, leaped and tossed. Night fell and we were still driving. We stopped talking, each wrapped in our own silence and tiredness.

We drove into the night, bathing in space, like a spaceship entering a new galaxy. We became conscious that our headlights were piercing the darkness and were visible for hundreds of miles. When we had almost reached the top we could make out the dim light of a campfire across the plain below us—the only sign of human life in the vast land which stretched at the foot of the hills.

It was probably a camp of Masai Morans, where they had had an *olpul*, the slaughtering of a goat. By now they were probably slowly eating the whole animal by the fire after having drunk its blood. This was what Moranhood prescribed: to sleep and eat only among Morans, away from the eyes of women and children. Almost as if they—having reached the status of demigods—could not be seen performing human tasks such as putting food in their body and giving it a rest. I thought of Lenjo and his tales. I missed his assuredness, his gentle smile. Suddenly I longed to be sitting around that fire with those Morans in the plain, in the midst of their smoky scent, to be lulled by their husky language, which is lean and fast, which leaps and falls like a Masai when he dances. I knew that those Morans this very minute were staring up at our distant beams. They probably knew it must be some crazy *wazungu*. Nobody else would head in that direction at night.

But Adam loved to be as far away from humans as possible, no matter what it took.

As we approached the top in the stillness of the night, our tracks leaving scars on the fresh grass, we both felt conscious of violating the integrity of those remote hills.

At last we pitched our tent, stumbling in the fierce wind, and crashed directly to bed, too tired to eat.

When I awoke at dawn, it was freezing cold, and my bedroll was damp. From inside the tent I could make out Adam next to the fire, a mug of hot tea in his hand. I waited for the sun to pierce the clouds before I could face the temperature.

The view was staggering. As the mist slowly lifted, we could see Kilimanjaro perfectly silhouetted against the sky and make out the snowy streaks on its top. Below us, soft and full like women's breasts, the round hills rolled and gently sloped down into the vast plain, like a sea of green. It was like sitting on the very top of the world.

"*The Green Hills of Africa*. That's it!" I said. "This is where Hemingway got the title, right?"

"Except he never saw them from up here, for sure," Adam said. "Nobody has ever enjoyed this view before, I can promise you."

He kept his eyes on the plain below, slowly sipping his tea, remote and exultant, like a child who has proved something which matters only to him.

But he was wrong. Someone had, and not long before us. Somebody not so interested in the view.

We had gone for a walk the next morning. Adam carried the shotgun because the place was swarming with buffaloes, and high-altitude lions were known to be nasty. We walked carefully and in silence. Suddenly the wind changed, and the smell hit us like a slap in the face.

"What is it? A lion's kill, you think?" I asked.

We walked slowly towards a patch of trees in the grassland. The stench became unbearable, I had to cover my nose with my shirt. As we drew near the trees we heard the buzzing. It was as if a million bees and flies were at work.

"Shit," Adam said, pushing a handkerchief over his mouth. "I think I know what this is."

Inside the thicket was a gigantic shape like a small mountain, some black thing twitching and throbbing as if it was still breathing.

Then I saw that the twitching was caused by a thick layer of maggots, worms, flies—millions of swarming insects—buzzing about the decomposed flesh of a carcass. It was a huge elephant.

The poachers had carved away the tusks and fled.

It looked like an eerie totem, something out of the worst *Lord of the Flies* nightmare. Something humans were not supposed to lay eyes upon.

My blood froze, and I was overwhelmed by an irrational fear—as if we had stumbled upon some terrible omen. I had to escape, and without uttering a word to Adam, I ran, clenching my fists, all the way back to camp, not worrying about the buffaloes or lions hiding in the grass.

Once at camp I warmed a bucket of water on the fire, then stripped naked in the grass and washed, pouring water on me out of a tin mug. It was still fairly early; the air was crisp and the green hills were imbued with a warm golden glow. A family of impalas across the valley stared frozen at my bush shower. But all I could think of was that throbbing black shape.

I was sitting in front of the fire with a cup of strong instant coffee, drying my hair, when Adam appeared at the top of the hill. He walked slowly, his shoulders slightly hunched.

"Don't run away like that," he said, putting the shotgun across the armrests of a safari chair. "It makes me nervous to lose track of you up here. Okay?"

He did look worried.

"The poachers must not be far," he said, scanning out with the binoculars. "They shot him with machine guns."

"Great," I said. "You mean it could be us alone with a bunch of crazy poachers armed with AK47s?"

He didn't answer.

"You mean we could be *raided?*"

He didn't answer that either.

"We must go down and report this to the KWS people," he said.

"Let's go." I instinctively stood up.

"Wait. We can spend the night and go tomorrow morning—"

"No," I interrupted him. "I don't want to spend any more time up here close to that *thing*. I want to go. *Now*."

He sighed.

I was happy to take the responsibility for our defeat.

We broke camp and drove down into the plain to the nearest park gate, and told the Kenya Wildlife Service rangers how to find the elephant.

We sat in the car next to the gate, sipping hot Fantas. Adam had spread out one of his old maps over the dashboard and was absorbed in its mysterious symbols. A naked child stepped out of one of the tin sheds provided for the KWS staff. I heard him cry, desperately, as he stumbled into the blinding noon light.

"Let's go home," I said. "I want to sleep in my bed."

Adam looked startled.

"You really want to go back to *Nairobi?*"

I knew I was disappointing him. I didn't care. I had depleted all of my physical and mental energy.

"Yes, we could be there by six. We'll have a hot bath, have a pepper steak and red wine at the French restaurant at the race-course. Please. It sounds *so good*; say yes."

He sighed and looked out the windshield. The child was still crying, his skinny little body covered with red dust. Adam folded the map and slipped it into the glove compartment.

"All right. If that's what you want."

Then he reversed the car, a bit too fast, and headed towards the north.

I was relieved: it seemed plausible and simple that once back home we could shut out whatever had burdened us since he had come back. That disturbing sensation of ominousness, that indecipherable pain. Whatever that feeling meant, it would be easier to hide it within the four walls of our house than under that glare.

Looking back now I can see that it was probably that moment when we began to withdraw and to lie to each other. Ever since then we've chosen to keep our eyes shut tight, even though the poison started dripping—slowly, drop by drop—as we pretended to have quietly fallen asleep.

CHAPTER THREE

In beauty, may I walk
On the trail marked with pollen, may I walk
with grasshoppers about my feet, may I walk
with dew about my feet, may I walk
With beauty, may I walk
With beauty before me
with beauty behind me
with beauty above me
may I walk

ANONYMOUS, FROM THE NAVAJO

"Esmé? Hunter here," a voice said into the telephone. It was before eight; the ring had woken me up. An operator had asked for my name, giving it the most imaginative pronunciation, and put me on hold, switching to unnerving Muzak.

"Hunter?" My heart skipped a beat.

I had not heard from him again since that night at my house almost two months earlier; he had completely disappeared. Back to Rwanda, back to Somalia, back to Zaire. Back to wherever the bad news was.

"Yes, Hunter Reed," he said, formal as if we were back to being just vague aquaintances. "Listen, I'm in Kinshasa now; I'll be in Nairobi tonight."

"Yes . . ." I said obediently.

"I was calling to see if you could give me a hand. Are you free tomorrow?"

"Tomorrow?" I tried to sound suspicious. "Um . . . yes, I think so. What do you need?"

"I have to run a story on this Italian missionary priest who lives in the slums. I'm told his English is not fluent, so I thought maybe you could, you know, give me a hand with that."

"Translate? Yes, of course. No problem."

"Great."

There was a pause. Obviously he wasn't in a loquacious mood. So I hastily tried to reach a conclusion.

"Okay then, how shall we . . . I mean, what's the plan, then?"

"Come to my place tomorrow. You know where it is?"

"No."

"Colobus Lane? Second driveway on the left. There's a little sign which says Wilkinson—that's me; I never bothered to change it. Eight o'clock too early?" He really sounded like a journalist now. On the case, and no time for bullshit.

I tried to sound just as efficient.

"Not at all. Wilkinson. See you at eight tomorrow."

"Great. See you tomorrow."

"Ciao," I said, and immediately regretted it.

"A *job* with Hunter Reed?" Adam was shaving, getting ready to go to his office in town. He turned around, surprised. "What *kind* of a job?"

"Oh, just translating. He has to interview this Italian missionary who doesn't speak English."

"You mean he's *paying* you to do it?"

"Paying? Well . . . no . . . I don't think so, he didn't mention anything like that."

"Oh, okay." He went back to his reflection in the mirror, lifting his chin. "Then it sounds more like a favour to me."

"Yes, I guess you're right."

I paused; then, as if to find an excuse for my enthusiasm:

"But I think it should be interesting. No?"

I watched him as he ran tapwater over the blade.

I love to watch men shave. There is something so attractive about the sequence of perfectly identical movements in which they all engage with lather and razor. The way they tilt their heads, looking sideways, how they splash their faces and sigh with satisfaction. How fresh and good they smell afterwards.

"It should be interesting to meet this man," I insisted, since I wasn't getting enough of a response. "He lives in the slums. Extraordinary, don't you think?"

"Yeah," Adam said, unimpressed, wiping his face with a towel. "Those missionaries can be pretty amazing guys."

He walked briskly past me and into the bedroom, opening the closet to choose a clean shirt.

"You know, I was wondering if you could go to the industrial area today and pick up those paints I need for the car and the pickup. Wilson has the list."

"Yes, no problem," I said meekly.

The honest-to-God truth being that what *actually* sounded interesting to me was to spend a whole day in the company of Hunter Reed.

Lonely men live like wolves.

Their houses are only a place to come back to at night, to collapse on the forever-unmade bed and lose consciousness. There's nothing for them to do inside those rooms during the day: there's never any food in the fridge, not even fresh milk for a cup of coffee; no comfortable sofa, no soft light filtering through a lampshade, no wood for fire.

Only the smell of stale food and unwashed socks.

The bathroom is bare: a tiny piece of cheap soap yellowing on the sink; an old toothbrush, its bristles spread open; a half-empty bottle of shampoo. What else would a man need to get clean? The stark emptiness of their houses haunts them at times. It's not clear how, in which way, but things around them could be arranged differently in order to produce some comfort. They know what it should feel like—they see it all the time in other people's houses. The smell of fire, meat sizzling in the oven, soft music in the background, children running around before going to bed. One can feel the entire household breathe, exude warmth. It's just a matter—they sometimes think—of filling up the fridge, replacing the lightbulb, changing the sheets.

And in fact every once in a while they attempt to recreate the same warmth they have seen elsewhere and which they secretly long to obtain by fulfilling these small tasks, but the result is always cold, almost inert, as if it had no life of its own. None of the objects gently blend with the others to generate that same secret harmony, not the lampshade with the pillow, nor the books with the shelf, nor the carpet with the floor. Not even the milk with the coffee. Each molecule of these separate bodies obstinately stiffens and rejects the others. Nothing mates or remotely suggests the idea of an internal rhythm, of a spark of life.

It's only a matter of days before the dirty clothes pile up again on the floor, along with muddy boots, empty glasses and overflowing ashtrays. It will feel cold and uncomfortable as ever. Everything will have either been flung, thrown or crushed, as if nothing, absolutely nothing, deserved any care.

This was how Hunter's place looked to me the first time I saw it. The empty den of a wolf.

There I was, at eight o'clock sharp, taking mental notes like a diligent detective checking out what this place could further disclose about him.

Its barrenness didn't scare me away; actually it looked familiar. I recognized the same distrust Ferdinando had in the seduction of comfort and the same excitement for what lured him out into the streets.

But I was now beginning to recognize a pattern in Hunter Reed's behaviour—which I not only found puzzling but was starting to resent: he seemed to have obliterated what had occurred between us in our previous encounters. Each time I saw him he acted as if he were meeting me for the first time. He showed absolutely no recollection of our earlier exchanges.

I wasn't expecting a declaration of love, but after all, not so long ago we had spent what I considered an incredibly emotional few hours together. He had unloaded on me some heartbreaking, harrowing tales, while I had been sobbing in his arms. He had fallen asleep on my sofa holding me close to his chest and had left me what I would call a rather intense note. That's pretty intimate stuff, at least in my book.

Yet to my astonishment, as he walked towards me offering me a cup of lukewarm Nescafé; none of that memory seemed to transpire in the way he acknowledged my presence.

"Ready to go?" he said with the same affection a cameraman would show a new assistant.

"Ready." I promptly put down the coffee I had just received from his hand.

He took a thorough look at my outfit, a soft flowery dress which I had painstakingly selected in front of the mirror while Adam was still asleep. I'd done my best to look sexy without giving away that intention.

"I should have warned you to wear something less . . ."

"Less what?" I asked defensively.

"Well, less *stylish*."

"Oh, it doesn't matter," I brushed the hem of my very expensive Belgian designer dress. "This is just a rag, really."

"We're going to the city's main garbage dump. I mean, it's *seriously* disgusting."

"Oh. I thought we were going to the *slums*," I said, as if "slum" meant somewhere posh.

"That's where the slum is. Right on the edge of the garbage dump," he specified with a hint of impatience. "We're both going to smell pretty bad, let me tell you."

"Okay, then lend me a pair of jeans and a shirt," I said, shaking off my docility and using a more resolute tone. I was tired of acting so lame in his presence.

"And a belt, too," I added forcefully, lighting a cigarette and shuffling my feet.

Fifteen minutes later I was sitting beside him in the car looking like a plumber in my oversize outfit. But I liked being inside his clothes: it felt intimate and naughty.

"So what have you been up to?" I asked casually, like someone politely starting a conversation.

"Oh, you don't want to know."

"No, I *do* want to know."

"I was in Rwanda, most of the time. Watching more bodies rot and more hacks lose their sanity. That's why the paper agreed to let me come back for a few days and do this slightly more optimistic story in Nairobi. They have to give us a break every now and then or we'll stop functioning. You tell me what you've been up to; I'd rather listen to that.

I could feel that this time he really didn't want to talk about it and was keeping himself at a safe emotional distance from me. I felt disappointed, like I had lost ground. But I tried to overcome his aloofness by telling him about my safari with Adam, how we had had to physically rebuild part of the tracks which had been washed out long ago. I longed to grab his attention by making my life sound interesting and adventurous.

"We camped in sites where nobody's been for a very very long time, it was incredible. From the top of the mountain you could spot a campfire a hundred kilometres away. And seeing it made quite a difference. Suddenly you know you are not alone."

"Amazing," he said, shaking his head with a smile.

"Yes, *so* amazing." I was eager to get to the dead elephant bit; I thought that might impress him.

"I mean that it's amazing how for the majority of people here, *whites,* I mean," he stressed. "The whole point of living in this country is to avoid the sight of other human beings."

"How so?"

"If we could press a button and pulverize the humans who happen to spoil the view, we'd happily press it. That's the whole point of going on safari, isn't it? Not to meet a single soul."

"Well, yes," I admitted cautiously. "I guess that's part of the reason why one goes through that much trouble. In order to find areas which are really remote and . . ."

"Not even a Masai herdsman, God forbid. I bet you *hate* it, in fact, when Masai show up at your camp with their cattle. Overgrazing the land and destroying the bush. Right?"

He was referring to Adam. I could feel it in his voice.

"Which is a fantastic paradox, if you think about it, since this country happens to be one of the fastest-growing in the world. Kenya has one of the highest birthrates; and in fact what this country is *really* about is not wildlife, but overpopulation."

"Yes, but—"

"But everyone," he interrupted, "absolutely *everyone* writes about and celebrates and describes East Africa as this virgin paradise, this Garden of Eden. Every bookstore in the first world is inundated with pretty books on Kenya, tales of man and wilderness and shit like that. I guess nobody bothers to read the figures or to take a look at places like the one where we're going now."

I hadn't read the figures, nor had I ever been to the slums before, so I had no argument, as usual. That was how Hunter Reed had always made me feel: pushed against the wall, with nothing to fight back with.

"I guess you're right," I admitted, to negotiate some breathing space. "On the other hand, that's why Kenya sells well over the counter in the West."

"Sure. But what amazes me is the people who *live* here. Nobody, but *nobody* here gives a fuck about Africans, let me tell you." He shook his head and patted his pocket in search of a Rooster. He lit it and went on lecturing me.

"After all, the only reason why white people came to live here, apart from making money off the land and the cheap African labour, is the scenery and the wild animals. And today still all they're concerned about is how to preserve the bush and the wildlife. You've heard them: at every dinner party in this town someone complains that where their father used to go hunting in the good old days it has turned into endless *shamba*s. They go berserk if anyone dares to plant a potato to feed their family. I mean, how on earth do we expect these people to *eat?*"

I wished I had never mentioned my safari in the wilderness and the dim fire in the distance. I wished I had never chosen to wear that silly dress and I wished I had read something to counter his argument about overpopulation versus wildlife in East Africa.

"I don't know," was all I could say, surrendering.

I already felt tired, and we had barely gotten started. I leaned back in my seat and looked at him as he kept his eyes on the road. His profile reminded me of those heads you see on Roman coins. A young consul. I had to close my eyes. Why was Hunter

Reed always *such* hard work?

Father Marco, the Italian missionary priest, was waiting for us outside the church in Kariobangi, on the outskirts of town. He was a good-looking man in his early fifties, small and muscular, with the energic gait most Italian mountaineers have. Deep blue eyes sunk in a bony face, round glasses, flowing grey beard and long hair. He wore a faded T-shirt and chinos and carried a small rucksack on his back which gave him an odd, schoolboy-like air.

"Marco," he said, extending his hand and gazing at me from behind his lenses with the shy look of a man not used to women. Still, he looked nothing like a priest. Rather like an aging hippie. His fingernails were filthy, as were his feet. He smelled, too.

His English was basic but rather fluent, so it turned out that I didn't need to translate much. Marco had lived in East Africa for the past twenty-five years and spoke fluent Swahili.

"That's all one needs to speak if one wants to be close to the people here," he said with a shrug. "And to say Mass in their language, of course.

The slum, Korokocho, started just beyond the church of Kariobangi, and stretched all the way to the garbage dump, a mountain of toxic waste and poisonous fumes. Marco said it would be safer to drive there than to walk, even though it was a short distance from the church. As he stepped into the car, he added shyly:

"Better lock the doors." He smiled. "One never knows."

"Why?" I asked.

"Not many cars come into Korokocho. Not many whites," he said, as if apologising for even naming the risk that might be involved. As we slowly drove into the slum on the main road, my feet went cold. I felt every stare and every gaze registering white skin. We drove in silence, negotiating our right-of-way with the people who clogged the road. The faces inspecting our car were not the same faces one would see in downtown Nairobi. These said "What are you doing in this neighborhood? How much do you have in your wallet?" As we advanced I felt further and further distant from what I thought I knew about the city. This place felt totally different, hostile, out of control.

Someone, as we slowed down over a pothole, banged on the hood. Suddenly we were surrounded by a mob. Faces and hands pushing on the windows, grins and sneers, blows on the sides of the car. Neither Hunter nor I flinched. I was paralysed, drenched in cold sweat. Marco kept still, as if nothing special was happening, until someone in the crowd recognized him and waved. We were free again. I held my breath until we reached Marco's place. When we finally got out of the car my legs felt weak.

Marco lived in a shed made of *mabati* and plywood, like the rest of the shantytown. It overlooked the valley which had become the city's garbage dump. There was no electricity or running water; open sewers ran all around. The air was filled with acrid fumes drifting from the perpetually burning garbage heaps. Children in filthy rags, skinny women in tattered clothes gathered around to see the *wazungu* who had come to see the Father. Everything looked sad, as if someone had painted a grey film over the bright colours of Africa. Inside the shed there was only a small cot, kitchen utensils hanging from nails on the walls, a couple of pots and pans, books piled on the floor and on top of the only table. Marco's few clothes hung on the back of the door. He pulled out a folding chair for Hunter; he sat on a low stool and I sat on the edge of the bed.

Hunter took out his cigarettes and offered him one.

"No thank you," said Marco, putting a hand on his chest. "I had to stop when I came to live here. You know, the fumes . . . we all suffer from lung infections."

He had a terrible cough, like the children who had sneaked in and were now giggling in the dark. And the women outside. All of Korokocho were coughing into each other's faces the most disgusting viruses from the burning waste.

Marco had been living in this shack for five years. He had decided to leave the mission in the rural area near Mount Meru and come to share the life of the real poor.

"Because you see," he said politely in his thick Italian accent, "this is the future, this unfortunately is what Africa is going to look like in a few years. Not the village life, not the witch doctor, or the cattle grazing. Urbanization is the big problem we have to face. All these people come to the big city, expecting to find a job, to get rich. But there is no job, there is no money. Not even to go back to the village. So they end up staying here because they have nowhere to go. And here they lose their identity, their tribal ties. They become scavengers. There is more need of God here than in the villages. There is more need of God in places where there is less hope, right?"

I nodded. He had a radiant smile.

"So men become criminals, women become prostitutes. Most of them have AIDS. This is what is going to happen to all of them." He pointed out, towards the dump which filled the valley. "When they have no money at all they turn to the garbage. They go hunting for food there and compete with the vultures. That's the lowest stage. Otherwise they pick up scrap metal, or paper which can be recycled, and I help them sell it. We have a small cooperative, as you know."

Hunter was jotting down notes. He wanted to hear about the cooperative, how much it made, how many people it managed to feed. The figures were still very low.

"But it will get better," said Marco. "The people are only beginning to understand what it means to work for the community, to join forces. You see, these people have all been traumatized; as I said, they have lost all sense of identity. These children," he pointed at the ragged kids giggling in the dark room, "they never had a family. How can you instill principles— not only religious principles, but basic ethical principles—when there is so much damage, so much trauma?"

We sat in silence, not knowing how to answer.

Marco stood up.

"Come, you have to see where we work to understand what I mean."

We followed him outside and down the filthy alleys which led to the valley. The fumes from the mountain of burning garbage thickened the air; grey ash burned my eyes. Drenching my clothes, insinuating itself into my throat and lungs, was the sticky smell of death and putrefaction. We waded down into the steep slope of garbage, our feet deep in the filth. The marabou storks flew low, clapping their heavy wings, and gathered in groups on the heaps of waste.

In the distance, like figures out of Dante's Inferno, one could see men crouched under the weight of huge sacks, moving against the smoke. They were the garbage collectors.

We stood still, looking at one of the men who slowly moved towards us. He recognized Marco and they exchanged a few words. The man raised his head from under the heavy load, and we saw his eyes. He had the crazed stare of someone who has gone beyond any reasonable experience and will never come back.

"When you spend the whole day amid filth and waste, it's very difficult to retain your dignity," said Marco as the man went off, bent nearly horizontal under the weight. "At the moment these people are outcasts, the lowest of the low. But you know, they can make their way back up the ladder. Garbage collecting can become a way to earn decent money. It's a dirty job to collect scrap metal, but it's a beginning."

We walked slowly back to his shack. Hunter asked Marco how long he planned to stay on in Korokocho.

"As long as I hold out. My lungs are very bad. And as long as they let me stay here. The government is not very happy about what I'm doing. They send informers to church when I say Mass. They claim I incite revolt in the ghetto."

"Do you?" asked Hunter jokingly.

"Of course not. I am just trying to explain basic political principles to these people. Like, for instance, that the government has to allot us the shacks we live in. We are squatting on government land, you see. They keep threatening to evict us. Now, even in the favelas in Brasil, or in Soweto, people own their shacks. Nairobi is the only place in the world where—"

"Oh, then you *are* inciting the ghetto!" Hunter interrupted him and laughed. "They are bloody well right to want to get rid of you!"

Marco smiled, amused.

"Do you speak good Swahili?"

"Good enough," said Hunter. "Why?"

"Then come to Mass on Sunday and listen to my sermon. We'll discuss the eviction problem."

"Sounds more like a party cell committee than a religious gathering to me."

"Yes. Except I act on behalf of the Party of God." Marco grinned.

We shook hands, and promised to come back. Hunter said he'd send him a copy of his article. Marco kept my hand in his and smiled.

"*Torna presto, e comportati bene. Ci vuole coraggio, sai, per capire.*"

"*Lo so. Grazie davvero.*"

We got back into the car and drove out of Korokocho in silence, anxiously checking the expression of every black face which bent down to peep inside the window, holding our breaths until we reached the church and the roundabout; and suddenly there we were again, reemerging on the familiar roads of Nairobi, at a petrol station where the black attendant smiled courteously as he held out his hand for the car keys. Back in the world of Memsahab and Bwana.

"What did he say to you in Italian?" Hunter asked me.

"He said 'behave.' And then he said one needs to be brave to acknowledge it all."

Hunter fell silent for a while. Then he shook his head.

"Africa is the one place which makes you want to believe in God. I guess it's the only way to accept this amount of despair." He turned to me with a faint smile. "But unfortunately no member of the Western press is allowed to fear God's wrath. It would undermine our ability to lie."

I smelled my clothes, my hair. The sickly sweet smell of putrefaction had glued itself onto me and was making me nauseous.

"Let's go to your house and take a shower," I said. "I have to get rid of these clothes fast."

"It's not an easy smell to get rid of, I warned you. I've got used to it by now. All of Rwanda smells like this, ten times stronger."

The rotting victims of the Hutu madness, the rotting carcass of the elephant, the rotting mountain of waste and desperation. The same smell of death, the same buzzing of flies.

"Why did you take me along today?" I heard myself ask aggressively. "He spoke fluent English; you didn't need my help."

Suddenly I was angry. Why had he dragged me into such hopelessness? Writing stories was his job, he was rewarded for it. But, what was in it for me, other than a slap in the face? And why me, of all people?

"Because I wanted to see you again," he answered, keeping his eyes on the traffic light, perfectly cool, almost annoyed by my petulance. As if that was the obvious and only answer.

"You could have asked me out to lunch instead," I said, trying to sound unimpressed by his revelation. Trying to keep to my point while my heart had started skipping beats again. "I mean, you could have said—"

"I didn't want to *say* anything," he interrupted, still not looking at me. "I just wanted to *see* you. And I also wanted you to see Korokocho. I thought you ought to."

"Why?"

"What do you mean, *why?* Because you live here. Because of what Marco just said to you: it takes guts not to *avoid* it. Maybe I think you have the guts it takes."

"Sounds more like you want to share all this pain with someone else."

"Yes. Maybe that too."

He shrugged, as if I was beginning to make him impatient. He pulled his hair behind his ear. It looked so thick and lustrous, I felt like touching it.

"It doesn't make much difference *why.*" Then he looked at his watch. "Listen, I really need some lunch, how about you?"

"I . . . I . . ."

"If I don't eat I won't be able to think," he said grumpily, keeping his eyes on the road. Then glanced at me, a worried expression on his face. His eyes were a dark grey.

"Christ. You are *much* more beautiful than I remembered."

Hunter said the paper would pay for lunch and we agreed we needed a treat. We sat across from each other at a table on the perfectly manicured lawn of the Safari Park Hotel, enveloped by the sound of the waterfall trickling down the rocks of the Japanese garden. All around us the reassuring presence of waiters in starched uniforms, and tourists in their childish fluorescent outfits, snapping pictures of each other eating hamburgers. Neither of us commented on the contrast, only five miles away from Korokocho; it was too obvious. We ordered lavishly. The waiter kept at a distance while taking the order. I saw him whisper something to one of his colleagues. They looked at us.

"I bet he just told him we smell," I said.

Hunter didn't answer. I feared his mood might change again and he would snap out of what he had started in the car. Which instead was all I wanted to know. Had he really been thinking of me, as he had written in his note? Or was he just saying things at random, throwing out these astonishing lines merely to catch me off guard? Was there a thread, an organizing principle, a reason for him to act like that? What was his volatile behaviour supposed to mean? Was he shy, or was he playing a game with me?

He was looking around with an absent gaze, not paying any attention to me. I had to resort to cliché.

"What are you thinking about?"

I wanted to shake him and pull him out of whatever distant place he was sinking back into.

"It's funny, what you said earlier in the car," he replied. "About my wanting to *share my pain* with someone. That's probably a very appropriate way of putting it. I think I have always felt very lonely in the way I perceive this country."

"Why is that?"

"Because I have always been in a very different position than anyone else; I never really fit anywhere. There was never anyone who shared my situation, and in retrospect I think I found that very unfair. Especially when I was younger."

"Why do you say you were in a different position?"

"It's a long story."

"Tell it."

I was eager to hear him disclose something about himself, stop behaving like this undecipherable mystery.

He lit a cigarette and leaned back on the chair, fixing his grey eyes on mine. He started telling his tale in the patient tone one would use with a child.

"When we went to live in South Africa, I was about ten, my mother and father split up. My mother had fallen in love with another man. Back in the sixties that was bad enough, but what my mother did was even worse. Because the man she had fallen in love with was black. And if *that* was not enough, not only was he black, but he was a militant activist in Black Consciousness, Steve's Biko's party, which saw all whites as their enemies without exception. So you see, my mother did the worst thing a white woman could have done back then and there."

"Oh. How did you feel about that?"

I had to fake my look of surprise. I didn't want him to know that I had gathered this information earlier on.

"My brothers and I were told only much later. At the time of the separation we didn't put two and two together. We knew she saw lots of Africans; it was part of her job. She worked for BBC radio—both my parents were working for the press and had always been extremely liberal. But in those days of course in South Africa it was illegal for a black man to have sex with a white woman, they could have gone to prison if they had been found out, so they had to keep it very secret. Even from us. The odd thing was that he had to keep it secret from his people as well. It was totally against Biko's beliefs that a black man would have anything to do with a white woman. To them whites were all equally bad, no matter how liberal they professed to be. A lot of white liberals called Biko's party black racists. So in a way they both turned into social outcasts by falling in love with each other."

"But how did you feel when you did find out?" I insisted.

"In a way I had always known. It was one of those things we just never talked about. Then one day Simon, the man she was in love with, was arrested. My mother lost it, she thought she'd never see him alive again. So she told me. I guess she needed some moral support, and felt that I was mature enough to give it to her."

"Were you?"

Hunter remained silent, pondering my question. Then he nodded.

"Yes, I think I was. It made me sad to see her like that. Rejected by her own people, rejected by his people, left only with a young boy like me to turn to. But it wasn't easy. I remember the secret police coming to the house with search warrants, raking through my mother's papers. By then my younger brothers and I knew exactly what was going on; we always feared they would put her in jail. We hated the secret police. We knew they were after us as well now. Our life changed overnight. Our white neighbours looked at us with contempt. We started receiving anonymous calls in the middle of the night, then threatening letters. So in a way I think I resented my mother for jeopardizing our life. Ultimately when you are a kid you want to be like everyone else, have the same life as your classmates. You didn't want to be the child of this mad woman in love who believed in the revolution, especially if you lived in Johannesburg. Everywhere we turned there was this incredible hatred. The whites hated the blacks, and hated my mother as well; the blacks hated my mother and hated Simon. We all suffered, in the name of *love*. It was ironic, really. So I grew up with such mixed feelings of guilt and hostility, of love and fear, all intertwined."

"What about your father? Where was he when all this was going on?"

"My father eventually remarried in England. He always respected my mother very much and has always spoken very highly of her. You see, at the time when they went to live in South Africa they were very young and idealistic. I think my father especially, he was in love with the black resistance, with the ideals of freedom and justice . . ."

He smiled, with a mocking expression, and took a sip of his cold beer.

"He loved the idea of being a white liberal democrat truly in love with Africans. It made him feel like such a hero."

"And what about your mother? Didn't she also—"

He interrupted me in that manner he had, almost as if my physical presence were insensible to him, as if by now the logical sequence of his narration had become more important to him than my listening.

"But in fact what had happened was that my mother completely outdid him: she *physically* loved an African. She actually *fucked* one."

He stretched out the word, as if he needed to emphasise the outlandishness of her act. As if he needed to make it sound obscene, unpleasant to hear. I sat frozen by his intensity, while the waiter delicately placed our avocado and shrimp salad in front of us. Hunter continued, unaware of the food.

"It was no longer a cause, it had become an individual, you see. That's much more concrete, such a *reality* to contend with. She had trespassed a boundary where my father could no longer reach her. I think he knew he couldn't win her back. So he left, defeated. I gather he realised my mother had a strength he would never have. To really commit herself, not just to play a role which looked good back home."

"And to face the consequences as well," I added sotto voce, to let him know I was getting the point, that he hadn't shocked me.

"You bet. I mean, I always admired her for that. She went ahead and did it, nobody could have stopped her. Not apartheid, not her own children. She was possessed.

I could tell he wanted to sound magnanimous. As a matter of principle, yes, he admired her. As her child, it must have been tough.

"And what happened to her and Simon?"

"Eventually Simon was released from jail, but it was obvious that they were not going to leave him alone ever again. That he, like all his comrades, would be imprisoned and tortured numberless times. That was the fate of all those black militants. Plus, Biko had been killed. So my mother finally persuaded him to leave with her for England. She managed to make him leave South Africa. I think he has always wondered whether that was the right thing to do. To leave his country, his brothers, to be forever in exile. For this white woman."

I remained silent. There was so little I could say. The more Hunter revealed himself to me, the more terrified I was of him. He seemed to come from a world where everything had been drawn in extremes.

I tried to eat, but the food stuck in my throat. Hunter looked at me as if he didn't know me, as if I had turned into some stranger overhearing his conversation on a train. He kept talking as if to an imaginary friend.

"Now they are this middle-aged couple living in the country in England. They go to Johannesburg every now and then, and whenever they go they have tea with Mandela and stuff like that. They are treated like celebrities." He chuckled. "Romeo and Juliet woken up from sleep thirty years later. They make very good press for South Africa, now."

He smiled wistfully and looked into his plate. He decided after all it was time for the avocado salad.

"Would they go back, now?" I asked.

"No. What for? They have a perfectly organized life in England. They both find Jo'burg way too dangerous. If you saw them at the local supermarket on a Saturday morning, pushing their cart, you'd never know these two are the same people. It's funny what age does; it dilutes everything."

"I guess one becomes tired of fighting. And it would seem they've had their share."

"Yes, I think they're tired. One can change sides in politics, one can change one's husband or wife, one's country or religion, but one can't change *race*. Class struggle, Buddhism, socialism, Catholicism—nothing has been invented to solve *that* problem. All one can do is get as far away as possible from its source."

He looked up from his food at me with a strange vacancy, as if he had just woken up.

"Aren't you hungry?" he said gently, glancing at my full plate.

He looked wonderful to me then, his long black hair falling over his quicksilver eyes.

And I was in love with him. One, two, three. Just like that.

"No . . . yes . . . I was listening to you so I forgot to eat."

"Do you want me to shut up so you can eat?"

I felt the tenderness in his voice. Yes, he could be tender and warm, not only terrifying and drastic. And I wanted desperately to feel more of that tenderness, to draw it out of him, and I prayed he wouldn't withhold it from me. I wanted to find the warmth and tenderness deep inside him. I needed to be certain it was there, now that I had reached that frightening place where the winds meet—admitting to myself I was crazy about him at last—and I knew there was no turning back.

"No. Please talk to me. I'm much more interested in you than in the food. I couldn't *bear* it if you were silent," I said impulsively.

The intensity of my voice startled him. He pushed away his plate.

"As a matter of fact, I'm not hungry anymore either."

There was a pause. Then he said:

"Shall we go?"

"Yes. Let's."

So we left, silently. And we drove to his house in silence, as if quietness had descended upon us like snow, to cool and shroud the ground, to disguise our tension and muffle our thoughts.

I didn't go there lightly. I knew even then that this was the beginning of something very hard to reverse. But I couldn't do otherwise: I too was possessed.

At his place we took long showers by turn. I scrubbed myself under the hot water, but the smell still clung to my hair and skin. It no longer bothered me. Instead, the sight of my naked body under the shower worried me, because I knew that in a matter of minutes, maybe, he was going to look at it and touch it.

I entered the living room with my hair dripping wet on my dress. He was sitting at his desk, his hair wet and ebony black. The house was wrapped in silence.

I sat across the desk from him. We studied each other for a minute or so. Then he raised his hand and lightly touched my cheekbone with his fingertip. Slowly his hand went over the planes of my face.

"What are you going to do now?" he asked.

"What do you want me to do?"

"You *know* what I would like you to do."

I didn't stir. I closed my eyes and felt him move away from me. He wouldn't push me, he obviously wanted me to be fully aware of what I was getting myself into. I hated his taking his hand from me.

"Why are you like this?" I said, almost angry again.

"Like what?"

"Always closing up, like a snail in its shell. One minute I feel you so close, it's incredible, and the next you look like you're dying to get rid of me."

"The only thing I have been dying to do is make love to you," he said quickly, matter-of-factly.

I almost couldn't bear to hear him say the words. He never seemed afraid of what he said. Unlike me, enervated by my own waiting and postponing. The time had come for me to give in.

"Then do."

It kills me to think of that afternoon. As if it couldn't possibly have been me, the same person I am now.

Now that I am left without a trace of it, with no claim to it, it seems incredible that once—not long ago—I felt so much love and passion coming from Hunter.

We were so greedy for each other that first time. As we held and touched and kissed and felt each other's body, it seemed impossible that we had waited so long, that we'd managed to sleep and eat, and talk and laugh with other people, and yet repressed that desire. I knew instantly that from now on that desire would be impossible to ignore.

I kissed him again and again: how foreign he was, what a stranger, once his face was that close to me. His lean body had surprised me: it spoke the language of small imperfections, it had the uniqueness of flaws. I was stunned by its newness.

Yet there was no barrier between us after we had made love: it had crumbled forever and I could touch him at last without fear. So I pressed my fingers to his eyes, his nose, his lips, his neck, like a blind person. I needed to memorise him, to make him intelligible, to make him familiar. I needed to imprint him in my hands, as completely as possible. I ached already at the thought of having to leave him.

We made love, desperately, intensely, always looking at each other. But we kept silent, never pronouncing the dangerous words lovers whisper in the dark. Words which bind you and smash everything that existed before, words which lift you and thrash you into the waves where any minute you can drown.

If the first time I made love to Adam I felt like I had finally reached somewhere—had *come home* into his arms—as soon as Hunter touched me I felt forever ripped apart from where I thought I belonged. He tore me away from all that preexisted, even from the simple concept of time. I saw from the start that from now on there would be only waiting, nostalgia for his potential absence, endless days filled with longing.

I had fallen out of my secure world, precipitated beyond the territories I had only begun to control so skillfully. What a foolish step to take. What an insane move to make.

"You are so beautiful," Hunter whispered, his hand sliding over my hip, slowly discovering me, taking me in. There was none of that fear in him. He was fullfilled, content.

I remained mute, drugged by his physical presence, unable to speak. I watched his body relax, until he fell asleep next to me. I hated seeing him slip into another world, so far away from me, while I was cast into this new darkness, which I knew nothing about. I felt jealous of his ability to dream, to breathe like a child. Angry—furious—to see him sink into sleep and drift so far away.

We will never be together. The phrase flashed through my mind as I watched him sleep. It hurt to admit it—we would never, not even when we're closest, not even when we were making love.

But, maybe the recognition of that painful truth was what lured and tempted me. One had to learn to live without illusion. No one ever became one with another. There *was no* coming home. There were no roots, no tree to hold on to.

One had to learn to love without feeling safe and secured to the ground, to accept being cast into the darkness, where no one knew what it was going to be like, at that dangerous place where the winds meet.

CHAPTER FOUR

When lovely woman stoops to folly and
Paces about her room again, alone,
She smoothes her hair with automatic hand,
And puts a record on the gramophone.

T.S. ELIOT

The shadows are lengthening under the trees; it must be getting late.

I must have slept: I know I have dreamt again. My sleep is filled with such rage, I actually need to wake up in order to give my mind a rest.

I walk around the empty house, smelling the sticky scent of my own sleep, as the wood boards creak softly under my bare feet.

Wilson must have gone for his nap in the "servants' quarters". Don't you hate the expression? How ludicrous, how Doctor-Livingstone-I-presume.

After all, it's the weekend, and nothing is expected to happen. It does feel like a Sunday Bloody Sunday. Same suicidal instinct. Except here one can't even look at the paper and choose a good movie. Or buy good drugs and veg out zapping channels. Or see a show at the National Museum, go skating, go out for pizza. Or just walk down the streets of a city mingling with the more-suicidal-than-you weekend crowd, or disguise your anguish in the subway.

Here, in a place where people have "servants' quarters" on their compounds, the alienation of a lone human being is not even contemplated. Here you are supposed to be a family, a unit, an association of some sort. Everyone is a pioneer here, and pioneers have no time for existential brooding. How I hate the ferociously optimistic attitude of the white tribe of East Africa, their idiotic pragmatism, their absolute lack of self-deprecation! How I wish I could call up Ferdinando and have a chat with him instead. Wouldn't he have loved to hear how nauseated and unhappy I felt on this weekend below the equator! He would have laughed at my little-house-on-the-prairie, my blind faith in the healing power of nature, my attraction to the primal. He would have found it so utterly naive. So *girlish*.

Instead I get into my car and go to see Nicole, the only person I can bear to show myself to. Another single woman in Africa. One of my kind.

She's on the verandah, cleaning her brushes, wearing only a tattered old Indonesian sarong wrapped around her tiny waist and a very short pale green jersey. There's tea and cake on the table. I can't help thinking that Nicole's afternoon looks far more acceptable than mine.

I envy her ability to spend so much time on her own. I think that's possible only if you have a passion like the one she has. A goal, I should say, something through which she'll always be able to feel fullfilled and self-realised without the need of others. I've never had that: my kind of passions, if anything, have only managed to make me feel lonelier and totally useless.

A big, unfinished portrait of a girl sits on the easel. It looks strangely hyperrealistic, as if it has been painted from a photograph.

"Who's that?" I ask.

"Do you hate it?"

"No, I don't *hate* it. But it's not my favourite."

She sighs and looks at it, biting her lower lip.

"Oh, it's so hideous, I can't bear to look at it. You know, I have had a commission to paint the whole De Vere dynasty. This terribly rich family who lives in a ranch near Nanyuki. This is one of the daughters." She makes a face. *"Edwina."*

"I've heard of them."

"The mother is loaded, I mean *loaded,* an American. She married De Vere in the sixties when William Holden was here and it was very Hollywood to live in Kenya."

"How many portraits did they commission?"

"Five so far. Mother, father and three daughters."

She falls into a chair and lights a cigarette.

"Edwina, Imogen and *Venetia.* How ludicrous is that?" She sighs and shakes her head. "But they're paying me a fortune."

"So, what's the problem?"

"They want to look good. Royal. They want me to paint them exactly the way they aspire to look. Like these gorgeous blond princesses. I have the mother on the phone every day, directing me long-distance. If she lived here she would be on my verandah personally mixing the colours. She thinks I'm the family's *makeup* artist. It's unbelievable."

She imitates a slow nasal drawl:

"Darling, please be careful with Venetia's nose, it gets kinda puffy around her nostrils, see if you can do something about it. She speaks of her own daughters like a vet speaks of *horses."*

"Would you like some tea?"

"No thank you, I'm fine."

I look again at the portrait. It's dull, empty. It says nothing. So different than Nicole's other paintings.

She pulls out a small square canvas from a pile leaning against the wall. It's a painting of a very thin girl sitting cross-legged on a Turkish carpet. She wears a sleeveless dress in black and orange stripes, against a bright apple-green background. Her hair is pulled back, revealing her long neck. On the carpet there is a small plate with a cigarette burning. The thin bluish smoke is the only moving element in the stillness of the painting. The girl looks morbid, mysterious, almost frightening.

"This is Imogen," says Nicole. "Or at least, this is how I painted her."

"Oh yes! This *is* beautiful!"

"The mother *loathed* it and sent it back in a flash. She had a fit when she saw it." Nicole giggles. "I nearly lost the job because of poor Imogen."

"She looks like one of those skinny prostitutes in Vienna, you know, more like an Egon Schiele model, rather than an heiress in Nanyuki."

"Absolutely. But that's exactly the point! Imogen is *completely* fucked up. She is on smack, has a very decadent Indian boyfriend, but she told me she actually likes girls. She's beautiful, much more interesting than the other two, but she is *suicidal*. I promise you."

Nicole looks at the painting and smiles.

"It's very good, isn't it? I really like it. Look at those thin arms. The arms of a junkie, so white, frail, so abused."

She places it on top of her work table, leaning it against the wall so that we can both see it better.

"Can you believe that the mother now wants me to repaint her, wearing jodhpurs and a denim shirt, with a view of acacias in the background? She even decides *wardrobe* now. Some people's arrogance is amazing: they actually assume reality can be painted over to match their will, just because they have money to pay for it."

We are silent. The sun has disappeared behind the Ngongs, it will be dark very soon. I can sense someone inside the house placing logs in the fireplace.

"Come," says Nicole, "let's sit inside and have a drink."

Her house is small and cosy, smelling of wood wax and incense. She goes to mix two vodka tonics by her drinks tray.

"You know, Esmé," She has her back to me now. "After Iris died I decided I was going to start doing portraits of white people who lived here. But my idea was . . ."

She hands me the drink and crouches on the sofa, shivering.

". . . my idea was that I was going to paint only people who had been hurt. Whites who had been bruised or wounded. You know how everyone here is always getting cut, slashed or hit? People are either crashing their cars, getting into motorcycle accidents, knifed by bandits, trampled by wild animals. My concept was, white people in Africa constantly get physically hurt.

Does this make any sense to you?

"Yes, of course it does, completely. Wounded whites."

"What this idiotic woman doesn't understand when she calls me up screaming that I should make her daughters more beautiful, is that the only real possible beauty in Africa is the beauty of destruction. Any other beauty here is false, petit bourgeois, frumpy. A white man's lie."

We fall silent, watching the fire.

"You should go back to Europe, Nicole," I say.

She stiffens. I know she hates to hear this.

"You're so wasted here."

"I'm not good enough for Europe."

"Yes you are."

"Well, even if I was, there are too many good painters there, I would have to join such a long queue." She shakes the ice in her drink impatiently. "I'm too spoiled."

"But what's the point of working like this? Nobody wants to hear about "the beauty of destruction" here. They want to hang portraits over the mantelpiece and pretend they live in castles. You'll become the court painter of Kenya ranchers."

Nicole laughs.

"Court painter of Kenya ranchers, my God! That really sounds final and hopeless."

Immediately I regret what I've just said. Who am I to preach what Nicole should do? Have I showed any more guts, done any relevant work, produced *anything* that contributed to something, since I've been here? Not really. Whereas Nicole has always been on her own, earning her living, she has never been helped by a man. She's been much braver than I have.

"What have you done to Miles?" Nicole asks, changing subject and showing no resentment for my aggressive behaviour. She's so good, that way. "He came around earlier and said you'd been throwing coffee mugs and chairs at him."

"I did. I hope you didn't give him the cooler."

"Actually I did. Was I not supposed to?"

"He was going to take Claire and that American photographer for sundowners on the Ngongs. He was keen on showing off his safari skills and serving chilled drinks on the mountain."

Nicole raises an eyebrow. I can tell Miles still has the power to annoy her.

"I mean, frankly . . . what a dickhead. He didn't say what he needed it for."

She stares for a second into her glass, then shakes her head and forces a bitter laugh.

"Sunset on the Ngongs! I've heard *that* line before. Don't tell me he wants to seduce Linda now."

"Of course he does. He would seduce Claire as well, only he can't."

"Oh *please*, what is this? Happy Valley? White Mischief? Does anyone *ever* give up instant sexual gratification in this country? Really," she giggles, "I should have thrown *more* chairs at him, *plus* the teapot."

The phone rings and she jumps up to get it. I shuffle through her CD collection and play an old Van Morrison song which reminds me of Hunter, just to check how unbearable it is to hear it again. I'm flooded by nostalgia. Thank God Nicole comes back and immediately lowers the volume. She looks elated.

"That was Kevin."

"Kevin who?"

"Kevin Steinberg."

I look at her blankly. She tries again, impatient:

"The screenwriter you met last night at Nena's."

"Oh God, yes. Unbearable."

"Don't be so fussy, Esmé." Nicole smiles mischievously. "I rather liked him."

"Really?"

It still amazes me the way people in this town keep popping up in different combinations, like reshuffled cards.

"Yes, I think he's sexy, and I love his wit. I'm *mad* about it," she adds.

Kevin Steinberg reappears as the King of Hearts.

"Anyway," Nicole says with a shrug, "he's taking us out for dinner tonight."

"What do you mean, *us*?"

"I told him you were here and he said great, I'd love to see her, she's so interesting, so smart. He obviously didn't realise you found him unbearable, so please try to be charming. Unfortunately, he said he wants to eat African food."

"African? But *where*?"

"God knows. It's maddening when people come to town and want to go native. It's like going to New York and begging people to take you to Harlem. There's nothing good to eat in an African restaurant except for chips and goat stew. But one doesn't want to sound so African-unfriendly with an American, does one? He may think we are hideous right-wing colonialists."

"So what? Do we have to go to some *nyama choma* place on Dagoretti Road?"

"Let's, so that we don't contradict him. He probably doesn't eat meat and will be easily persuaded to take us somewhere else on his platinum card."

"Let's hope so. I'd love some Thai food."

"What an excellent idea! I better get ready, then." Nicole runs into the bathroom and lets the water run into the tub.

How I wish I could feel that light again, could be interested in new people. How I miss getting ready for an evening with a sense of expectation, flinging open the closet door, feeling that the outcome of the evening depends on the dress I wear. Now it seems impossible that this will ever happen again. That I will ever care to wear one dress rather than another.

Nicole reappears three songs later, perfectly groomed and made up, wearing the sleeveless orange-and-black-striped dress of Imogen's painting. She must have lent it to her for the sitting. It's so Nicole, in fact, something one would never dare to pick up in a flea market, but which looks perfect on her.

"I should warn you that Kevin is taking us out because he wants to do a little research work," she says, pinning up her hair in front of a mirror.

"Does he *ever* stop researching, I wonder."

"He's just come across Iris's books, and now he's terribly excited. In fact he called me to ask if I happened to know her. He thinks she would make a terrific story for Hollywood."

"Oh God, Nicole, I really don't think we should be doing this."

"Relax, okay? Let's hear what he has in mind, first. Plus, if he wants to do it he'll go ahead and do it, the books and the photos are out in the shops, it's not as if we can keep him away from it."

"I really don't feel like discussing Iris as an Hollywood script, and I can't believe you—"

"Esmé, you've become more sanctimonious and moralistic than Hunter Reed ever was. Just shut up, put on some lipstick and be quiet, will you?"

I obey without uttering a sound. I don't know anymore what I should be thinking. I feel like I have lost the plot.

As I'm putting one of Nicole's darkest lipsticks, I hear her voice behind me. I can feel her eyes dancing.

"Iris as a Hollywood script. She worked *all her life* at it, it was such a perfectly rehearsed screenplay. Finally this successful writer comes along, happens to see a book of hers at the hotel shop, reads it and dreams of turning her into the Karen Blixen of the year two thousand, and *you don't want to help?* She's probably cursing you from Heaven, my dear."

CHAPTER FIVE

I wanted everything for a little while.
Why shouldn't I?
I wanted to know what it was like.

EVERYTHING BUT THE GIRL

Yes, everyone does try to have a go at history here.

Maybe it's because we live so far away from the action, and the only payoff is to sell our lives as monuments back in the first world to make our time here worthwhile.

Even though wilderness as such no longer exists anywhere in the world—save maybe for the Arctic—our prestige depends on the assumption that *this* is the last outpost of wilderness and we are the last batch of Romantic Heroes. Most of us have built our careers around this assumption, and now entire families depend on it.

Yes it's true, cheetahs in the Masai Mara have changed their hunting habits: now they stalk their prey in the heat of the day, when the tourist vans are back at the lodges for lunch and they can be left in peace, without hordes of paparazzi following them. Large areas in Tsavo and Amboseli have been so seriously scarred by the cars' tracks that they have had to be shut down in order to heal. Masai and Samburu cattle herds have died because their only reliable water hole in the dry season now fills up the swimming pools of the lodges in the parks where they are no longer allowed to graze. Many Morans go as far as the coast to find a job to survive. They will be employed as watchmen in the cheap packaged-tours hotels; soon they will end up escorting older women from Frankfurt or Milano and will learn to wear designer jeans and mirrored shades.

I had discovered that a lot of people in Nairobi were suspicious of Hunter because he seemed obsessed with shattering the precious assumption that we lived in Paradise and showed pleasure in doing so. He always knew facts and figures, so that it was hard work to contradict him, unless of course you were in the field. He had become a prophet of doom, and not everyone liked having him spoil their view of the future.

"Why doesn't he go back to South Africa, then?" Peter the Elephant Man had once said. "He's a political animal, he has a passion for humanity on a *War and Peace* scale. Marine turtles and rhinos to him are simply not worth the effort."

Now my heart sank whenever anyone pronounced his name.

He hadn't called me after the day we had spent together. At first I had been relieved, because I was terrified of what had happened. That day I had gone home to find Adam smiling and cheerful, ready to have a drink with me by the fire. Instead I had zoomed past him, muttering something about the squalor and hopelessness of the slum, as an excuse for my aloofness and lack of concentration. I desperately needed a bath before anything else, I said. I wanted to be alone in order to go over what had just happened and pull myself together. I lay in the tub for an hour, praying that this new lunacy would dissipate with the steam.

But it did not.

Soon Hunter's silence started to oppress me. As I had foreseen, I stopped having a life of my own and began a life of waiting. I found the wildest excuses to stay home as much as possible in the vain hope the phone would ring, I would check my mailbox obsessively, grill Wilson on whether anybody had left a message while I was out. I couldn't stop thinking of Hunter: he had invaded me, his day had become my day. I kept trying to guess where he could be and what he could be doing, as if I had a parallel watch on my wrist. I knew he was still in town, I kept track of his moves via Miles or Nicole, but I knew he wouldn't be much longer. Rwanda was about to swallow him back.

What his silence meant, I told myself, was either that I was the one supposed to make the next move or that I had simply vanished from his brain again. I couldn't decide which hypothesis terrified me more.

One morning I saw his car parked outside the Horseman's Restaurant. The thought that he was *there,* just behind the gate and the ferns, gave me a rush and I broke into a cold sweat like an ex-junkie who has spotted his old drug dealer.

I've got to see him now, just to talk to him, nothing more, I told myself.

I walked up the path lined by lush plants along the small pond and stepped under the thatched roof of the open restaurant. It was early, and almost all the tables were empty. My heart sank when I spotted Hunter sitting across from a woman who had her back to me. As usual, he was totally absorbed in a conversation, gesticulating animatedly. I couldn't make out who the woman was, but before I could turn and run, he saw me and called me over.

His date turned out to be a fifty-year-old German reporter, an old acquaintance. They both insisted I join them. The woman seemed friendly and pleasant.

"Ulla," he explained to me, "is writing a story on the Goldenberg scandal."

"Really?" I tried to feign interest, not having the faintest idea what the Goldenberg scandal was. About which, needless to say, Hunter had the minutest details. I sat back with a frozen smile and pretended to follow their conversation.

I had no will of my own, no desire except to intercept his movements across the table and try to get in his way, to steal an opportunity to touch his knee, brush his hand, smell his hair as we were passing each other lighter, cigarettes, menus. I could only concentrate on keeping the level of our sexual tension charged by constantly feeding it with my body language. Nodding like a moron whenever Ulla made a significant comment or he said anything I gathered was seeking approval.

By the end of the meal I was furious with myself; I'd never known I had this in me. The sight of my own passivity—animal subjugation, almost—frightened me. I'd never thought I could become so naked and exposed, so oblivious, as if nothing else mattered, nothing and nobody. All I could feel, all I *had become,* was this pulsating sexual energy—carnal, raw—which had taken control of me to the point that I had to get away from it, physically. I literally needed to walk up the wooden staircase which led to the washroom and look at myself in the mirror.

"Stop this. You are *pathetic,*" I commanded my own reflection.

I walked downstairs again determined to regain control of myself. Hunter meanwhile seemed perfectly relaxed, not in the least emotionally altered to see me. Why did I have to fight these titanic battles completely on my own whenever I was around him?

The whole thing was hopeless, and I was behaving like a neurotic. *This needs to stop right now,* I ordered myself. What I hated most about the situation was his adamant concentration on the Goldenberg case, as if nothing was more important to him than proving his theory about who was most corrupted and who had made more money at the expense of whom, for Ulla's article.

I was starting to loathe his self-righteousness. He would say the same things, with the same fervent passion, to anybody who came along, just to hear himself being outraged or passionate about an issue. Only a few days earlier he had talked to me with the same intensity about his childhood, his mother and father, had made me feel like he'd chosen me because I had something *special.* And there he was, his hands flying, looking at Ulla like he'd never had an object in his life other than the Goldenberg scandal. Suddenly I found myself detesting everything about him—his furiously bitten fingernails, the way he held his cigarette in the corner of his mouth, even the colour of his shirt. I'd been right from the beginning: there was a priggish narcissism about him that one didn't really want to put up with.

I looked at my watch.

"Hunter . . . I think I'd better get going—"

"No, wait," he said in a flash, and his hand landed on my wrist like a handcuff. "We'll go together in a minute; just let me give Ulla these contacts."

As he scribbled phone numbers of people who would spill more beans on the Goldenberg scandal, he firmly locked my ankle between his feet under the table.

All my hatred instantly melted like mist in the sun. I sat back, watching him hand his notes to Ulla, a besotted grin on my face.

He wanted me. He wasn't going to let me go.

And then and there I was back to being the happiest woman in all of Karen.

Later, at his house, after we had made love again, he said:

"I missed you, I kept dreaming of you."

"I missed you too."

"I was hoping you would come here. I waited for you."

"Did you?"

"Of course."

"I was afraid of coming back."

"Afraid of what?"

"Oh. Well," I stared at him. "You know . . ."

We said nothing more. There was very little either of us could say, after that. Neither of us wanted to get into the details that revealed the pettiness of our situation. Neither of us wanted to face what the situation demanded. But I knew it had to be me; I was the one who was living with another man. I was the one who had to lie and deceive. And it was up to me to say what I was prepared to do.

But I didn't want to say anything, yet. I wasn't prepared to say that what we were doing was wrong and had to stop right away, nor that it was what I most wanted and that I couldn't live another day without it.

Instead I turned to him and kissed him slowly. I felt the warmth of his body. I slid my fingers inside his shirt and caressed his lean flanks. I lied to myself, thinking that if I could make love to him just one more time, I would go home fullfilled and satisfied.

I knew I had trespassed into the illicit, but the junkie in me said, You can get off the stuff whenever you like. Just take another hit now, and you won't think about it again. You'll be fine, you won't get hooked on just one more hit.

The junkie in me is such a devious liar. By the time I was back in my car I knew I was hopelessly intoxicated. Yet I realised that I could survive the addiction only if I pretended it was just *physical*. I couldn't let it slip into falling in love.

Thus, equipped with all these custom-made lies, tailored to fit what my situation required, I believed I had managed to get on top of the situation once again. I went home, proud and elated, as if I had just learnt a really good trick.

CHAPTER SIX

Why, what could she have done, being what she is?
Was there another Troy for her to burn?

W. B. YEATS

Cassandra lay asleep in the temple.

Apollo appeared and offered her the gift of prophecy, in exchange for lying with him. She accepted at first but then went back on the bargain. Apollo begged her for at least one kiss, and as she agreed he spat in her mouth as revenge, so that nobody would ever believe her prophecies or go near her. Nobody likes the company of a doomsayer. I've always sympathized with Cassandra. Especially since I've been spat in the mouth by Hunter.

So let's see. I'm going over and over the story looking for at least one redeeming factor hidden in its folds. Maybe my storytelling is a bit like sifting river sand hoping to find at least a handful of gold.

But so far all I've managed to see is how we have reached the point where the paradise is decaying faster than our decadent minds.

We, who thought Africa was going to turn us into better human beings, more wholesome and in tune with our instincts, seem to have instead progressively showed our basest nature. But in fact I am convinced that we who live here end up looking more ruthless, narcissistic and deceitful only because this place has fewer distractions and diversions, and very little available camouflage. So Africa only turns out to be a higher observation point, where it's possible to cast a wider glance at human nature.

I knew exactly what had happened: I had so much time to think and brood. The analysis of why I was so desperately attracted to Hunter and so incapable of leaving Adam had become my favourite pasttime.

Yes, each name contains a destiny, and only now I see how Hunter stalked me from the very beginning, as if he could smell the Ferdinando genes in me. He knew right away I was an escapee, a renegade from the coldness of intellectual control seeking refuge in a purely sensual life. He picked me out of a crowd and said, Stop disguising yourself, I know where you come from, *you are not one of them*. As he said that I likewise recognized the familiar traits of my own tribe in him. And I followed.

Ironically, between Adam and me it had worked the other way round. It had been the distance I felt from him which had made me trust him. I knew that even if I showed myself naked to Adam, he wouldn't be able to really make me out. Such a deep understanding wasn't necessary, because our attraction was founded on a completely different principle: it sprang from instinct, an animal chemistry. But then I had failed in the logical consequence of that principle: I had failed to be an alpha woman and have his child.

So I was instantly flattered by Hunter's recognition—for whatever reason, he wanted me because of my mind, he wasn't remotely interested in the breeder in me—but I knew that once I'd shown myself naked in front of him he'd decipher me to the minutest particle. And that scared me.

Therefore I quickly had to learn how to lie, not only to Adam but to myself, pretending that all we wanted was quick sex and soon we'd have had our fill of it. I escaped to see Hunter whenever I could, while Adam would dash out of the house every morning before eight smelling of shaving cream, leaving yet another scribbled list of provisions to buy for the camp and things which needed fixing.

This is what lovers do in the stillness after they have made love.

They say *I love this bit of you.*

Which?

The nape of your neck.

And I love this, right here.

Why?

Because it's so soft, so vulnerable.

What else?

Your shoulders. I'll never forget when I saw your bare shoulders for the first time.

What is it about them?

Hunter touches the roundness of the muscle, then the hollow over the armpit. I feel his finger trace the line of my collarbone.

I don't understand what he means, don't care. He is kissing my bones, laughing. I never want it to end.

"I want to take this away with me," he says, cupping my shoulder in the palm of his hand.

"What a boring part of my body to take on a trip."

"You have no imagination. There is much more to anatomy than you think. Let me show you."

As I drive home in the dusk I hold you in my head: the image of your eyes—such a strange shade of grey—as you look into mine while making love. I never thought it would be possible to fix a single image in one's mind for so long. The sound of your voice as you whisper:

"You. You."

You don't even dare pronounce my name.

This is what I go home with almost every day now.

219

For the first couple of weeks I had felt almost brave in being able to lie to Adam. I found it easier to feel cold rather than ashamed. But it didn't last.

The mornings were the most difficult. That's when Hunter would come back to me most vividly, in fragments still tangled up in my dreams. It was like reemerging from under water, enveloped in his scent, specks of him still sticking to my skin like weeds. It was so hard to extricate myself from it, and that's when I felt most vulnerable under Adam's gaze.

"Why don't you move to the camp for the season?" he asked me one morning out of the blue as we were having breakfast.

"What? For the *whole* season?" His question took me completely by surprise. I could feel myself blushing. His eyes were inspecting me, testing.

"Yes. You could help me manage the camp."

"I wouldn't . . . I mean I don't think I would be able to, really. I'm so useless at keeping accounts and stuff like that."

"Come on, Esmé, you'd just have to play hostess with the clients at dinner, make a bit of conversation. You wouldn't have to keep the books or manage any of the business. You'd be great." His voice held an insistence which worried me.

"Would I? I'm not so sure," I said feebly.

He poured himself some coffee and stirred it a while too long. I felt tension creeping up my spine.

"It's a real job. I mean, the company would have to pay you for it," he said without lifting his eyes from the cup.

"*Come on,* it's not a matter of paying me. It's—"

"Otherwise we'll be apart too much of the time," he finally admitted. And he looked at me with an open stare which meant much more than he was prepared to admit.

I started inspecting my fingernails, pretending to be evaluating the offer. I knew that Adam was asking me to leave town, to leave whatever was keeping me away from him.

"It's so beautiful up there now, so green and lush, full of game—"

I *knew* it would be beautiful. But I wasn't interested in the beauty anymore. I had entered a different realm, where that beauty would have driven me insane.

"I don't know," I said. "I'd like to think about it. It's a bit of a commitment."

He looked at me and suddenly I felt he knew everything. He must know, I thought, how could he *not*?

"Yes it is," he said. "It is a commitment."

East Africa could be the worst place on the planet to have a secret affair. No out-of-the-way restaurants, no movie theatres, no romantic hotels or cosy cafés where they wouldn't know you or your lover.

So Hunter and I didn't attempt to hide, but simply pretended to have become really good friends, which allowed us to be often seen together having lunch or hanging out without raising particular suspicions. That we had become so close didn't surprise anybody.

"You two," Nena once said to me, "are both so *cerebral*."

"What do you mean?" I said, alarmed at the mere fact that she had thought of us as a pair.

"Well, you know, Hunter has always complained there was never anyone around he could talk to. I think he loves your company, the way you two always exchange opinions, how you can go on and on about *ideas* for hours. It's so rare here."

"Come on, you have opinions about things too. You read a lot."

"Only cosmetic labels, lately." She shrugged. "Anything else feels like too much effort."

It was amazing how nobody saw the obvious. Which was that we were made for each other. That it wouldn't have been possible for us *not* to be lovers. At the time I couldn't see it clearly myself. Probably, like every other junkie, I was in denial.

Meanwhile Hunter came back from Rwanda each time more distraught. As time went on I could feel that he was about to break down. It was as if something inside him had slowly given way, and now was bent beyond repair.

Those afternoons after we had made love, he always started to talk in that particular way of his, almost to himself. We were on his bed; he was lying sideways, resting his head on his arm, as I was slowly getting dressed and ready to go.

"The incredible thing is that while you are there, witnessing the horror, you persuade yourself that as soon as you file what you have just seen the whole world will come to a halt, and everyone will jump on a plane and come to help to stop the slaughter."

He looked away from me, as if he didn't want to see me getting ready to go.

"But instead nobody gives a damn. Nobody is even willing to call it a genocide."

He got up and quickly crossed the room stark naked. He wrapped a *kikoy* around his waist and sat at his desk, his back to me, and started to roll a joint.

"It's so fucking hopeless. People wrap up their china with my articles, and eighty percent of the foreign-news-page readers still don't know which one is which. You know," he faked an American accent, "who are the bad guys, the Hutus or the Tutsi? Can't get these African names straight."

I sat on the edge of the bed, suddenly feeling desolate.

"You must feel I'm so far away from it all."

I could see him lick the edge of the rolling paper. But he still didn't look at me.

"You are. But not in the way you think."

The room fell silent.

When he spoke again his voice had softened:

"Actually I'm lying. We never think of the readers when we're there."

He lit the joint and turned to me, waving away the thick smoke.

"We go to those places, right? Miles, Ruben, Bernard, me. We see those things. It's not even for the excitement or the danger, why we want to go."

"What is it, then?"

"I don't know. Isn't it weird?" He shook his head with a vague smile. "t's like . . . we all have this *secret*."

"I don't understand."

He took a deep drag and passed me the joint. Then he looked away from me again.

"I think at heart we put ourselves in those places because we are lonely."

"Lonely?"

"Yes. I think that's what the secret is: we go because we live other people's wars, we're involved in other people's pain. We can forget about our own, that way."

We smoked in silence. I wanted to say something, but I couldn't. I just sat there feeling impotent. And guilty, because of my impotence.

I looked at my watch. It was getting late. I stood up to go.

I walked up to his chair and we stared at each other without saying anything. I remember thinking, *Me too, I am your loneliness, you want to forget about me as well, don't you?*

But I couldn't make myself say it.

He touched my shirt, lightly. And slowly undid the buttons one by one, keeping his eyes fixed on me.

"Hunter . . . I really need to go," I whispered, imploringly.

My shirt slipped lightly onto the floor.

"No." He slid his fingertips on my naked shoulders. "I really need to make love to you. Now."

I knew he resented the way I always had a watch to obey.

But I resented with equal passion the way he disappeared from one minute to the next, just like that. How he never said he was going to miss me. Or when he would be back. Maybe we both secretly wished one of us would get rid of the other so we wouldn't have to feel any more of that anger.

"Why is it that everybody around me always has more important things to do than brood and pine like me?" I asked Nicole.

We were having cappuccino in the French Café in a brand-new shopping mall in Westlands. Housewives' paradise: the best butcher in Nairobi, the German bakery and a health food store all under one roof.

"Because you should start doing something meaningful with your life, you fool," she said. "Having an affair is not what I call an occupation."

"I know. And it takes up all of my energy, besides."

I had told her everything about me and Hunter and she had begged me to be careful. She didn't want anyone to get too hurt.

"Then I guess I should accept the job at the camp and work with Adam, shouldn't I?" I said gloomily. "I really can't go on like this, it's too demeaning."

"I don't know about the camp," said Nicole hesitantly. "Can you see yourself putting up with the clients and all that?"

"No. I would do it only because I feel guilty." I sighed. "In fact I'd much rather do something on my own, completely apart from any man I'm involved with."

"I agree. That would make much more sense."

Nicole blew on her hot cappuccino, lost in her own thoughts. Sometimes I feared that my nonsense might be starting to get on her nerves. But she wasn't like that.

"There's this postproduction company in town, Right Track it's called," she said. "They do news for KTN, all sort of freelance work, some advertising. I know they're looking for somebody to manage the place. You should go talk to them. I think you could get a pretty good salary. Jason Winters, this filmmaker who moved here from London, he works with them sometimes. A seriously bad city boy, for a change."

"Sounds like fun," I said, trying to sound excited.

But the conversation had sunk me into a dark mood again. I nibbled at a piece of croissant and put it down.

I was quiet a moment too long. She suddenly broke the silence.

"What are you going to do?" she asked me. "You can't keep this up much longer."

"I'm going to have to stop it. It's hideous having to lie to Adam."

"But why don't you tell him the truth? You're not married, you don't have children. I mean, nobody's marriage is going to—"

"No," I interrupted her vehemently. "You don't understand. I *love* Adam. Between Hunter and me it's only this . . . this . . ." I struggled for the word. "Mad attraction. I could never have a life with him."

"But why?"

"Because he'll hurt me," I said without thinking. And wished I could take it back.

"What do you mean he'll *hurt* you?" Nicole shook her head. "Good God, Esmé, sometimes you are twisted!"

"No, it's just that . . . oh I don't know how to explain this." I sighed, and looked through the glass door of the Uchumi Supermarket, at the people on line for the cashier.

"Hunter somehow . . . he scares me. He does something to me, I don't know what it is, I think he did it to Iris as well. He makes me feel like I'm drowning. Like we could never be happy."

Nicole raised an eyebrow.

"I think you're being unfair to him."

"Why?"

"He may hurt you only if he can't *have* you. And you'll do the same to him."

"Great," I said impatiently. "Then we've been locked in the wrong position right from the start and we'll never get it right again. It's too late now."

I hadn't met Jason Winters yet; he'd moved to Kenya only two months earlier, on a whim. A true Londoner, a pure Notting Hill Gate swinger, he'd given up his status of struggling director in the video clip industry in England to become the trendiest director Kenya ever saw. He tied his bright red hair in a long ponytail, wore only Agnès B linen shirts and jackets, outrageous Jean Paul Gautier suits, and red or emerald green cowboy boots. Every advertising agency in Nairobi wanted him.

Nicole asked him to meet us for lunch the next day at Leone's, an Italian deli in town. She reckoned he'd be the right person to help me get the job. Jason emerged from a silver 1960's

American car with tailfins and a complicated array of taillights, wearing shades and a black beret.

"Sorry I'm late, girls, but I went to sleep at six," he excused himself. "All-night editing."

He turned to Nicole with a conspiratorial grin.

"Thank God our friend Boniface has just been successfully shopping in Lagos."

The same coke dealer: that's how they had met, I figured.

Jason proceeded to order the most expensive white wine on the list, fussed until he obtained a sufficiently chilled bottle, and had us completely drunk by the time the antipasto arrived.

"You'll get the job no problem, Esmé," he said, picking a sun-dried tomato with the tip of his fork. "If anything, you're overqualified."

"To be honest with you, I've never worked in films in my life."

"That's not the point," he said, waving the tomato in midair and spraying oil onto my shirt. "You have style, which is what the film industry *always* needs."

When I did get the job with Right Track, thanks to his introduction, and told Jason I had no clue what postproduction really meant, he said:

"Who cares? You're not a technician. They pay you to run the place, to be the hostess, to make everyone feel a tingle of Hollywood."

Right Track Productions was a tiny studio on the tenth floor of a glass tower in town. Two rooms, neon lights and lino floor; the only concession to Hollywood a *Casablanca* poster. Their main feature was a brand-new Avid machine which was state-of-the-art equipment for Kenya, and drew a lot of customers: correspondents from foreign TV news desks, local advertising agencies and so forth. Sometimes the occasional journalist would pop in and cut some Rwanda or Sudan footage in a rush, sometimes it would be a *mzungu* director like Jason who had just shot a local ad for underarm deodorant or aspirin. I sat at the reception desk, took the bookings, chatted with clients, made sure things got done according to schedule, and soon even started learning how the equipment worked.

It was absurd. To live in Kenya and be shut up inside a dark room all day listening to the maddening sound of cereal jingles, or to the hypnotic sound of the president's official speech inaugurating a fertilizer factory.

I loved it when Jason booked the Avid for one of his silly ads. We would have eggs Benedict and Bloody Marys sent up from the Norfolk bar. Jason's continental charm made up for the job's lack of glamour, but above all he provided an escape from my extremely polarized life. He had no idea what was going on in the bush or in Rwanda, and didn't particularly care. It was refreshing to hang out with him. He had the flavour of London, film festivals, art galleries, seriously good restaurants, new books, European gossip. Whenever I spent any amount of time with him, Nairobi instantly became a very simple place to live.

Adam was about to leave for the camp with the first clients of the season. My decision to stay and pursue my new career in an office building rather than follow him to the freedom of the bush had puzzled him.

"People pay thousands of dollars to come on safari and escape from jobs like the one you just got," he said shaking his head.

"Exactly. I don't want my life to be like an expensive holiday."

"The camp is not a holiday. It's your *home*," he said, and then looked away, out the window.

A home? Was the camp my home too? The idea struck me as odd. I'd never thought of it that way, but somehow I knew it was a mistake to feel always so removed from him and never able to accept completely what he had to offer me.

"Adam."

He turned towards me. There was distance now in his eyes.

"Please don't misunderstand me," I said. "I need to do something which is entirely mine. It doesn't matter what it is; I just need to be proud of myself for having done something on my own here."

And as I said that I realised how true it was. My absurd job in town had not only released me from the feeling of dependency, but it had created a space—however small and insignificant—where I wasn't just passively surrendering to my emotions.

"I know," Adam said, forcing a smile. "It's just that I'll miss you and I'm being selfish about it."

"But I'll come and see you whenever I can," I said. "I'll miss you too, you know."

We kissed, as if to seal a newly made pact. But I moved away from him a bit too soon, and I think he noticed my slight impatience to get our parting over and done with, to go on with my life and my new arrangements without having to discuss them again.

I think that's when Adam sensed he had lost me. He didn't yet know to whom or to what, but he was aware of my withdrawal from him. He wouldn't force the issue, it wasn't like him to do that, and I knew it only too well. His inability to express himself with words worked to my advantage now.

I did visit him every weekend like a dutiful wife. I would get on a small six-seater every Friday afternoon and fly to the camp. The pilots were all friends with Adam so I hopped in as if on a bus and got a free forty-five-minute lift to the airstrip, where Adam or one of his drivers would be waiting for me.

I had it all worked out. By the time Friday came I was always ready to see Adam. Our time together was always perfect: I gave him all my attention, I was always in a perfect mood, my guilt was so strong that our sex life turned out to be revived by my betrayal. But the thing is that I did love him.

I loved him even more than before for having accepted my loss without making claims of any sort. Now I know that he was not just passively giving in, he was only waiting: he knew that only by being strong and patient could he eventually win me back. And now it is so clear to me how I too wanted him to succeed. Since I could no longer find my way back to him on my own, I needed him to be the one to break the spell. In fact we had been silent accomplices all along, both pretending that nothing was happening, that by saying nothing about it, the thing would simply go away as it had come.

Our obliteration of the truth had a psychological and financial payoff as well.

The clients at the camp invariably left saying how they envied our lifestyle. To them Adam and I were the incarnation of the perfect movie cast, a romantic, adventurous and good-looking couple. And to us they represented the perfect audience: always happy to pay the ticket price, invariably thrilled with the show, always asking about a sequel.

Nobody wants to see such a good story end.

CHAPTER SEVEN

Touch me,
touch the palm of your hand
to my body as I pass,
Be not afraid of my body.

WALT WHITMAN

I remember this.

A beautiful day in September, Sunday lunch at the Dawsons' farm on Lake Naivasha. Children running around on the lawn, grown-ups slowly getting drunk around the long table laid with hibiscus flowers.

Nena has put one in her hair and looks like a Spanish dancer.

I catch Hunter looking my way across the table. I'm wearing a sleeveless dress and Adam's hand rests for a few seconds on my shoulder as he smokes a cigarette after coffee. The bare shoulder Hunter once said he wanted to take away with him. The shoulder he loves to kiss.

His part of my body.

Feeling Hunter's eyes on me, I immediately have to stand up and walk away from the table. I move away with such unnecessary energy that my chair falls over.

"Sorry. Oh, sorry."

Adam picks it up and looks at me.

"Are you all right?"

"Yes. Just feel like moving."

These are the moments when the hideous pantomime is forced upon us. These are the moments when I realise how impossible it is not to hate it.

Heather Dawson had taken me and Nicole for a walk around the farm before lunch, had showed us the rare species of birds, the gazelle droppings, the resident giraffes. In Africa people don't show you their interior decoration; you don't have to sigh with admiration when your hostess flings the door open onto each new room and expects you to congratulate her on her colour combinations. Here your hosts show you animals.

My giraffes, *my* buffaloes. And we also have a *leopard.* He was here last night, came right to the doorstep. Come over here, see these tracks?

Oh God, isn't that wonderful.

When we came back from the walk Hunter was sitting around the table with the others. He had turned up unexpectedly.

"Hunter, what a marvellous surprise!" Heather Dawson hugged him. "This beautiful man no longer shows his face. He used to come around so often a few years back. You and Iris, remember?"

Everyone remembers Hunter and Iris. There is a history of them as a couple in this country.

The history of Hunter and Esmé on the other hand—already two months old—is still sealed inside a bedroom. Nobody will remember the two of us together, nobody will ever have seen us.

It felt so wrong, suddenly, that we should have this secret. That we should hide it from everybody. That it should stay underground and never see the light.

I suddenly felt like shouting *We are lovers, we are mad about each other, I make him very happy.*

Instead I kissed him chastely on the cheek.

"Hello Hunter, good to see you."

Hunter got rapidly drunk and unpleasant at lunch. He started a furious argument with Peter the Elephant Man on the subject of lifting the ban on hunting. Adam sat sphinxlike at the end of the table, keeping his eyes fixed on Hunter. He made it obvious he didn't want to be dragged into the conversation. He sensed that Hunter's rage was directed at him.

"Ranchers have been culling game anyway, so it's just a matter of calling it hunting and letting a client pull the trigger instead. At the moment they make about four thousand shillings per zebra once they sell the meat and the skin. If you had the same animal shot by a client you could make six, seven times as much."

"It would be the beginning of the end, you just have no idea," said Peter, irritated.

"It would be a way for the African landowners to finally make a buck from wildlife. It would give them a reason to look after it, instead. It's such hypocrisy."

He turned to me. Sneeringly.

"Come on, let's hear a woman's opinion on this."

I shrugged, feeling uneasy.

"I don't really have an opinion. I mean, I can see your point but . . ."

I sighed, as if begging him to leave me out of his rage.

"I don't think I know enough."

"It's all right. You don't need to have an opinion about *everything*" he said curtly. "I guess one doesn't have to take responsibility for every single issue."

"Good. Because I can't." My voice had hardened.

"Right."

He took a another swig from his glass and looked somewhere past my head.

"I wouldn't expect you to."

Later that afternoon I lay in the sun watching the children play with bows and arrows. I was exhausted by the constant sensation of Hunter's body around me, as if an internal radar kept measuring its distance from mine. I flattened my head in the grass, seeking refuge in the minute business of insects lulled by their laborious buzzing.

Peter's voice shook me.

"Like this, Toby, try to keep it straight, yes, that's it!"

He was showing little Toby how to string a bow. They were deeply absorbed in the experiment, crouching on the grass, their heads close together. I watched the two of them for a while. They looked so similar—same colours, same seriousness, like two children of very different sizes.

"There you go, Tobes! Excellent job!"

Toby ran to show the other children his new toy. Peter caught my glance and came to sit next to me on the lawn.

"Are you all right here all by yourself?" he asked.

"Yes. I was just enjoying the sun."

He stared at me.

"Are you sure?"

"Absolutely. Why?" I asked defensively.

"I don't know. You seemed a bit sad at the table."

"Oh . . . no . . . I was just feeling . . ." I suddenly blushed. "quiet, I guess.

His attention made me uneasy. Paranoia seized me. Could Nena have told him she suspected something was up between me and Hunter? Women usually could tell these things.

"Yes, I've noticed how you can be very quiet at times," he said in a friendly tone, lowering his voice.

Heather came running towards us.

"Come on, I'm taking a group photograph on the verandah, everyone get ready. We can't miss this light!"

We all stood obediently in the five-thirty light, like extras on a set, while Heather shuffled us into different positions.

"There, Peter, you take Natasha on your lap, like that. Adam, come over here, you sit down, yes, perfect. Esmé, come forward a bit, I can hardly see you. Gosh, you *are* gaunt, my dear! Don't smile, everybody, I want you to look serious, this is a Victorian portrait."

Hunter's shoulder touched mine. Then, as the camera

233

clicked, I felt his fingers pressing hard, angrily, low on my spine.

"Good. So now our duplicity is on record," I heard him whisper as we all moved away from the camera.

"Why do you hate me so?" I stormed into his house the next day.

"What are you talking about?" He was sitting at his desk, his index fingers flying across the keys of his laptop. He hardly raised his eyes to look at me.

"You were so hostile. It kills me."

"I would never have come if I'd known you'd be there with Adam."

"We can't really avoid it, can we? This is such a small place, we're bound to stumble into each other a lot."

"Still, it bothers me."

"You knew this would happen when we started."

"That's especially why it bothers me."

"Can you stop writing for a second?"

"Not really, I've got lots to do."

"Please."

He continued typing.

"All right then, I'll go," I said.

"Esmé."

"Yes?"

"Don't go. Come here. Sit down."

"Why are you like this?"

"Because I live here, because this is my home. And you're making it impossible for me to go anywhere without feeling *illegal.*"

"I think you have started to resent me."

"I do, sometimes."

It infuriated me to hear him say that. As if it was only my fault, and I had ruined his life.

"Let's stop seeing each other, then," I said. "This just isn't going anywhere."

"No. Nowhere at all."

There was a long silence.

I wonder now why we always made the whole thing sound so impossible. We seemed to enjoy the feeling of being stuck in a situation with no exit. It was like being prisoners and discovering that the jailer had drowned with the key. I guess we did it because we believed we'd passed the point where being rational was possible, and now all we could do was try to keep alive, no matter what it took. It felt like total liberation in a way, because there were no longer any rules.

"Come here," he said.

Once you eliminate all the rational possibilities of escape within your mind, all you are left to escape with is your body.

I closed my eyes as I felt my dress slip off. His hands caressing my spine. His mouth.

Only when we stopped talking could we get close again. We would find our way back into each other through the silent language of sex.

It was the language we invariably started to speak whenever we came to the end of our options.

What's the point of remembering? When something is lost forever, its memory only makes you feel lonelier.

Even though I had promised myself to avoid doing so, since Claire has arrived in Nairobi (only yesterday morning!), I haven't been able to resist the temptation to take every piece of the story out of its box and look at it once again.

Now I know why I wanted to go and pick her up.

I needed to make her real. I wanted to smell her skin and hair, to see what her mouth, her legs, her breasts were like. So that her realness would finally hit me like a blow and force me to bury everything for good.

So that I can finally have this little funeral.

Meanwhile, I'm faking it pretty well: Nicole, Kevin Steinberg and I have just had a delicious Thai dinner in Westlands

and I think I've managed to conceal my angst rather successfully. We've drunk a few tequilas at the Mayfair Casino bar,
watching rich Asians lose fortunes at blackjack and roulette,
and now we're having a few more at the bar of the Mud Club.
Tonight it's packed with Kenya cowboys and young Sikhs on ecstasy, drunken Hillcrest School girls, a few Rastas on ganja, all
dancing to techno music.

Over dinner Kevin has become progressively convinced that
Iris would make great Hollywood material.

"We need a contemporary heroine. Period movies are expensive, and then after *Out of Africa,* I mean, what do you do? Forget it. It's like trying to do another great film about the South
after *Gone With the Wind.* You can't beat *that.*"

Nicole and I nod sympathetically.

"Yes, that's the irony, isn't it?" Nicole says. "That whites in
this country should need another movie to feel *real* again."

Kevin laughs and looks at Nicole. It's obvious he's mad about
her. She must look so different to him than any other woman
he's met. So unconceivable that a girl like that should live here,
all alone in the middle of nowhere, in a country which doesn't
add up except as a movie set. She defeats him, and for a split
second I catch him looking at her in awe. Then he regains his
confidence.

"Only she can't possibly die in a car crash in the middle of
town. We need something a bit more epic than that. Another
round?"

We nod and he signals the bartender for more tequilas. I see
why Nicole finds him attractive. Thin lines around his eyes, salt-
and-pepper hair, well-exercised body, self-confidence and wit
oozing from him. But there's also a softness in him which I
didn't see last night at Nena's, busy hating everyone in sight and
feeling sorry for myself as I was.

"Don't forget the lemon, girls," Kevin warns.

We lick the salt and bite the lemon slice before tilting our
heads back and gulping the shot.

And all of a sudden I think *How incredible*: how much life is
actually going on outside of here, people, deals, ideas, conversa-

tions. My brain has become anorexic, it has shrunk into this tiny uninteresting thing. Wouldn't it be a dream to sit inside a dark movie theatre, take in someone else's vision and let it fill me up slowly till I was satiated and full to the brim with tears and emotions which would have—for once!—nothing to do with *me*? Wouldn't it be heaven to be inspired by someone else's intuitions rather than obsessed by someone else's *body*? The brutality of my mere sensual life has hardened me like arid soil.

"Look who's here," says Nicole, as we lean against the bar. Miles is dancing with Linda and Claire. We wave, nonchalantly.

Another card combination: Miles and the girls.

It's taken them only twenty-four hours to become this silly trio. We are always striking alliances of some sort, just in case we can profit from it. Us and the Hollywood Screenwriter, he and the Blonde Babes. Petty manoeuvres of a small small town.

"See," I point out to Kevin a series of bodies leaning against the walls or dancing in the dark. "That's Jason, the director I work with sometimes; that one in the red is my hairdresser, she cut my hair this morning; the African girl with the braids waxed my legs last week; and the man in the red turban talking to the girl in the green, that's Doctor Singh, my gynecologist. Between the four of them they could win a quiz game on the subject of my body surfaces."

"You can't get away much in this town, can you?" he says.

"No, we're stuck in this deadly proximity. Relentlessly mixing our juices. And that girl in black, Claire, the one dancing with Miles, you met her last night at Nena's, she's now sleeping with the man I'm madly in love with."

I'm so drunk now, I feel like I could say or do anything. I must look menacing and wild. But Kevin Steinberg is smiling at me. Slightly incredulous.

"So nice to hear the words."

"Which?"

"*Madly in love.*"

"Why?"

"Nobody says that anymore."

"*Madly.* I swear to God. So mad about him, it's absurd."

"Does he know?"

"Not really. It's too late now anyway. I totally blew it."

Kevin hands me another tequila and a pinch of salt. He shakes his head and looks over at Nicole, who's talking to Miles in a dark corner.

"You girls are lucky. You wouldn't be talking like this if you were at a party in London or New York. You probably wouldn't be mad about much there. I kind of envy that."

I follow Kevin's gaze in in Nicole's direction. We watch her as she gesticulates animatedly; it's an intense conversation she and Miles are having, and it looks pretty final.

"Take her home," I say to Kevin. "Don't wait around. Just tell her you're mad about her."

Kevin grins.

"I'd like to do that, actually."

"You should. She's the best." I take another swig. "Just go for it, will you?"

He looks at me defiantly and steps down from the bar stool, with the amused, concentrated expression of a child performing a task in a game. He moves swiftly through the crowd, crosses the dance floor and lands gracefully next to Nicole. He's smiling, and is feeling totally sure of himself. Miles looks up at this handsome older man, slightly annoyed by his intrusion. I watch Kevin as he gently taps Nicole's elbow and whispers something in her ear, I intercept the surprise on her face and the smile. They're off. It's taken only thirty seconds.

This is one of the many ways you can change your life.

If you want to.

Miles walks slowly over to me. He hops onto the stool beside me with a smile.

"I'm afraid you've lost your ride home tonight."

"I'll get another one."

"Shall I take you home?"

"No."

"Why?"

"You already have a car full of groupies."

"Esmé, listen. I know what you think."

"What do I think?"

"That I'm unsensitive, vain, hopelessly panting after every new girl just to satisfy my ego."

"Funny you should say that. It's exactly what I think."

Miles shakes his head and chuckles. I know I amuse him when I'm rude.

I catch a glimpse of Claire looking at me and Miles from across the dance floor. We stare at each other, perfectly still. I know she knows. And worst of all, I know she doesn't fear me.

Miles follows my stare and sighs.

"Listen, I hate to sound annoying, but I think I know why you are so upset."

I stiffen.

"It must be the best-kept secret in town, then," I say bitterly.

"Stop being so proud." He squeezes my arm. "I'm your friend, I do care about you, all right?"

"All right. Then get me a drink."

He bolts happily to the cashier. I keep my eyes on Claire as she goes back on the dance floor. I watch her step under the lights, like an actor on stage. Performing for me.

She has no sense of rhythm, she's too stiff, she doesn't let go. Funny to lose Hunter to such an uninteresting woman. But she has something I've always lacked, a blind determination which tells her to hold on to the raft and never let go. She's learned the lesson: Don't make a fuss when you find someone else's love letter inside a drawer, don't ask, never doubt. The less you flounder, the less likely you are to drown. Just hold on.

I didn't learn that lesson. I drowned a long time ago, my lungs full of water.

CHAPTER EIGHT

And I sing this
for the heart with no companion
for the soul without a king
for the prima ballerina who cannot dance to anything.

LEONARD COHEN

Then came Goma. Divine retribution.

Hunter had been there since day one and he hadn't come back yet.

The truth was I couldn't care less about the destiny of those people. I just wanted the whole Rwanda chapter to be over and done with so that I could spend a few days with him far away from all the bad news. I dreamt of escaping with him to the island of Lamu and waking up in a beautiful room overlooking the Indian Ocean. I dreamt of watching the dhow sails come back over the horizon at sunset, of making love to him without having to speak about war and death. I dreamt of being careless and selfish, like all lovers are.

I had these silly dreams. I just had no idea, of course.

Instead the swearing in of a new government in Kigali had pushed one million Hutu refugees into Goma, Zaire, in only thirty-six hours. After the genocide, now even the exodus of the killers had taken on a biblical scale, as if nothing about Rwanda could ever be less than apocalyptic. The human mass which had crashed into this dilapidated ex–French colony lacked every-

240

thing. The vegetation had vanished overnight because a million people needed firewood. There was no water, no food, no latrines, no clean water, no shelter. The cholera epidemic broke out almost immediately. After a week there were six hundred deaths a day and after two weeks three thousand.

Hunter was right: readers must have thought they definitely could never get these African names right when they saw the cover story on *Newsweek*. Weren't the Hutus the bad guys?

What on earth was happening? How could the killers have turned into victims overnight?

The press loved it. It was such an unexpected twist, like Kevin Steinberg's stroke of genius at a Hollywood meeting. Newspapers and TV reporters had a field day in the midst of this new carnage. And when the volcano which had been dormant until then suddenly awoke and started spitting lava and the sky turned orange, they thought, great, what next? The deluge? Nobody could have invented better headlines.

As far as I was concerned I loathed reading their reports and kept thinking of history as my personal calendar, always weighing the chances that if the Hutus stopped dying so fast Hunter might come back sooner and we would have at least one more afternoon together.

Then out of the blue he was gone.

One evening, I think it was in November, I had come home after work to find him sitting on the sofa, a beer in his hand. He had been waiting for me. His bags were on the floor, he looked utterly worn out as if he had come from very far.

"Hunter. When did you get in?"

"Just an hour ago. I came straight here from the airport. I've got very little time."

"You're going out again?" I could feel something was up.

"No. I'm *leaving*."

"Leaving what?"

"Africa. My job." He almost sniggered. *"You."*

I sat down across from him, my knees faint, my palms

sweaty.

"What do you mean—when? What's going on?"

"I resigned from the assignment. I just can't deal with Goma, I had to get out. So they're sending me to Afghanistan on Tuesday."

"*Afghanistan?*"

"Yes. They figured I could cope with that." He looked at me with a funny smile, like a child caught doing something wrong. "I'm flying to London tomorrow, and then out to Kabul."

"But *why?*"I felt a lump form in my throat. He couldn't go. Please. Not just like that.

"Because I will not write another word about the Hutu refugees. What's happening out there right now, all that fucking media craze, is plain disaster pornography. I won't contribute to it. These people on the first page of every newspaper are the ones who have perpetrated a genocide, they are not *these poor victims.*"

"Yes, but . . . what do you do, you want them all to die like that?"

'Listen, you haven't been there. You haven't seen them at work. I did. Now that the killing is over it seems like it's no longer the issue. Well, it is for me, and for a few others who were in Kigali three months back. I *hate* these people, I *don't* want them to be saved, I *don't* want to tell the world how they need to be fed. This is where I stop being a journalist, all right? I'm sick now, so sick of what I have seen, I have no pity left in me. I'm *tired.*"

"I know you are."

I took his hand and held it in mine.

"It's madness." It's like a nonstop cocktail party in that hotel: every night new reporters check in from all over the world, they all know each other, they're thrilled to meet again in Goma. In the dining room all you hear are glasses tinkling and corks popping. And let me tell you, you've never seen *any* of these guys in Rwanda before. Three months ago they were probably covering the Cannes Film Festival. So now they're all in seventh heaven, sexing up the story because Goma is easy, no risk of getting killed and you have Pulitzer-quality footage right outside your hotel door."

"But isn't it always like that? Why are you so outraged, as if you didn't know how the press worked . . ."

"Because with all their cameras and satellites they're twisting the facts in a way I will not contribute to. We didn't have any images of the killers in Kigali when they were clubbing people to death, we didn't have cameras rolling when they slaughtered thousands in the churches. We don't have the genocide on film, so in a way it's never been *real*. People believe things have actually happened only if they can watch them on television before supper. The dying Hutus are becoming the real Rwanda tragedy now, only because they are getting this incredible media coverage. Suddenly everyone's concerned with their plight, humanitarian organizations flocking in, everybody happily making a million bucks a minute, while the murder and the genocide slowly slides out of focus. It's already wrapped in fog." He shook his head. "I won't do it. I'm out of here."

I didn't know what to say, didn't know how I felt. I could feel a wave of panic about to submerge me, and I fought back with as much strength as I could muster. I couldn't believe he was leaving like that.

"When will you be back?"

"*Back?* You don't understand, Esmé. This is like a major crisis with the paper. They don't like it when someone pulls out of a story and I don't think they're going to send me back to Africa for a while. I'm replacing their correspondent in Kabul only until the end of December and then we'll see." He shrugged and looked out the window. "They may post me back in London as far as I know. If I keep the job."

Then he looked at his watch, impatient and uneasy.

"Listen, I have to have something to eat and I have to have a bath. I have very little time left to do a million things."

He was already far away, his brain focussed on the logistics of airline tickets and what to pack.

"I'll run you a bath and see if there's anything to eat in the house."

We became very quiet and mimicked a domesticity we'd never had. I sat on my bed and listened to his body moving in the water through the bathroom door. I didn't dare go in. It would have disturbed me to see him lying in the tub, the steam rising like I'd seen Adam so many times. No, we'd never allowed ourselves to feel that intimate and tranquil, and it would have felt like a sacrilege to let it happen now. I sat on my bed and waited.

At last I realised what had always scared me about Hunter: he could do without me in the name of a principle. Nothing and nobody could have held him back now. He was prepared to go away, the lone wolf again. Africa meant something to him. His life had been shaped by it, like his mother's, and he would leave it rather than betray it.

I didn't have that. I was a weak, selfish and self-obsessed creature who had adjusted an immense African tragedy to her petty needs. I lacked his strength, his rigour, and ultimately—for that very reason—I didn't believe someone like him could ever love, trust or need me.

He came into the bedroom, his hips wrapped in a towel, and sat beside me on the bed, his hair dripping on the sheets. The proximity of his body threatened me. I wanted him to get dressed as fast as possible.

"Come with me," he said.

I looked at him incredulously.

"Where?"

"To Kabul, to London. Wherever."

"Are you *mad*?"

"You don't *have to* live in Africa."

"Hunter, it's impossible."

"Why is it impossible? You could make it very possible if you wanted to."

"What makes you think I could leave, just *like that*?"

"I don't know. My ego, in the first place." He smiled, but I could see he was feeling vulnerable.

"And in the second place, I think Africa is just an escape for you. But you're not like everyone else here, Esmé."

"What am I like?"

"This won't ever be enough for you. You're more complicated than that."

"What are you trying to say?"

"Adam won't ever be enough."

I stiffened, I didn't like hearing him say Adam's name in our bedroom. I didn't like him half naked in my house giving a label to my life.

"What do you mean, *enough*?" Suddenly I felt angry. Angry at him for leaving me, angry at myself for letting all this happen without foreseeing the consequences.

"You don't *measure* people like that. And what do you know about my relationship with Adam, anyway?"

I thought that would close the subject. But he didn't seem to be afraid of losing now that everything was at stake:

"I think he's making you feel secure and loved. But I don't think you are *in love* with him."

I shot up and away from him. It drove me wild that he would discuss Adam and me like that, sitting on our bed, as if he'd come to officially take over.

His sudden resolve scared me. All we had silently agreed to ignore and conceal up till now, all the words which were never said, he was now calling up one by one and giving each one of them its name. I knew this was a dangerous game: once you give things their name, they refuse to go back into Pandora's box.

Words flew out of my mouth like desperate, blind blows.

"So what," I asked bitterly, "do you think I am in love with *you*?"

He stood up and began to put on his shirt. He looked drained.

"You are very acrobatic, Esmé. All these pirouettes and somersaults you do in order never to say anything, bouncing back questions like a juggler. You should have been English, it would suit you much better." He looked at me defeated. "I'm not the one to answer that for you. *You* are."

I could have turned my life around in thirty seconds. I could have said Yes, I love you. I've been in love with you since the first three seconds I saw you. And even though you ask so much of me, even though it scares me to follow you so blindly wherever you go, I'll come with you because otherwise I'll spend my life regretting it. Here I am, Hunter Reed, it's as simple as that.

But I didn't.

I stood speechless by the door and watched him put on his clothes, paralysed by the fear of losing him, hypnotised, like someone leaning over the rail of the Empire State Building, down into the void. If only he could disappear now, it would be like having a leg amputated. The whole thing would be over and done with. Then maybe, once by myself, it would be easier to deal with the pain.

CHAPTER NINE

This is my black. I alone
Am the authority, and I know no further
Than I've got, if that be anywhere.
I inherited no maps.

U. A. FANTHORPE

The next day I took off from Wilson Airport after five.

I sat in the copilot seat of the Cessna next to Peter, the Elephant Man. He was in the midst of his elephant-counting survey and for the last three weeks he'd been giving me lifts to Adam's camp. We didn't talk much during the flights, but these little trips had created a kind of intimacy between us. It was nice to be just the two of us in his small plane. He would gently tap my elbow and point down at game, and he glided over the plains, tilting his wings in the wind like a ballerina. Usually he played opera as he flew low over the long grass, and I couldn't resist singing along to Verdi in a poor crescendo as we floated above the jumping herds of zebras and wildebeests. I loved the way he always made our flights such an exhilarating transition.

But that afternoon I was mute, sunk, drained. *Dead.* I think Peter detected the hollow note in my silence and he didn't even try to get my attention as we flew in the golden light.

I kept my eyes on the small plane's shadow as it lifted off the ground until there was no more surface to reflect itself upon and its silhouette vanished among the clouds. Such a liberating feeling, to unbind and let go, almost weightless, without even your shadow to pin you to the earth. I exhaled deeply, as if I needed to get rid of the air inside my lungs.

It felt good to take off. I needed to lift myself out of it, pierce the clouds and see it all from above. To see it all from up high so one could learn to love it again.

Yes, it was good that Hunter had had to leave like that. That we had been brutally forced into this unexpected separation. That we'd also managed to show each other how ugly it could turn between us; our unpleasantness had helped ease the pain of having to part.

The night before, he had rung me from Kenyatta airport where he was about to get on the midnight British Airways flight.

"Since I doubt that I'll ever see you again, I thought I'd let you know what I've learned from our last little rendezvous, Esmé."

He had been drinking, his voice was strident, menacing. He was as wild and dangerous as anyone who has nothing left to lose.

"Hunter, don't. There's no need to make this more difficult than it already is."

"Difficult? You've just solved it brilliantly. In fact, congratulations."

"Please—"

"Here's what I learned," he recited. "Some men can't ever be husbands. They'll always be lovers."

". . . . ."

"Are you there?"

"Yes."

"It's extraordinary, you know. That you should think of yourself as this romantic, passionate character." I heard his bitter, husky laugh; "The Poet's Daughter."

"Hunter, will you listen to me for—"

"Considering that instead you have the nature of an insurance agent, I'd say you suffer from delusions of grandeur. The way you evaluate all the risks, the costs, the consequences, I mean, you should sell policies, Esmé. Nobody could resist you."

"You're drunk."

"Yes. But I see everything very clearly through the vodka haze."

He coughed and cleared his throat.

"Seriously, now. It's going to work really well for you. Adam is your friend. He'll probably become your husband. You'll eat fish cakes and chips in front of the telly. Whereas I, Esmé . . ." he paused, emphatically. "I may never be your friend, but at least I've been your lover."

His voice ended in a slur:

"Whateverthassupposed to mean."

"All right then," I asked angrily, "and what *do* you think that means?"

"I don't know yet. That we were only meant to fuck and then get fucked in the end? Dunno."

I've got to go now.

"Wait! You can't go like that."

"Of course I can. *I have to.* They're calling my flight."

I lost it.

"This is so fucking unfair! To call me just to be mean, as you're boarding a plane, so I can't even—"

"I'm afraid I'm too drunk to evaluate the consequences of this phone call, sweetheart."

"Hunter, wait!"

"*Ciao bella.*"

He hung up.

Such arrogance, to vanish like that and leave me stripped bare by his sarcasm. And I badly needed my resentment in order to start writing him off.

The land stretched out under my eyes, rich in its red colour, unending. As we flew over the Rift Valley I felt a longing to be back with Adam in the way we used to be. I was tired of the hopelessness and the despondency Hunter had infected me with. Being in love with him had only meant insecurity, nostalgia, fear of losing him. All my feelings towards him had pivoted around what we *couldn't* have.

Suddenly it all seemed luminously clear. Love had very little to do with fear and emotional sabotage; love had to do with trust.

I longed to be back with Adam in the beauty of Africa because I needed to believe in it again. After all, there is truth in beauty as well as in despair. Perhaps I could finally learn that.

It was a boys-and-cars world again up at the camp; I'd almost forgotten. When I arrived Adam was lying under one of his trucks, surrounded by greasy spanners and tools neatly arranged on a piece of green canvas. All around him the usual circle of guys in overalls, the lean Turkana and Samburu staff who'd been with him for years, with whom he spoke in incomprehensible tongues and cracked mysterious mechanical jokes. I could see only his legs and part of his bare back caked with black grease and dust sticking out from under the car. His body looked fit and fresh, his skin soft and lightly tanned. Even dirty and sweaty he still smelled like a snowflake.

He looked up from under the body of the car. A glimpse of his green eyes. He eased himself out and rubbed his forehead with the back of his greasy hand. I felt his hot sticky skin through my shirt. His lips quickly on mine.

"You got in early."

"I came with Peter."

"I'm nearly finished with this. Go have some tea and I'll be right with you." He smiled, amused. "We had this huge lioness roaring right in the middle of camp last night. It was excellent. The clients went *mad*. Had to give one woman a couple of Valiums."

It was like watching him for the first time all over again, like I had that evening a long time ago, me in the role of the Lonely Crazed Surfer and he acting the Beautiful Stranger.

I looked at his clothes scattered around the tent. His threadbare khaki trousers falling to pieces, his old mended shirts, his worn-out boots. Everything had been moulded by his shape and said something about his body, his good smell, his manliness. I studied his handwriting on a pad, I picked up the book by the nighttable, shuffled through his music. He had been listening to the Chopin sonatas. I checked his toothbrush, his shaving cream, the joint butts in the ashtray. I took in all the small details which had something to say about his life without me in that tent. It felt to me now that we'd spent only fragments of time together in the last few months, to the point that by now I seemed to know too little of what he did all day. And suddenly it seemed like such a waste that we should have been apart, and that I should have stopped looking at him with the attention I once had and which had made my life so full. I felt as if I'd come to reclaim my happiness, like something precious I'd left behind in a store.

He came into the tent as the light was fading. He quickly stripped naked, chatting about the lioness and the clients under the shower in the rear of the tent.

I wasn't really listening. I watched as he vigorously rubbed his head and skin under the water. His strong hands were much browner and harder than his lean white flanks. Those secret parts of softer skin of his body I used to know so well, millimeter by millimeter, which I used to kiss slowly in the dark.

The insides of his wrists. The back of his neck. The palms of his hands.

I'd worshipped every inch of his skin and muscle, every curve or bone or nerve, I'd known it like one knows his way home in the pitch black. Bit by bit, step by step.

Adam's body, this body which sang, lately had lost its arias and hidden melodies and had gone back to be silent again. Had I been the fool who'd slowly turned down the volume? Obviously yes. I longed desperately to hear it sing again.

He held out his arm and I handed him a towel, which he wrapped around his waist, and he briskly walked past me. I went to kiss him, I wanted to smell the fresh water on his lips, but he went on looking for a clean shirt and gently pulled me away.

"You're going to like these clients, they're from New York, pretty cool people. The husband deals in art, big auctions, something like that. If say you have a Rembrandt or a Velasquez, he'll flog it for you. It's such an amazing world, total spy book material. The wife is much younger, very good-looking, I think she's involved in publishing, and they have these two incredibly clever kids in their early twenties. I wish we'd always have people like that around, it would make everything so much more amusing."

I looked out the tent. The camp felt very quiet.

"Where are they now?"

"I sent them on a game drive with Morag, they'll be back any minute."

"Who is *Morag*?"

Adam looked at me hesitatingly, then waved vaguely.

"Morag is this hunter from Tanzania who's been hired to cull zebras at the Copelands' ranch."

"Oh, okay. I never heard of him."

"Because she's been down there only in the last two months. Shooting every day."

"*She?*"

"Yeah. Morag is Scottish for Mary. She's a huntress, to be exact. Quite an amazing shot, as a matter of fact."

I watched him as he brushed his hair with his fingers and tied his old leather belt around his hips. I felt alarmed.

"And how come Morag takes your clients on game drives?"

"Because she often comes into camp once she's done her daily zebra quota and she's perfect for the clients, they love having a girl like that show them around."

"You mean she's working for you?"

"No. She's only doing it because she enjoys it. She's shooting and sitting all day in a huge pickup truck filled with smelly bloody animals and flies. I promise you it's not a lot of fun. Here she can relax, have a drink, listen to good music and have some interesting conversation. She takes them on a drive in the evening, they seem to have lots of fun together, and that gives me a break if I have things to do back here."

"Right."

It sounded like a great arrangement. Yet this Morag and her killing skills worried me.

"It's a pretty amazing job to kill ten zebras in one day and be finished before tea, let me tell you," said Adam, trying to make me like her and creating the opposite result.

"Yeah. I bet."

The micropause which followed seemed to stretch out a little too long. Then, thank God, we heard the car come down from the hill. Female giggles and male laughter, brakes on the rough surface and the solo sax from "Take a Walk on the Wild Side" blasting from the stereo.

"I thought you didn't allow clients to blare music in the bush."

"Did I say that?" Adam grinned a naughty smile and took my hand. "I must've been in a very bad mood when I made that rule, then. Come have a drink, city girl."

Morag definitely was an amazing shot. Alarmingly good-looking for starters. A Helmut Newton model lookalike, Botticelli blond curls and marble skin, the long white jodhpurs drenched in zebra blood, heavy black boots. No eyes, just that Hockney swimming-pool look with no ripples. The eyes of a drowned Ophelia. Or of dead fish if one didn't care to be so romantic about it.

She offered me the tips of her thin fingers to shake, and a blank look. This girl was not interested in sisterhood, and to be honest in her case neither was I. Morag the huntress was possibly the last person on the planet I wanted to have sitting in camp that night between me and Adam. I felt like kicking her in her bloody jodhpurs and calling her a fraud, then radioing the Copelands to come and collect her for good. That was how threatened she made me feel. The clients were clearly mad about her, they'd spent three days in her company and couldn't imagine a cooler woman than this twentieth-century Greek goddess. Pure mythology at your feet. You should have heard them, the New York Upper West Side Intellectual Family, Morag said this that and the other. Blah blah blah.

Adam was right; they looked interesting and clever, they

didn't wear stupid clothes, they had a wild sense of humour. I wanted them to like me as well, but when they asked me what I did and I said I worked in a postproduction company in Nairobi, they looked at me with the same embarrassment and pity as if I'd revealed I had a slow but fatal disease.

Morag went to shower somewhere in the staff quarters and reappeared beautifully wrapped in black, a fat cigar sticking out of her breast pocket. I wanted to scream with rage and smack her in the face.

Why couldn't one ever relax in this country? Why was it always like a crazy film without an ending, where new characters kept popping up nonstop just when you thought you'd reached the climax and were only waiting for the grand finale? Your two heroes finally reunited against the African sunset, kissing passionately, music levitating as tears rolled along with the credits.

But no.

This fucking long-legged Artemis appears, who has shot buffaloes in Zimbabwe all her life.

Frankly, one feels like giving up.

Adam was busy creating the perfect atmosphere, making everyone lethal drinks, selecting music, lighting candles. I hadn't seen him so full of energy with clients in a long time. But more than that, I'd never seen Adam so concentrated on a woman since the day we met.

At dinner I sat next to Brian, the art dealer, and across from his younger wife, Anjelica. Morag sat between Brian and Adam, the two clever boys who obviously adored her.

Brian started elucidating just how extraordinary he thought Morag was.

"She's incredibly brave, considering the chauvinism of the hunting world. Seems it's quite difficult for Morag to get proper professional clients."

"That doesn't surprise me. No guy who pays thousands of dollars to shoot a buffalo wants to listen to a twenty-five-year-old angelface tell him when's the best time to pull the trigger. It's too demeaning," I said. "You want some rugged guy to be your guru on a hunt, someone who looks like Clint Eastwood and makes you feel just as cool, don't you think?"

Anjelica nodded, whereas Brian went on championing Morag's position in a man's world.

"I wouldn't mind at all going hunting with a woman. I wouldn't find it demeaning in the least."

"Yes darling," said Anjelica with a grin, "but you are a vegetarian and wouldn't even know how to kill a bird, so you hardly count as a potential client."

Morag was busy discussing ammunition with Adam and pretended not to be listening. I overheard her invite him to join her on the zebra shoot at the ranch next week, after the clients had gone. He said he'd definitely come, that he loved the idea of doing a bit of hunting.

"She's completely ridiculous," I said to Adam after Morag had finally left to go back to the Copelands' ranch late that night, her shotgun nicely propped behind her seat. The Intellectual Family had turned in much earlier, and I'd had to sit through a tedious conversation about shooting techniques and bullets, the advantage of soft-nosed bullets versus solids, Remington guns versus Holland.

"Why do you say that? She's just really into it, she has a real passion for it."

"She's obsessed."

"I agree," he conceded. "But I like that kind of obsession in a girl. I think it's attractive."

I felt murderous. I literally had to sit still and breathe to calm down. I felt I was losing everything at an impossible speed, like a Black Friday nightmare on Wall Street when your stocks tumble on the screen and there's nothing you can do but watch your fortune sink.

Yes, love was about trust. Not about fear. Not about emotional sabotage. Love was about things people could *do* together, not about what they *couldn't* do.

How long had it been since Adam had felt he could trust me, how long since he hadn't felt lonely without me, how long since we'd done anything together? Why was I expecting him to keep loving me like day one? What was so unfair about Adam finally finding a buddy in the bush to listen to his favourite Chopin with and talk about boys' stuff, someone who on top of everything had the curves of a model?

Morag must have been sent by a goddess who particularly hated me.

We heard the lioness grunt in the distance.

"I promise you, she was right in the middle of camp last night around three. Woke everybody up, it was total mayhem for a while. I wished you were here."

"Did you?"

"What?"

"Wish I was here?"

"Yes," he stared at me. "I *always* wish you were here."

I stared back at him. Tears slowly started trickling out of my eyes. He wiped them off with the back of his hand.

"Don't," he said, "there's no need to cry. Everything's all right."

"I'm not so sure about *that* anymore."

"Come on, Esmé. You *know* it is. You're the one who's been away. I've always been in the same place." He waved in the dark. "Right here."

He said it with such a melancholic look in his eyes it scared me. Now it was impossible for me not to see the nostalgia, the loneliness my absence had inflicted upon him, and I was so afraid to think of the scars my carelessness had left.

I started unbuttoning his shirt.

"I want to make love to you."

He took me by the hand and we went inside our tent. We undressed each other slowly in the warm light of the kerosene lamp. There was a certain roughness in the way his hands touched me now, how they held me beneath him. We made love with impatient passion, as if we both wanted to see the end of it, to confirm that we still owned each other in the same way as ever and that nothing had changed. We didn't care to linger, to wait, to smile at each other, to postpone the conclusion. We wanted to get it over and done with.

In the darkness I brushed his ribs with my finger and kissed the inside of his forearm. No, nothing would ever be the way it had been, before Hunter. I had been mad to think Adam and I could make it through undamaged. We were no longer the same two, and now we both knew it. It wasn't necessarily the end, but it was pointless to pretend nothing had been broken. And the job of mending whatever was salvageable was entirely mine, I realized.

"Adam."

"Yes?"

"Maybe I could keep my job part-time, follow only some of the clients, like Jason for instance. That would give me much more time to be here. Would you be happy if I did that?"

"Yes, of course I would. But I would want you to do it only because you wanted to, not because you felt you should."

—I know. But I do want to. I do want to be here with you. I'm so tired of being away from you. From here."

The lioness grunted again; she'd gotten closer.

"Maybe she'll come into camp again," said Adam. And he turned to me, his eyes shining with childish joy in the dark.

"Let's hope she does."

We fell asleep and her rasping growls woke me before dawn. Adam was standing, watching her through the netting. This big dark shape, this wild intoxicating smell. I couldn't believe how close she was to our tent. We both stood watching through the netting without moving, till the sky turned grey and we could make her out completely. She was lying under a tree, sniffing the breeze, flapping her tail. Then she got to her feet and disappeared into the thickets. I felt blessed, welcomed again. I gently pulled Adam back onto the bed and we lay next to each other for a while, without talking, feeling the warmth of our bodies close together, letting our different thoughts dart like swallows and dissolve in the early morning light.

I left my job at the office and worked on a freelance basis

with Jason Winters, on postproduction of his ads. He paid me little but pampered me and kept me in an excellent mood. We'd spend long hours together in front of the Avid machine, then go to the Mud Club and dance ourselves stupid.

The rest of the time I was with Adam at the camp, entertaining clients at dinner and becoming rather good at it, climbing the escarpment with Lenjo and getting the names of the plants and birds right once and for all. The Christmas holidays went by, and still we had bookings until Easter. Adam said he'd never had such a good season.

My instincts told me the time had come for me to mark that territory, make it mine, before I lost my foothold. Therefore I concentrated on keeping Morag at bay, not letting her annoy me more than I could bear. Her zebra-culling job had come to an end, but apparently the Copelands loved having her around, so she was still living with them at the ranch. I knew she came around the camp a lot more often whenever I was in Nairobi, and it infuriated me that I didn't seem to intimidate her one bit.

I couldn't help thinking she and Adam were having an affair. Why else wouldn't she leave? I couldn't make myself ask him; I still had much too much to hide from him myself.

"Why doesn't she go back to Tanzania, where at least it's legal to shoot? She insists on hanging around in a country where hunters are loathed, killing animals is taboo, and she whines about it nonstop. What's the sense of it?" I asked Adam.

"I think she wants to get a job with me," he said, as if admitting something. That's why she's sticking around. She's totally broke.

I felt no sympathy for her poor financial state.

"Well, there are millions of safari companies who would love to hire her. She's *stalking* you, that's what she's doing."

He laughed, as if I was being outlandish.

"Come on, Esmé, what's wrong with you? I can't believe you're *jealous*."

He was absorbed in yet another manual operation and went back—innocently—to unscrewing some tiny bit from the radio. I watched him closely. Suddenly I saw his embarrassment. Yes, they had slept together. I could feel it.

"I am not. I just find her incredibly irritating. And she's so *stupid*," I said, wanting to goad him. I did feel a pang of jealousy now and it hurt, but at the same time I was relieved: if Adam had had a fling with Morag it evened the scales. Not only did it make me feel less guilty, but it also gave me motivation to win him back.

I needed that motivation, I needed the spur. It was part of the regimen I'd put myself on the day Hunter had left Africa.

I made myself never think of him.

Not his voice, not his eyes, not his smell. I never opened the shoebox where I kept his few letters, never dared glance at his tiny handwriting or at the only photograph I had of him—I loved it because he was smiling—it was black-and-white and slightly out of focus.

These were strict rules. One had to forget.

I had found, unexpectedly, an internal delete button. I had to be careful never to fiddle with it, otherwise the whole thing could come back in one go. One huge overwhelming wave of desire for Hunter would have drowned me on the spot. I couldn't afford to be that suicidal.

But it wasn't easy.

Even if you want to, for some reason it seems impossible to lose track of anyone if you live in Africa.

You'd imagine it would be the opposite, that once someone leaves here, he or she vanishes into the unknown. Instead not only it is virtually impossible to disappear from view within this vast and wild country—your car will always be spotted, even in the Chalbi Desert, by some Ker and Downey safari guide who will report your exact location for the sheer pleasure of keeping track—but you're even less likely to vanish once you've physically left the country. There's a very good overseas network which keeps every bit of info regarding Kenya residents circulating daily.

I never asked, but I would meet Ruben or Miles and they would say nonchalantly:

"Hunter's doing a really excellent job in Kabul, they want

him to stay on. He says he loves it."

"Oh you heard from him?" I would say with a quiver.

"Got a fax the other day." Sounds pretty wild over there.

"Right," I would say and then change the subject, trying to overcome the faint feeling that always took over me anytime his name was mentioned.

Kabul sounded safely remote and unreal. Then one day one of them would slap me with a new piece of information.

"Hunter's back in London for a couple of weeks. They may post him in Moscow, you know."

"*Moscow—?*" I would pretend to find that amusing. "Will he like that, you think?"

And my heart would sink again, as I felt his presence suddenly near, his voice within reach: London.

One could be there in eight hours and track him down in two minutes. The mere thought elated and terrified me at the same time.

At such moments the junkie in me was back: she'd been on strict rehab, but she knew she could start it all up again in a second, and she'd be right back where she'd left off. There with all the guilt and the passion, the ecstasy and the wickedness, the frightening chaos.

Whereas now I'd become this heavily sedated patient, fed three times a day, on sleeping pills, who no longer cracked a decent joke.

Yes, the guilt and the chaos had slid out of me, but life had as well.

Chapter Ten

Since there's no help, come let us kiss and part,
Nay, I have done: you get no more of me,
And I am glad, yea glad with all my heart,
That thus so cleanly, I myself can free.

MICHAEL DRAYTON

Jason had rented a grand old house in Karen.

"Just for a laugh," he said, then began the tour, proudly showing me the dining room panelled in dark oak, the imposing fireplace in the sitting room, the wraparound verandah with old stone pillars covered in creepers.

"An expensive laugh, this must be," I said, having counted four bedrooms, three bathrooms, a huge salon, sitting room and dining room.

"What the hell. We're doing Omo next week, Tampax beginning of next month and probably Smirnoff."

Jason and I had become a good team. I was working as his assistant on the shoots now and I sometimes helped to dress the sets, bringing things from home. My teapot had been immortalized on a breakfast cereal commercial, my leather armchair had been the pièce de résistance of a particularly atmospheric brandy ad.

He shrugged as he showed me the vast kitchen.

"Plus my girlfriend is coming in June. I need to impress her to persuade her to stay."

"You have a girlfriend in London?" I don't know why, but I had always assumed he was a single-minded bachelor having a good time on his own.

"Daisy. She's a costume designer. I kind of miss her, you know."

"How come she didn't move out here with you?"

"She has *tons* of work in London," he said, as if to justify the fact Daisy wasn't right there, knitting by the fireplace. "Actually she thinks I'm mad to have moved here. Careerwise."

We sat by the fireplace in the huge living room and Jason slipped the *Out of Africa* tape into the VCR.

"Oh please," I said, "let's watch something else."

"I just want us to get ideas for sets and costumes, in case we end up getting the Smirnoff job."

"All right then." I sat next to him, pad and pen in hand.

I tried to watch the film with a professional eye, but by the time Meryl reads the poem on Finch-Hatton's grave in the Ngong hills, whispers *"He wasn't mine"* with a dead stare and walks away in the grass, Jason and I—the deserted souls—had used half a roll of loo paper to wipe away our tears.

"I wonder what it means when you feel that schmaltzy film plots are starting to fit the plot of your life," I said, drying my eyes and getting up to go home.

"I don't know," said Jason, shaking his flaming red hair and blowing his nose. "But, it doesn't sound good."

March came, the rains were about to start again. Every morning we'd wake up to the distant rumbling of thunder and smell mist in the air. Adam closed camp once more and drove to Nairobi with all the equipment in his truck.

The day of the first downpour I sat on the verandah clutching a mug of hot tea, looking at the muddy pools in the garden, and realised this time for sure my brain was going to rot. I couldn't stand the thought of all that water pounding on my head for months to come. I hadn't been home in almost two years. I needed to get out.

I phoned Teo.

"Come, my love," he said. "You're the only person I want to be with for the rest of my life.

Oh, my beautiful magic child brother.

"Say that again," I begged him with a laugh. "I can't believe I've managed to stay away from for you so long."

"Just come. But this country is hideous, I warn you. You mustn't read the papers or watch television, *ever*. If you do you'll run away immediately. You must promise to do only what I tell you."

"Oh, I've missed you so much," I said in a small voice, and suddenly realised how insane it was to have been away from him all that time.

It started pouring. Roofs leaked, cars got stuck in the mud, phones went down, power got cut, it was one red-bucket day after another, but I couldn't care less. I had my ticket: all I was dreaming of was a fresh European spring, away from the darkness, the snails and the frogs.

I hadn't ask Adam to come with me and meet my brother, as we had planned the summer before. I needed to go alone now. I wanted no witnesses.

He drove me to the airport. I detected a hint of apprehension in him as he saw me to the check-in counter: he could only vaguely imagine what Italy looked like, let alone Teo, my other friends, my whole life there. As he saw me gabble in Italian with the Alitalia staff, my foreignness must have suddenly startled him.

"Don't stay away too long," Adam said when we kissed goodbye.

Only at the passport control did I realise how long I had been broken.

How much I wanted out, how I needed to be healed.

"I want you to come back soon, all right?" he whispered.

And it was strange, but as he said that I felt that I could very easily disappear, slip out of that life and never come back again.

The plane was full of tour groups avid to show their tans at the office on Monday, with nothing else to thank Africa for.

It was the basest company you could conceive of for leaving a place you loved. Nothing felt right: not their accents, not their clothes or the emotions they expressed. It was like travelling with criminals.

When you leave Africa, as the plane lifts, you feel that more than leaving a continent you're leaving a state of mind. Whatever awaits you at the other end of your journey will be on a different order of existence.

The Italian tourists hadn't a nanosecond of feeling for what they were leaving behind. That was the advantage of travelling with criminals: their heartlessness prepared you for the lack of emotions ahead.

At the other end of the tunnel, thank God, there was Teo in a crumpled white shirt looking like an archangel who had just been woken up. He was leaning sleepy-eyed on a rail in the arrivals hall among the waiting crowd, looking so different than everyone else. He held a long shoot of wistaria which he must have cut from a garden wall on the way. There was still a small leaf on his shirt. I picked it off, mechanically, as he hugged me and I smelled his familiar scent: what was it? Damp wood, ferns, rain?

"You've changed," he said smiling as we got inside his old Beetle.

"How?"

"You've lost weight. But it's more like you've lost a layer. Now it's the very essence of you."

"And what does that look like?"

"It's scary. You look feral, like you're mad or something. But it's beautiful."

I laughed and squeezed his arm. It felt good to be back with him, speaking our secret language. He had changed too, or maybe I just didn't remember how much he reminded me of Ferdinando. Suddenly the unbearable fact hit: I was home but I would not see him or hear his husky smoker's laugh again.

We drove into the center of Rome to Teo's flat near Via Giulia, past marble palazzi and fountains and tritons and cupolas and pigeons, across the green river and through the busy flower market, into the baroque piazzas, skirting the outdoor cafés. I saw pretty girls on bicycles who'd just bought flowers, sexy boys on scooters on the way to deliver groceries, older couples walking their dogs, nuns from the order of Santa Brigida rapidly crossing the square, children playing football in the courtyard of an old building covered in ivy, carpenters and carabinieri and thieves and beggars. I smelled lime tree blossoms and moss and freshly baked bread and rotten river. It all felt wonderfully tamed and graceful. To think that it had all continued to be there while I had been under that glaring light, the alleys and the spurting fountains and the pretty girls on bicycles and the nuns and the thieves, all these parallel lives, seemed incredible, nearly science fiction.

Would there be room for me now, for my animal-like madness, would my body adjust again to these perfectly sculptured corners and intricate labyrinths? It looked magnificent, but it looked crowded.

And it looked *small*.

The first few weeks I felt like an beast trapped in a cage. Everything seemed so fragmented: the flow of conversations, all bits and pieces, always interrupted, phones ringing nonstop, sounds overlapping, everything and everybody endlessly crossing and bumping into each other.

I wandered the streets and into the shops. There was so much of everything, I didn't know where to start. I devoted hours to staring at different shades of lipstick, and flicking through hundreds of CDs and books. Each title sounded better than the next. I couldn't decide what I needed; I needed everything because I had come back with nothing, but the options confused rather than attracted me. I invariably gave up and walked out of the store empty-handed.

I would try on masses of shirts, dresses, shoes. Each time my image in the mirror of the shop struck me as new. Yes, I had changed: under the bright lights of the dressing room, unlike in any mirror in Africa, I saw at last how my hair had bleached, my skin had darkened, my eyes had sprouted thin wrinkles all around. I had been too long under the sun.

The expensive, well-cut shirt didn't blend with this new me; it stuck out, in all its freshness and composure. I invariably handed it back to the salesgirl.

Yet it was heaven to be back with Teo, like being put on an IV drip of some magic substance. Every day his presence infused me with a sense of belonging, not to a place, but to a way of being. It was like finding Ferdinando again through him.

Every morning he'd wake me up with a cup of tea, and sit on the edge of my bed.

"Get up, Esmeralda," he'd say playfully. 'Let's go look at beautiful things.'

We'd peer inside small churches, he'd show me statues I had never even heard of.

"Never seen the *Ecstasy of Santa Teresa*? You must be joking! Come on, hurry, the light will be perfect only for a bit longer.'

He'd take me into a museum only to show me that one painting. One particular *Judith Holding the Head of Holofernes* by the school of Caravaggio, her face lit sideways with that unmistakable light.

"The rest you can skip, it's all boring stuff." And from the wonderful penumbra of the Galleria Corsini we'd dash out into the sun again.

"That's the therapy," he said. "You're only allowed to look at beauty—well, at whatever is left of it, and you must ignore the rest."

I rang Adam a couple of times and attempted to describe what I was doing, what Rome looked like, but I knew I failed to convey my real feelings. It was as if I took for granted that he wouldn't know what I was talking about.

"What's going on in Nairobi?" I would ask.

"We haven't had this much rain in twenty-five years. It's a flood. All the fields have been drowned upcountry. All the bridges are washed out. You can't even reach Nanyuki. It's amazing."

The fields, the river, the bridges. We had these farmerlike conversations.

"Anything else?" I'd ask.

"I miss you."

"Me too."

I wasn't sure it was true, but it felt good to say it.

After about a week Teo and I drove to the Amalfi Coast, in a childish Kodachrome mood. We blasted old James Bond music in the car and belted out "Goldfinger" as we sped along the road that wound along the edge of the precipice over the sea. We'd rented the old house where Ferdinando used to take us in the summer when we were children.

We sat on the eighteenth-century terrace propped on the cliff, looking out to sea. It all came back, the scents and colours of my childhood. The smell of dampness exuding from the thick walls, the vaulted ceilings over the shady rooms, the crumbling stuccoes, the cracked blue tiles. The whiff of jasmine at night. The wild fennel sprouting from the cracks in the terrace floor.

"It's so completely *settecento napoletano*," I said to Teo, as we sat on the terrace after sunset.

He seemed amused by such a discovery.

"But of course," he said with a smile.

"Strange. I grew up in this and I never saw it."

I looked down at the cupola of the church covered in old tiles which, as a child, had reminded me of the green scales of a snake.

Now that I had come back with the greedy eyes of the exiled, everything I saw touched me and tore me to shreds.

"I feel so broken away from it all," I said in a whisper.

Teo leaned closer. It made him sad that I should say that.

"But why?"

"I don't know. Maybe it's the feeling of being back in a place where you belong which is no longer yours. The more you rediscover it, the more you see how you've lost it."

We sat bathed in the soft light of dusk which in Italy, unlike Africa, lingers on and on.

"Perhaps after all it's not good for humans to live in more than one place at the time," Teo said. "I think we were designed to be territorial."

"Yes. Perhaps one should never have more than one home," I paused, and something made me smile wearily. "and certainly never more than one love."

Once back in Rome we often ate in the old trattoria where we were not allowed to pay the bill, and drank with Ferdinando's old friends. When they asked me about Africa I never knew what to say. I couldn't think of a single image to deliver. It was as if Africa had vanished from my speech, it had become untranslatable, too private to be shared with strangers.

I did talk about it to Teo: I knew he would understand me.

"It's in your face," he would say. "All that space. It has deranged you completely."

"But what is it?" And I would look at myself in the mirror. All I could see were my eyes, the same wild stare as Judith's as she brandishes the head of Holofernes.

"Ferdinando would have loved to see you like this."

"I don't know if he would understand why I want to go back there. He'd think I was being melodramatic or something silly like that." I imitated his sarcastic drawl: "He'd say 'Stop acting like you're inside a Russian novel *right now!*'"

"No he wouldn't. After all you are simply trying to do what he always did, I think."

"Which is?"

"Being bigger than life. Except you have been able to do it in a purely geographical way. He had other ways of doing it. I mean, *he was* a living Russian novel, for Christ's sake. He only pretended to be cynical."

I didn't say anything for a while.

"And how do *you* manage to be bigger than life here?"

"Oh. I don't." He sighed. "I just fall in love."

Teo had a lover, Pascal, a dark-eyed, slender dancer. He was French, but originally came from Algiers. They had met at some music festival a year earlier, after I had gone.

Pascal would come with us sometimes, and he was so quiet

one would almost forget he was there. Yet, even though they hardly spoke to each other in front of me, I knew there was more than just sex between them, there was a deep bond of tenderness and love. It was very simple and beautiful to be around. I envied what they had.

"I wish I could be like that," I said to Teo one evening after Pascal had gone. We were lying at opposite ends of the sofa, our legs stretched out under the yellow light of the lampshade, each trying to read a book.

"Like what?"

"Like you and him. I wish I could love someone without having to get into his head with a can opener and take inventory each time I'm in there."

"What a frightening concept."

"But you know, that's what I wanted to have with Adam. I thought for once I could be in love without my head. It was such a relief. Just the physical aspect of things."

"It's never just physical. That's such a cliché. It's always more complicated than that, for everyone. Even for me and Pascal, you know."

"All right. Maybe I mean that I see how love can actually be *easy*. And I wish I—"

"But you've never liked *easy*, Esmé," he interrupted me. "Why don't you stop trying always to be someone else? And then," He propped himself up and gently pushed my book away with his toes. "go ahead and *do* something about this unhappy love life of yours, instead of moaning about it. You have become such a bore."

At the end of the day everything softened again, because I always dreamed of Africa. It would come to me every night. The space, the silence, the sky, the crisp morning air. While asleep that feeling of being voraciously alive bit into my heart, filled my lungs to the brim and pumped blood in my veins. For a few minutes every morning I was shocked not to find myself there, to wake up in the soft white light filtered by the mosquito net of my bed.

But then, as time passed, the dreams became fainter, like a memory which slowly fades away, and it made me sad to be left alone in the city without them, as if along with the dreams I would lose the glow.

Then one night Teo tapped lightly on my shoulder and woke me.

"Telephone. For you."

"Who is it? What time is it?"

"Late. Around two."

"Oh God. Who—"

"Hunter. It's Hunter Reed."

My heart stopped. I leaped out of bed like a wildcat and grabbed the receiver.

"Hunter?"

"Did I wake you?"

"Yes . . . no, it doesn't matter. Where—"

"Listen, I'm on my way to Rome tomorrow, I thought I'd stop and see you, if it's all right."

". . . . ."

"Esmé?"

"Yes."

"Would it be all right?"

"Yes."

"Are you sure?"

"Hunter."

"Yes?"

"I can't believe it's you."

"You better believe it. Give me the address."

"No. I'll come get you at the airport."

"No, give me the address."

"It's impossible spelling, you'll get lost, let me come and get you." Sudden panic seized me. What if he couldn't find the house?

"*No.*" I was annoying him already. "Just spell it for me and I'll get there.

"What time will you get here? Where are you anyway?"

"Moscow."

"*Moscow?*"

"Why don't you just give me the address and stop asking all these questions?"

I did. I spelled *Via degli Orti d'Alibert* three times.

"Hunter."

"Yes."

"I can't wait to see you."

"That's good."

Beep. He was gone.

I howled, I screamed, I jumped, I smoked a pack of cigarettes, I laughed hysterically until Teo had to give me a sleeping pill.

"You are fucking *mad*."

"No, you don't understand! I thought I'd never see him again." I seized his arm with violent energy. "I thought he had started to hate me, that he would never want to see me again, and now the gods are giving me a chance. It's like winning the lottery, one chance in a million."

"Well, you better not blow it this time," Teo said, disentangling himself from my grip.

I spent all the next day on the phone with every obscure airline that could possibly fly into Rome from Moscow, in an attempt to track down Hunter on a passenger list. I couldn't make myself do anything else besides stare at the telephone or at the door, waiting for either of them to ring. I kept rehearsing lines out loud, then looking in the mirror while delivering them, trying on different clothes, sighing, smoking, laughing, driving my brother nuts until he had had it.

"I am leaving you here. I'm leaving you the whole house." And off he went.

When Hunter finally walked through the door eighteen hours later—by which time I'd driven myself crazy with terror, envisaging his plane crashing or being hijacked by terrorists—the reality of him shocked me. I felt like I was seeing him for the first time: his dark hair cut short now which made his eyes look brighter, his long skinny legs in the old khaki pants hanging loose at the waist, his full soft lips, his old military boots. He threw the bags on the floor and held me for only a second. We both felt shy of each other physically now. New rules had to be established, new boundaries had been marked. We no longer knew where we stood in relation to one another.

"Shall I get you a drink?" I asked him. Maybe alcohol would make us more relaxed, I thought.

"Yes, please." Then I caught him staring at me. "I had forgotten what you looked like, Esmé."

"Oh," I smiled, "that's terrible."

We exchanged a long stare and our eyes shone.

I feared he might remind me of our last bitter words to each other. But in typical Hunterstyle, he seemed to have forgotten all about that. And most probably he had, considering how drunk he had sounded at the time.

We sat out in the terrace, overlooking the Gianicolo hill. It was one of those Roman evenings blessed with a rich golden light: all Pompeian red façades, swallows cutting the air and distant church bells. Hunter pointed to the lush gardens below us.

"What's that? The Villa Borghese?"

"No. These used to be the gardens of Christina of Sweden. She lived in that palazzo over there." I pointed at the light pink façade of an imposing seventeenth-century building. "She was a big patron of the arts, and supported Michelangelo and Raffaello. They say she was a lesbian. Now her park has become the botanical garden, and her palazzo is a . . . how do you say pinacoteca?"

He nodded, amused.

"It's interesting to see you here. A lot more of you makes sense," He waved towards the view. "in this."

"Yes?" I smiled, trying to look enigmatic. "But you know, I'm longing to go back to Africa. I miss it already."

"So when will you go back?"

"Soon, next month maybe."

We paused. I was afraid to say anything more. I sipped my drink slowly and made myself wait.

"I'm on my way back to Africa right now," he said.

"Are you?" Everything was falling into place. "I thought you never wanted to—"

"I'm an African boy after all, you know." He smiled. "Ultimately, no matter what I plan, I always end up getting homesick."

"I'm so happy you're coming back." I touched his wrist very lightly. "I've missed you."

"The paper is posting me back to Nairobi." He squeezed my finger between his for one second and then let it go.

"They decided after all I'm the best African correspondent they will ever get after I wrote that piece on the Rwandan anniversary."

"When was that?"

"Right after you left, in April. The paper asked me to go back to write a story about Kigali a year after the genocide. I came through Nairobi for a day. You'd just left, I missed you by only a few days."

"Oh. I had no idea. I heard you were going to Russia. I thought I'd never see you on the face of the earth again."

"Oh well, I hope *that* made you a bit sad."

"It did as a matter of fact."

I stared at him, proud of what I had just said. He smiled, then lowered his eyes and started fiddling with his lighter.

"Well, it was a last-minute thing, I was the only staff who had been in Rwanda during the massacre, so they sent me in a flash when they realised that every network and magazine was going to do a story about the anniversary. I found myself back in Kigali twenty-four hours later."

"Did you hate to have to go back?"

"Yes and no. I needed to see it again, in order to wipe out some of those memories. We were all back there, in the same hotel, a year later. The last time I had been there the owner had fled, leaving me and Ruben and Miles and hundreds of refugees without food or water, living in this abandoned place like in a trench. The place smelled of urine and blood. And it still smells like that, I recognized the smell immediately, the walls and the carpets are impregnated with it. I couldn't believe this time they made us *pay* to stay there. Credit card machines and all."

"Amazing," I said, looking into my half-empty glass.

I realised I wasn't prepared to listen to this again. All I wanted was to hear he had missed me as I had missed him.

"Now the lawns are clipped, the hairdresser is back in the hotel shop, the shell-shocked gardeners are back at work. You'd never know anything had ever happened. It was like superimposing a totally different picture in your brain. Like when I walked into the swimming pool and I saw this crowd of happy-go-lucky aid workers swimming and splashing around, getting a tan, I couldn't cross out the memory of those hundreds of refugees actually fighting to *drink* the water out of that pool, only a year back."

"It must have been inspiring for your story."

"It was. And it was therapeutic too, in a cruel way. That everything ultimately can be wiped out and will sink into oblivion."

He looked at me sombrely.

"How you can actually forget *anything*?"

"But can you really?"

"Yes. Of course. We all do. The more painful the memory, the faster you want to forget. You just replace the scene, superimpose another face."

"Are you talking about us?" I don't know where that came from. It flew out of my mouth.

"I am talking about a lot of things at the same time."

I felt his eyes on me. I didn't look; I knew my question had annoyed him. But I couldn't help it.

Why had he come here like this, out of the blue? Had he planned this all along, going back to live in Africa and coming to track me down on his way? Or was this just an unexpected stopover between flights? It was always the same story with Hunter: he took me by surprise, in *controtempo*, and caught me unequipped with a decent strategy.

"Will you spend the night with me?" I asked abruptly.

"Yes."

We let that hang in the air for a bit. It was comforting to

stand on solid ground for a minute or two. Now at least we knew we had the night. And once you have the night, you can—theoretically—have much more.

"I have to leave very early tomorrow around six, though," he added, slightly defensively. "I'm taking the early-morning flight to London."

"It's all right, I'll book you a cab."

I leaned closer to him, slowly traced the line of his collarbone with my fingertip and slid it in the hollow of his throat, feeling his blood pulse. It was getting dark. I didn't want to waste time.

We kissed at last. Slowly, as if we had all the time in the world. I felt a warm flush hit the nape of my neck, then spread smoothly into my bloodstream. It was like thawing from hibernation.

Then, I don't know, it's impossible to remember. Our eyes locked, as if we were trying to keep each other from slipping away and vanishing again. We kissed and made love slowly, knowing we would start again as soon as we finished, and we kept smiling and whispering to each other, saying each other's names over and over and shaking our heads as if in disbelief at the miracle of being together again, of touching each other, kissing, embracing; and as if to say *oh no*, there was no way we could be apart for so long ever again.

At last we lay still in the darkness. I don't think I've ever felt so happy.

"Hunter," I whispered, "do you love me?"

"Yes," he said.

"That's good. Because I am crazy about you. And I love you."

It felt wonderful to finally say it. It was so simple, such a gift. I never wanted to hold it back from him again.

There was a short silence. I stroked his hair with the tip of my fingers and then his forehead and his lips.

We had finally reached somewhere together. Yes, now we would have to discuss the logistics, but that aspect of things didn't scare me any longer. I would move out of Adam's and . . .

He gently moved my fingers away.

"Esmé. I am coming to live in Nairobi with someone. Her name is Claire. You don't know her."

Suddenly the room was empty, we were inside a vacuum. As if someone had sucked out the sweet air, the magic mist, and the room had turned into a hollow cave. Cold and empty.

It was like a crystal smashing. It shattered in one second. Painful like a thousand blades through your heart. It makes me nauseous to remember it.

"I met her in London a few months back. I've asked her to come live with me. She's someone I really care about."

Every word he said fell in the room like a pebble on a marble floor. It had weight, it made a noise, one couldn't misunderstand or be confused by its meaning. That was the unmistakable, hideous sound of the truth. Unevocative, pragmatic, straightforward. *Hard.*

Claire.

The syllable which destroyed my life.

I sat there frozen in the dark. What does one do, what does one say? Is one allowed to cry, to scream?

"But why did you come, then?" I managed to whisper, forcing my voice out of my dried lungs.

"I came because I needed to see you again before I—"

"Because you needed to make sure you had wiped me out," I interrupted him. "Like Rwanda. You came on the anniversary."

"Don't be like that. Don't be bitter."

I turned away.

"I'm not bitter. I'm *destroyed.*"

That silenced him. He lit a cigarette, blew out the smoke in a sigh.

"Why now? Why only now are you ready to say how you really feel about me?" he asked.

"Why did you make love to me *like that*?"

He didn't answer. He looked at the ceiling, I knew his eyes were full of terrible sadness.

"What makes you think there is always an answer for everything one does?" he said slowly. "We are not these perfect machines performing rational tasks all the time."

"But how can you say you love *me* and then plan your life with someone else?"

His voice hardened and his eyes went cold:

"How can you say you love *me* and live with another man? You forget that you have been in this very predicament since the first day I met you."

But it seemed so foolish, so absurd, that now he would make the same mistake.

"So what is this? Revenge?" I asked, my voice hardening too.

"I'll tell you what it is. It's very simple, maybe too simple for you. It's only that I want to have a life, just like you do. I want to come home from all these terrible places where they send me and find someone smiling, happy to see me. I want to be with someone who doesn't feel tortured or guilty for loving me, who doesn't look at her watch. Who doesn't need to lie. Does it sound terribly prosaic? Is that too homey for you, not glamorous enough?

I put my hand over his mouth.

"Don't. Please don't say anything else to hurt me."

We fell silent for a long time. I stopped my brain from thinking and put it in neutral.

I knew the light would come soon, I could hear the the birds in the trees and the garbage truck making its way down the alley. He would be gone then—at the break of dawn—just like a character out of a nineteenth-century novel. I could always run to the station and do my Anna Karenina bit on the tracks. But the image didn't amuse me. I was too drained to invest any energy in trying to make myself smile.

I needed to say something final which would allow us to go our separate ways. It didn't matter at this point if it was another lie. I just wanted to be able to breathe after he was gone. I needed desperately to lie in order to get some air back into my lungs and fool myself that I could accept his loss. The existence of Claire.

"Maybe that's the best solution. It probably would never have worked between us anyway," I said. "I'll just have to get used to it."

He didn't say anything.

"I'm not angry at you or anything," I continued. "I'm just sorry we made each other so unhappy. I wanted the opposite. But our timing has always been wrong, right from the start."

"Yes. *Timing*," he said, with a slight sarcastic inflection. "One always underestimates it."

I got up and walked away from the bed. Away from him. For the first time I felt we really were no longer allowed to be that close, that we hadn't the right. I turned on the shower and let the hot water wash away the pain.

The pink light seeped through the blinds and infused the room, but our faces were frozen. He got up and I watched him get dressed. He looked staggering in that soft light, I couldn't bear it.

We heard the cab downstairs, then he kissed me very quickly on the lips.

"I'll see you in Africa."

And he was gone. I felt brittle. And then cracked.

CHAPTER ELEVEN

The force that through the green fuse drives the flower
Drives my green age; that blasts the roots of trees
Is my destroyer,
And I am dumb to tell the crooked rose
My youth is bent by the same wintry fever.

DYLAN THOMAS

Now I think I've learned the lesson of the drug abuser.

The whole point of going cold turkey is to shock your body in such a way that the stupid junkie in you will think about it twice before getting in that kind of trouble ever again. You cannot endure that pain more than once. I must have been a pretty tough case since I made myself go through it twice with Hunter. The second time—after he left me in the empty apartment in Rome—as he closed the door behind him, it actually felt like my heart had been shut forever inside a freezer. I remember the clang of the heavy metal door.

The sudden change of temperature cracked it.

I didn't break down, I didn't go to pieces. I ended up with this very fine scar.

I learned to live with it and eventually even found it rather attractive. The crack made me feel stronger, it gave me an unusual resolve. I felt like an old Japanese cup determined to outlast the new ones. All the more valuable for its unique seam.

"Are you sure?" Teo asked me when I told him I was ready to go back to Africa. "If you stayed a bit longer we could go to

Stromboli, the water's divine in June. We could rent an old house from a fisherman, go out in the boat every morning, then have lots of chilled *moscato* wine. We could climb up to the volcano crater under a full moon. We'd have such fun."

It did tempt me, the sound of yet another mild Mediterranean summer. Maybe if I stayed longer I would eventually succeed in resurrecting my earlier self, and shed that excruciating feeling of loss. My earlier life seemed so much more tame, so exquisite, so tasteful. There seemed to be no risk of ever falling apart.

Then one night Nicole rang from Nairobi.

"Nena, Miles and I went to Laikipia for the weekend, got stuck in the mud, we broke down twice, it took us twelve hours to get up there. We got charged by a buffalo while we were changing a tire, I swear it nearly fucking killed us, we had to fly on top of the roof of the Landcruiser and sit there for three hours under the rain, getting smashed on vodka, waiting for this monster to leave us alone. It's been a safari from hell, but we did have a blast after all. In Nairobi it's still pouring and getting really cold. You don't want to come back here, the weather is so miserable and everyone is in a bad mood."

It sounded wonderful.

I suddenly longed for the smell of wood smoke in the rain— must be the acacia bark burning because you only get it in Africa; for the vast sky hanging low and wide over your head; for that feeling of danger and space. I wanted to feel that fear again, the fear of being smashed in the waves.

"No. I don't want to swim in the Mediterranean," I said to Teo. "It's too polite."

A week later I was back on a crowded plane, squeezed among a batch of ferocious holiday makers decked out in leopard prints and straw hats. They were loud, boisterous, and determined to get the most out of their two weeks on Malindi beach. This time I didn't mind their company: their childlike expectations charged the aircraft with a cheerful energy.

At the first light of dawn I opened my eyes to find we were over Ethiopia. The light broke the spell of the night flight, when it seems impossible ever to reach a destination, encapsulated as you are in a spaceless dimension, surrounded by aliens. An odourless and timeless transit. Suddenly coming out of the darkness and finding myself on top of Africa, I swear I could smell it.

As we flew over Lake Turkana and I made out its shape in the desert, I felt immensely moved. Now I knew exactly where we were as I looked down at the scarred ground. The land below had ceased to be an abstraction.

Loyangalani, South Horr, Baragoi, Barsaloi, Wamba, Archer's Post. I whispered the names one by one. Here we go, I thought, now I too can sing my bit of Africa.

How absurd to feel that I was coming home again. This place couldn't possibly be home. But then why was it making me so weepy?

The peroxide blonde in leopard Lycra sitting next to me tried to concentrate on her precooked scrambled eggs but kept checking me out. "Are you going on holiday on your own?" she asked me suspiciously.

"No, actually I live here."

"You live *there*?" How outlandish. To her Africa was just a brochure. White people didn't *live* there, they just went on holiday.

"Do you work there?"

"Sometimes."

"Are you married?"

"No."

She gave this some thought, then shook her head.

"Then *why* do you live there?"

I didn't answer her, I don't like discussing my life with strangers.

But I'll tell *you* why.

It's because of love.

Nobody ever moves to Africa for any other reason. It doesn't have to be a woman or a man. It's because of love itself. But I've just learned this. This answer is the gift I've just been blessed with. That day on the plane, when the woman in the leopard print asked me, I didn't know it yet.

So I got back and Adam was there behind the glass door at Jomo Kenyatta airport in a brown moth-eaten sweater. His unshakable confidence in me, in my coming back to him no matter what, moved me almost to tears.

And then the smoky smell of firewood and cow dung and rain greeted me out on the road.

This was what I kept thinking coming back to Africa would feel like, and I was right.

I have been quiet and patient since I've been back here.

I have been this woman with a very fine scar. It is a secret scar that nobody else can see. I look at it when I'm naked and I have learned to love it.

It gives me power.

I have been wounded and the wound has made me stronger.

This is also what I've learned in Africa: the only whites who will heal are the ones who let themselves be wounded.

Now it's July again, the coldest month of the African winter.

Nicole is right, the weather is miserable still and everyone has been in a rather bad mood.

It was July when I first came here two years ago, like Napoleon on a new campaign, moving his armies. I was so excited then that I don't remember feeling this cold in my bones, like I do now.

Adam is back at the camp. Morag got a job with him after all and the clients apparently love her.

I suspect Adam does too.

I look at them together when I'm at the camp and I can't help thinking they're made for each other, and the realization doesn't make me too sad nor angry anymore. Her swimming-pool eyes with no ripples still annoy me, she's a harder Iris without gracefulness and without warmth. But she will be loyal to him as I have not been.

Adam and I are still in love in the way lovers who have lost each other are. Haunted by nostalgia: we both know that any-

282

time now—anytime now—we're going to have to part.

Hunter has been around town, jumping in and out of planes to his unpleasant destinations, and we've met several times since I've been back. We run into each other at the Karen *dukas*, at dinner parties, standing by our cars in the parking lot of the bank, keys dangling on fingers. We have adjusted to meeting like this, like two neighbours who greet each other in haste.

Now that we have sealed each other off, our hands never dare touch, we never get close enough to be able to smell each other. We avoid looking into each other's eyes for more than a second or two. Our bodies are off-limits, and we keep that a very strict rule.

But I know he must be walking around this town with a very similar scar to mine under his clothes. I do not want to see it. I am not allowed to see him naked ever again.

"Claire will arrive next Friday."

We were standing in front of the petrol station. Hunter and I. Barely a week ago.

"Oh."

We paused, I felt terribly nervous. I was holding a bunch of pale orange roses I had just bought. Having the flowers in my hands made me feel strangely vulnerable. As if they had been a gift for him, something he'd refused to accept.

"I'll be in Kampala. I leave the day after tomorrow."

"You mean she's not going to find you when she arrives at the airport?"

"No. There's very little I can do about that."

"I'll go get her."

"You don't need to do that."

"I know. But I can."

"Why you, of all people?"

"It's all right, Hunter. I guess it's all part of the process."

"Which process?"

"I mean . . . I have to get used to a lot of new things around here. Since I'm going to meet her anyway I may as well do something useful."

He looked down at the roses I was holding, as if seeing me again had punctured all his energy. I was plucking nervously at the flowers and unconsciously pulled one out of the bunch, as if to offer it to him.

"Come on. I'm not going to *bite* her. I'll just take her to your place and make sure there's something for her to eat in the fridge."

"She knows nothing about you."

"She never will. Don't worry about that."

He stared at me. I was suddenly aware of the temperature of his body next to mine. Too close. My internal alarm started to flash its red light.

"All right then," he said and clenched the orange rose from my hand. "It's the British Airways morning flight. Next Friday. I'll tell her what you look like."

I smiled.

"Right. But you better not tell her how beautiful you think I am."

And I ran away fast, a whirl of petals falling from my arms.

So I've taken you full circle, and now we're back to where I started.

It's nearly five in the morning in Nairobi, I'm coming home from the Mud Club, still pretty high on tequila. Peter the Elephant Man is driving me. He's been dancing all night with lots of girls and he's had a few drinks too. I don't think I've ever seen him so out of control. Not sloppy or anything, he's simply loose, more boyish than I've ever seen him, as if the alcohol has thawed the veneer which usually protects him.

"Why didn't Nena come tonight?" I ask.

"We had a hideous fight."

Peter is driving with a smile on his face, swaying slightly. He's never said anything so private to me before.

"Did you? I hope it wasn't too serious."

"Well, I guess I'm supposed to say it wasn't. But the truth is it was pretty bad."

Then he adds:

"I hate to tell you, but I think we may have to split up."

"*What?* . . . Shit, Peter. I always thought you and Nena were . . . Slow down darling, we're going to fall in the ditch."

"Don't you worry, I'm perfectly capable of driving. Yes, I really think we are going to split up. Does that shock you?"

I can't believe he wants to discuss his marriage with me at five A.M. But he obviously does. So I take the bull by the horns.

"Is there anyone else?"

"Why do you ask that?"

"Because usually married people with children split up only if they are in love with someone else."

"You mean you don't think it's worth breaking up a marriage just to be happier and feel alive again, on your own?"

"No, wait, I do. But most people don't. They think they alone are not worth all that trouble."

"Hmm, that's an interesting theory. You're saying a lot of people stay in an unhappy marriage because of what the shrinks call low self-esteem."

"Something like that. And fear, of course. Fear of a leap in the dark. But if you have an object of love, well then, you have an objective, right? That makes everything easier."

He nods pensively. Then he turns to me, brisk and sober.

"Listen, do you really feel like going home now?"

"What's the alternative? I mean, it's daybreak, Peter."

"Why don't we go somewhere beautiful and have a cup of coffee?"

"Fine, somewhere beautiful. Except I can't think of anywhere beautiful where we can have coffee right now."

"I can. We must hurry, though, before it gets light."

He wheezes off down the Langata road, into Wilson Airport's gate.

"I'm going to *fly* *us* somewhere beautiful and see the sun rise."

"Peter that's terribly grand, but are you sure you're not too drunk to fly?"

"Stop worrying about my alcohol intake for a minute."

He parks the car in front of the Africair hangar. It's still dark. There are a couple of Africans in overalls inside a tiny office behind a glass window. Peter honks lightly and they wave at him.

I don't know what it is about Wilson Airport, it must be combination of the hangars, the small planes, these tall men in old-fashioned overalls, but it instantly puts me in a black-and-white movie mood.

Peter rummages in the back seat of the car and emerges holding a flask.

"Go in and ask those guys to fill this up with Nescafé. I've got biscuits and sugar in the plane.

"Do you like Hobnobs?"

"I love Hobnobs. It's *just* what I feel like eating."

The sun on the equator always rises at six. No matter what.

Peter and I have flown over the Rift Valley in the first light of the day, to the sound of the Brandenburg Concertos.

Suddenly the tequila fumes have vaporized, and with them my sadness. We have flown low over Lake Naivasha, skimming the water with our wings, and then brushed the tops of the yellow fever trees as the first rays of the sun touched their bark and turned them gold.

I am suddenly happy.

How can I explain this? Why is it you can never hope to describe the emotion Africa creates?

You are lifted.

Out of whatever pit, unbound from whatever tie, released from whatever fear. You are lifted and you see it all from above. Your pit, your ties, your fear. You are lifted, you slowly rise like a hot-air balloon, and all you see is the space and the endless possibilities for losing yourself in it.

"This country was created to be seen from the sky," I shout to Peter. "Everyone here should have wings."

"Why not?" He laughs. "We should all have the right to be angels, since we live in Paradise.

Peter has managed a landing in the grass without too much jolting, and we've walked to the top of a boulder with our breakfast and a blanket. Now we are sitting on a flat rock, hundreds of kilometers from Nairobi, looking down at the early-morning view and sipping our Nescafé. You can cast your glance all the way into another country: Tanzania is on the left, behind those deep purple mountains. Mount Kenya is coming out through the clouds, we'll be able to make out its tip very soon.

The plane is right below us, it looks like a dragonfly. Something out of of a children's book. A magic toy in a fairy tale.

"You know, you could fit the length of Manhattan at least twice between here and those mountains," Peter says. "The whole island, with all its cars, and offices, and telephone cables and faxes and electric wires."

"With all the the people, all the noises they make, all the problems, the sex, the crime, the business."

"And the banks, the books, the art, the shops, the furniture, the clothes, the gadgets."

"Imagine. The amount of stuff."

"Unbelievable. The concentration per square meter."

"And instead, from here to there, there's absolutely nothing."

"Us two, and a few animals."

"Fucking amazing."

The sun is still low and radiates an orange light on the plain. Impalas and gazelles graze in the distance. They will shortly come to the water hole below us. Its surface is perfectly still like a mirror, doubling the sky above us with an amazing sharpness.

"Thank you, Peter, I couldn't think of a better place for a cup of coffee. It puts everything back in its right place."

He nods and sips his coffee. He lights two cigarettes and hands me one.

"I'll tell you what it is about this place," he says. "It sentences you to freedom."

"Yeah. It can be a sentence, rather than a liberation, can't it?"

"Sure. A lot of people can't take it, it frightens them. That's why a lot of people drink so much in Africa, it's one way to smooth the vertigo. But you know, for those who can bear to ride the wave, I think what happens is that here you are constantly reminded of what it means to be free and to be alive. And then it becomes very difficult to settle for anything less than this. You want to live with that awareness all the time. You want to be able to sit on this rock at dawn and feel *this* happy over and over again."

He pauses, lost in his thoughts.

"That's why sometimes I need to come and look at things from here. It puts everything back into perspective, somehow. This I mean, look at this. Frankly I'd find it very hard *not* to feel happy in a place like this."

"Yes. But it can also be very cruel. I've been incredibly desperate here. I felt exposed as nowhere else."

We feel the warmth of the first rays touch our skin. Peter fills up my cup with steaming coffee.

"You know, Esmé, when I first saw you," he says gently, "I thought: *She's going to be thrashed.*"

"Did you?" So surprising, that he should say that.

He nods.

"Come on, Peter. Did I look *that* naïve?"

"No. You just looked like someone who wouldn't put up any resistance. Someone who had come intentionally unarmed. But I knew you'd come out the other end."

"Have I?"

"Yes, I think you have. The difficult bit is over."

He knows everything about me. Doesn't everyone here? But he's been gentle, he's been watching me with care. I'm touched by his attention.

I raise my head, impatiently, as if driven by a residual ripple of anger.

"Sometimes I think I should leave. Sometimes I think I won't be able to bear all of this," my arm sweeps over the plain below us, over the grass swept lightly by the wind, "on my own."

I want him to reassure me.

"You'll be all right. You don't have to leave."

But I need to insist.

"I feel like I've lost everything now."

He shakes his head. He's smiling.

"No you haven't. That's the point I'm trying to make. You *think* you are here because you are in love with someone and then maybe because you fall in love with someone else. But what you don't understand is that you've been here all along for a different reason. It has nothing to do with people in your life, but with your ability to feel."

He looks at me, waiting for me to say something, but I can't. I lower my eyes to the ground because his gaze is making me uneasy.

"Are you no longer in love with Nena?" I ask him quickly, in a whisper, as if the answer will bind us forever in a secret it scares me to share.

"Love." He pronounces the word as if casting a rock down from where we sit, listening to it slide in the silence. "Of course I still love her and I always will. But Nena and I have stopped *feeling* for each other. We've been slowly clipping each other's wings, one could say. It happens a lot, to people who spend many years together. You *erode* each other."

I take another sip of coffee. Incredible how I have never paid any attention to Peter. How I always took him for granted, as if he needed no further investigation after my first scan of his personality. The Elephant Man, Ideal Husband and Ideal Father, No Further Desires. Rather presumptuous of me.

"You know, Peter, very selfishly, in a way it makes me feel better to know that you and Nena aren't this ideal couple, and that your life is still going through changes. That you too are . . ."

I can't find the appropriate word.

"*Struggling,*" he says. "Hey, isn't it what we are all doing?"

We sit in silence, listening to the breeze gently shaking the grass.

Then these birds come forward, in a perfect V formation, and glide over the water hole. The water surface reflects them like a mirror, and for a moment it is impossible to distinguish how many they really are. They drift very low, like choreographed dancers, and in the perfect stillness we can hear their wings flapping. The sound in this light stops the heart.

"Look now," says Peter, as we hold our breath, feeling that any second one of them will break the surface of the water.

And there it is, the sound of feathers against water, the ripples, and the sky now breaking in whirls, all its soft purples and pinks in overlapping motion.

"Amazing, isn't it?" he says. "And it's always like it's happening for the first time."

I see it now, and I don't think I will ever forget it.

In a way everything here always happens for the first time.

How the birds fly, the clouds move, the sun rises. Each time it's like watching a miracle happen.

You will never get used to it.

It will always be new.

ACKNOWLEDGEMENTS

There are many people I need to thank, who have helped me during the writing of this book. I am in debt to all of them for their support, and for the inspiration they have given me.

To Dominic Cunningham-Reid, Anna and Tonio Trzebinski, Emma Marrian, Judy Walgren, Mark Huband, Sue Fusco, Saba Douglas-Hamilton, Stefania Miscetti, Pasquale Plastino, Claire and Bernardo Bertolucci, and Melissa North, who have all, in different ways, contributed to this book.

To Simon Evans and Kerry Glen, for the perfect writer's retreat at Ol Laro Camp. To Mrs Nancy Camm, for her wonderful house in Naro Moru. A special thanks to Ali Masumbuko, Ali Mwyini and Mzee Salimu, for putting up with me and always making my life a lot easier.

To my agent, Toby Eady, for believing in the book right from day one, and to Robin Desser, my editor at Pantheon, whose indomitable wit and passionate enthusiasm have carried me through.

ABOUT THE AUTHOR

Francesca Marciano was born in Rome and has worked in both films and television as a writer and filmmaker. She divides her time between Kenya and Italy.